DEAD
NORTH

"In this new anthology of mostly original short stories we see deadheads, shamblers, jiang shi, and Shark Throats invading such home and native settings as the Bay of Fundy's Hopewell Rocks, Alberta's tar sands, Toronto's Mount Pleasant Cemetery, and a Vancouver Island grow-op. Throw in the last poutine truck on Earth driving across Saskatchewan and some "mutant demon zombie cows devouring Montreal" (honest!) and what you've got is a fun and eclectic mix of zombie fiction, with a special interest in environmental issues and the sometimes thin line that separates the quick and the dead."

—*Toronto Star*

The zombie stories in *Dead North* invoke many forms of dread – including the dread of living – and present different takes on what a zombie is. Moreno-Garcia has curated a collection that not only presents a diversity of horrors, but also a multitude of cultures existing across a wide Canadian landscape... *Dead North* is an excellent Canadian anthology, incorporating stories set across Canada and exploring diverse cultures and themes. It's also an excellent horror anthology, with some truly disturbing, and yet enticing, tales."

—*Paper Droids*

Braaaaiiiinnnnns, eh? New *Dead North* anthology puts the zed in zombies [while] featuring quirky tales of the undead that are uniquely Canadian... It's a perfect antidote to the American mythos presented in such pop culture zombie hits as *The Walking Dead* – which is all suburbs, shopping centres, traffic jams and jails. Oh, and guns... *The Walking Dead* gives a new twist to the old slogan, "You can take my gun when you pry it from my cold, dead hands." *Dead North*, on the other hand, features a distinct lack... of automatic weapons when facing actual zombies. That's right, zombies aren't just an American thing."

—*The Province*

DEAD NORTH

The *Exile Book of* Anthology Series

Number Eight

CANADIAN ZOMBIE FICTION

Edited by Silvia Moreno-Garcia

EXILE
editions

Fiction, Poetry, Translation, Drama and Nonfiction

Library and Archives Canada Cataloguing in Publication

Dead north : Canadian zombie fiction / edited by Silvia Moreno-Garcia.

(The Exile book of anthology series ; number eight)
Contributors: Tyler Keevil, E. Catherine Tobler, Gemma Files, Ada Hoffmann,
Melissa Yuan-Ines, Simon Strantzas, Jamie Mason, Jacques L. Condor,
Richard Van Camp, Claude Lalumière, Beth Wodzinski, Chantal Boudreau,
Michael Matheson, Rhea Rose, Carrie-Lea Côté, Ursula Pflug, Kevin Cockle,
Brian Dolton, Tessa J. Brown, Linda DeMeulemeester.
ISBN 978-1-55096-355-7 (pbk.).--ISBN 978-1-55096-381-6 (pdf).--
ISBN 978-1-55096-382-3 (epub).--ISBN 978-1-55096-383-0 (mobi)
1. Zombies--Fiction. 2. Horror tales, Canadian (English). 3. Short stories,
Canadian (English). I. Moreno-Garcia, Silvia, editor of compilation.

PS8323.H67D43 2013   C813'.087380806   C2013-903998-8
                                                      C2014-908309-2

SECOND PRINTING
Design and Composition by Mishi Uroboros / Cover Art by Szymon Siwaks
Typeset in Fairfield and Trajan fonts at Moons of Jupiter Studios

Published by Exile Editions Ltd ~ www.ExileEditions.com
144483 Southgate Road 14 – GD, Holstein, Ontario, N0G 2A0
Printed and Bound in Canada in 2014, by Imprimerie Gauvin

We gratefully acknowledge the Canada Council for the Arts,
the Government of Canada through the Canada Book Fund (CBF),
the Ontario Arts Council, and the Ontario Media Development Corporation,
for their support toward our publishing activities.

Canadian Sales: The Canadian Manda Group, 165 Dufferin Street,
Toronto ON M6K 3H6   www.mandagroup.com   416 516 0911

North American and International Distribution, and U.S. Sales:
Independent Publishers Group, 814 North Franklin Street,
Chicago IL 60610   www.ipgbook.com   toll free: 1 800 888 4741

To Antonio, who is lovely and not a zombie.

CONTENTS

INTRODUCTION

There have been a plethora of explanations for the popularity of the zombie sub-genre. Some people believe it is based on the economic downturn, that bad financial times engender survivalist fantasies. Others see zombies as the antithesis to the beautiful, gentler vampires of paranormal romance.

The popularity of zombie stories has given way to certain "zombie rules," some inspired by George Romero's *Night of the Living Dead*, and others that morphed and mutated after the release of this film, but were not actually in the black-and-white flick. For example, in Romero's original movie, a zombie bite is not the only way to turn into a zombie, though it becomes *de rigueur* in other movies and stories.

For this anthology, I sought stories that went beyond the Romero-inspired survivalist scenario. After all, two of my favourite zombies stories, "Lazarus" by Leonid Andreyev and "Pigeons from Hell" by Robert E. Howard, are far from Mad-Max-Meets-the-Undead. Of course, there are some zombie fans that might counter that those are not "real" zombies, but zombies have no rules. Just like vampires, we have crafted, forged and re-forged horrors that reflect the fears of our time.

Thus, *Dead North* goes beyond the usual brain-chomping undead you might expect. Yes, there are zombie apocalypse tales, like in "Escape," where a survivor is trapped in the Montreal Biodome. But there are also stories where Aboriginal myths and legends give rise to the undead, like in "Those Beneath the Bog," inspired by the Abenaki and Algonkin legends the author heard in his childhood. Sometimes it's not just humans who are zombies, as Claude Lalumière proves when cows attack in "Ground Zero: Sainte-Anne-de-Bellevue." And, because this is Dead North, all stories take place in Canada. From marijuana-happy British Columbia to the freezing Yukon.

Canadians like to say that our country is like a mosaic, with a mix of ethnic groups, languages and cultures that co-exist within society. Fittingly, *Dead North* also works as a mosaic, a contrasting picture of dread. For it is dread that I believe ultimately draws us back to the zombie genre. The undead are the blank slate upon which we project our anxieties. Whether these are fears of technology (medical experiments turning people into monsters), an economic collapse (the zombie apocalypse scenario), a runaway consumerist society (zombie consumption generates more consumption) or simply our fear of death and the corruption of our bodies, the zombie serves as a vessel for our collective dread.

In conclusion: dig in and discover the darkness at the heart of the Great White North.

Silvia Moreno-Garcia
April 2013

THE HERD

Tyler Keevil

I can see them in the distance, moving over the tundra with that familiar, dopy stride. Aping the shapes of men and women, and still moving as if they have some purpose. I know better. Their only purpose – like mine, like anybody's in this wasteland – is to find food. It is a full-time occupation, something that consumes you. Living to eat, and eating to live.

I'm hunched in a snowbank, my skis and sled beside me, watching through my field glasses. I count maybe two dozen of them, all relatively healthy. They are grouped in a loose cluster. Not even walking in file, which would make it easier, in the snow. And not using snowshoes, either. Every so often one of them sinks in up to his thighs, and thrashes around in confusion and frustration. Once when this happens, another goes to help, and they both end up struggling together, until they start punching and biting. It's funny, really. The intelligence of deadheads can vary, depending on the strain they've been infected with. I've seen one trying to operate a snowmobile. Unsuccessfully (the battery was dead), but still. These ones look to be about as smart as dogs.

To the south, I catch a flicker of movement. I sweep my binoculars that way. It's a wolf. Just the one. A rogue. So lean his ribs are showing through his skin. He is following the herd of deadheads, in a low crouch, padding noiselessly over the snow. It is like watching a ceremonial performance, an enactment of one of our old legends. The wolf trying so hard to play his part, to stalk quietly. He doesn't need to bother. He could be snarling and howling at them. If he did, the deadheads would probably howl back. I snicker, thinking about that: all of them howling like animals, which is what they are, now. As it stands, they just keep plodding along, the wolf picking his way after them, paddy-pawing the snow.

◀ ▶

The deadheads are heading north. The wolf follows them, and I follow the wolf: stepping into my skis, draping the sled harness around my torso. I adopt an easy rhythm, sliding my skis back and forth, back and forth. The snow has a glittering crust, easy to traverse. I trail the herd at an angle, moving in parallel rather than directly behind them. They haven't noticed me. The wolf may have, but if so has decided – for the time being – to focus on easier prey. The prey walk and walk and walk. They have great endurance, mostly because they don't know any better. They are fully capable of hiking all day, but every few hours they take a break. There is never any discourse about this (some of the deadheads are capable of basic communication – grunts and guttural sounds) but they all seem to know instinctively when to stop. It's that pack mentality they have. They form a circle and crouch, squat, or kneel in the snow, backs turned to the wind. They're smart enough for that, at least. They rest for fifteen minutes, like automatons recharging their batteries.

Then they get up and keep moving.

It's hard to say what this group were at one time. They are all pale-faced whites – except for those too stupid to cover their faces, which are now blackened by frostbite. They are outfitted well, in parkas, toques, mitts, boots. Some are in worse shape than others: their clothing torn or falling off, bits of goose down puffing from the seams like fungus. They might have been the inhabitants of some town, or outpost. Could be they ate their way through it, and have now moved on. The towns got infected first. The tribes, and my people, later. When it first started to happen, I would meet others on the tundra, in passing. The last of our kind. I'd explain to them about the sickness, the hunger, but they wouldn't believe me. They had stopped trusting me long ago. Even the ones not of my tribe had heard about me, and feared me. But of course they all learned soon enough that I was telling the truth.

Not that it did them any good.

◀ ▶

The wolf is desperate. It will not wait long to attack – it cannot afford to get any weaker – and by mid-afternoon the opportunity presents itself. One of the deadheads is flagging, faltering, trailing behind the others. There is something wrong with his left leg. It looks to be lame – from frostbite, or gangrene, maybe – and he is limping. He is quite small, too. Not a toddler, but a child. Seeing its chance, the wolf slinks up, shoulders hunched, gaze affixed on its prey. It is so intent on its purpose that it doesn't notice me coasting closer, soft and silent on my skis, or understand that it is not hunter, but hunted.

When I am within twenty yards I stop and unsling the bow from my shoulder. I reach up and ease an arrow from my quiver, notch it to the bow, draw the shaft to my cheek. Then I whistle, soft and high – a sound only the wolf will pick out over the wind. It looks back, confused, and my arrow catches it clean: burrowing into its chest, punching out through its back. It drops, whimpering and snarling. The deadheads haven't heard; they continue trudging, oblivious. I wait until the wolf stops twitching before I approach, then jab it once with my spear to make sure it's dead. Only then do I put down my weapons, get out my tools: an ivory knife, a stone-bladed *ulu*, and an *umiuk* made out of bone.

I lay the wolf on its back, and with the knife slit it from its throat to its groin, being careful not to slice the stomach and intestines. There isn't much muscle on the wolf – it's all skin and bone – but there's enough for a decent meal. I've never been fond of wolf meat. It is tough, and sinewy, particularly in an old beast like this. But it's food, at least.

And now the competition is out of the way.

◀ ▶

By the time I finish with the wolf, I can no longer see the herd of deadheads on the horizon, but their tracks are easy enough to follow. I start after them. My stomach is making strange burbles and groans, spasming and cramping. After weeks of nothing but stale pemmican, it's having trouble digesting wolf meat. I can feel it sitting in there, a hard ball. My stomach used to regurgitate food after long periods of fasting, but I've learned to take it slow, and control that reflex. I got tired of eating my own vomit.

I skate with my head down, pushing hard with my poles, falling into a smooth and steady rhythm. The landscape is overwhelming. The horizon flat in every direction. The sky a veil of grey. Behind it, the sun gleams like a tarnished coin, so dull you can look right at it without hurting your eyes. Those who haven't been here, and seen it, simply cannot imagine the endless expanse of white. It is stark and harsh as a blank page, or a map with no borders, no boundaries. No sense of right or wrong. In this blighted snowscape, anything is possible. Here you are free to cross over, to transgress. It is a map of madness that I negotiate alone.

The flats of my skis, waxed with fat, make satisfying hissing noises as they glide back and forth beneath me. I lose myself in that motion, feeling the terrain sliding away behind me, as if it is moving, not me. My sled is light enough right now that it isn't much of a burden. No stores of food to weigh it down, aside from a few cuts of wolf meat. At other times, when hunting is good, it gets so heavy that I feel like I'm dragging a tree behind me.

Years ago I kept a dog to pull it for me. A beautiful creature. Part husky, part wolf. Fierce, loyal, protective. And warm, too. His fur soft as ermine. We made a good team, traversing the Arctic together. He had a brilliant sense of direction, a great nose for tracking food. And he was much better at pulling this sled than me. But times grew lean, food scarce. We both shrunk, our skin tightening over us, hugging bone. Skeletal creatures. One night I woke to catch him regarding me in the darkness. He had enough wolf in him for that. The next morning, as I put him in his traces, I slit his throat with my knife. A nice, clean cut. Quick and relatively painless. For him, at least.

Now I am the one pulling the sled, but I like to think he is with me, in spirit. I wear his hide on my back, as a parka. His teeth dangle from the leather necklace around my throat. We still stalk this tundra together, seeking food.

He tasted different than wolf. There was something more wholesome about the flavour, as if the muscle was seasoned by all that love and loyalty, the bond between us. I think he would have appreciated my eating him. I took him inside myself, made him part of me.

Alliances up here are fleeting, friendships temporary.

◄ ►

Evening is coming on when black dots appear on the horizon. As I get closer, the dots grow into the stumbling shapes of deadheads, their figures shimmering as if in a haze of heat, or a mirage. When they stop for the night, I do too. After pitching my tent, I watch them for a time. In the fading light, I can see them getting into their huddle formation. Every so often they change positions – the ones on the outside going to the centre, the others shifting out. It's like observing a flock of penguins, each taking turns to act as the windbreak. It's interesting behaviour, and effective in fighting the cold. At times I think they might be developing, evolving. Getting smarter. I hope not. It would make life that much more difficult.

That night I sleep soundly, the flapping of the tent gentle and soothing as a lullaby. Perhaps because I have been thinking of him, my dog comes to me in my sleep. My brother, too. For a time, the three of us are traversing the landscape together. It is spring, the thaw. Food is plentiful: there are tubers lying on the ground, berries hanging from bushes, deer leaping onto our spears. My brother is laughing. It is good to have companions again, even if only in a dream.

For most of the following day, and the next, I keep pace with the herd. I am cautious, waiting. I am in no rush, and the last scraps of the wolf meat keep me going. A shift in the weather is coming. It is something you grow to feel, after years on the tundra. It is nothing tangible, just a sensation. A heaviness in the air, a change in temperature, the wind, the look of the clouds. I know it is going to snow, and it comes in the early morning, just after the herd has set out. It arrives, first, as a brief sprinkle – the flakes light and peppery. Then a lull, the air charged with a static crackle. Next, the first real flurries. Some of the deadheads stop, confused, and look up at this white confetti raining down. Soon they are overwhelmed by the snowstorm, swirling in the air like a swarm of frozen locusts.

Visibility is reduced to ten feet. I lose sight of the herd, but can hear them calling to each other, mooing and moaning in confusion. I ski forward, closing the gap, moving softly, softly. A few shadowed shapes begin to emerge again, some faint, others more substantial. I focus on one shadow, separated from the others, and move towards it. It is stumbling along, looking left and right, calling for its kin. As I glide in, I transfer both my poles to my left hand. I reach for the axe at my belt, heft it and swing it smoothly down atop the deadhead's skull. It makes a dull crumpling sound, like a watermelon being split, and he falls to the ground. I stop, kneel in the snow in a telemark position, next to my kill. I can still hear the others over the howl of the wind. One passes within a few feet of me, but notices nothing. Then he – or she? – keeps walking. The calls and moans fade away.

When I'm sure they're gone, I dig a trench for the corpse, and a snowcave for myself to weather the storm.

◀ ▶

The deadhead is a big man, well over six feet. A white man like the others. His nose is slightly black, his beard clotted with snot and frost. He hasn't lost much weight, and is still bulky and muscular. This herd can't have been infected for long. His parka has a small red cross stitched over the heart. He must have belonged to a rescue crew of some sort. I wonder if that's what the group are doing: still wandering the wastes, dimly but diligently following their old purpose. I have seen this before. In the towns, the deadheads return to their homes and offices to putter aimlessly. They wash dishes in empty sinks, push lawnmowers through the snow, stand and hammer pieces of wood as if driving in an invisible nail. It could be that certain parts of their brain – those to do with learned reflex – are unaffected by the sickness. Reason and rationality are gone. All that remains is appetite, instinct, muscle memories.

The snowstorm has stopped, the herd has moved on. It's time to get to work. I lay him flat on his back, unzip his parka. With my knife I slice through his undergarments. The sight of his pale abdomen – still fleshy with fat – triggers a low rumble in my belly. I take my time, stripping him completely. Then, with my axe, I dismember him: hacking through the limbs, lopping off the head, then halving the legs at the knees, and the arms at the elbows. He is already stiff with rigor mortis, the blood dense and congealed.

The thick thigh muscles – gluts and quads – make the best meat. I start there. The left thigh first. With my *ulu* I remove the skin, which I lay aside, to be dealt with later. The layer of fat beneath the epidermis makes good lamp oil. Then I cut large strips of meat off, rectangular in shape, about the size of T-bone steaks. A big thigh will yield four of these.

I do not know if I'm the only one who has discovered this, but it is the sole reason I have survived so long. Deadhead meat is edible, if treated properly. The bacteria or virus or parasite that causes the sickness can be killed. Either with heat, by cooking, or with cold, by freezing for several hours. My people have frozen meat like this for centuries, to preserve it.

Each part of a deadhead has its uses. The bones make arrowheads, spears, needles, blades, parts to repair my sled. The intestines are perfect for stringing my longbow. The skin is useless for warmth, compared to wolf or fox or bear. But it makes good leather. My tent, once rough canvas, is now almost entirely a patchwork of deadhead skin. The top of the skull can be used as a bowl, in a pinch. The fat for lamp oil, the hair as thread. You can derive salt from the blood. The body of a deadhead is like a walking cache of practical provisions.

At the moment, however, I am well-stocked in terms of tools and equipment. Some of this will have to be buried, and returned for if and when the time comes. Right now my priority is food. It is a long and arduous task, to skin and clean and butcher an entire body. It takes me most of the day. By the time I'm done, the snow all around me is bright with blood. A large patch has formed in the shape of the dismembered corpse, like a bloody snow angel. After, I wearily set up camp, digging a snowcave and windbreak, and erecting my tent within.

Only then am I ready to eat a proper meal.

Most of the meat has been frozen long enough to be safe. It is not something to be rushed, a feast of flesh this fresh. If I gorged myself I would puke it back up immediately. So I eat slowly, as darkness falls, savouring every bite, letting it thaw and melt in my mouth so I can appreciate the texture, the flavour. The selection is rich and varied. There is the muscle meat, of course, and the sweet bits of fat – so necessary to prevent protein poisoning. The organs are even more important. The liver, in particular, is very rich in minerals, and vitamin A and D. The kidneys are a great source of iron, the brain loaded with vitamin C.

It is a good meal. After, I hunker in my tent and with my oil lamp heat a cup of frozen blood until it is steaming, simmering. I sip this slowly, savouring the salty flavour. I can feel the warmth in my belly, helping digestion, radiating outward, and the strength it infuses in my limbs. Then I douse my lamp, strap down the flap of my tent, and wrap myself up in furs. I lay there, satiated, too full to even sleep. There's nothing quite so satisfying as a deadhead feast.

◀ ▶

The next morning I load up my sled with stacks of meat – cuts of all sorts – separated by layers of skin and packed with snow. Preservation isn't a problem. You do not need a fridge, or a freezer. Up here, in the winter, negative twenty is a mild day. The meat will keep, and feed me, for several days – a week if I eat sparingly. And there are many more deadheads to sustain me after that.

For the next few weeks, I follow the herd north. In the same way, my ancestors used to follow the herds of caribou that once roamed the tundra. Like them, these deadheads are my roving food supply. Every few days, I cull the herd by picking one off. Taking the weak, the lame, those being left behind. Or striking under the cover of night, or using the weather as I did the first time. They must be vaguely aware of me – some of them have seen me – but their memories are short, their capacity for problem solving minimal. They soon forget me, and what has become of their missing companions. They continue plodding along in stoic, blissful ignorance. I am very aware of the irony of this. It was when the whites first came that the caribou started dying out. Now the whites have become my caribou. They are far less noble, and far more stupid, but just as nourishing.

◀ ▶

I can see something on the horizon which doesn't blend into the natural contours of the landscape. A low oblong, squat as a concrete block. It is towards this that the deadheads are moving. As it grows larger, I see that it is a man-made structure, quite large. It looks too big to be a weather station. It could be an old outpost of some sort, or a research base.

The deadheads trudge steadily towards it. They must remember it. This must be what they have been heading towards so purposefully all along. As they get closer, I notice movement out front of the building. I stop, kneel, and raise my field glasses. Somebody is standing there, in a blue jacket, toque, and scarf. It's hard to tell but by the features it looks like a woman. She has binoculars of her own, and has them trained on the approaching herd. I remove my skis and lay myself flat in the snow, in case she scans the terrain. She is sentient, a survivor. I know that much already. She watches them for some time (counting numbers, maybe?) before ducking inside. The door – a makeshift piece of ply-board – is shut behind her. There are storm shutters on the windows. Hands appear to close them, latch them. There looks to be several people inside – I count at least four – and they seem to know what they're doing.

It takes another ten minutes for the herd to reach the station. I stay where I am, watching from a distance. The building itself is solid. They will not get through concrete. But the door is a weak point. The windows, too. The storm shutters are designed to keep out wind and snow, not half a dozen clawing, hammering hands. And of course it is to these openings that the deadheads are drawn. When it comes to self-preservation they're useless, but they do have a certain animal cunning where food, and prey, are concerned.

Three or four of them are already battering at the door, leaving bloody handprints, but it is one of the shutters that goes first. A weak hinge snaps, and the whole thing comes away. Behind it there is only a pane of glass, which the dead-heads punch through heedlessly. A hand appears, swinging a club to keep them at bay. It's a brave but fairly stupid idea. They grab the club, and then they grab the hand. A man is dragged through the window. They fall on him, clawing and biting and tearing. Arterial blood sprays wildly, spattering the snow.

From within the hut, a ball of flame blossoms forth: somebody has fired a flare. Not as an alarm, but as a weapon. It smashes into one of the deadheads and gets lodged in his jacket, which promptly ignites. He wanders around, wailing, his torso engulfed in flames, trailing a column of smoke. But if the survivors have other flares, they don't have time to use them. The deadheads have begun scrambling through the open window. The door is in danger of collapsing, too. From within the shelter, I can hear the sounds of struggle. Shouting, smashing, that dull animal wailing of the deadheads. But no gunshots. Apparently these survivors aren't all that well equipped. I wonder if they've been waiting for this rescue party – if they sent out some kind of SOS. Imagine their surprise, then, when the rescuers arrived, intent on eating them rather than saving them. I could step in here to help, but the situation is too uncertain and chaotic. It is better, and safer, to let it play itself out.

A trio of survivors emerge from inside. One is wielding a fire axe – either painted red, or already red with blood. The other has a two-by-four, which is fairly useless. The third – the woman in the blue jacket – has a hammer and knife. The one with the axe looks to be injured, his arm bitten and bloody. There are half a dozen deadheads out front. Upon seeing the people, they rush in. It's surprising how fast they can move when they want to. At first the survivors fare quite well. One deadhead is neatly decapitated by the axe. Another gets cranked by the two-by-four. I watch all this through my field glasses, the images reaching me before the sounds. An odd disparity between image and noise.

But more deadheads are converging. The wounded man makes a desperate, heroic effort – waving the others away. He swings his axe, dropping a third deadhead, then turns to take on a fourth. This time, the blow comes down on its shoulder, cleaving into the chest, and gets embedded there. The man struggles to tear it free. He's still trying as two others fall on him, bear him down to the snow. He flails and fights, biting and clawing back at them, and for a few moments it's hard to tell which is human, which is deadhead.

The other two survivors are trying to flee. But the snow is deep, and they are slow. The deadheads have the benefit of following the tracks plowed by the fugitives. When the man with the two-by-four stumbles, sinking into a drift up to his knees, the woman stays behind to help, trying to drag him on. The few remaining deadheads catch up. Then there is a futile, final skirmish, which seems to go on endlessly. All this flailing around in the snow, this bloody thrashing. Even if the people survive, they'll both be infected.

I rise and brush the snow off my parka and step into my skis. I skate forward at a good clip. By the time I reach this last struggle, both the humans are dead. Three of the dead-heads are feasting on the fallen man. They hear me coming and stand up, curious, and look at me as dopily as deer caught in high beams. There is blood trickling from their chins, flesh hanging from their maws. I plant my poles and unsling my bow and notch an arrow. When the first deadhead drops – with an arrow through its eye – the others howl and begin wading towards me. But they are easy targets, compared to the wolf. Two more arrows sizzle through the air, embedding themselves in the throat of one, the chest of the other.

I reach for another arrow, and look around.

The man they were feeding off is a mess – his head caved in, brains spilling like porridge across the snow. The woman looks done, too. One of the deadheads, though, is crawling around, keening. It has been blinded somehow. Maybe stabbed in the eyes and face. I step out of my skis, pad up behind it, and tap the back of its head with my axe.

Then I approach the hut. The snow here is soaked in blood, more red than white. There are eight or nine bodies – both human and deadhead – out front, all motionless. But I can hear noises coming from inside. Clattering and banging. Something's still alive in there.

I plant my bow upright in the snow, leave my quiver of arrows beside it. It would be useless in closer quarters. I take my axe with me instead, and my *umiuk*: my long-bladed skinning knife. I also tug a leather gauntlet onto my left forearm, and lace it snug. Outside the caved-in door, I crouch and squint into the darkness, allowing my eyes to adjust, before scuttling inside.

The area just within is a kitchen of some sort. One of the deadheads is standing at the stove. He has a pot on the burner, and is stirring it aimlessly. The burner is out, the pot empty. To one side, next to him, he's got what looks like somebody's arm. I'm so struck by the oddness of this sight – and the comedy of it – that I almost get taken by surprise.

I am saved by a tin can. A soup can, actually. I hear it rattle, and turn left to see hands reaching for me from the shadows. One is missing a finger, and that detail, for some reason, stands out. I duck and swat the hands aside. I stab up with my *ulu*, into and under the chin of an Asian lady, then swing around with my axe, catching her temple clean. There is the familiar sound of bone breaking. My axe is blunt and dull, deliberately so. I find it the most effective way to minimize blood spray. Blood is a carrier, too.

As that deadhead drops, I turn back to the chef. He is right there, now, lunging for me, practically on me. I get my left arm up in time. He bites into the gauntlet and I swing down, over the top, tapping his scalp. It crunches, and he crumples. But his bite is so hard that his teeth stay fixed in my gauntlet, pulling me down to a crouch. To free myself I have to pry his jaws apart, like a dead pitbull's.

I scan the rest of the room. Opposite the kitchen is a living room, with a tatty old sofa, a TV with a broken screen, some bookshelves. Sprawled on the floor are three bodies. They're so bloody and mutilated that it's hard to tell if they were human or deadhead, and it doesn't matter. I give each of their heads a tap with my axe, just in case. Then I check the other rooms. One is a bunkhouse, with six beds and some gear lockers; the other is some kind of lab, with microscopes, monitors, computers, technical equipment. Both rooms seem to be empty. When I've made sure of this, I lower my axe and check my gauntlet. The bite broke through the leather. I pull the gauntlet off, roll up the sleeve of my parka, and study my forearm. The faint indent of incisors – a twin set of white lines – is visible, but the skin is not broken. I wipe at them to make sure, but there is no blood. A millimetre or two was all that separated me from becoming one of them.

Then, a groan from out front. I stand, taking my axe, and step outside. The woman in blue is still alive. Barely. She is bleeding, her torso torn open. Guts spilling everywhere. Grey tubes snaking across the snow. Her teeth chattering from cold and shock. She sees me approaching. I wonder what I must look like, with my weapons and weather-blasted face. My eyes two slits, my mouth a slash. A death mask. I stand over her and raise my axe.

Then I hear: "Stop!"

In the doorway behind me is a boy. Maybe eighteen or nineteen. He's got a flare gun in his hands, though it's probably the one they shot off. I look at him. The woman at my feet does as well.

"That's my mother," he says.

"Not for long."

"It's okay," the woman says. To her son, I think. "It's okay."

I shrug, lower my axe, and step aside. Still pointing the flare gun at me, the boy makes his way to his mother. I leave them, let them have their dramatic moment, their sentimental goodbye.

While they do, I go around tapping heads, making sure all the rest are fully dead. Then I begin dragging the bodies into a pile by the door. The next time I look at the boy, he is kneeling in the snow, his shoulders shaking, sobbing silently. He has let the flare gun drop at his side. I go and pick it up. Just in case.

◀ ▶

I set up a makeshift work area in their lab: clearing the equipment off a desk, shoving all the electronic detritus into one corner. Without power, it's useless anyway. Then I drag the first body inside and heft it onto the table. It's a scrawny white man. Or it was. I strip him down, slice him from throat to groin, and begin the arduous chore of dismemberment. Hacking through muscle, sawing through bone. Tearing tendons and cartilage.

I'm in the process of scraping the fat off a strip of back skin – using my *ulu* – when the boy appears in the doorway.

He takes a look at me, at the tool in my hand, at the blood on my forearms, at the mutilated body in front of me, and he pukes. Or retches. Not much comes out. He doesn't look like he's had a lot to eat. None of the humans have. They were wasting away up here, without a clue as to how to survive once their supplies ran out. The deadheads will make better feeding. The corpse on my table is gaunt and scrawny.

"What are you doing?" the boy asks.

"We have to eat."

"But these are *people*."

"They were people. Now they're meat. Just like the dead-heads out there. And you look like you could use some meat."

"I know him!"

I shrug. "I don't."

I turn my back, and resume my work. He watches, dumb-founded, then stumbles away. I hear him retching in the kitchen. Then I can hear him sobbing again, like a child.

◀   ▶

The stove in the kitchen – the one the deadhead was using – is a two-burner camp stove. It attaches to a propane tank beneath the sink. The gauge reads half full. They ran out of food, apparently, before they ran out of fuel. The stove even has a lid, like a barbecue, for baking and broiling. There is salt and sugar, too. For the thaw, I'll be able to make smoked meat, and jerky. The summer months, and the mild weather, bring different challenges. Food is more readily available – tubers, berries, other animals – but it doesn't keep so long when the world isn't one big freezer.

After burying the majority of the meat cuts and organs out back, I turn on the stove. On one burner I fry a sirloin, on the other I boil a leg bone, halved, in water, seasoned with blood and salt and kidneys. It should make a good broth. When the pot starts steaming, I lean over it and breathe in deeply, savouring the scent. I'll be eating well for some time.

I'm standing like that, leaning over the stove, when the boy tries to kill me. He makes a clumsy job of it, swinging the fire axe I saw one of the survivors using. But he is noisy, and slow. I sidestep, and the axe plows into the counter – splintering the laminate. Before he can swing again I step into him, bodychecking him. He is so light and scrawny he bounces off me, sprawling out on the floor and smacking his head. He lies there, groaning, gazing up at me with dull eyes. Not even particularly angry, or scared. Just empty.

I leave him lying there. My steak is nearly done. Since it's human, and fresh, I've left it a little raw. It should be uninfected. I was careful not to take a cutlet from anywhere near a wound. There's always a chance, of course, that I'll catch something, but I enjoy the thought of that risk. It's like eating blowfish, or whatever it is. The one that's poisonous if prepared improperly. I put the steak on a plate, pour myself a bowl of broth, then step over the boy and go to sit at the table. I have not sat down, eaten like this, for years. I saw into the steak like a proper white man. Appropriate, since I'm eating white man.

There's nothing quite like fresh human meat. Partly it's the fact that I don't have to eat it seared, or frozen. The meat is tender and soft, the juices salty as gravy. It tastes better than wolf, better than deadhead, better than seal or fish or whale. Better than anything. It is, and has always been, my favourite meat. All the more delicious for its scarcity.

I am aware of the boy watching me, from the floor, lying there like a hungry dog. I cut off a sizable chunk, pinch it between my fingers, and hold it out to him, right at eye level.

"No?" I say.

He doesn't take it. Not until I make as if to pull it away. Then he snatches it from my hands, tears off a bite, chews and gnaws and swallows hurriedly.

"Go slow," I tell him. "You'll make yourself sick."

He bites again, and again, eating it all at once, as if he needs to before he can think about what he's doing, about what – or who – he's actually eating. I can vaguely recall that feeling – that revulsion – but to me it seems almost quaint, now. Naïve. When he's finished, he falls on his side, clutching his stomach, squirming and moaning.

"You made me do it," he says.

I saw off another chunk for myself. Pink blood leaks across the plate.

"Life feeds off life," I say. "Besides – I didn't even kill these people."

I don't tell him that I have, more than once. I first got the taste when my brother and I were stuck in a blizzard, on a hunt. Separated from the rest of the tribe. Days stretched into weeks, the snow raging on and on. And the two of us, in a small ice-hut, getting thinner and thinner. It was him or me, or both of us. I think I saw relief in his eyes when I finally went after him. He thought it was better, perhaps, to die than live as what I'd become. Initially I thought he might have been right. When I returned to my tribe I saw the horror in their eyes. I was too tainted even to be killed. Once the devouring spirit is in a body, nobody wants to be the one to set it free. Who knows where it might settle next? So I was pushed out, exiled. Left to wander the waste alone. Feeding off whatever – or whoever – I could find.

When I'm finished my steak, night has fallen. I go to get my lamp, light it, and put it on the table. The boy is still lying on the floor. I pick up an overturned chair, set it upright, and motion towards it. He crawls over, pulls himself into it, gazes at me across the table. The air smokes black between us. His eyes settle on the flame, drawn to it like a moth.

"You found paraffin," he says.

"Fat makes good oil."

"Human fat?"

"Deadhead fat, this time."

He does not seem so surprised by this. I offer him a bowlful of broth, which is still steaming. He doesn't ask what it is, and instead sips it. Tentatively at first, and then more hungrily. It will be easier on his stomach than the meat.

"How long have you been out here?" he asks.

"Since before the sickness."

He thinks about that, peering at me.

"What tribe are you?"

"Would you know the name of any tribes?"

"My mother was an anthropologist." He is cradling his soup bowl, soaking up its warmth, still looking at the flame. As if it can distract him from the reality of what he's saying, what he's been through. "She was studying the Inuit, and their stories. Collecting some of the legends from the oral traditions. I came up to help, as part of my university degree. We were talking to a bunch of different tribes, so I know a few of them."

I nod towards my makeshift abattoir. "What about all that equipment?"

"She was part of a team. The others were doing carbon dating on bones and tools. Learning about the history of your people."

"They are not my people anymore."

He sips, watching me over the rim of his bowl. The room is cold, now, and the temporary heat given off by the stove is dissipating. We will have to repair the door, the windows.

He says, "A tribe told us about a man, one of their hunters, who had been cast out. They said he still wandered the plains. He had been possessed. He had gone *wendigo*."

"*Wendigo*," I repeat, like an invocation. "The evil spirit that devours mankind. That is what the name means, in our language. But we are all *wendigos*, these days. Humans and deadheads alike. When there is nothing left to eat, we eat each other."

"Not everybody turns cannibal."

"No?"

He meets my eyes briefly, then looks away.

I say, "Human, deadhead, animal – it's all the same to me."

"You eat the Zeds, too?"

I frown. "Zeds?"

"Zombies. You know. Zeds."

"If you cook or freeze the meat, it is safe."

"How did you find that out?"

"I took the chance. It was that or die."

We finish our soup in silence, the only sounds that of our slurping, like a subtle and subliminal conversation. Then I put my bowl down, lean back in my chair.

"I could use your help, if you're willing."

He puts down his bowl, too. I explain to him about cutting and preparing all the meat – both deadhead and human. We can freeze what we'll be able to eat over the winter. There is enough food, though, and enough propane, to cure and season a large portion to last during the summer thaw. There is plenty to do, plenty to eat. Supplemented with hunting and gathering, the two of us should be able to live off the spoils for six months or more.

"Or one of us could live off it for a year."

I smile at him. He is not stupid, this one.

"Even frozen or cured, meat doesn't last indefinitely."

"What about when we run out?"

"Then we will find other sources. There are herds of deadheads – or your Zeds – all over the tundra, and in the towns. And wolves, ravens, hares. Other animals."

"Other people?"

"If need be."

He nods, accepting this. Or pretending to. He will do fine, for what I have in mind. I will feed him, make him strong. I will train him. I have been alone for so long, it will be good to have a companion again. But I will not teach him all my skills, all my tricks. When the lean times come – as they inevitably will – I want to make sure I have the upper hand.

Alliances up here are fleeting, friendships temporary.

THE SEA HALF-HELD BY NIGHT

E. Catherine Tobler

Esteuan sees the bent figure at dusk and thinks nothing of it. His day has been long, beginning before the sun brightened the sky, ending as the sun takes a last gasp and puts herself away for the night. Exhaustion bends his broad shoulders against this darkening sky and he presumes it is another man much like himself, wearied from a day on the ships, amid the tryworks. The stench of his body, streaming with sweat, blood, and whale oil, masks anything else he might discern from the evening. Esteuan brings these scents home and even when he emerges from the bath some time later, he smells of whales, of sea, of hunting. I see the figure three days later; when I mention it to Esteuan, his head lifts from the tub of water and his eyes bore into me, as if what I have said makes no sense. There were only exhausted men; he tells me of the one he saw. I tell my story twice, and neither time does it change.

Coming home from the harbour, my hands and arms still caked with spermaceti, I see the figure wandering the rocky shore. Here, the shoreline is strewn with the corpses of whales, flesh melting from stark white bone into the waters where it turns green and black with rot. The water glimmers at all hours of the day with those colours. If one is new to Red Bay, the scent is vile, causing eyes to water and stomachs to heave; when one has been here for years as we have, this scent fades and becomes common. I smell at least as bad, spending most of my days curled inside whale heads to scoop the spermaceti into buckets which never quite contain it.

This figure – this man – stumbles. Perhaps on a rock, perhaps on an exposed whale vertebra. He doesn't catch himself, but staggers half a dozen steps, arms shaking. His shoulder knocks into the arc of a whale rib which rises from the mud and he stares at this shape for a long while. Even standing, his body seems oddly liquid, flowing. He is wet from the sea, I think; he is tired from a long day of hauling whales from the waters, his shirt streaked with whale blood, other debris. My mind fills in the information I cannot know with what I do know: long days of hard, awful work. This man doesn't lift his head and look towards any destination, but he turns, as if knowing he's going the wrong direction. These staggering steps lead him away from the whale corpses, back to the glimmering water.

He walks into the water and I think surely he will stop. He will realize his error and turn back yet again, towards the houses which scatter the land for certainly one is his own, but he doesn't. He walks until I can see nothing more of him; the water swallows him bit by bit, hips and belly and narrow chest. His head vanishes and though there should be bubbles of breath to mark the surface of the water, there are not. He sinks and is gone. Ghostsong rises in the air a breath later; this eerie sound is like the groaning of masts and sails, like the roll of thunder before a storm, but it is something else entirely. I think it is the whales, weeping in agony at what we do to them.

◀ ▶

Esteuan refuses to talk to me about the man. He says I imagined him walking into the ocean. This is the only answer that makes sense to him. Where would he have gone, he asks me. I do not know. I cannot give him an answer. When I shake my head, Esteuan grunts and leaves the house, headed for the harbour. I follow; my work is there, too.

When a whale is taken, it screams. Esteuan tells me I am a fool for describing it this way, for imparting such a human sound to a monster, but this is only what it is. The rip of harpoon and drogue into flesh sound like nothing else. The tearing of fabric? No – it is not that. It is the opening of a life, one body sundered into two things. The spill of liquid into liquid – life-giving blood into dark water. The animal makes this sound: black birds raking grey sky, a mouth smothered beneath a hand, a child running until the world around it is unknown. Esteuan calls me a fool.

Our *chalupas* are small compared to the whales, and fragile. When captains are carelessly eager, we lose many ships. I used to go out into the waters with them, but now I do not. I wait in the harbour for them to return with the kill. Other than the young boys, I am the only one small enough to easily fit inside the split heads when they return with a sperm whale. I am the one they want scooping the soft spermaceti out by the bucketful. They train the boys to be men; train them to sail the *chalupas* and take the beasts in the open waters. Other wives stay home. They try not to see me most days, but when they do look, their eyes are mournful.

But this is why we came: to hunt the whales. I was seventeen my first summer, having come with my brother Joanes and his crew of six hundred men. Esteuan was among them and had not yet taken me for a wife, though the long looks he gave me said he wished this very thing. Among my brother's men, he was the least offensive – high praise, indeed – but the long journey across the Atlantic gave us time to learn one another. His mouth was coarse in all ways, but in those days his hands were patient, coaxing shapes and images from whalebones before gifting them to me.

The first time Joanes took me to a hunt, the violence captivated me. The claiming of such beasts by mere men held a strange poetry; the manner in which we trailed the creatures, the way harpoons and ropes pulled them in. The great whales would bleed to death on the journey back to shore; would float once dead and unresisting. It was Joanes who cracked the head of the first sperm whale we brought back; the beast steamed in the cool autumn air and smelled like hot meat. It was Joanes who showed me the compartments inside that great head, the way the oils collected there. It was Joanes who first dared me to crawl inside.

When you stand inside one of these animals, you almost cannot believe it. You are aware of your own breath for it sounds very close in your ears, aware too that these walls around you are not walls at all, but flesh that once lived and carried breath of its own. If you spread your arms wide, you cannot touch each side of the chamber; you must rock from one side to the other to touch the damp walls. At first, they feel warm and then the heat bleeds out, until only cold remains. The colder it gets, the thicker the oil which clots this compartment, so you work quickly, scooping bucket after bucket of spermaceti out, so that it may be purified, turned into rare oil for lamps and candles.

The Bible tells its story of Jonah who was swallowed by a whale and thus saved, but standing within the creature is nothing like that. You do not feel as though you will be saved. This animal will draw you down if it can, so best you get there first. Standing inside, you still will not believe it, that you triumphed, but you did, and so you don't mind the smell at the end of the day. You don't mind the loss of occasional ships. This is part of the price to be paid for small miracles.

◄ ►

Esteuan marries me that first winter, when the harbour freezes so hard we don't think we will survive. We can go nowhere, our ships frozen in place, and the whales have stopped coming. We can only hold on until the thaw and pray the beasts return and we can hunt them again.

Esteuan marries me in the shack that will become our home. The wind is awful, blowing in a fresh storm which will leave two feet of snow on the ground come morning. The wind slips in between the wood slats, causing every flame in the room to shudder. The room is painted in shivering gold, every lamp in the camp brought here because it was my foolish wish. I did not ask for every candle – we would need something to see us through the winter dark – but I wanted every glass lamp. Each is filled with our most precious oil, bright honey in colour. The other wives and I spent the afternoon filling them and setting wicks.

This oil burns without scent and its colour is clean, bright. It is the best marriage gift anyone could have given me. In this light, the shadows of Esteuan's face are erased and he becomes a gilded being. Joanes stands at his side, offers my hand into his, and words are spoken. Words that, in that moment, seem easily kept. But after winter's thaw, spring's bloom, and summer's harvest, there will come the autumn that will change everything. Joanes will leave us. He will cross the Atlantic in the *San Juan*, carrying casks of the oil we have made. Others will come in his place. He will return, in another year. Perhaps. Although there are days ahead of us, I already mourn his leaving.

Esteuan seems to understand. I find it strange that he does, for sailors come and go so and this is also his way, but after our wedding, after our friends and fellow workers each set into the storm with a wedding lamp in their hands, Esteuan offers me another gift. It is a whale's rib, an unbroken length that has been smoothed by his hands. He has carved images and words into it: my likeness and his own are there, and so too Joanes, his nose crooked from a fight he lost years ago. The images are darkened with soot, rubbed so deeply in it seems part of the bone itself. I mean to thank my new husband, but already he has moved on, to close the door so the snow does not come in, to extinguish the lamps because he needs no light to claim me as his.

◀ ▶

The stooped figure returns at sunrise. I am home today because Esteuan refuses to let me do my work. He refuses to let me do my work because I think I may be with child. I am sick these past two weeks and my courses have not come. We argued all night. I did not want to stay home – will I stay home for my entire pregnancy, should there be such a thing? Esteuan tells me I will. Marina, who has surely heard our arguments, comes to console me, but I don't want consolation, so when the figure of the man returns, it is with relief I point at him and show Marina. She is slow to rise from the table; her hands are fisted in her skirt, because she has likely heard Esteuan and I argue over this man, too. Our houses are not so close; it is only that at night, the land is quiet and the walls thin. Voices carry.

The man is farther inland than I have seen him before, his eyes seeming to rest on the house. My house. I shudder at that idea and Marina reaches for me in fear. He will not run, I tell her. I do not know this for certain, but I remember the way he moves. He moves that way now, lumbering as though his body weighs him down. He is ill, Marina says, and we should ask Gil to come. I only stare at her. Gil is an old man; I am not certain what she thinks he can do, but I am insulted she believes he can do more than we can.

For now we only watch the man as he shuffles about. When he goes to our supply shed, I move to the back door. Marina tells me no, tries to hold my arm, but I pull from her grasp and open the door. I do not yell at her, but instead at the man who seems intent on looking through our tools, our stored oil and wood. He does not react to my voice, his focus falling to the pale curve of whale rib which stands upright against a wall. It is the rib Esteuan carved for me. His hand falls to it and a rough sound pours from him. I scream at him to leave it alone. His sound – it changes, rises to the sound the whales make at slaughter.

Leave us alone! Marina cries and it's only then I realize she is there at all. She lifts a slat of wood and strikes the man, though he has done nothing. He turns and – half of his face is gone. From the cheekbone down, he has rotted away, his skin glimmering the way the water does from the whale rot. I can see the curve of a bone and where the muscle once connected; the muscle is familiar, having worked with whales so long. Having cut them apart. His eyes are milky, waxy, soft. I think I could scoop them right out the way I scoop spermaceti from the whales' heads.

Marina strikes him with the slat and he goes down at once, a pile of bones barely held together with muscle and fabric. His bone-thin fingers claw at the wet ground, towards my feet, and Marina jerks me backwards when I can only stare in silent regard. She hits him again and still he reaches for me. Tota, run, she tells me, but I cannot, because I cannot stop staring.

It was like this with my first whale. I should have been frightened at the way the men split the body apart, by the blood and other fluids that spilled everywhere. The head cavity only ever seemed like a cocoon to me, a place where one could be away from the noise of the world, a place where I might bury myself so I would not have to experience Esteuan's anger when my monthly blood came. It is what a woman's body does, I tell him. To him the blood only means no sons, no one to carry on the work when he no longer can. This man, I think, disappeared into the sea. What must it be like beneath those waves? Where the noise of the world also must vanish, where great beasts move through cold waters as grey shadows.

Marina hauls me back to the house, screeching. There is no lock upon the door; she wedges the slat of wood against it and pulls me towards the counter. Where did he touch you, she asks, over and over, and she dips a cloth into the bucket of clean water. What did he do to you, where did he touch you, and I cannot answer, for my attention is still anchored with the man who picks himself up from the ground and stares longingly at the whale rib before he shuffles away, towards the sea.

What did he do to you, Tota? Marina cries. She shakes me hard enough to steal my focus and I don't understand what she means until I see the bloody footprints on the wood floor. My footprints, my blood. I press a hand to my belly. Tomorrow I will be back inside a whale.

◀ ▶

The man from the sea is only the first of many who come to our camp. At first, the men refuse to believe it. They think the women are suffering from a shared illness. The men have not seen these strangers from the sea, therefore they cannot exist. They are a dream, Gil says, and he is so old and weathered that every younger man cries out in support of his words. Marina only stares with hard eyes; her own husband does not believe her, either.

Esteuan, who has seen the same strange man I have, says nothing. Why do you not speak of what you have seen? I ask him when we return to our home. Esteuan pours himself a cold bath and tells me he has seen nothing. His hands shake and he shoves them into the icy water as if it will numb him to the truth. He says we women have grown sick because we do not bear our husbands sons.

Though it is growing colder, I spend that night sleeping in the shed. I have no wish to lie beside Esteuan when he says such things. In the dark, I hear a rustle and I listen, to see if it is one of the sea strangers. The sound does not come again, but the low ghostsong rises up from the harbour to wend through the tryworks, the houses, the sheds where we store the casks of oil. I close my eyes and listen and am still listening when I wake at sunrise. I do not see Esteuan before I flee to the harbour where the men have brought in a whale already.

The men are triumphant, singing and hoisting harpoons into the air. These men have never brought in a whale before and though Arnaut was lost in the battle, the battle is still considered won. This is not a right whale or a bowhead; this is the treasured sperm whale and when Berasco sees me, he gestures for me to come, come, because they want only me to crawl inside. God help me, I long for that, to retreat from everything else if only for a little while.

The cool of the morning is erased inside the whale's body. The body is so fresh I find myself sweating from the heat of it as I work. Some days it is mindless, the stretch of arms and bucket into the waxy innards, but today I am aware of every motion. Aware of the strength in my limbs and this strange ritual. I murmur a thanks to the whale, lift up another bucket, but find myself holding it too long. Where has Berasco gone? I peer up and he is not perched on the whale's head. He is gone.

I climb my way out to find most of the crew gone. Young Dat hovers nearby, but his attention is not on me. Deeper in the harbour there is a flurry of activity and I think perhaps another whale has come, but it is not a whale. It is the strangers from the sea. I cannot count how many there are, but it reminds me of a flood of fish, so many that they wriggle one atop the other, unsure of how they are suddenly on land and not in the water. These men look much like the one I have seen; they are in various states of rot, some worse than others, but all of them gleam with the sheen of whale oil.

Dat looks at me when I emerge, filthy from the whale's innards. He offers me a wet rag and I wipe my face clean; the rest does not bother me and can wait. You can come, I tell the young boy as I move past him; I have no idea what we might do, but I want to get closer to see the furor. He follows me, mostly I think because he was charged with staying close. He wishes they would let him crawl inside the whales, but I know they will not; he is destined for greater things, they say. They say this of all the young men.

We round the tryworks and ships, working our way closer to the shallows where the furor is greatest. Our men are beating the strangers back into the water, with fists and clubs, with harpoons and oars. Esteuan is there and his oar connects with one rotting head; the head bursts under the contact and the body collapses. For a moment, Esteuan looks victorious, but two more strangers step up to take the place of the first and he hefts the oar once more.

There is a frantic sound to the confrontation. It reminds me of men taking a whale in open waters. That scream, the opening of one body into two parts. Though our men are killing these rotting bodies, our men are also being devoured. This is the only word for what I witness. It occurs to me to reach for Dat, to cover his eyes, but he has already seen the horror. These rotting men are devouring the healthy flesh of the others. Ripping into them the way a harpoon would, tearing, sundering.

The strangers do not stop and our men continue to fall. The women stream into the harbour now, roused by the sound, the screams. I leave Dat, trusting him to not be a fool as I am about to be. I cry for Marina, for Isabel and Andere, and anyone else who can come. Marina sees me – she feared I would be trapped in a whale! She cries, but I silence her and drag her towards the casks of oil.

She guesses what I mean to do because she protests. Isabel and Andere seem less worried over the loss of the oil – they each grab torches from the rendering fires as if they already know what must be done. We keep the tryworks, large iron tubs wreathed in brick, near the shore to try out the oil close to the water where the whales are kept. It lessens the work, for we haul the whales less distance than other stations must. It also adds risk, keeping this much oil near this much heat.

I grip Marina's hands and tell her to quiet. I speak to her as one might a child and slowly she understands we must do this. The strangers are gaining on our men and what shall we do if this station is lost? She moans and I stroke a hand over her tear-streaked face. I know, I know. But when we roll the casks towards the combat, she is steady and true and silent.

On the long tongue of bridge that connects the docks to the land, we haul the casks onto the railing. Below us, the conflict continues. There is only that awful, furious sound – if there is a scent to the spilled blood, to our precious dead, we cannot smell it above the normal stench of this place. Isabel nods at me and I at her. The moment I push the cask off the edge, she touches her torch to its gleaming side. The cask drops into the fray, streaming oil which catches fire, bursts. Our men who have not fallen run the other way, but the strangers take no notice. They are wrecked and fall burning into the shallow waters.

After, the silence is staggering. So too is the reek of burnt, rotten flesh, which I can now distinguish above the usual stench. It is Dat who runs down first, crying for his father. And soon after we are all there, wading through the charred and floating dead. Marina's husband scoops her up from the water, carries her from the shore though he is streaming with blood. Isabel's husband is covered in slash marks that call to mind the battle scars we see on whales. I imagine these men carrying these marks the way whales do, for the rest of their days – which they will do, but these days become short indeed.

Of Esteuan there is no sign.

◀ ▶

Marina and Lope take me to their house. I hear myself protest: if Esteuan should come home, I should be there to greet him when he does; there should be a warm meal and a wife. There are many shoulds. While I speak these words, another part of me is numbed to them. Where has Esteuan gone? Which ship took him? Was there a whale? I ask Lope, for they work together every day. Certainly he will know where my husband is. Lope quiets me, settles me into a chair beside their hearth. In the warmth of the fire, my thoughts come into some better order. Esteuan was not on a ship, there was no whale; the strangers have taken him, devoured him.

There is a warm meal here, warm soup and Marina's best bread. My hands smell like whale oil; they are steady when

I break my bread, though Lope's begin to shake then. He begins to have trouble feeding himself and Marina helps, her hand steadying his and the spoon. Still, the soup drops down his chin as though he were an infant and not a grown man. This frustrates him. He shakes her hand off, pushes away from the meal, and stalks across the room. This room is not large. I can smell him where he stands. He is rotting.

Once Lope is in bed, I suggest to Marina that we leave. She should not see what he will become. Though I do not know, I suspect. His flesh will fall to ribbons, his eyes will go milky and sightless. I do not say this to her, but Marina refuses. I cannot say what I would do in her place. She rests beside him, her hand upon his chest when he stops breathing in the night. She shakes him, pleading for him to wake and when his eyes come open, it is a sobbed laugh that escapes her. He loves to play, her Lope.

But these eyes are no longer his. Their green spark drowns in a haze of milk and I try to pull Marina away. Away before he can latch onto her. His movements are slow, the bedcovers confound him; I have Marina almost off the bed before she realizes I am taking her from her husband. She screams no, reaches for him. Lope groans and strains towards her. They are two lovers kept from one another, but she cannot see what has become of him. Perhaps she does not care. She wrenches from my hold and stumbles back to his. His rotting mouth glances her cheek and then sinks in.

It is that sound, the sundering. The ripping apart of flesh. Lope becomes the sharp harpoon and Marina the bloodied whale; he pulls her under. He breaks her open and scoops out all she is and no matter how I strike him, I cannot dislodge him. He is newly made, not wasted like the first man I saw, and terribly strong. I cannot separate her. Marina screeches and yet I see the way her hands hold fast. She holds to his arms to say she will not be parted even if this is how it ends. Until death, she swore to him.

Lope reaches past her for me, but I move towards the hearth. Towards the lamp which sits on the mantle. I throw the lamp into the fire and the oil bursts, licks up the walls and across the floor. The fire behind me throws my shadow across the grass. This shadow me staggers away into the night, hands held over ears as if this can forestall the wet screams that bleed into the dark.

◀ ▶

The man waits near the supply shed. He stutters, the rut in the ground saying he has been here a while, pacing and waiting while others of his kind flooded the harbour and ate our men. When he sees me, he stops. I wonder what I look like through those milky eyes, though perhaps I am not so different from most days I come home from the whales, coated in cooling spermaceti. This man screams at me. Spittle flies and his jaw unhinges on one side. The rot devours him; he's melting before me, but still lifts a hand, gestures. The whale rib rests on its side on the ground. Smears of blood and muck coat it, as though he tried to hold it. Oil gleams on the likeness of my brother.

Two years ago a storm pounded Red Bay; it was autumn and Marina and her chandlers had finished the candles we would need to see us through winter. These candles were shelved in pantries and cellars, wrapped in soft linen and

closed away from the light of day. The excess were boxed in
the hold of the *San Juan,* who stood ready to make her return
across the Atlantic with Joanes as her captain. That return
would never be made, for the storm did what she would with
the ship, forcing her into the depths before she could leave.
She went down with all hands, more than two hundred casks
of whale oil, and all of Marina's candles.

Whale oil drips from the man's hand, into my out-
stretched palm. Not water or blood, but oil, and one look at
what remains of his crooked nose tells me: this is Joanes. The
men who have come back from the sea are our own men,
dead and yet living still. Far behind us, someone screams –
oh, it sounds like Isabel – and another house erupts in scouring flames. Joanes's fingers rest in my palm, as cold as dead
whale flesh. He has no strength to grip my hand. He turns
and his fingers slide away, but he looks back at me once.
Come with me, Tota, I can hear him say. I dare you.

I follow him to the shore, through the rotting carcasses
and oily water that licks the rocks. Smoke roils through the
air now and fire illuminates the sea in long golden strips, in
bright blotches between the stones. We move slow, because
he doesn't lift his feet. He drags one then shifts his weight to
drag the other. We played this way as children, pretending
injury he can no longer escape. He wades into the water and
I hesitate. Joanes is waist-deep in the golden water when he
realizes I am not there. He turns. Moans. I want to push his
jaw back together, mend what the sea has broken. I extend a
hand to him.

Joanes comes back to me. Difficult, slow, terrible. I make
him drag himself through the water back to me, and picture
the many times he has come to shore already, how demand-

ing each journey was. The effort makes even me tired and I am reminded how my arms felt of lead after my first afternoon inside a whale. How I could not move the next morning and how the men laughed at me. They only ever laughed once. My brother lifts his arm with the same difficulty now, resting his dead fingers in my hand.

Something in the bones is familiar and I hold tight to him as he walks back into the sea. Every step takes me deeper, until the ground slips from beneath my shoes and I paddle. Joanes sinks, hand slipping from mine, and I can't go under, I can't, until I do. I take a breath and dive and spy him in the gloom beneath the surface. He walks as if anchored to the bottom, towards things I cannot see. When I do see them, my breath bubbles out of me and my chest screams a protest. I swim deeper.

Whales swim in the depths here, dead and yet living. These whales are injured, carrying harpoons that in turn carry ropes, weeds, moss. Some whales are split open across their broad heads, exposing the chambers where I would spend my days scooping them clean. The whales watch me with their unblinking eyes, steady, knowing all that I cannot know. My brother strides into the depth and I see others like him, drowned sailors all, shuffling amid the whales, broken casks of oil, strewn candles.

Do I drown? They will say so. It is the easiest explanation, because though I tell my story twice and it never changes, it never makes sense to those who remain. Isabel, her face scarred from that long ago night, refuses to believe, even when she leaves me bowls of warm soup in winter. Isabel's daughter (gifts of bread), granddaughter (gifts of oil), great-grandson (gifts of candles), great-great-granddaughter (gifts of drawings – a tall house with a light that I think is a dream, but I see the light scrape the sky).

I watch them all and they say I am a ghost, a girl who drowned because she could not give her husband sons. Esteuan knows better. He watches as I crawl into the dead whales. Watches as I stretch from side to side and expand to fill this chamber, and, at long last, in the cold waters of Red Bay, feel saved.

KISSING CARRION

Gemma Files

*Q: Are we living in a land where sex and horror are the new
Gods?*
A: *Yeah.*
—FRANKIE GOES TO HOLLYWOOD

I am persecuted by angels, huge and silent – marble-white,
rigid-winged, one in every corner. Only their vast eyes speak,
staring mildly at me from under their painful halos, arc-weld
white crowns of blank. They say: *Lie down.* They say: *Forgive,
forget. Sleep.*

Forget, lie down. Drift away into death's dream. Make
your…final…peace.

But being dead is nothing peaceful – as they must know,
those God-splinter-sized liars. It's more like a temporal
haematoma, time pooling under the skin of reality like
sequestered blood. Memory looping inward, turning black,
starting to stink.

A lidless eye, still struggling to close. An intense and
burning contempt for everything you have, mixed up tight
with an absolute – and absolutely justified – terror of losing
it all.

Yet here I am, still. Watching the angels hover in the ill-set corners of Pat Calavera's Annex basement apartment, watching me watch *her* wash her green-streaked hair under the kitchen sink's lime-crusted tap. And thinking one more time how funny it is I can see them, when she can't: They're far more "here" than I am, one way or another, especially in my current discorporant state – an eddying tide of discontent adding one more vague chill to the mouldy air around her, stirring the fly-strips as I pass. Pat's roommate hoards trash, breeding a durable sub-race of insects who endure through hot, cold and humid weather alike; he keeps the bathtub full of dirty dishes and the air full of stink, reducing Pat's supposed bedroom to a mere way-stop between gigs, an (in)convenient place to park her equipment 'til the next time she needs to use it.

Days, she teaches socks to talk cute as a trainee intern on *Ding Dong the Derry-O*, the world-famous Hendricks Family Conglomerate's longest-running preschool puppet show. Nights, she spins extra cash and underground performance art out of playing with her Bone Machine, getting black market-fresh cadavers to parade back and forth on strings for the edification of bored ultra-fetishists. "Carrionettes," that's what she usually calls them whenever she's making them dance, play cards or screw some guy named Ray, a volunteer post-mortem porn star whose general necrophiliac bent seems to be fast narrowing to one particular corpse, and one alone…mine, to be exact.

Pat can't see the angels, though – can't even sense their presence like an oblique, falling touch, a seraph's pinion-feather trailed quick and light along the back of my dead soul. And really, when you think about it, that's just as well.

I mean, they're not here for *her*.

Outside, life continues, just like always: Jobs, traffic, weather. It's February. To the south of Toronto there's a general occlusion forming, a pale and misty bee-swarm wall vorticing aimlessly back and forth across the city while a pearly, semipermeable lace of nothingness hangs above. Soft snow to the ankles, and rising. Snow falling all night, muffling the world's dim lines, half-choking the city's constant hum.

Inside, Pat turns the tap off, rubs her head hard with a towel and leans forward, frowning at her own reflection in the chipped back-mirror. Her breath mists the glass. Behind her, I float unseen over her left shoulder, not breathing at all.

But not leaving, either. Not as yet.

And: *Sleep,* the angels tell me, silently. And: *Make me,* I reply. Equally silent.

To which they say nothing.

I know a lot about this woman, Pat Calávera – more than she'd want me to, if she only knew I knew. How there are days she hates every person she meets for not being part of her own restless consciousness, for making her feel small and useless, inappropriate and frightened. How, since she makes it a habit to always tell the truth about things that don't matter, she can lie about the really important things under almost any circumstances – drunk, high, sober, sobbing.

And the puppets, I know about them too: How Pat's always liked being able to move things around to her own satisfaction, to make things jump – or not – with a flick of her finger, from Barbie and Ken on up. To pull the strings on *something,* even if it's just a dead man with bolts screwed into his bones and wires fed along his tendons.

Because she can. Because it's an art with only one artist. Because she's an extremist, and there's nothing more extreme. Because who's going to stop her, anyway?

Well. Me, I guess. If I can.

(Which I probably can't.)

A quick glance at the angels, who nod in unison: No, not likely.

Predictable, the same way so much of the rest of this... experience of mine's been, thus far; pretty much exactly like all the tabloids say, barring some minor deviations here and there. First the tunnel, then the light – you rise up, lift out of your shell, hovering moth-like just at the very teasing edge of its stinging sweetness. After which, at the last, most wrenching possible moment – you finally catch and stutter, take on weight, dip groundwards. Go down.

Farther and farther, then farther still. Down where there's a Bridge of Sighs, a Bridge of Dread, a fire that burns you to the bone. Down where there's a crocodile with a human face, ready and waiting to weigh and eat your heart. Down where there's a room full of dust where blind things sit forever, wings trailing, mouths too full to speak.

I have no name now, not that I can remember, since they take our names first of all – name, then face, then everything else, piece by piece by piece. No matter that you've come down so fast and hard, fighting it every step; for all that we like to think we can conquer death through sheer force of personality, our mere descent alone strips away so much of who we were, who we *thought* we were, that when at last we've gotten where we're going, most of us can't even remember why we didn't want to get there in the first place.

The truism's true: It's a one-way trip. And giving everything we have away in order to make it, up to and including
ourselves, is just the price – the going rate, if you will – of the
ticket.

Last stop, everybody off; elevator to…not Hell, no. Not
exactly…

…goin' down.

Why would I belong in Hell, anyway, even if it did exist?
Sifting through what's left of me, I still know I was average, if
that: Not too good, not too bad, like Little Bear's porridge. I
mean, I never *killed* anybody, except myself. And that—

—that was only the once.

Three years back, and counting: An easy call at the time,
with none of the usual hysterics involved. But one day, I
simply came home knowing I didn't ever want to wake up
the next morning, to have to go to work, and talk to people,
and do my job, and act as though nothing were wrong – to
see, or know, or worry about anything, ever again. The mere
thought of killing myself had become a pure relief, sleep
after exhaustion, a sure cure after a long and disgusting illness.

I even had the pills already – for depression, naturally;
thank you, Doctor. So I cooked myself a meal elaborate
enough to use up everything in my fridge, finally broke open
that dusty bottle of good white wine someone had once given
me as a graduation present and washed my last, best hope for
oblivion down with it, a handful at a time.

When I woke up I had a tube down my throat, and I was
in too much pain to even cry about my failure. Dehydration
had shrunk my brain to a screaming point, a shaken bag of
poison jellyfish. I knew I'd missed my chance, my precious

window of opportunity, and that it would never come again. I felt like I'd been lied to. Like I'd lied to myself.

So, with a heavy heart, I resigned myself once more – reluctantly – to the dirty business of living. I walked out the hospital's front doors, slipped back into my little slot, served out my time. Until last week, when I keeled over while reaching for my notebook at yet one more Professional Development Retreat lecture on stress management in the postmillennial workplace: Hit the floor like a sack of salt with a needle in my chest, throat narrowing – everything there, then gone, irised inward like some silent movie's Vaseline-smeared final dissolve. Dead at twenty-nine of irreparable heart failure, without even enough warning to be afraid of what—

—or who, in my case—

—came next.

Am I the injured party here? I hover, watching, inside and out; I can hear people's thoughts, but that doesn't mean I can judge their motives. My only real option, at this point, is just what the angels keep telling me it is: Move on, move on, move on. But I'm not ready to do that, yet.

There were five of us in the morgue, after all, but the bodysnatchers only took two for her to choose from. And of those two...

...Pat chose me.

◀ ▶

Lyle turns up at one, punctual as ever, while Pat's still dripping. She opens the door for him, then drops her towel and stalks naked back to her room, rooting through her bed's topmost layers in search of some clean underwear; though he's obviously seen it all before, neither of them show any interest in extending this bodily intimacy beyond the realm of the purely familial.

Which only makes sense, now that I think about it. In Pat's mind – the only place I've ever encountered Lyle, up 'til now – their relationship rarely goes any further than strictly business. He's her prime "artistic" pimp, shopping the act she and Ray have been working so hard to perfect to a truly high-class clientele: One time only, supposedly. Though by Lyle's general demeanour, I get the feeling he may already be developing his own ideas about that part.

Pat discards a Pixies concert tee with what looks like mould stains all over the back in favour of her Reg Hartt's Sex and Violence Cartoon Festival one, and returns to find Lyle grimacing over a cup of coffee that's been simmering since at least eight.

"Jesus Corpse, Pats. You could clean cars with this shit."

"Machine's on a timer, I'm not." Then, grabbing a comb, bending over, worrying through those last few knots: "Tonight all set up, or what?"

He shrugs. "Or what." She shoots him a glance, drawing a grin. "Look, I told you it was gonna be one of two places, right? So on we go to Plan B, 'sall. The rest's still pretty much as wrote."

"'Pretty much.'"

"Pretty, baby. Just like you."

And: Is she? I suppose so. Black hair and deep, dark eyes – a certain eccentric symmetry of line and feature, a clever mind, a blind and ruthless will. Any and all of which would've certainly been enough to pull *me* in, back when I was still alive enough to want pulling.

The angels tell me I'm bound for something better now, though. Some form of love precious far beyond the bodily, indescribable to anyone who hasn't tasted it at least once before. Which means there's no earthly way I can possibly know if I *want* to 'til I'm already there and drinking my fill, already immersed soul-deep in restorative, White Light-infused glory...

Convenient, that. As *Saturday Night Live*'s Church Lady so often used to say.

Oh – and "earthly," ha; didn't even catch that one, first time round. Look, angels! The corpse just made a funny.

(I said, *look*.)

But they don't.

Pat tops her shirt with a sweater, and starts in filling the many pockets of army pants with all the various Bone Machine performance necessities: Duct tape, soldering wire, extra batteries. Lyle, meanwhile, drifts away to the video rack, where he amuses himself scanning spines.

"This that first tape he sent you?" he demands suddenly, yanking one.

"Who?"

He waggles it, grinning. "Your boyfriend. RAY-mond."

A shrug. "Pop it and see."

"Pass." Which seems to remind him: "So, Patty – realize you two are sorta tight and this comes sorta late, but exactly how much research you actually do on this freak-o before you signed him up for the program?"

Pat's bent over now, hauling her semi-expensive boots up with both mittened hands. "Enough to know he'll fuck dead bodies if I ask him to," she says, shortly.

"'Cause he *wants* to."

A short, sharp smile, orthodontic-straight except for that one canine her wisdom teeth pushed out of line, coming in. "Best way to get anyone to do anything, baby. As you should know."

Of course, Pat's hardly objective. Seeing how she's in lust with Ray...love, maybe, albeit of a perversely limited sort. Much the same way *he* is, truth be told—

—with "me."

But Lyle, obviously, doesn't feel he can argue the point. So he just returns her smile, talk-show bland and throat-slitting bright, as she reaches for the door handle: Lets them both out, side by side, into a world of gathering cold. All bundled up like Donner Party refugees, and twice as hungry.

And: *Don't follow*, the angels advise me, uselessly. *Don't watch. Don't care.*

But the fact is, I...don't. I really don't. Don't feel, or know what I don't feel. Let alone what I do.

D-E-A-D, but way too much still left of me. I'm DEAD, so let me lie. Let me *lie*.

Please.

Pat and Lyle, struggling up the alley and down to the nearest curb. Ray, his obtrusively unobtrusive car – the Rich Pervertmobile itself, far too clean and anonymous to be used for anything but life's dirtiest little detours – already there to meet them, pluming steam.

And somewhere, awaiting its cue, the reluctant third party in this little triangle-cum-foursome: My body, a water clock full of blood and other fluids, forever counting down to an explosion that's already happened. A psychic plague-bomb oozing excess pain, a hive for flies, all slick, lily-waxen and faintly bruised in the wake of rigor mortis's ebb, even before

Ray's hot mouthings gave birth to that starburst of pale lavender hickeys around what used to be my trachea.

It's not *me*, not in any way that counts – but it's not NOT me, either. And I just, I just…

…don't…

…want…

…them *touching* it anymore.

Either of them.

◀ ▶

Going back – as far back as he can, at least – Ray tells Pat that he thinks the first time he really began to understand the true nature of his personal…distinction…must have been when his parents insisted he visit his beloved grandfather's freshly dead body at the local hospital: Washed, laid out, neatly johnny-clad. His parents had already forewarned him it would look like a mannequin, like something made of plaster, an empty husk. But it wasn't like that, not even vaguely. It looked oddly magnetic, oddly tactile; nothing rotten, or gross, or potentially contagious – soothing, like an old friend. And its only smell was the familiar odour of shed human skin.

He wanted to lie down with his head on its sternum, breathe deep and let it cool his fever, this constant ceaseless hammering in his head and heart. To free him, for once and for all, of the febrile hum and spark of his own life.

Since then, Ray's never been able to decide what arouses him more: The concept itself, or the sheer impossibility of its execution. Because anyone can fuck the dead, if they only try hard enough – but the dead, by their very nature, can never fuck *back*. Which is why it has to be guys, though he himself is – in every other way than this – "straight." If that term even applies, under these circumstances.

Their superiority. Their otherness. To him, it's only natural: The dead know more, and knowledge is power. And power, as that old politician once boasted…is sexy.

So: Fucked in slaughterhouses, under the hanging racks of meat. Fucked with decay smeared all over them both, in graveyards, animal cemeteries; sure, buddy – just gimme my cut, you freak, and bend on over. Fucked in mortuaries, the "other" corpses watching impassively. Corpses taking part in his own taking, silent voyeurs, sad puppets in countless sweaty *menages à mort*. Fucked by guys wearing corpses' skins – and wow, was *that* expensive, mainly because it went against so many kinds of weird sanitation strictures; public health, and all that. Same reason you can't just drop your granddad in the garden if he happens to croak at your house – or die at home at all, these days, for that matter.

Fucked by the dying – guys so far gone, so far in the financial hole, they'd do anything to make their next medical bill. A charge, but not quite the same; not the same, and never enough. And finally, back to the morgue alone with condoms and trocar in hand – here's an extra hundred to leave the door ajar, I'll lock up as I leave. No worries.

Money's no problem; Ray *has* money. Too much, some might say – too much free time, and a bit too little to do except obsess, jerk off, plan. The idle rich are hard to entertain, Vinnie…

Things do keep on escalating, though, often and always. And escalation can bring a bad reputation, especially in some quarters.

Which made it all the more lucky Ray and Pat happened to find each other, I suppose – for them both.

And for Lyle, of course, albeit from a very different point of view…Lyle, to whom falls the onerous yet lucrative task of facilitating this genderswitched postmillennial *Death and the Maiden* tableau they've played out every day this week, give or take; same one that would surely rerun itself constantly behind my eyelids if only I still had either eyes to see with, or lids to close on what I didn't want to see. Same one you might well already have seen, if you're just hip and sick enough to have paid Lyle's "finder's fee" up front – or bought the bootleg DV8 tapes he peddles over the Internet, thus far unbeknownst to either of his silent partners.

Like Lyle, I never saw that original "audition" tape on Pat's shelf, either. But as the rundown above should prove, I've certainly heard its précis often enough: Why I Like To Get Screwed By Dead Bodies For The Amusement Of Total Strangers Even When The Money Involved's My Own, in fifty thousand words or more. Ray's confession/manifesto, re-spilled at intervals – after various post-postmortem Bone Machine-aided orgies, usually – over binges of beer and weed which sometimes culminate in fumbling, gratitude- and guilt-ridden, mutually unsatisfying attempts at "normal" sex. Pat lying slack beneath a sweating, huffing Ray, trying to will her internal temperature down far enough to maintain his shamed half-erection even as her own orgasm builds, inexorably. Cursing the demeaning depths this idiot hunger for him can make her sink to, while simultaneously feeling her fingers literally itch to seize the Machine's controls again and do the whole damn thing over *right*.

Part of me wonders exactly how much detail I need – or care – to go into here, vis-à-vis Pat's "art" and my rather uncomfortable place in its embrace. But then again, close as "I" may get to it in flesh, most of the Bone Machine's complex structural workings will probably always remain a mystery to me. Bolts screwed directly into bones, wires strung like tendons, electrical impulses jumping from brain to finger to keypad to central animatronic switchboard...

Pat pulls the strings here, as in all else. When my dead body's making "love" to him, it's her moves, her ideas, her smoothing, gentle touch translated through my flesh, which keeps Ray coming back time and time again; I'm just the medium for her message, a clammy six-foot dildo powered by rods and pistons. A deadweight sex-aid soaked in scented lube to hide the growing spoiled-meat smell, the inevitable wear and tear of Ray's increasingly desperate affections.

But Ray, like any true fetishist, ignores whatever doesn't contribute directly to the fulfillment of his motivating fantasy. He knows our time together's on a (necessarily) tight schedule, so he tries to wring every extra ounce of pleasure he can out of the experience while Pat watches and fumes, trapped behind her rows of switches. He loves the mask, not the face; the made, not the maker. Decay's his groom, and he doesn't want even the shadow of anything else getting in the way of this so-devoutly desired consummation, this last great graveyard gasp.

It'd be sort of tragic, if it wasn't so – mordantly – funny. Together, Pat and Ray have all the requisite common interests and obsessions, plus a heaping helping of that brain-to-groin combustive spark which so many other relationships are made from; if she was dead (or had the right equipment required to rock his world), they'd be perfect for each other. But her hole just doesn't fit his socket, or vice versa. So the only way she can touch him...and make him *want* her to, at least...

...is with *my* hands.

And more and more, that very fact is already making her dream happy dreams of someday taking a bone-saw to "my" wrists. Of burning them in some HazMat crematorium's fire, like plague-infected monster grasshoppers.

Ray told Pat he was literally up for her ultimate piece of performance art, to bravely go where none of her other co-conspirators were ever willing to, not even with three con-doms' worth of protection. She told Lyle, who instantly cheered her on, visions of Ben Franklin dancing in his money-coloured eyes; he paged his pals down at the M.E.'s office, and the deal was struck – cash for flesh, tickets at the door and a fresh new co-star every week, after the old one finally started to rot.

And so it went, a neat little cycle, a perverse new rhythm method. Pat called the shots, Ray did the dance, Lyle racked up the take; they soon got into the habit of partying later, while Lyle was on his way to the bank. Pat, using Ray's addic-tion to feed her own, like any pusher trading "free" product for not-so-free favours, while Ray replays his own earlier per-formance for both their benefits.

It was, and is, a match made in Gomorrah, or maybe Gehenna: Pimp meets girl meets boy meets corpse(s). And everybody's happy.

Everybody alive enough to count, that is.

All that changed once Pat and Lyle fixed Ray up with my mortal coil, though, and he "fell for" it...telling her, feverishly, and repeatedly, how this hunk of otherwise nonde-script white male meat which just happened to come with my restless spirit attached was the end of his search, the literal em*bodi*ment of all his most cadaver-centric daydreams. Suddenly, his fetish had narrowed and shifted to allow only this one particular corpse or nothing at all.

And: "You know tomorrow night's gonna have to be curtains for Mr. Stinky, right?" she asked him, briskly, after yesterday's post-show pas de deux.

Ray, frowning: "How so?"

Pat reclipped her bra, sponged sweat from her cleavage; I saw the angels' halos reflected in her throat's shiny hollow, a wet white crackle of phantom jewelry. "'Cause he's starting to fall apart, same as the others. Already had to rewire his joints twice just to get him limber enough to limbo – and his scalp's starting to peel, too. Now it's just a matter of time."

"But if you're keeping him refrigerated...."

"Yeah, sure; but there's only so far that goes, Ray. No freezer in the world's totally fly-tight. Nature of the beast, man."

A pause. Ray stood silent as Pat wriggled back into her jeans, then shot him the raised eyebrow: You comin', or what? Shook his head. And replied, finally—

"Then I guess we're looking at goodbye for me too, Pat."

At that, Pat turned fully, *both* eyebrows up. "You're kidding."

"No."

Because...this is the *one*. Remember? The one and only. No substitutes need apply, not even—

(well, *you*, sweetheart)

Ahhhh, true love.

He feels like he's having a dialogue with it, that's what he's always told her. Like he's finally being privileged, through this nightly series of gag-makingly contortionate sex show antics, to vicariously experience the ecstatic transformation my corpse is already undergoing – the transition from flesh to fleshlessness, an all-expenses-paid tour through time's metaphorical flensing chamber. To share in the experience as it sloughs the residue of its own mortality off like a scab, revealing some clean, invisible new form lurking beneath.

My body, my husk. My shucked, slimy former skin.

It's not *pure*, though, for fuck's sweet sake. It's not *perfected*. It has no "secret wisdom" to impart. And as for powerful, well…

If it really *was* powerful – if *I* was – then we wouldn't be here, would we?

Any of us.

The argument went on for some time, back and forth: Pat's voice soaring snappishly while Ray stayed quiet but firm, unshakable. There was an element of betrayal to her mounting disbelief, as both of them well knew. Suffice to say, Lyle probably wouldn't have been too happy to find out his star attraction had decided to retire either. Not that Pat even seemed to be thinking of things from that particular angle.

"It's just a fucking *corpse*, Ray. You've done fifty of 'em already, most of 'em long before you ever met me—"

Ray nodded. "Because I was looking for the *right* one."

"And this is it?"

"In my opinion."

She stared, snorted.

"Lyle won't like it."

"Fuck Lyle."

A sigh: "Been there."

The unsaid implication – goodbye to it, to this, the nightly grind. To Lyle's meal ticket. And, by extension, good-bye…

(to me?)

Me meaning her. As well as me meaning "me."

Before, whenever Ray's beaux got too pooped to preserve, the routine took over. Lyle got on the pager again, handing out more of Ray's money; the bodies made their exit, stage wherever. Parts in a dump, an acid-soaked tub-ring, concrete at the bottom of a lake, with all trace of Ray's touch, or Pat's – or Lyle's, for that matter, not that Lyle ever *touches* the Bone Machine's prey – salved away in disposal.

Which should be enough, surely: Enough to wash this lingering wisp of me clean and let me rise. Sponge the finger-prints from my soul, and all that good, metaphorical stuff. But —

(but)

At first I just hovered above, horrified, longing for the angels to cover my see-through face with their equally see-through wings. So grotesquely helpless to do anything but watch, and wait, and watch some more. Wait some more, watch some more. Repeat, repeat, repeat.

But then, slowly…through sheer, profane will alone, one assumes, while my constant companions loomed ever closer in (literally) holier-than-thou disapproval…

Don't look.

But I have to.

Move on.

But – I CAN'T.

(Not yet.)

…I found myself starting to be able to feel it once more, from the inside out. The ghost of a ghost of a ghost of a sensation. Ray's mouth on "mine," sucking at my cold tongue like a formaldehyde-flavoured lollipop. "My" muscles on his, bunching like poisoned tapeworms.

Taking shaky repossession part by part; hacking back into my own former nervous system synapse by painful synapse, my shot neural net fizzing at cross-purposes like that eviscerated eight-track we had in the student lounge back at my old high school – the one you could only make change tapes by reaching inside and touching two stripped wires together, teeth gritted against the inevitable shock.

Pat sends her commands and I…resist, just a fraction of a micro-inch; she's off-put, suspects that her calibrations aren't quite as exact as she'd thought. But even as she re-works them, Ray strains towards me and I…strain back. Rise to meet him, halfway. I know he sees what I'm doing, if only on a subconscious level. Her too.

Because: It's like cheating, isn't it? Always is, when love's involved. And lovers *always* know.

"I want to do it," he told her in the car, on the way home. "I want to be the one, this time."

"The one to do what?"

"You know. Finish it."

Pat narrowed her dark, dark eyes. "Finish it," she repeated. "Like – get rid of it? Destroy it yourself?"

Rip it apart, tear it limb from limb, eat it (un)alive. If he couldn't have it…

Dark eyes, with green sliding to meet them: Money-coloured too, in a far more vivid way. Because it's not that Ray's unattractive, that he couldn't possibly indulge himself any other way. In fact, if you look at it too closely – closer than he probably wants you to, or wants to himself – you'd have to conclude that the *indulgence* is doing things the way he's chosen to.

"You're worried about what Lyle'd think?"

She shrugged. "His customers, maybe."

"Should be a hell of a show, though."

…should be.

Another cool look, another pause – silence between them, smooth as a stone. All that frustrated longing, that self-bemused *ache*; enough to power a city, to set both their carefully-constructed internal worlds on fire.

The angels ruffle their pinions, disapprovingly. But I was human once, just flawed and impermanent enough to understand.

I mean, we just want what we want, don't we? Even when it's impossible, perverse, ridiculous, we want just what WE want. And nothing else will do.

Move ON.

Be at PEACE.

But: I can't, can't. Won't. Because I want…what I want. Nothing else.

(Nothing.)

"You're the last of the red-hot romantics, Ray," Pat told him, eventually, knowing what she was agreeing to, but not caring. Or thinking she knew, at least. But knowing only the half of it.

She's had her dance, after all, like Ray's had his: Now I'll have mine, and be done with it. Change partners mid-song; no harm in that. And if there is…

…if there *is*, well – it's not like anyone'll be complaining.

◀ ▶

And now it's past midnight, the zero hour. Showtime. Lyle's customers file in as he sets up the cameras, trance-silent with anticipation: Stoned suburbanites, jaded superfan ultra-scenesters, unsocialized Western *otaku* with bad B.O. and worse fashion sense. Teens who followed the wrong set of memes and ended up somewhere way too cool for school, let alone anywhere else. Many seem breathless, barely able to sit still. Some – few, thankfully – have actually brought dates, rummaging absently between each other's thighs as they lick their lips, eyes firmly on the prize: The Bone Machine itself, a slumped mantis of hooks and cords; Pat, strapping "my" body in for its final run around Ray's block, suturing it fast with duct tape. Slipping the requisite genital prosthetic mini-bladder tube up the corpse's urethral tract and pumping it erect before condoming the whole package shut once more…

The Machine – model number five, rebuilt on-site by Pat herself, due to be broken down to component parts and blueprints when the spectacle's dollar value finally wears itself thin – occupies a discontinued butchering lab somewhere in the Hospitality area of a shut-down community college campus: Ray's coin bought a deal with security guards who let them in at night after the campus manager went home, as well as access to a walk-in fridge/freezer just big enough to keep their mutual "carrionette" pliant. It's a vast, slick cave of a place whose dark-toned walls are hung with 1960s charts of cartoon pigs and cows tattooed with dotted "cut here" lines, whose sloping concrete floor still sports drains and runnels to catch blood already congealed into forty years' worth of collective grease-stink. Under the heat of Lyle's lights the air is hot and close, smell thick enough to cut: Meat, sweat, anticipation.

Transgression a-comin'. That all-purpose po-mo word poseurs of every description love so well. But there are all kinds of transgressions, aren't there? Transgression against society's standards, the laws of God and man, against others, against yourself…

Here's Pat, gearing up – eyes intent, face studiously dead-pan. Here's Lyle, all sleaze and charm, spinning his strip-club barker's spiel. Here's "me," slug-pale and seeping slightly, yet already beginning to stir as the connections flare, the cables pull, the hip-pistons give a tentative little preliminary thrust and grind. And—

—here's Ray, nude, gleaming with antibacterial gel. Right on cue.

See the man, see the corpse. See the man see the corpse. See the man? See the *corpse*?

Okay, then.

…let's get this party started, shall we?

Jolt forward, pixilate, zoom in – not much foreplay, at this stage of the game. Just wind and wipe into Ray bent L-shaped and hooking his heels in the small of my jouncing avatar's back, clawing passion-sharp down its slack sides. Pat puppets the Machine's load forward, digging deep, straining for that magic buried trigger; Ray scissors himself and "me" together even harder, so hard I hear something crack. And blood comes welling: Fluid, anyway, tinged darker with decay. Blood already starbursting the cilia of "my" upturned eyes, broken vessels knit in a pinky-red wash of old petechial haemorrhaging—

Ray groaning, teeth bared. Lyle leaning in for the all-important E.C.U. Pat, bent to the board, her hair lank and damp across her frowning forehead.

Ray, grabbing at "my" hair, feeling its mooring slip and slide like rotten chicken-skin. Taking a big, biting tug at "my" bile-soaked lower lip, swapping far more than spit, before rearing back again for a genuine chomp. Starting to – *chew*.

Pat gags: Ewwww, rubbery. You kiss your girlfriend with that mouth?

(Not any more, I guess.)

First the bottom lip, then the upper. A bit of "my" cheek. Sticky cuspids and canines like stars in a gum-pink evening sky. Ray's tearing at "my" sides, "my" chest, "my" throat, as the audience coos and gasps; Lyle's still filming. And Pat's twisting knobs like a maniac, trying to match Ray's growing frenzy, fighting with all her might to keep the show's regularly scheduled action on track: Destruction, ingestion, transgression with a capital "T." Fighting *Ray*, really, as he guides "my" exposed jaws to his own neck again and again, like he's daring "me" to – somehow – bite in, bite down, pop his jugular and give all his fans the ultimate perverted thrill of their collective lives.

Because: Ray feels himself going now, in the Japanese sense. Knows just how late it's getting, how soon the high from this last wrench and spurt will fade. Knows that no possible climax to this drama will ever seem good enough, *climactic* enough, no matter WHAT he does to "me." I can see it in his eyes. I can—

(*see* it.)

See it. "I" *can*. And "I," I, *I*…

I feel myself. Feel *myself*. Coming, too.

Feel myself *there*. At last.

Feel Ray hug me to him and hug him back, arms contracting floppily – feel that pin Pat put in my shoulder last time snap as the joint finally pulls free, and tighten my grip with the other before Ray can start to slip. Feel my clotty lashes bat, a wet cough in my dry throat; the sudden gasp of breath comes out like a sneeze, spraying his face with reddish-brown gunk. See Ray goggle up at me, as Lyle gives a girly little scream: Cry to God and Pat's full name, reduced to panicked consonants. HolyshitPahtri-SHA*FUCK*!

Pat's head comes up fast, hair flipping. Eyes so wide they seem square.

My tongue creaks and Ray hasn't left me much lip to shape words with, but I know we understand each other. Like I said, I can SEE it.

Gotta go, Ray. You want to come with?

Well, *do* you?

And Ray...nods.

And I...

...I give him. What he wants.

And oh, but the angels are screaming at me like a Balkan choir massacre, all at once – glorious, polyphonic, chanting chains of scream: Sing *No,* sing *stop,* sing *thou shalt thou shalt thou shalt NOT.* Their halos flare like sunspots, making the whole room pulse – hiss and pop, paparazzi flashbulb storm, a million-sparkler overdrip curtain of angry white light.

(Sorry, guys. Looks like revenge comes before redemption, this time round.)

Ray pulls me close, spasming, as my front teeth find his Adam's apple. Blood jets up. The audience shrieks, almost in unison.

I look over Ray's shoulder at Pat, frozen, her board so hot it's starting to smoke. And I smile, with Ray's blood all over my mouth.

So hook *him* up to the Bone Machine now, Pats – make a movie, while you're at it. Take a picture, it'll last longer. Take your turn. Take your time.

But this is how it breaks down: He's gone, long gone, like I'm gone, too. Like *we're* gone, together. Gone.

Gone to lie down.

Gone to forgive, to forget.

Gone, gone, finally—

—to sleep.

◀ ▶

Aaaaaah, *yes*.

The sheep look up, the angels down. And I'm done, at long, long last – blown far, far away, the last of my shredded self trailing behind like skin, like wings, a plastic bag blowing.

Done, and I'm out: Forgiven, forgotten, sleeping. Loving nothing. Being nothing. Feeling none of your pain, fearing none of your anger, craving none of your – anything. Anymore.

Down here where things settle, down below the bridge, the weighing-room, the House of Dust itself – down here, where our faces fall away, where we lose our names, where we no longer care what brought us here, or why…I don't care, finally, because (finally) I don't have to. And in this way, I'm just the same as every other dead person – thank that God I've never met, and probably never will: No longer mere trembling meaty prey for the thousand natural shocks that flesh is heir to; no longer cursed to live with death breathing down my neck, metaphoric or literal.

Which only makes the predicament of people like Ray – or like Pat, for that matter – seem all the crueller, in context. Since the weakness of the living is their enduring need to still love us, and to feel we still love them in return; to believe that we are still the same people who were once capable of loving them back. Even though we're, simply…

…not.

Down here, down here: The psychic sponge-bed, the hole at the world's heart, that well of poison loneliness every cemetery elm knows with its great taproot. Here's where we float, my fellow dead and I – one of whom might *be* Ray, not that he or I would recognize each other now.

The keenest irony of all being that I suppose Ray killed himself for *me*, in a way – killed himself, by letting me kill him. Even though…until that very last moment we shared together…we'd never really even met.

Come with me, I said. Not caring if he could, but suspecting—

(rightly, it turns out)

—I'd probably never know, in the final analysis, if he actually did.

Down here, where we float in a comforting soup of non-description – charred and eyeless, Creation's joke. Big Bang detritus bought with Jesus's blood.

Ash, drifting free, from an eternally burning heaven.

AND ALL THE FATHOMLESS CROWDS

Ada Hoffmann

Queen's University
Department of Survival
SURV 110
Final Examination
April 21, 2031
Professor Lita Yao
Name: Sandra Chakarvarthi
Student Number: 1715-5730

Written Component, Part 1
Q. When is it advisable to use deadly force against a Non-Mind?
A. When you are threatened, and not before. Attempting to exterminate Non-Minds on sight is a sign of Romero Disorder. In the days immediately after 12/12, many human survivors developed this disorder. The sheer number of Non-Minds overwhelmed them, and each human died of exhaustion mid-rampage – if the Non-Minds didn't get them first. Arguably, Romero Disorder itself is a form of Mindlessness.

◀ ▶

Practical Component, Part 1

Five hours, forty minutes, and fifty-eight seconds to go.

Your first destination is City Hall, and you've picked a lake-side route because that's what gets you top marks: Professor Yao needs to know you can deal with any terrain. There are plenty of creatures on land who cannot enter running water. But there are creatures in the water as well. You split the difference and jog along the wave-lapped rocks, past the Time Statue, which was once a pair of simple metal blocks but nowadays dances to its own irregular ticking sounds, half-melted. Sunlight glints off the water, drawing your eye to the storklike walk of the windmills on the other side.

First lesson: Apart from the insides of Certified Homes, everything is alive.

Confidence is more important than speed. You can't look like you're fleeing. So you jog along, not too fast, and fix the thought deep in your centre. *I am safe in this place. I refuse to be afraid.*

It's not like you haven't walked this route before. Even walking from your residence to the classroom is a form of practice. All year you've gathered your friends on assignments and walked all around the city: visiting shut-ins in their Certified Homes, harvesting resources from emergency stores, gaping at the beauty of the lake and the old buildings. But alone, with the clock ticking and your grades at stake, the trip gives you jitters.

I refuse to be afraid.

A tentacle of pure water rises out of the waves and gestures to you. You wave back, but don't look at it long. Be polite, says the rule, but don't get them too interested. The tentacle dissolves back into the lake.

A few blocks on, a small crowd of Purples emerges from City Park. You see Purples at least once a week around campus: violet-skinned, young and beautiful, except for the matted, paint-coloured hair. You wrote your ANTH 101 midterm essay on Purples, on how they retain just enough Mind to ape human sociality. They crawl out from the trees, howling and hooting and slapping their jackets on the ground. One calls to you.

"*Oil Thigh na Banrighinn!*" It's the only thing Purples ever say.

It's a crapshoot with Purples. You can ignore them and risk their ire. Or you can interact – even a little – and risk being swarmed.

I refuse to be afraid.

"*A'Banrighinn!*" you call back, grinning jauntily. Not breaking stride. Making it clear you're on your way someplace else.

The Purples cheer, and the rhythmic *thunk* of jackets slapping on the ground follows you all the way to the harbourfront, where twist-sailed boats mutter unintelligibly to each other. When the sound dies away, you glance over your shoulder: they aren't following. Not a threat.

You look forward again and there's a dead woman standing there.

You freeze. You stare. You've heard of zombies before, but never seen one up close. She's not pretty like Purples, not ethereal like the tentacle. She's foul-smelling and swollen and bluish, with a rigor mortis smile. Bits of her have come off or rotted away: you can see the bones of her knuckles.

You've seen other disgusting things since you came of age and left your Certified Home. The disgust by itself would not stop you. You stop because you know those eyes. You know the red sari she wore to your sending-off, which the robots dressed her in again before they lowered her body into the earth.

You're suddenly not thinking of the exam rules at all.

You open your mouth:

"Mom?"

◀ ▶

Written Component, Part 2

Q. Briefly list the major known causes of Non-Mundane Events, including the creation and control of Non-Minds, and explain the implications for the Minded.

A. 1. The mental energy of the Minded. (Fear, faith, desire, and other strong emotions, as well as deliberate spellcasting.)

2. The pseudo-mental energy of Non-Minds. (Different from Minded. Poorly understood.)

3. Ordinary physical processes working with Non-Mundane sources. (e.g. infection with Non-Mundane viruses; operation of Non-Mundane mechanics and circuitry; Non-Minds reproducing sexually).

4. Divine intervention (rare).

In special cases the Minded have some control over 3, but in a normal situation, 1 is the only way we can hope to have a say. This is why any Minded venturing out of their Certified Home must learn to control their mental energy above all else.

◀ ▶

Practical Component, Part 2

Your mother's corpse follows you into City Hall. You haven't been able to make her speak. After the third inarticulate groan you started to ignore her. You can't get too fascinated with the Non-Minded, even if they look like your mother. Maybe especially if they look like your mother.

City Hall is a big limestone building, domed and pillared. When you were too little to leave your Certified Home, your mother showed you a picture and told you they used to administrate all of Upper and Lower Canada from here. You misunderstood at first. She had to explain that this was long before she came to Canada, long before her own parents were born. By 12/12 the place was mostly a tourist attraction.

She had to explain five times what a tourist attraction was.

"And," she whispered sometimes, "not everything was Mundane, even then. There was always a little magic. But it was different. Hidden."

The next page of your exam lies neatly on the front steps. When you've answered the question, your next destination blooms on the paper. *The altar at St. Mary's.*

You goggle at the page. The church district is the second-worst part of the city. Worst are the prisons, of course, but no sane professor would send you there in your first year. A sane professor wouldn't send you to the churches either. In a place like that, belief metastasizes.

But that's what the page says. That's what you have to do.

You rise to your feet and march down the steps. Worrying will only waste time. You breathe deeply. You stay in your centre. *I refuse to be afraid.*

Your mother's corpse trails after you. Groans again.

"Go away, Mom," you say through your teeth. She shambles along in your wake, undeterred.

Almost everything is dangerous when provoked, even your mother. You think of the question on Romero Disorder. You wonder if she will attack you later, if Professor Yao will grade you on whether you made the transition to combat at the right moment. *Am I going to have to kill my mother?*

Then you close your mind on the question. Thinking it might make it happen. You do times tables. You recite poetry. You breathe deep.

You detour around the hospital, which is the third-worst part of the city, and venture into the bowels of the church district. Your mother has shown you pictures of how it looked before 12/12 – like normal buildings, lined up along the street and neatly separate, their steeples and stained glass the only hint of magic. You've never seen a church in real life that still looks that way. They're overgrown and bulbous, intersecting at odd angles and growing knots around the connections. Between Sydenham Street United and First Baptist there's a place where needlelike stones wave in a slow-motion battle, the remnants of sectarian disagreements no one remembers anymore.

The street itself grows over with Gothic arches until you can't see sunlight. You've never gone this deep into the church district. You don't know what church this stretch of the road belongs to this week, but it's candlelit and lined with icons: St. Francis and the Animals, St. George and the Bulldozer, the Warrior Angel of the Three-Headed Sharks.

Your mother trails behind you, staring into space. You wish she would go away.

There's a rumbling sound.

You think they're Minded for a second. Pilgrims. There are religious people crazy enough to try to live in these places. The creatures creeping out of the walls look almost like humans. Broad, clean faces, smiling, in the whole range of human colours, not purple, not grey and rotting like your mother. Covered in robes: white, blue, and burgundy.

But they lurch while they walk. They hum dully together in the ghost of a hymn.

Pergolesi's *Stabat Mater*. The Non-Minds have a sense of irony.

And they are coming right for you, their fingers out-stretched in claw shapes.

You're outnumbered. You don't know how powerful they are. You should run or call the emergency robots. But you *have* to get to the next question. You're so close. You can see the arched nave of St. Mary's just past them. And you don't know any other way in.

You are too tempted.

You know how to jump and how to balance; you did gymnastics for years in your Certified Home. You can stand on the railing and run past them. It's ambitious, but you can do it. *I refuse to be afraid.*

You hop up onto the railing with ease.

The closest Non-Mind grabs your shin and pulls you back down.

In an instant they're all over you. Heavy robes and grabbing, tearing fingers. You roll to your feet and punch out at them blindly. In American schools the students have guns for this, but Professor Yao doesn't allow them. They make you arrogant and a lot of the interesting Non-Minds are immune to bullets anyway. So it's back to your punches, blocks, kicks, and throws.

You get one in the nose, one in the neck, and they stagger backwards. You trip another one behind you. A jab from your elbow and a fourth goes down. But every time you hit one, two more grab you.

There are too many. They're coming too fast.

You punch out again, but your arm doesn't even fully extend before a group of three Non-Minds grab it away. You panic. Try to peel them off with your other hand but they trap that one, too.

You fall. The floor hits your shoulder and they're on you. Their mouths gape open, the ghost of the *Stabat Mater* still echoing in the air. Blunt teeth close on your shoulder.

Then there is a roar.

Your mother plows into the fray, tossing Non-Minds aside like Styrofoam. Her half-rotted fingernails tear their flesh. A hand lets go of you, then another, and you leap to your feet. Adrenaline surges through you. You punch and kick and shout alongside her, but it's her they run away from.

And run away they do. Until the arched-over street is empty again and you're catching your breath in silence.

Your mother has no breath to catch.

You don't know if you just failed your exam. You don't know if it's safe to touch your mother. But oh, God. It's your mother. She's saved your life.

You wrap her in a bear hug the way you used to when she was alive. She smells horrible, like meat left out on the counter too long, and you don't care.

◄ ►

Written Component, Part 3

Q. What would you have done in that fight if your mother had not been there?

A. Did I just fail? Did I fail because I got in a fight? It wasn't Romero Disorder. They actually attacked me. Did I fail because I fought instead of running away? Did I fail because I didn't beat them on my own?

Q. What would you have done if your mother had not been there?

A. Did I fail?

Q. What would you have done if your mother had not been there?

A. You're not even going to tell me if I failed, are you?

I might have waded in anyway, but that would have been really stupid. It's important to know when you're outnumbered. What I *should* have done is run away. If there was no suitable escape route, I should have called 911. Emergency robots are not a sure thing, but if they get there in time, you'll probably survive. That is what I should – would have done. Avoided the confrontation.

No human can win against everything. Knowing when to back off is as important as knowing how to fight. And so is knowing who to turn to for help.

◄ ►

Practical Component, Part 3

Fort Henry Hill. A cakewalk compared to the churches.

You were scared of the Hill when you first came to Queen's. The squat fortress on top was paced by uniformed Non-Minds and cannons that rolled along of their own volition. Every so often a thundering boom echoed from the ramparts. You pictured it worse than the churches or even the prisons, a place infected with the brutality of war. Professor Yao had to explain to you that the war was over long before 12/12.

The Non-Minds here are friendly, as Non-Minds go.

You stride up the hill, one hand held in your mother's, keeping an eye on the cannons. Showing fear is not recommended here. Neither is excessive speed, furtiveness, belligerence, or the carrying of weapons. They're friendly, but you don't want to get them excited.

"Left! Right! Left!" barks a small group of Non-Minds marching past you, ramrod-straight in bright red. It's like the Oil Thigh: the only thing they can say.

The swing bridge holds as you creep across the protective ditch. The Non-Minds have left the front gates open. Easy. The interior is an ancient limestone courtyard, grey and stately.

You try to catch your mother's eye in triumph. Which is when you notice the flesh sloughing off her face.

She was rotting before. But the blood of the Non-Minds at the church has done something. Acidic, maybe. She's coming apart where it splashed her. No one's skin should peel off like that, even if they're dead already.

You bite down the panic. Panicking will attract all the fear-seeking Non-Minds for miles. But you're already walking faster, aiming for the Lower Fort. Maybe they'll have something. A washbasin. Water.

What if they don't have water? The lake is close by. You can take your mother there. If running water doesn't drive zombies off. If the sharks and tentacle-things don't get you.

If water can get the blood off at all.

You duck into one of the fort's corridors. They're narrow and short, and torchlight creeps across them. There will be a washbasin in here somewhere. Or at least the next page of your exam. But it may be too late.

◀ ▶

Written Component, Part 4

Q. Tell me about your mother.

A. What does this have to do with the course?

Q. Tell me about your mother.

A. She's dying.

Q. Tell me about your mother.

A. Is this part of the exam? Did you bring her here somehow? A spell?

Q. Tell me about your mother.

A. You have to be sure I can control my energy. So you purposely give me something that will make my HEAD EXPLODE. To see if I can control THAT. Is that how things are?

Q. Tell me about your mother.

A. No.

Q. Tell me about your mother.

A. She came to Queen's from India two years before 12/12. For graduate school. She was studying chemistry. She was home with morning sickness when it happened. She still wasn't sure if she was really pregnant or if it was stress and bad food. The other two RAs in her lab got eaten when the hydrochloric acid came to life. My father died a few days later.

She survived. Flying home was out of the question. So was giving up. Even without her parents, without my father, she knew she had to make a life for me.

She learned VAL3 and OpenRDK so she could help program the emergency robots. She designed some of the first Certified Homes and did some of the first mapmaking on the post-12/12 city and its hazards. She took me to see the local shut-ins, and she said, "That's no life. It's good we have these homes. You can't imagine life without them. But when you grow up you have to go further, or what's the point? You're my strong, smart, brave little girl. You can go wherever you like, if you are prepared."

I went to school because of her. She was so proud of me. She made me stay in residence, even though she lived in town, just so I'd know what it was like to live without her. She came by every weekend with curry. Everything she did was for me.

By Thanksgiving, something had started growing in her lungs.

I watched her die. I watched the robots put her body in the ground. And now, you bastard professor, you're making me do it again.

◀ ▶

Practical Component, Part 4

You stop writing. Writing is making you angry. Anger will attract Non-Minds full of rage, and you can't afford that now. You go into your centre. Breathe deep.

Fort Henry has hot and cold running water, it turns out, but no amount of washing will get the blood out of your mother's skin. The flesh is coming off her arms altogether now, exposing bone.

You want to ask if it hurts. You're afraid to ask. She groans, long and loud, again and again, but you don't know if that's because it hurts, or because that's the sound zombies make.

Back to campus, says the latest page of the exam, *by way of Aberdeen Street.*

You slip out of your centre for a moment. You want to tell Professor Yao you don't care where she wants you. You don't care about this stupid exam anymore. But that's an angry thought. You have to let it go.

Aberdeen Street is the densest haunt of the Purples. It's literally crawling with them. And that makes sense, if you think about it calmly: Professor Yao wants you to walk through the Non-Minds' nest, staying in your centre, even though your mother is coming apart. If you can do that and live, you can go anywhere.

"Would you like to stay here?" you ask your mother. "Would that help?" You don't want to drag her across town in the shape she's in. Walking might make it worse.

She gives you a piteous look. The skin around her eyes is rotting and sloughing off, but you can still see pain in them. Pain and terror.

You don't know if that's a yes or no to your question.

You look away.

"Do whatever hurts less," you say. "Please. I'll be all right." And you start to walk.

Your mother shuffles slowly behind you.

You barely see the roads go by as you walk. Your feet are already aching, but you don't care. All your energy goes to putting one foot in front of the other. Keeping your breathing going. Keeping your emotions at bay. Not looking over your shoulder.

It's only when Aberdeen Street looms up right in front of you that you work out what's wrong.

The street is there – sort of. The close-set red-brick houses. The thick groups of Purples lounging in nests, tossing garbage around, climbing through the windows or slapping their jackets. But something *else* is there. It's not just a nest for Purples today: the bulldozers have moved in, bringing a maze of scaffolding and temporary wire fences with them.

These things roam the outskirts of campus. Digging up roads and putting them back. Smashing old, living buildings and assembling new ones. Something hovers around the university that is insatiable, that cannot stop building, and the bulldozers are its midwives.

You almost fall back and detour. But Professor Yao is too good to send you here by mistake. She has a virtual map keeping track of the bulldozers' migrations. She wouldn't have sent you to them unless she wanted you to face them.

Still, you falter. You risk a look over your shoulder.

Your mother has come entirely apart. Barely more than a skeleton now, dusted with clumps of black hair, fragments of the red sari.

You squeeze your eyes shut.

"Go back," you whisper. "Please."

She gives you the same pain-and-terror look with those empty sockets. You never studied how zombies are made, what spells are used. Maybe she can't go back. Maybe the same force that brought her to life keeps her cloven to you.

Your hands are shaking. You breathe as deep as you can. You have to fight your way to the centre now.

You walk forward.

The bulldozers rumble and roll of their own accord, chattering to each other every so often with piercing beeps. You walk into their midst, into the wire-fence maze.

Your presence makes them pause. It turns the Purples' heads. They stare at you. Murmur to each other. A few shift like they're thinking of getting up.

You fight down panic. You're not quite in your centre. You're radiating too much emotion and they're noticing you too fast.

What did Professor Yao tell you to do in a situation like this? Better meditation? A detour? You can't remember. You hardly care. It's hard enough to put one foot in front of the other, let alone think of other options.

You put one foot in front of the other for a while. And then the maze comes to a dead end.

You pause. Try to retrace your steps. But looking carefully, there is no way forward. There's a wire fence here stretched all the way across the street. No opening. No gate. You're stuck.

You waver.

And then, before you can stop her, the skeleton of your mother leaps up and begins to climb the fence.

You rush after her. You're not the best climber. But you're suddenly frantic to reach her. Little slivers of bone are clattering to the ground now as she hooks her fingers into the links. "No," you whisper. "No, no, no!" But she climbs faster than you. You're up at the top of the fence, nearly at her, before you can think straight. She wobbles. You reach out to steady her.

Before your fingertips reach her, she falls forward.

You leap. It's only eight feet down from the top of the fence to the other side. Not enough to do more than jar you, with your gymnast's sense for landings. But where your mother hits the ground there's suddenly nothing but red fabric and broken fragments of bone, rolling outward in all directions.

You land on your hands and knees. You stare at the red fabric in disbelief. You scrabble at it, like you can put her back together again.

Where is your centre? You can't find it. You can't even imagine where it would be. All you can do is crouch on the ground, staring, shivering.

The Purples, in your peripheral vision, are all crawling towards you.

Fine. You have no centre. You can't even bring yourself to get up. You don't care. So the Purples will take you. There are too many of them to fight, and not enough time for the emergency robots to get here. There's nothing you can do. You can refuse to be afraid. You can't refuse to grieve.

You hunch down and wait for them. A violet hand, surprisingly warm, grips your shoulder.

"*Oil Thigh na Banrighinn*," murmurs the Purple. As though it's sad.

"*A'Banrighinn*," echo the others. And there's a slow, rhythmic *thunk* of jackets on the ground.

Not an attack. A dirge. They are mourning with you.

You bury your face in the Purple's shoulder and weep.

◀ ▶

Written Component, Part 5

Q. Do you think you have passed your exam?

A. I think I have survived.
   I think Non-Mind is the wrong name for them.
   They're not safe. Their minds are not like our minds.
   But sometimes they are just close enough.

WAITING FOR JENNY REX

Melissa Yuan-Innes

Anorexia nervosa came first. She was the first and the best. But then I'm biased, since I also like to think she came back for me.

The autumn day she walked into my life, and back to life in general, started off as usual in the *Ottawa Citizen* newsroom. I was cutting two hundred words out of my movie review. It was raining hard outside, but I hardly noticed until my screen died and the room went black. In that astonished moment, a shadowy, angular form appeared in the doorway.

Her heels clicked as she walked to the centre of the room. Her voice was young and clear. "Hello. My name is Jenny Reed. I died from anorexia three months ago, and I've returned to be a spokesperson for the disease."

Marsha, our sports editor, was the first to recover. "Excuse me. You said you died from anorexia?"

"That's right. I died in the Ottawa General Hospital and I was buried in Beechwood Cemetery. Here's a copy of my death certificate. You can ask me questions and get a doctor to prove that I am a) dead and b) Jennifer Emily Reed. But I'll only spend an hour on that sort of proof. I want a front page story with a maximum of 35 percent of the column space devoted to the fact that I'm dead. The rest of it must be on anorexia. And I get to approve the final copy."

I had to ask. "What if we refuse your conditions?"

"I walk out of here, leaving you with nothing but a nice anecdote, and I go to the *Ottawa Sun*."

"Wait. No need for that. Josh is just being cautious," Marsha soothed, casting me a glare. "But I'd say we need an hour for the medical exam alone."

"Well." She cocked her head to her side. "I can see how you'd want to be sure I'm dead. All right. An hour medical." We negotiated an hour for Q&A on her former life, including research time, and voted to go for it. Then the lights came on.

My breath caught. She was so thin that her temples were concave and her cheekbones protruded obscenely beneath her glittering brown eyes. Only thin brown wisps of hair remained on her skull. I could almost count the bones in each hand. She wore a navy pantsuit which mercifully hid the rest of her body.

She let us look our fill, then, surprisingly, grinned. "Anorexia isn't pretty, and now I'm taking it out of the hospitals and into the street. If you guys want in on it, you'd better hurry up."

We dug up her medical records, her death certificate, even some school records of Jennifer Emily Reed, dead of anorexia at the age of twenty. A doctor began the physical exam. She had no pulse or blood pressure. Her temperature was only 20°C. Her eyes jerked slightly as they moved and did not respond to light. Her mouth was dry. No heart sounds. Her reflexes were delayed and faint. Her sense of touch was diminished. She let him do a heart tracing (flat-line) and a dental X-ray, but drew the line at in-hospital tests.

He inserted a needle in her arm for a blood sample. He tried twice more, and she didn't flinch, but said, "That's enough. I don't heal like I did when I was alive."

"One more time—"

"You can't get a blood sample. That's the point!" She sighed. "Okay. I know this isn't what you learn in medical school. How about this. If you promise to sew me up afterward, you can cut my arm. A *small* cut."

The room was quiet as he wielded his scalpel. Then he yelped, and we gathered around Jenny, with her smiling above us like a pale saint. The vein on the inside of her elbow was neatly cut in half. So was the blood in her arm, which was a solid instead of a liquid. We were mesmerized, and people started arguing over whether we should do another cut, just to be sure. She shook her arm to get everyone's attention. "That wasn't the deal. Show's over, folks. Could you sew up my arm, please, Doctor?"

"I still have fifteen minutes left!" he objected.

"You still have to sew up my arm, and I want you to do a good job." He protested until she took ahold of his chin with one of her skeletal hands and made him look her in the eye. "Now."

He blanched. So did the rest of us. He sewed her up in silence. I walked up beside her. I could actually see her teeth through her sunken, grey cheeks. She jerked around to return my gaze. Her over-bright eyes were frightening, but I said, "Hi. I'm Josh Kleinedler. I like your style. It could have worked against you, though. What if none of the newspapers had agreed to your conditions?"

"Oh, even the more conservative papers like to have something weird and wonderful." She huffed slightly over her words, more noticeably at the ends of her sentences. "And Plan Z was the Internet."

"Why didn't you go there in the first place?"

She shrugged and grinned. Her gums were pale. "Too many kooks there already." She nodded approval at her arm, refused a bandage, and turned to the fully assembled group. "Time for the interview. Remember, I'll only answer questions about anorexia and my past life. You already have enough for the zombie angle. And there'll be plenty of time for that later." She spoke of a lonely childhood with parents who pressured her to overachieve. "That joke about getting a 97 and them asking 'What happened to the other 3 percent?' was serious. If I got a 100 in English, they would demand how I was doing in math. Or pressure me about my extracurricular activities. Or about my weight. That was the one area where I could never, ever please. I had a pretty normal build, but my mother was a really skinny teenager, much smaller than I ever was, so she thought I was a freak. She literally watched what I ate."

Jason Delaney prompted, "And your father?"

"Well, he was more concerned about my marks, but he never stopped my mother's nagging. Once I appealed to him, and he said, 'Well, you probably could stand to lose a few pounds,' then went back to reading the paper. So finally I thought, if everyone cares so much about losing weight, I'll be the best weight watcher that ever lived." She smiled grimly.

"So you'd say your parents were responsible for your anorexia?"

"No. At least, not completely. But they definitely got me started by making me hate my body and convincing me that nothing I did was good enough."

◀ ▶

I waited until most of the crowd died down to make my way over. "What are you doing afterward?"

"Researching anorexia."

"Could I treat you to dinner first?"

She looked amused. "I don't eat anymore."

"Oh," was all I could say while my face turned red.

"Sorry."

"Well, could I help you do your research?"

She cocked her head. "You want a scoop on zombies, or are you that hard up?"

Shot down by a dead woman! I stared at her.

"I'm sorry." She reached out and caught my arm. Avoiding her weird eyes, I studied the skeletal hand on my arm. Her skin was cool, almost cold. I felt vaguely repulsed until I saw her very human expression. "That was rude," she said, "but I've had a long day. Everyone wants an exclusive, and they think they can buy it out of me with everything from dinner to plastic surgery."

"Plastic surgery?"

"Yeah. So I would look more 'normal.' I told him it was a bit late for that, seeing as how I was dead and all."

"Did it bother you?"

"A little. But not as much as when I was alive. I have so much to *do*." She smiled so radiantly then that I forgot her haggard face. After a minute, she said, "You're staring at me."

"I'm sorry. You just looked – nice. I mean…"

"You mean instead of like a skeleton." She cut off my apology. "Forget it. I spent my life worrying about not being

pretty enough. I have better things to do now that I'm dead."
She gave me a curt nod and left.

◀ ▶

For two weeks following her *Ottawa Citizen* debut, my contact with Jenny was limited to TV and newspapers. The people who couldn't get a direct line on her were cashing in on
the interest with stories on eating disorders and zombies.
One guy wrote acidly, "Amidst the hoopla, the fact remains
that the most interesting thing about Miss Reed is that she is
dead, which enables her to capture everyone's interest with
the subject foremost on her mind, namely, anorexia. In her
latest speech, she said 'anorexia' an average of four times a
minute. Congratulations on your fifteen minutes of fame,
Miss Anorexia 2002." But mostly, they loved her. Some took
to calling her Jenny Anorexia, which turned into Jenny Rex.
She adopted that for her web page. She wrote, "I like being
called Jenny Rex. It seems fitting to be renamed after the
cause that I'm fighting for. It's a lot catchier than Reed, anyway." I clicked on the icon to send her mail, despite the warning that she had little time to answer. I sent some advice and
my phone number.

The next week, she called, sounding hesitant. "Josh
Kleinedler? This is Jenny Rex."

"Thanks for calling. How are you doing?"

"Fine. Ah, I got your email. You think I should do school
tours?"

"I *know* you should do school tours. The talk show circuit
is fine for reaching a mass audience, but the more you're on
TV, the more you turn into a media icon. You need more

interaction. You need to convince people you're real." She was silent. I added, "And you want to reach young people, right?"

"Well, not just them, but…yeah."

"They'll lose interest first. Get 'em while you're hot."

She sighed. "You have a point, but I don't have the time."

"You can make the time. Start small. If someone flies you out for a speech, talk at one of the local schools afterward. You can build from there."

There was a short silence. "Why are you telling me this?"

"I like you. I liked you ever since you walked into our blacked-out newsroom and started telling us what to do."

She laughed reluctantly. "I think I remember you. You're the guy with glasses who asked me out, right? I thought you were shy. What happened?"

"I took a course: *How to Be Aggressive*."

Long pause. "You're kidding, right?"

"Yes," I deadpanned. "It was actually *How to Be Assertive*."

She groaned. "Okay, whatever. Do you want to help me organize this? I might be able to scrape up an honorar-ium—"

"That's not what I'm looking for. I just want to be your friend."

"Okay." She sounded surprised but pleased. "We can see about that over dinner."

"I thought you didn't eat."

"I don't. But you do. And I can talk while you eat."

"You've mellowed."

"Yeah, I took a course: *How to Mellow Out*."

◄ ►

"Did you see this?" Jenny Rex waved *People* at me indignantly.

"That we've been an item since you were resurrected? Yep. Good picture, eh?"

"You know I hate pictures of me, but that's not the point. Everyone thinks we're going out, even though I keep saying we're just friends. And the *National Examiner* thinks we're having kinky sex!"

"Hey girl, I'm surprised that they're not saying you're pregnant with a zombie love child. I think it's because you're so straightlaced, not to mention an anorexic zombie."

She stared at me. "You're enjoying this!"

"Well, it's sort of funny, don't you think?"

"No! I want people to believe what I say about anorexia, not make up lies about my sex life!"

"Welcome to the real world, Jenny. People like romance. No one wants to hear about eating disorders twenty-four hours a day. It's getting kind of tired."

"What!"

"Haven't you noticed you're getting less play, and the stories they do run are about you, not your disease? You're still hot, but if you keep up this 'talk about anorexia, never mind that I'm dead' 24/7, you'll be in the 'what's not' column soon."

"Well, excuse me for having a message instead of endless B.S.!"

"That's fine. But don't freak out over fluff. It shows people you're human. And they need to hear that because you're, well, *not* human. You don't sleep, you don't eat, you're above romance because of your holy message…"

"Shut up!"

"Oh oh, the saint is enraged…a fit to kill…Now, that would really get you in the news: ANOREXIA KILLS…HER BOYFRIEND!"

"You are not my boyfriend!"

"No? Why not?"

"Because…because I have work to do!" We stared at each other, and then she finally started laughing. I put my arms around her, which made her laugh harder, and then I gave her small, thin lips a light kiss. Her eyes turned serious. "Josh…"

"Yes?"

"I'm tempted. I – never really had a boyfriend. But—"

"I won't distract you from your mission. I'll just hold your hand as you go from school to school."

"Well…okay." And she kissed me back.

As predicted, our romance created a small flurry of renewed interest. So that was just peachy for her mission. She worried too much about what she was doing, though. One of the things that bothered her was blaming her parents for her anorexia. She wanted to talk to them about it, but they were trekking in Nepal and couldn't be reached.

"Well, there's nothing you can do about it now. You left your messages at the hotel. They'll call you when they get back," I assured her. It was sort of weird. She didn't feel right living at home, since her parents didn't know she wasn't still six feet under, so she was living from hotel room to hotel room and constantly calling her parents' answering machine to update her number. I said she could crash at my place whenever she was in town, and she almost bit my head off.

Whenever I could, I travelled with her. The *Citizen* was pretty understanding as long as I sent them copy every week. I, we – I think we – fell in love. Yeah, like some bastard said, she had the face to shrink a thousand dicks. Even now, once in a while, I'd be shocked by something like her hand in the air, her skeletal fingers pressed together, but so painfully thin that light shone through the gaps in her fingers. But I loved her. I was willing to try and show her that her body wasn't just something to starve, or to carry her around so she could spread the word.

I kissed her. She kissed me back, just for a second, long enough for me to bring my hand up to touch her cheek. Then she turned away, like she always did.

I let her go. "Jenny, why are you so scared?"

She shook her head. Finally, she burst out, "I don't want you to see me!"

"Why?"

"Because I'm ugly!" She hid her face in the pillow. I stroked her wisps of hair.

"You're not ugly to me. I love you. To me, you look…"

She jerked up and watched me with glittering eyes.

"Like you," I finished weakly.

She smiled bitterly. "Like a skeleton, Josh."

"Yes. But—"

"But what? I'm an ugly skeleton. I can hardly feel it you when you touch me. That's never going to change. I'll be an anorexic zombie forever! So why bother!"

"Because I love you. And I'll love you no matter how you look, because you're – you." God, that sounded cheesy. No response. She burrowed under the blanket. She was shaking, but she yelled, "Don't touch me!"

"Jenny, for God's sake…"

"No, it's not for God's sake, it's for your sake. If you loved me, you wouldn't need sex. Just loving me would be enough."

I stared at her. "You've got it backwards. If I didn't love you, I'd just get sex somewhere else."

"So go, then. Get out."

I paused. "Jenny, we're not even talking about sex, just let me hold you."

Silence.

"Jenny, you spend so much time telling women they should love their bodies. Why can't you? "

"Get OUT!"

◀ ▶

Except for those fights, the weeks were pretty wonderful. I loved her drive, her sass, and funny little streaks of innocence. And she could be coaxed into walks, and we would read to each other, and we had a great time painting a mural together as part of a fundraiser for anorexia. I decided that I had been pushing too fast. I was nine years older than her, and I had to ease up. Everything would come, eventually. I just had to win her trust.

Then one day, she was unusually quiet. She rushed right home after her speaking engagement, and asked me to call the newspaper for breaking stories. It was busy. "That's fine," she said absently. "Thanks." She went and sat by the television, curling her legs beside her, intent. At 3 p.m., the story broke. It looked like there was a new zombie. He was wasted but slightly paunchy, with a moustache, deeply etched wrinkles, and pale skin. He swayed a little as he spoke. "My former name was Franklin Miller," he said, looking into the camera earnestly, "but I'd like to forget about that life. I just want to tell people that smoking kills, and I want to help them quit or, better yet, don't even start."

I groaned. Jenny glanced at me. "Bad?"

"Yep. A weird-looking guy with message we hear all the time. Not a good combo. You knew about this?"

"No. I just had a...feeling. Maybe you could help him market himself?"

"I thought you didn't believe in marketing."

"I don't. But if you're right, and people don't like him, soon they won't listen to him. Or to me."

◀ ▶

When we spoke to Frank, he said, "I have a vision. I have to save people from tobacco. Once you can't breathe, you'll never forget it."

"I'm sure," I said. "But—"

"I started coughing up blood...I lost thirty pounds...My chest X-ray was so bad..." Blah, blah blah. "So I want to tell young people, don't start. Smoking kills."

"Right, Frank, but—"

"My name's not Frank. Not anymore. Frank is dead. I want a name that will convey my message, like Mr. Butt-Out or something."

I stifled a laugh. "Well, maybe you'd want something a little less obvious."

"Mr. Kleinedler, I want to go the whole hog. Unlike some people, I have no attachment to my living name, and no desire for romance. This crusade will rule my life. After all, that's why Jesus returned me to this earth."

"Jesus sent you?" Jenny stared at him. "How do you know that?"

"I was a good Christian all my life and I know that He must have had His reasons."

"Oh." She was very quiet.

◀ · ▶

ZOMBIE II SAYS BUTT OUT
JESUS SENT SECOND ZOMBIE TO STOP SMOKING
ZOMBIE PART DEUX: NO SMOKING, PLEASE

These headlines were shortly followed by editorials and letters to the editor alternating between "Right on, Frank!" and "It's my body and I'll smoke if I want to." Jenny Rex was not amused. "People aren't so interested in anorexia anymore."

"Honey, it was happening already. Can't you see how funny Frank is? He's like the Zombie Ned Flanders!"

"No, I don't think it's funny at all, Josh. And neither would you if you took eating disorders as seriously as I do. Now, if you'll excuse me, I have a speech to write."

"Jenny, everyone has heard your message," I called after her. "Now you have to let them do what they want with it." She didn't answer.

◀ ▶

So she kept touring and fundraising, but her agenda had more and more blank spots. Of course, Frank was even less popular, unless he was preaching to the converted (whether they were non-smokers, ex-smokers, Christians, or all of the above). Maybe it was the dip in zombie demand, but in any case, less than a week after Frank arrived in New York, Heart Disease (a.k.a. Ruby Smythe) showed up in Toronto. She was a scrappy woman, grey-haired, sixty years old when she died, and she was fighting mad that there wasn't more heart disease research money devoted to women over fifty. She was well-received by seniors and feminists, and most people seemed willing to listen to her, if not rave over her, as they had for Jenny Rex. Ruby called and suggested that they "band together for a panel discussion. After all, three zombies are better than one." The threesome negotiated a time and place and a network.

I flew to New York with Jenny Rex. She was edgy in the studio. I tried to distract her. "Hey, did you see the hate mail I got today? A woman called me a zombie lover and said I should save myself for the living, and the picture she sent was—"

"Glad you enjoyed it." Her teeth worried the edge of her lip.

"Hey, stop biting, Jen, or we'll have to get a doctor to sew it up." She shrugged. I pretended to leer at her. "Darling, don't. You must look beautiful for the camera."

She whipped around to glare at me. "Shut up!"

"It was a joke."

"The beauty myth is not a joke." She settled back morosely and started tapping her fingers.

"I love you," I whispered.

Her eyes were sad. "I know."

She went on the show a few minutes later. They each made a speech, then opened it up to questions. The first few were like, *What do you guys think about each other?* Then a young Asian woman spoke at the microphone. "I think you three are doing a good job of raising awareness about the diseases that *you* died from, but it's become such a fad that the non-zombie causes aren't getting any money." A few people booed, a few applauded, but most of them waited.

"I don't consider ourselves a fad," Ruby objected. "We're educating people."

The young woman was unrepentant. "What's the bottom line? Donations to eating disorders have gone up 700 percent, and I'm sure the Lung Association and Heart and Stroke Foundation will be happy, too. But I work for the environment, and our donations have dropped like a stone."

"Well," Frank began, "I'm sorry about the other problems out there, but I can't do everything. Smoking is such an evil that I have my hands full helping people quit."

Jenny just watched.

The moderator spoke up. "Here's an email from Seattle. 'I am a forty-year-old smoker. I know the health risks, but I'm not going to stop smoking. After all, my car is dangerous and causes air pollution, but I don't see anyone taking away my right to drive it. I will quit smoking if I want to, not because you tell me to. And so I say to the zombie formerly known as Frank Miller, *you* butt out.'"

Frank blustered on. The moderator asked if Jenny Rex had anything to say about the smoking issue.

"Not really. Well, I think it's wrong, but we have to make people want to stop, not shame them into it."

"Are you suggesting that's what I'm doing?" Frank demanded.

Ruby stepped in. Jenny hardly glanced at them.

Another studio audience member said, "I'd like to add to the point that the other woman was making. All of you are white, middle class North Americans promoting your own problems. I'm not saying you shouldn't, but anorexia doesn't even exist in developing countries. What about malaria and diarrhoea? We don't have zombies for those, but worldwide, those are the real killers!"

While the other two took her on, Jenny started to shake. I ached to comfort her. I started towards her during the commercial break, but some television aide was already there, whispering. She started. Her eyes met mine, briefly. Then she tore off.

Her taxi beat mine back to the hotel, her door was chained, and she let the phone ring. Finally, she ripped off the chain and opened the door, and went right back to folding her robe without meeting my eyes.

"What are you doing?" I yelled at her.

"I'm packing."

"I know that. Why?"

"Because I don't know what I'm doing here anymore. I don't know why I came back. Taking food out of the mouths of starving children—"

"She didn't say that!"

"She didn't have to."

"You know you did the right thing."

"Do I? I just woke up and it felt right to tell everyone about anorexia. But look at Frank. He thinks he was heaven sent. Maybe he was, but maybe it's just because of what he believed before. Maybe anorexia was just my personal demon, and I made everyone else live through it."

"Jenny, there was nothing wrong with what you did—"

"No? It wasn't wrong to turn eating disorders into the disease of the month, so that people jumped on that bandwagon and forgot everything else?"

"It wasn't your fault."

"And what about my parents..." Her voice faltered and broke. "They called today, during the show. They're back. I have to talk to them. I complained about them in front of the whole world! It wasn't enough that their daughter died, and that she came back from the dead. No, I had to tell the world that they killed me."

I grabbed her and shook her. "Jenny, they hurt you, too! So, okay, now they have to deal with that. Would you quit feeling guilty about everyone else on the planet and start thinking about yourself?"

"I already did! That's the problem!" she screamed in my face.

I was stunned.

She pushed me away and steadied her breathing. Then she started packing again. "I'm leaving, Josh. That's final."

"Jenny..." Then I saw that she had packed everything except the gifts I'd given her: a little owl "piggy" bank, books, a picture of us, and a huge stuffed panda bear that she lugged around even though she pretended to hate it.

She half turned. "I thought I'd leave you your stuff."

"It's yours." My throat closed up.

"No, that's okay. I'll have a hard time carrying everything by myself."

"I'll come with you."

"No."

My voice was hoarse. "I'll send it to you."

Silence. "All right. If you want to."

She added the picture of us and the owl bank to her luggage and zipped it. I drove her to the airport. I waited with her, holding her hand so tight even she could feel it. And I said goodbye, choking. "I love you, Jenny Rex. Forever."

"Oh, you'd better watch out, Josh. The way I'm going, forever could be a very long time." She touched her hand to my cheek. "I'll call you someday. I promise. I just need to work things out with my family, and think about what I've done, and…maybe decide what to do with the rest of my life. I'll let you know when I decide." She paused and kissed me. A sound broke from my throat. She looked at me and whispered, "I wish I could cry." Then she stepped away, clutching her handbag, and looked back once before boarding the plane.

◀ ▶

It's been a year. Ruby has become a lobbyist for heart disease and other women's health issues. Frank pops up here and there at anti-smoking rallies and hogs the microphone until someone cuts him off. Jenny has all but disappeared. Once in a while, she writes a piece for one of the eating disorders newsletters or websites, but she no longer makes public appearances. In the little bio at the end of one of her articles, she said she is looking for peace. I guess she hasn't found it yet. I haven't contacted her. She's had enough of other people telling her what to do.

The other day, I overheard my co-workers joking about what kind of zombie's causes they'd come back as: Marsha said she'd be "equal funding for women's sports" zombie, and someone said Jason Delaney would be "find a cure for baldness" zombie. They shut up when I came in, but in my head, I had my answer: heartbroken zombie. So I wait. And I smoke. I eat too much, or too little, and I laugh at the irony. I write my crappy little columns. And I remember. And I wait. For Jenny Rex.

STEMMING THE TIDE

Simon Strantzas

Marie and I sit on the wooden bench overlooking the Hopewell Rocks. In front of us, a hundred feet below, the zombies walk on broken, rocky ground. Clad in their sunhats and plastic sunglasses, carrying cameras around their necks and tripping over open-toed sandals, they gibber and jabber among themselves in a language I don't understand. Or, more accurately, a language I don't *want* to understand. It's the language of mindlessness. I detest it.

Marie begged me for weeks to take her to the Rocks. It's a natural wonder, she said. The tide comes in every six hours and thirteen minutes and covers everything. All the rock formations, all the little arches and passages. It's supposed to be amazing. Amazing, I repeat, curious if she'll hear the slight scoff in my voice, detect how much I loathe the idea. There is only one reason I might want to go to such a needlessly crowded place, and I'm not sure if I'm ready to face it. If she senses my mood, she feigns obliviousness. She pleads with me again to take her. Tries to convince me it can only help her after her loss. Eventually, the crying gets to be too much, and I agree.

But I regret it as soon as I pick her up. She's dressed in a pair of shorts that do nothing to flatter her pale, lumpy body.

Her hair is parted down the middle and tied to the side in pig-tails, as though she believes somehow appropriating the trappings of a child will make her young again. All it does is reveal the greying roots of her dyed hair. Her blouse…I cannot even begin to explain her blouse. This is going to be great! she assures me as soon as she's seated in the car, and I nod and try not to look at her. Instead, I look at the sun-bleached road ahead of us. It's going to take an hour to drive from Moncton to the Bay of Fundy. An hour where I have to listen to her awkwardly try and fill the air with words because she cannot bear silence for anything longer than a minute. I, on the other hand, want nothing more than for the world to keep quiet and keep out.

The hour trip lengthens to over two in traffic, and when we arrive the sun is already bearing down as though it has focused all its attention on the vast asphalt parking lot. We pass through the admission gate and, after having our hands stamped, onto the park grounds. Immediately, I see the entire area is lousy with people moving in a daze – children eating dripping ice cream or soggy hot dogs, adults wiping balding brows and adjusting colourful shorts that are already tucked under rolls of fat. I can smell these people. I can smell their sweat and their stink in the humid air. It's suffocating, and I want to retch. My face must betray me; Marie asks me if I'm okay. Of course, I say. Why wouldn't I be? Why wouldn't I be okay in this pigpen of heaving bodies and grunting animals? Why wouldn't I enjoy spending every waking moment in the proximity of people that barely deserve to live, who can barely see more than a few minutes into the future? Why wouldn't I enjoy it? It's like I'm walking through an abattoir, and none of the fattened sows know what's to come. Instead they keep moving forward in their piggy queues, one by one meeting their end. This is what the line of people descending into the dried cove look like to me. Animals on the way to slaughter. Who wouldn't be okay surrounded by that, Marie? Only I don't say any of that. I want to with all my being, but instead I say I'm fine, dear. Just a little tired is all. Speaking the words only makes me sicker.

The water remains receded throughout the day, keeping a safe distance from the Hopewell Rocks, yet Marie wants to sit and watch the entire six hour span, as though she worries what will happen if we are not there to witness the tide rush in. Nothing will happen, I want to tell her. The waters will still rise. There is nothing we do that helps or hinders inevitability. That is why it is inevitable. There is nothing we can do to stem the tides that come. All we can do is wait and watch and hope that things will be different. But the tides of the future never bring anything to shore we haven't already seen. Nothing washes in but rot. No matter where you sit, you can smell its clamminess in the air.

The sun has moved over us and still the rocky bottom of the cove and the tall weirdly sculpted mushroom rocks are dry. Some of the tourists still will not climb back up the metal grated steps, eager to spend as much of the dying light as possible wandering along the ocean's floor. A few walk out as far as they can, sinking to their knees in the silt, yet none seem to wonder what might be buried beneath the sand. The teenager who acts as the lifeguard maintains his practiced, affected look of disinterest, hair covering the left half of his brow, watching the daughters and mothers walking past. He ignores everyone until the laughter of those in the silt grows too loud, the giggles caused by sand fleas nibbling their flesh unmistakable. He yells at them to get to the stairs. Warns them of how quickly the tide will rush in, the immediate undertow that has sucked even the heaviest of men out into the Atlantic, but even he doesn't seem to believe it. Nevertheless, the pigs climb out one at a time, still laughing. I look around to see if anyone else notices the blood that trickles down their legs.

The sun has moved so close to the horizon that the blue sky has shifted to orange. Many of the tourists have left, and those few that straggle seemed tired to the point of incoherence. They stagger around the edge of the Hopewell Rocks, eating the vestiges of the fried food they smuggled in earlier or laying on benches while children sit on the ground in front of them. The tide is imminent, but only Marie and I remain alert. Only Marie and I watch for what we know is coming.

When it arrives, it does so swiftly. Where once rocks covered the ground, a moment later there is only water. And it rises. Water fills the basin, foot after foot, deeper and deeper. The tide rushes in from the ocean. It's the highest tide the world over. It beckons people from everywhere to witness its power. The inevitable tide coming in.

Marie has kicked off her black sandals, the simple act shaving inches from her height. She has both her arms wrapped around one of mine and is staring out at the steadily rising water. She's like an anchor pulling me down. Do you see anything yet? she asks me, and I shake my head, afraid of what might come out if I open my mouth. How much longer do you think we'll have to wait? Not long, I assure her, though I don't know. How would I? I've refused to come to this spot all my life, this spot on the edge of a great darkness. That shadowy water continues to lap, the teenage lifeguard finally concerned less with the girls who walk by to stare at his athletic body, and more with checking the gates and fences to make sure the passages to the bottom are locked. The last thing anyone wants is for one to be left open accidentally. The last thing anyone but me wants, that is.

The sun is almost set, and the visitors to the Hopewell Rocks have completely gone. It's a park full only with ghosts, the area surrounding the risen tide. Mushroom rocks look like small islands, floating in the ink just off the shore. The young lifeguard has gone, hurrying as the darkness crept in as fast as the water rose. Before he leaves he shoots the two of us a look that I can't quite make out under his flopping denim hat, but one which I'm certain is fear. He wants to come over to us, wants to warn us that the park has closed and that we should leave. But he doesn't. I like to think it's my expression that keeps him away. My expression, and my glare. I suppose I'll never know which.

Marie is lying on the bench by now, her elbow planted on the wooden slats, her wrist bent to support the weight of her head. She hasn't worn her shoes for hours, and even in the long shadows I can see sand and pebbles stuck to her soles. She looks up at me. It's almost time, she whispers, not out of secrecy – because no one is there to hear her – but of glee. It's almost time. It is, I tell her, and try as I might I can't muster up even a false smile. I'm too nervous. The thought of what's to come jitters inside of me, shakes my bones and flesh, leaves me quivering. If Marie notices, she doesn't mention it, but I'm already prepared with a lie about the chill of day's end. I know it's not true, and that even Marie is smart enough to know how warm it still is, but nevertheless I know she wants nothing more than to believe every word I say. It's not one of her most becoming qualities.

The tide rushes in after six hours and thirteen minutes, and though I'm not wearing a watch I know exactly when the bay is at its fullest. I know this not by the light or the dark oily colour the water has turned. I know this not because I can see the tide lapping against the nearly submerged mushroom rocks. I know this because, from the rippling ocean water, I can see the first of the heads emerge.

Flesh so pale it is translucent, the bone beneath yellow and cracked. Marie is sitting up, her chin resting on her folded hands. I dare a moment to look at her wide open face, and wonder if the remaining light that surrounds us is coming from her beaming. The smile I make is unexpected. Genuine. They're here! she squeals, and my smile falters. I can't believe they're here! I nod matter-of-factly.

There are two more heads rising from the water when I look back at the full basin, the first already sprouting an odd number of limbs attached to a decayed body. The thing is staggering towards us, the only two living souls for miles around, though how it can see us with its head cocked so far back is a mystery. I can smell it from where we're sitting. It smells like tomorrow. More of the dead emerge from the water, refugees from the dark ocean, each one a promise of what's to come. They're us, I think. The rich, the poor, the strong, the weak. They are our heroes and our criminals. They are our loved ones and most hated enemies. They are me, they are Marie, they are the skinny lifeguard in his idiotic hat. They are our destiny, and they have come to us from the future, from beyond the passage with a message. It's one no one but us will ever hear. It is why Marie and I are there, though each for a different reason – her to finally help her understand the death of her mother, me so I can finally put to rest the haunting terrors of my childhood. Neither of us speak about why, but we both know the truth. The dead walk to tell us what's to come, their broken mouths moving without sound. The only noise they make is the rap of bone on gravel. It only intensifies as they get closer.

For the first time, I see a thin line of fear crack Marie's reverie. There are nearly fifty corpses shambling towards us, swaying as they try to keep rotted limbs moving. If they lose momentum, I wonder if they'll fall over. If they do, I doubt they'd ever right themselves. Between where we sit and the increasing mass is the metal gate the young lifeguard chained shut. More and more of the waterlogged dead are crowding it, pushing themselves against it. I can hear the metal screaming from the stress, but it's holding for now. Fingerless arms reach through the bars, their soundless hungry screams echoing through my psyche. Marie is no longer sitting. She's standing. Pacing. Looking at me, waiting for me to speak. Purposely, I say nothing. I'll let her say what I know she's been thinking.

There's something wrong, she says. This isn't—

It isn't what?

This isn't what I thought. This, these people. They aren't *right*…

I snigger. How is it possible to be so naive?

They are exactly who they are supposed to be, I tell her with enough sternness I hope it's the last she has to say on the subject. I don't know why I continue to make the same mistakes. By now, I'd have thought I would have started listening. But that's the trouble with talking to your past self.

Nothing, no matter how hard you try, can be stopped. Especially not the inevitable.

The dead flesh is packed so tight against the iron gates that it's only a matter of time. It's clear from the way the metal buckles, the hinges scream. Those of the dead that first emerged are the first punished, as their putrefying corpses are pressed by the throng of emerging dead against the fence that pens them in. I can see upturned faces buckling against the metal bars, hear softened bones pop out of place as their lifeless bodies are pushed through the narrow gaps. Marie turns and buries her face in my chest while gripping my shirt tight in her hands. I can't help but watch, mesmerized.

Hands grab the gate and start shaking, back and forth, harder and harder. So many hands, pulling and pushing. The accelerating sound ringing like a church bell across the lonely Hopewell grounds. I can't take it anymore, Marie pleads, her face slick with so many tears. It was a mistake. I didn't know. I never wanted to know. She's heaving as she begs me, but I pull myself free from her terrified grip and stand up. It doesn't matter, I tell her. It's too late.

I start walking towards the locked fence.

I can't hear Marie's sobs any longer, not over the ruckus the dead are making. I wonder if she's left, taken the keys and driven off into the night, leaving me without any means of transportation. Then I wonder if instead she's watching me, waiting to see what I'll do without her there. I worry about both these things long enough to realize I don't really care. Let her watch. Let her watch as I lift the latches of the fence the dead are unable to operate on their own. Let me unleash the waves that come from that dark Atlantic Ocean onto the tourist attraction of the Hopewell Rocks. Let man's future roll in to greet him, let man's future become his present. Make him his own past. Who we will be will soon replace who we are, and who we might once have been.

The dead, they don't look at me as they stumble into the unchained night. And I smile. In six hours and thirteen minutes, the water will recede as quickly as it came, back out to the dark dead ocean. It will leave nothing behind but wet and desolate rocks the colour of sun-bleached bone.

KEZZIE OF BABYLON

Jamie Mason

You can't call the RCMP when the zombies attack if you live on a grow-op. You just can't. It doesn't matter if the fucker shambles into your yard grunting and hissing and starts eating the dog – a call to the cops will only get you busted, even on Vancouver Island. Imagine a whole year's effort cultivating bud wasted because some asshole climbed out of his grave and decided to trespass on your property and start killing and there's nothing you can do about it (including call the cops) because the guy's already dead. Fucking zombies. Fucking cops.

There were already zombies on the mainland, of course. The Parliamentary Subcommittee on Zombieism recommended formation of a special RCMP Zombie Response Unit after the Toronto infestation and as usual BC's budget allocation came last (which meant the Island got its money last of all). No problem: West Coast zombies are different from the ones back East – slower, less resourceful, less of a menace to public safety. They don't work well in groups. And the ones we got on the Island are actually pretty ineffective, to tell you the truth. You can see them coming a mile away and they have a tendency to get distracted easily. They aren't very successful zombies.

So when Buzz dies, we bury him in the north field where we grow the best dope then head back to the farmhouse to get high (because that's what Buzz would have wanted). The wolf follows us. Buzz hated that fucking wolf because it killed that one sheep (his big experiment in legitimate farming) but the wolf seemed to like Buzz. It would appear on the ridge above the commune when Buzz was out doing chores. Buzz would scream and chuck rocks at it until the wolf got tired and ambled away. Only to reappear a few weeks later to torment him again. Now it follows us, watching. Keeping to the ridge as we return to the farmhouse. Fucking wolf.

Just ignore it, Kezzie says. That's Buzz's spirit animal. Nobody, even Deacon, says anything because Kezzie with her wispy blond boy-hair and John Lennon glasses is leader and controls the dope supply so we all want her to like us. After a pause she glances at each of us in turn and quotes the Bible to reinforce her authority: For they are the spirits of devils, working miracles, which go forth unto the kings of the earth and of the whole world. Fucking Babylon, children, and don't you forget it.

Kezzie likes the Bible. She believes part of it (the last book) is about her so she has memorized large chunks of it. Deacon says Kezzie is no different from that crazy Mormon sect up the road where men marry little girls and have more than one wife at a time. I never even had an opinion because I never read the Bible but I stole a copy from the drawer of a hotel room I help clean as a spot-labourer, got high and read the last book. It's really sick – full of whores and monsters and killing. All about the end of the world, if you want to know the truth. Kezzie likes that shit enough to become an expert in it; since the zombie infestation her power over us has only grown.

So we convene in the front room and Indian Sarah puts a fire in the wood stove and Kezzie breaks out the dope and starts rolling joints the way she does – real slow, taking her time and talking all about herself the way she does. We're her captive audience: me, Deacon, Indian Sarah, Rhonda, Rasta Bob and Tyler. But it's strange without Buzz. So in honour of him, during a lull in Kezzie's monologue, we begin talking conspiracy theories about the zombies.

Rasta Bob says it's something in the ground water, mon, but Tyler (nah!) says it's a government lab somewhere with a life-extension experiment gone wrong. Rhonda and me think it may be toxic contamination, and Kezzie? She sticks by her conviction that it's God's will. And soon Indian Sarah and Tyler start agreeing with her. After a time so does Rasta Bob. Rhonda stays quiet but you can tell from her facial twitches that she doesn't agree. Neither do I.

It says in the Book, Kezzie mutters, that at the end of days the Dead will rise from their graves, Praise God. And Alleluia and the wrath of the Almighty shall be loosed upon the world. We're living it now. The end of days. She tokes a joint to life then passes it.

And Deacon, in his sleeveless leather jacket and scraggly black beard, stays reserved as hell, giving up nothing. Nothing at all. Deacon plays his cards close (he is American, after all) – is quiet mostly while he watches Kezzie. But you can sense he's plotting. So when the joint comes to him he holds it hostage and asks:

Kezzie, who's to say it's religious? Maybe it's just crazy science gone wrong. Why does it always have to be God?

And in the silence of the record player's needle hissing between Beatles songs and the tendrils of smoke wafting around the mildewed wood of the parlour, Rhonda and I exchange a glance. Deacon would give Kezzie the gears more often than he does but Kezzie – Canadian Kezzie – wears the gun. And we know from experience she won't hesitate to use it. Not everybody is here because of Kezzie's "gift." Some of us just like the dope. And some of us, like Deacon, just don't trust her.

Kezzie's eyes slide towards Deacon, narrowing. And there fell a great star from heaven, she hisses, burning as it were a lamp, and it fell upon the waters. And the waters became bitter and the people died. Is that you, Deacon? You and your skookum-big fake plastic nation, falling from the sky to contaminate the earth and poison the waters?

And because we all share the traditional Islander distrust of Americans, you can feel the support in the room shift back in Kezzie's direction. In the breath-held hush while we await Deacon's reply Rasta Bob, a slender Jamaican silhouette by the window, exclaims:

Look, mon! Here come Buzz!

◀ ▶

We dug a shallow grave and did not bury him in a box because Buzz said he wanted to fertilize the Earth.

So when he reappears, wandering in and out of the mangy clear-cut on the ridge above the commune partially hidden in the autumn fog, his presence seems strangely ordinary. I keep thinking about medieval peasants goofing up and burying family members alive and how they learned to wait a while, placing bodies in coffins with little bell mechanisms attached to cords that rested in the passenger's hands. *Of course – he must have been in a deep coma when we buried him, then awakened and clawed his way out.* What else could it be? It's funny how the word "zombie" – despite all the Emergency Preparedness Drills and "New Government" pronouncements – is still just a little too alien to spring immediately to mind.

Is it—? Kezzie half stands. Grips the butt of the Browning at her hip.

It. I pause. It is. See the dreads?

It's Buzz, mon. (Rasta Bob's voice is soft with wonder.) And now there be that fucking wolf!

Head lowered, shoulders hunched, the wolf stalks out of the fog. Its movements are slow – almost hesitant. Buzz pauses in his shambling trot and faces the beast. The wolf raises its snout. And begins backing away.

What the—? I pluck the telescope -- the small fold-out one we use for star gazing – from its place on the sill and draw a bead on the wolf. He is definitely backpedalling – and fast. Eyes wide, hackles up. The way he might from an onrushing vehicle. I swing the telescope towards Buzz but he is a blur of movement then suddenly the room behind me is all:

What—

Hey, did he just—?

Ja rae!

I sweep the scope back and forth, its far end a swerving disk of daylight. The wolf's chest, then face, fill the lens. Jaws wide, but not to bite: the creature screams in pain. I lift the

scope as the first rivulets of its blood trickle down and…
There's Buzz, straddling the wolf's back, clawed fingers
gripping its forelegs, plunging forward to bury his face in its
neck.

Buzz. But not Buzz.

◀ ▶

There comes a moment in all disasters – like when the crew
of the *Titanic* understood they really *were* going to hit that
skookum-big iceberg, or when you realize halfway to the
ground the ripcord you pulled just isn't attached to your para-
chute anymore – that the full horror of your situation really
dawns on you, hey? Buzz was back from the dead. That was
bad enough. But it was only the beginning.

And behold, Kezzie whispers, daylight reflected in the
little round mirrors of her specs, the graves were opened
and Hell gave up the Dead, great and small, who were in
them.

The Toronto infestation, like 9-11, reverberates in our
memory – the newsbytes so deeply embedded as to be summoned by a glance. Standing frozen, recalling the headline
horrors, all of us are thinking: *So…it's finally come to the
Island.*

The death screams of the wolf seep into the room. The
turntable hisses, clicks…and then restarts "Piggies" from the
Beatles' *White Album.* For long minutes we watch the death
struggle on the ridge above. And then…

What the fuck we gonna *do*? Indian Sarah's voice is tense.

Call the RCMP! cries very white and very middle-'burbs
Canadian Tyler.

You can't call the RCMP if you live on a grow-op. You just can't, I say.

Well then what are we gonna *do*? Rhonda insists.

Repent.

Kezzie's soft whisper coincides with the pause in "Piggies" right before the ending. And catches us all by surprise. Like when she draws her gun and points it at us.

◀ ▶

The public safety bulletins explain the weird hissing noise zombies make as air, produced by muscle reflex, colliding with gridlocked lungs in a body no longer recycling oxygen to survive. Makes sense, but it doesn't explain the weird feeling it prompts in the listener. It feels like that uncomfortable warm tingle you experience immediately after cutting yourself. That. Magnified a hundred times. And stretched out. The zombie hiss intensifies when the creature scents blood, and the sound summons others to swarm.

Buzz begins hissing softly as we glare back at Kezzie, holding us God-hostage there in the room with her Browning and Bible verses. We know what she is about. It's obvious. Accept Jesus Christ as our Lord and Saviour lickety-split or be blown to bits. Or fed to the zombie. Simple as that.

This is bullshit, spits Rhonda.

This is a gift. Kezzie smiles dreamily. The Lord has given you time to repent and make yourselves right with Him before the oceans turn to blood and the moon to sackcloth and death takes you.

I got people. Indian Sarah stares very intently at Kezzie as she speaks, the way you might stare at someone very fragile. Not my band, but friends.

Rhonda and I glance at each other. The First Nations have fared better than most. Many bands retreated onto their reserves and barricaded the roads when the infestation started.

We can steal some canoes from the marina. It's just a short trip across the saltchuck to Quadra Island. They'll—

Those heathens? Kezzie's whisper is casually dismissive. (As she looks up, I imagine the hiss from Buzz as a light misting rain into which she gazes.) Children of Cain. They brought this on us with their pagan ways. A lightning rod for God's wrath! No thank you. I'd sooner push my face into a meat grinder.

Rasta Bob's eyes flick from Indian Sarah to Kezzie and back. What should we do? he asks. What *can* we—?

The hiss grows louder. Tyler is first to pivot to the window. Jeeezus! he exclaims, and I can see before even stepping beside him the horrific thing that has wandered out of the blasted tree line to stand beside Buzz – or rather, *two* things. And because one would be horrific enough, the presence of a second creature is sufficient to make me dizzy. I grasp the wall to stay upright. And force myself to look at the ridge.

One is Davis. He farmed the spread next door until dying over a month ago. Bone-splintered, the tweed of his good suit worm-eaten to tatters, he grins down at Buzz. A half-moon of flesh has rotted from his right cheek. The gaping black of his eye sockets roll like weird, sinister marbles beneath the brim of a new straw hat. And below him?

A maggot-infested barrel of ribs. Bone legs teetering on strips of flesh. A skeletal head of the type better suited to desert floors or the walls of western bunkhouses. A mammal abomination, every bit as much arisen from the grave as its rider…

And behold, Kezzie whispers, a pale horse. And he that rode upon it was named Death. And Hell followed him.

Deacon chooses that moment to act — just puts his head down and charges Kezzie in a classic football tackle. Almost gets there too. But Kezzie – gifted with the spooky awareness of the ultra-paranoid – spins, aims and fires. Deacon crumples with a grunt, hands spidering to stem the trickle from the powdery black hole in his thigh.

Blood. The hiss rises to a shriek as the creatures outside catch the scent. Buzz, Davis and the zombie horse start down the hill towards the farmhouse. Kezzie, looming over Deacon, grins and makes the sign of the cross with the gun barrel.

◀ ▶

Let us pray.

Under the circumstances, the dumbest idea I've ever heard. But Kezzie's tone is so firm, so serious that – even with zombies approaching and Deacon bleeding to death on the living room floor – I'm almost tempted to join Rasta Bob, Tyler and Indian Sarah as they bow their heads.

Almighty God, you have shown your great love for us in so many ways – by famine, war, pestilence, this zombie infestation…

You're fucking crazy. The tightness in Rhonda's voice could pass for self-control but I recognize it as panic. You're like those fuckers who pray over their sick kids rather than let them have a blood transfusion.

...and now merciful God you have granted us the privilege of watching the world die...

Deacon groans from his place on the floor. The pool of blood is spreading so fast that even an ambulance hauling ass full speed from Comox wouldn't get here in time to save him.

You have warned us time and again merciful God that only an ocean of blood can redeem the infinite sins of this generation of vipers. Kezzie marches to the military footlocker beside the old stone fireplace and twiddles the dial of the padlock. And in your benevolence, O Lord, you have promised that the faithful will be protected as beneath eagles' wings!

She drags the locker top open to expose the rack of weapons inside.

Behold the claws that lurk within the wings of angels! Kezzie drags out an assault rifle and hands it to Rasta Bob. A riot gun that she passes to Indian Sarah. An AK. It goes to Tyler. Then she slams shut the locker and re-locks it.

What about us? I ask.

You non-believers are on your own. Kezzie smiles.

I once lived in an apartment next door to a man who wept continuously. At first I thought the noise was some sort of machine – a broken air conditioner, perhaps. Until someone explained that the man had shared the place with his wife for forty years until she died. This knowledge placed the sound in context and gave it emotional depth. The same way that knowing the hiss approaching the house is caused by air hitting dormant lungs lends its scuba-tank sound a sinister quality. By some weird consensus we all keep our gazes fixed indoors, intent on the tight circle of mutual anger in the living room.

You're just going to let us die?

It is said that in the end of days those who do not profess the Son of Man shall be told to depart from him. Kezzie cocks her assault rifle. Dried sheaves cast unto the fire!

A clawed hand thumps the window – skeletal fingers gloved in decaying flesh. Kezzie raises her assault rifle. We duck. A hail of lead blows the window outward in a spray of exploding glass. A breathy shriek rises. Kezzie fires again, advancing on the jagged sill, face twisted in rage.

And in those days – !(she slams a fresh clip into the gun) – men shall seek death and not find it! Desire death and – (she cocks the action) – DEATH SHALL FLEE FROM THEM!

Gunfire. I grasp Rhonda's wrist and drag her through the kitchen doorway. The keys to the farm truck are on a hook by the stove. I grab the keys and haul open the back door. Panicked voices are erupting between bursts of gunfire. The truck crowds the narrow carport. Rhonda pulls away from me.

We're not LEAVING them—?

Fuck 'em. C'mon!

I push Rhonda out first. A cowardly move but one that, in the logic of the moment (wide truck, narrow carport, zombies busy) makes perfect sense. I hear the frenzied metallic clatter, then Rhonda screaming. I reach to pull her back and she is snatched around the edge of the doorway. I hear a noise like a bear howl — loud but compressed, as if the sound is being forced through the tin horn of an old gramophone. I am about to run after Rhonda when a mist of scarlet sprays the windows and driver's side door of the truck, driving me back through the doorway.

Coward! Frozen by a little blood? I crane around the edge and am rewarded by the sight of the zombie horse dragging Rhonda over the hood of the truck, teeth clenched in the nape of her neck. Its bony hooves make clattering sounds on the chassis as the beast balances on its back legs. The crimson eyes flash and the ropy hair of its mane – still inexplicably attached to a narrow strip of rotting skin on its upper spine – whips as it drags a still-struggling Rhonda out into the open beyond the carport. And what do I do? Grasp an ankle? Grab a carving knife from the cutting board and leap forth to put it point-first into the Hell-coloured eye of the zombie nag?

No. I retreat into the kitchen and flatten my back against the wall beside the doorway and wait until the racket subsides. Then I peer into the carport to see the death nag grazing calmly on Rhonda's eviscerated intestines. And shut the door softly before slipping back into the living room.

That image of the horse, head lowered, swaying slightly as he sucks up Rhonda's innards like spaghetti is frozen in my mind like a DVD player after you've hit pause. Dazed, I look up to discover I'm back in the living room. The couches have been upended into impromptu barricades. A spray of glass carpets the floor. Deacon, having bled out, lies blank-eyed and still.

Get down!

I glare towards the fierce whisper and glimpse sharp blond bangs, light reflected in little round lenses. In that moment I hate Kezzie more than anything – even the zombies. Two of us are dead because of her. How many more? I duck behind a bookcase.

The hissing outside roars like a gale-force wind. The ranks of undead summoned by Buzz and Davis shift and mutter in a cluster of indistinct figures beyond the fence. Closer in, hands – one bone, the other a shrivel of grey flesh – grasp at the windowsill. One lone creature, drawn by the prospect of live flesh, is willing to brave oblivion in order to feed. And the stench! Although cunning enough to remain out of the line of fire, the zombies can't hide their smell (moist earth, rotting viscera, decaying shrouds). It clots the room in a vile perfume.

Where's Rhonda? Kezzie demands.

Dead, I say quietly. Tyler opens up with a blast of sub-machine-gun fire and gore floods the sill and floor as the hands abruptly vanish from the window. All is silence, followed by the clank of Tyler's empty magazine hitting the floor.

For behold in those days, the winnowing fire—

Kezzie, I interrupt, what's the plan? (After a brief hesitation, the undead at the fence are shuffling forward with a chorus of renewed hissing. In the distance, bug-like, others break from the tree line to converge on the slope leading down to the farm.)

Why – (Kezzie blinks) – to wait here 'til Jesus comes to get us, of course!

Yeah! You got a problem wi' dot, mon?

Ah – no. No, not exactly. I was just hoping for something a little more practical...

Practical? You can think of something more *practical* – (Kezzie jabs her weapon skyward) – than awaiting the Prince of Peace?

One creature has gotten close enough to grasp the window ledge and lever a knee onto the sill. Pin-striped arms out on either side to steady itself, its dress pants threadbare around the meaty wreck of its knee, it hisses, throat working in a snarl of tendons.

Indian Sarah curses in Cree, pumps her Mossberg.

I and I!

Fucking death-critter...

What time (I pretend to check my watch) is the Jesus bus due, Kezzie? Cuz I think he better get a move on...

Indian Sarah's shotgun roars and the critter's head evaporates in a spray of bloody bone. Its body teeters on the sill for a moment or two before crumpling backwards. The others crowding in behind it release a collective hiss of displeasure before climbing over the corpse to take its place.

There's too goddamn many of them! Tyler grasps his gun and does a jig like an overgrown kid desperate to pee. Too goddamn many!

DON'T TAKE THE LORD'S NAME IN VAIN YOU GODLESS FUCK! Kezzie leaps to her feet and sprays a burst of machine-gun fire at the window. The nearest critters are driven back but it takes only a few seconds for a trio of them to reach the sill and begin fighting for dibs to climb inside.

What we gonna do, mon?

Quiet...QUIET! I need to think. Kezzie sticks a joint in her mouth and sparks up. The collective eyes of her followers follow its perfumed smoke spiraling upward as hungrily as the critters watch us. Kezzie takes a long contemplative toke and blinks at the approaching hordes.

Alas Babylon, she whispers.

A new zombie makes its bid. Despite its advanced stage of decay I can tell, from the apron and high shoes, that it is female – the undead corpse of an elderly woman. (Do zombies recognize distinctions of age?) It gets partway through the window before Rasta Bob steps up and blasts it back the way it came. In the silence following the weapon's roar a new sound intrudes – that of the front door being hammered.

Second floor! Kezzie grasps Tyler's elbow. Now!

Kezzie…maybe we *should* call the RCMP. I stumble on the word "call" and am forced to grab the banister as I stagger upstairs beside her. Indian Sarah runs ahead of us. Tyler and Rasta Bob cover our retreat at the bottom.

Call the fucking cops? Are you nuts?

I know we'll get busted but we've got bigger prob—

Indian Sarah screams. She stumbles back from the top of the stairs, something clamped to her left foot. At first I think it's an animal until I recognize the tiny hands, the little round head and the rotted lace of an infant's funeral dress. Sarah drops her gun and starts trying to pry the thing from her leg.

Fuckin' critter! Kezzie brushes past me, puts the muzzle of her rifle against the creature's skull and fires. Baby bits fly in a thousand blood-strewn directions. They musta' pitched the damn thing up through a second-floor window! Tyler! Check all the rooms!

Sarah sobs and drops to her butt. Kezzie bends over her, examining the raw wound at her ankle.

Ya got bit, Sarah.

Sarah presses her eyes shut against tears and nods as if moving her head is painful.

You know what's going to happen? Don't you?

Indian Sarah says nothing. But we've all seen the public service bulletins. Bites from undead cause a swiftly spreading infection that resembles gangrene. Within an hour paralysis spreads to the viscera and lungs and the body of the victim ceases to pump blood and process oxygen. It enters a death-like paralysis where it lays for a short time before reanimating as a zombie.

I'm finished, Sarah whispers.

Kezzie draws her Browning.

I am the Resurrection and the Life, she whispers, cocking the breech and laying the muzzle to Sarah's temple. He that believeth in me shall not perish but have eternal life.

I close my eyes and Kezzie delivers Sarah to her promised eternity.

◀ ▶

I'm gonna kill you: a common enough threat. I've thought it a million times. But in a world where death has grown legs and walks around like a mob of decaying meat puppets, that threat loses its force in a funny kind of way.

I want to kill Kezzie. But what good will that do? Really? She'll just come back from the dead. They all do. Her pre-emptive cancellation of Indian Sarah was an empty gesture because it's not Jesus who is the Resurrection and the Life anymore. Now there is resurrection but no life. And it's more than that. I don't want to just kill Kezzie.

I want her to suffer.

◀ ▶

Tyler has taken up a position beside the smashed window where the zombies pitched in their baby bomb. I stand nearby, my back against the wall until giving up to slide down and sit on my haunches.

We should have called the RCMP, Tyler. You were right.

Think they'd still come?

They have to. They got no choice.

I dig in my pocket as Kezzie's exhortations to Rasta Bob float up the stairs:

Be strong, as unto the warrior Joshua, the warrior Ezekiel! Let your sword flash swift in your hand, brother!

I draw out my cell. Dial 911. Wait. Then:

Nine-one-one. What sort of emergency? Police, fire, ambulance or undead?

Undead.

Please hold.

There is a brief pause before a male voice says firmly:

Zombie Response Unit. What's your location?

I tell him.

How many undead are present?

Dunno. Maybe...two dozen?

That many? (I hear typing.) Why did you wait to call?

This is a grow-op.

Are there weapons on-site?

Yeah. Pointed at the zombies.

Okay. (More typing.) We'll be sending an airborne unit. Nearest detachment is Campbell River. How long can you hold out?

I extend my cell so the constable can hear Rasta Bob's screams float up the stairs. When I put the phone back to my ear, he says:

Hold on. We're coming.

He clicks off.

Kezzie backs up the stairs, emptying her machine gun as she goes. She nods to Tyler who immediately jumps up and takes her place. Kezzie snakes up beside me, eyes jumping from my hand to my pocket as she reloads.

Who did you phone?

Dial-an-Atheist.

Mock as you wish, unbeliever. But it is the faithful who stand strong in this final hour!

You're really full of shit, Kezzie, you know that?

Tyler is singing between bursts of gunfire:

Glory, glory allelujah...glory, glory...

That's it, brother! Kezzie shrieks. Give them the full measure of God's wrath and splendour!

Tyler looses one final burst of gunfire before being engulfed. He manages a strangled scream before the hordes are fighting one another for a chunk of his body. His death has bought us, at most, a minute or two. Kezzie turns to me.

Will you accept Jesus as your personal lord and saviour?

What if I do?

Then I'll shoot you in the head.

Um, no thanks. As I glance out the window for signs of approaching choppers Kezzie asks:

What are you looking for?

Angels.

◀ ▶

They say suffering is good for the soul.

Do they suffer, these soulless creatures? Is feasting on us an expression of their anguish? Are they tormented by memories of their time among the living? I think about the human fear of extinction that elevated death into a religion of resurrection. Do the zombies have a fear of life that works the same way, only in reverse? That's when an idea occurs to me.

Kezzie?

Mm?

Doesn't it say something in the Bible about…preaching to the Dead?

She fishes a roach from her pocket and lights up. But she has cocked her head. I have her attention now.

Something I seem to remember, Kezzie, about the Dead being given the opportunity to accept Christ before the Apocalypse.

She takes a deep toke, holds it, exhales, then says:

I saw another angel fly in the midst of heaven having the everlasting gospel to preach unto them that dwell upon the Earth.

Yeah. The shifting and muttering of the zombies resumes on the stairs. They are done feasting on Tyler and are sniffing for what comes next.

They'll be coming upstairs soon. It's just a matter of time, Kezzie, before they get to us.

I continue:

I suppose the question is – who will preach the Gospel to them? Not me. I can't. I don't know the Word of God like you do. But what if you die first? What will that leave them? Without you, who will be their angel? Who?

The air outside is reverberating with the thrum of inbound choppers. Kezzie smokes meditatively. I can see the crazy logic of her insanity cross her face like cursive. She knows that her mission – her destiny – as the angel of the apocalypse is at hand. All the signs are present. The seals are broken. The vial of God's wrath has been poured. The Dead assemble, awaiting the Word. And the Dove of Grace hovers above the blasted landscape in a glowing golden cloud.

Will you, Kezzie? Will you be their angel?

Kezzie takes one final toke of her joint and crushes it underfoot. Then, turning to me with bloodshot eyes, she nods slowly. Hands her assault rifle to me. And marches towards the head of the stairs.

I am the Alpha and the Omega, she whispers. The beginning and the end.

Praise God! I smile uncomfortably.

Kezzie marches downstairs.

Her screams are drowned out by the roar of choppers. I glance out and see the RCMP response team disembark and advance across the yard in red HazMat suits wielding flame-throwers, scarlet angels brandishing tongues of fire.

THOSE BENEATH THE BOG

Jacques L. Condor ~ Maka Tai Meh

Prunie Stefan, wearing a plaid shirt and men's trousers cinched at her waist with a rope, toiled at flensing a fresh moose skin. Her hair was in two braids tied together across her back so it did not fall in her way. Her husband, Martin, trimmed sinews from a moose carcass hung on a crossbar in the forks of two trees. The work of trimming and flensing was tiresome, but necessary for both of them.

A campfire blocked the entrance to their campsite against marauding bears attracted by the moose kill. Prunie pushed the flensing tool against stretched skin to remove fat and fibres. The final tanned skin would be smooth as the velvet cloth sold at the Nelson River trading post.

Bot flies darted around Prunie's head and arms so she ran to the enveloping alder wood smoke of smudge fires where she was free of the buzzing pests. Prunie used the tail of her blood-spattered shirt to wipe her watering eyes. She left the smoke and walked to the river bank fifty paces away. Prunie scanned the lake. Something moved far out on the water. She shaded her eyes with her hands to make out the object. A freight canoe with a single sail moved far out on the water. The canoe came closer and she recognized the man at the tiller.

My Uncle Alex from Cranberry Portage, Prunie thought. *Coming to visit his relatives at Reed Lake.*

Wind scudded across the water and threw up spumes of white froth. The man turned the canoe into the sudden gust. The sail lofted. Prunie saw the painted clan symbol on the canvas and recognized several people in the canoe.

"Hey, husband," she called out. "People are coming: Uncle Alex and my aunties. There are other men with him."

Martin turned from his butchering. "They smelled my moose meat over there in Cranberry." He laughed. "I know your relatives. They can sniff meat twenty kilometres away. Am I wrong?"

"Yes, wrong. Perhaps they come just to visit," Prunie said.

"We'll feed them, no? It's good I shot this moose. You're lucky your husband is a great hunter." He planted a kiss on her nose and laughed. The woman laughed with him and rolled her eyes.

"You should get to cookin'," Martin said. With a knife as long as his wife's forearm, he sliced through the carcass and pried loose a section of ribs.

"I'll roast these over a slow fire," Prunie said. "But I need meat for stew. They'll need hot soup. It's cold on the lake." Martin cut several lean strips from the belly of the moose. Prunie went to her cooking fire with her arms full of meat.

Martin walked to the rock ledge boat landing at the river's mouth and waited for the canoe to nudge into shore. He saw the guns and the backpacks and knew the relatives were not just visiting, but hunting.

Old Alex climbed from the canoe bobbing in shallow water. The old man waded to shore. As tribal elder and leader of a hunting party, it was his duty to be the first ashore.

The old man shook Martin's hand. "Hello, my relative."

Prunie's cousins, both in their early thirties, greeted Martin.

"Remember me? I'm Peter and this is my brother, Freddie." Freddie pumped Martin's hand.

"Uncle, good to see you," Prunie embraced the old man.

"Good to see you, niece. It has been a year."

Martin waded out to the canoe and picked up an auntie in each arm and carried them to shore. There were squeals and laughter.

"Don't drop them!" Old Alex shouted. "They are the only ones to cook and take care of me."

Peter tried to help the third and eldest of the aunties ashore. The old woman waved him off. She crawled out of the canoe, lifted two layers of long skirts above her knee-high rubber boots and plodded through the water. A large black dog leapt out of the canoe and splashed behind her. One of the strangers whistled a shrill command. The dog dropped on his belly on the gravel shore.

The visitors followed Prunie to her campfire where they drank hot soup and warmed themselves. The oldest woman stirred the ashes of the fire with a willow stick before she dropped in a bundle of tobacco, cedar twigs and red yarn. Her offering flared for a moment and the fire smoldered as before.

"I had to do that, Prunie," the old Auntie Rose said. "That's my prayer offering to *Manitou*. I been prayin' since we left home. That lake is dangerous with the crosswinds rushin' in."

"Oh, Sister Rose, you worry too much about everythin'. You're always praying for somethin' or other," Alex said.

"Somebody's got to do the prayin' or we wouldn't have any protection at all."

"I'm glad you pray, Auntie Rose. It makes me feel safer," Prunie said. "Do you pray too, Auntie Sophia?"

"I sure do, but when Rose tells me I ought to be prayin' to the Old Ones, I get peevish. I'm a good Catholic, Prunie," Auntie Sophia said.

"Well I wish prayers could kill these pesky bugs!" Young Aunt Nettie swatted at a circling ring of black flies swarming around her head.

"Hard freeze works better than prayers on bugs," Uncle Alex said.

The youngest of the aunties made a sound like "Pish" and walked downwind of a smudge fire and let the smoke discourage the pests.

"We haven't seen moose on our side of the lake. Don't know where they gone to," Alex said.

"Alex is too old to hunt moose." Aunt Sophia said.

"I am not too old," the old man replied.

"If I say you are – then you are," Sophia replied. "That's why these two boys came along – to get some moose meat for us – forgot to introduce them."

"These boys are from our village," Auntie Rose explained. "The tall one is Nikolas. That black dog is his. It's a good duck dog. This skinny one is Ephraim. They is good boys."

"And good hunters, too," Sophia added.

The man called Nikolas whistled again and the black dog came and crouched at his feet. "This is River. I call him River 'cause he takes to water every chance he gets. Never go any place without him," Nikolas said.

"You never go any place without that silly cap either," Auntie Sophia pointed to the leather hat the man wore. It was decorated with fishing lures, bits of shell, dangling beads and animal fetishes. The hat was firmly tied under the man's chin with leather thongs.

"He sleeps in that damned hat," Alex said. "Come on, we got to talk huntin'."

"You're a pushy old man bringing up the main subject without first jest visitin'," Sophia said.

"And you won't let a man talk about huntin' in peace."

Sophia kicked at Alex's moccasin-shod foot and missed. She shrugged and walked away to join Prunie and Nettie at the cooking fire. As she passed her eldest sister, Sophia noticed that Rose held a spruce root basket in her hands and a tattered red blanket was draped over her arm.

"What you plannin' to do with that stuff, Rose?" Sophia asked, frowning. She recognized the divining tools and knew her sister intended to consult the bones and foretell the future.

"Leave me be, Sophia!" Rose croaked. "I'm gonna go off yonder and do me some prayin'."

"Prayin', I don't mind, Rose, but tossin' around them old bones and little coloured rocks is the devil's work in my way of thinkin'."

"Then stop thinkin'. Don't pay me any mind and let me do my *niganadjimowin* divinin' in peace."

"Oh go off by yourself and throw them smelly old bones all over the place if you want. My advice is to toss all that evil stuff in the Grassy River." Sophia turned abruptly and went to tend the roasting ribs.

Rose moved several metres farther away and spread her blanket. She peered inside the basket. The bones were there. The porcupine bones would tell her of hunting success and the beaver hipbone foretold the fate of all in the camp. The other tiny bones and coloured agate stones and the *pindjigossan* medicine bag helped old Rose with vague details of her divinations. She covered the opening of the basket with her hand and shook it seven times. She sang divination song-prayers before she turned the basket upside down and let the contents spill on the worn red blanket. Rose bent to study the pattern the bones made. She read the message:

Three moose will be taken – not by these hunters but by others. Danger surrounds this camp. Two hunters will die! "Ka! Kawin! Namawiya! Ka! Ka!" She cried out. "No! Oh my, no! Oh no!" and slumped to the ground.

Prunie saw her old auntie fall and rushed to her side.

"What is it, Auntie?" Prunie asked.

"I think she fainted," Nikolas said, hurrying to their side.

"I'm alright, you two." Rose allowed herself to be raised to a sitting position. "The bones' message scared me. I'm all right, but this camp and two of the hunters are in danger. Two gonna die!"

Nikolas shook his head, eyes growing wide. "Who? Which one of us is it? When? Who will die?" he asked.

"Foolish man!" Rose hissed. "The bones don't give me a time and a place! They don't spell out names if that's what you're thinkin'."

Prunie looked up into Nikolas's worried face and forced a smile. "Sometimes what the bones reveal never come true. Isn't that right, Auntie? Sometimes the bones reveal things that have already happened."

The old auntie did not answer. She gathered her divining items and replaced them in her basket.

Nikolas helped Rose to her feet. "Sometimes things you see don't happen?"

"Prunie said that. *I didn't*," Rose said. "I might read the bones wrong – but it doesn't happen often. I must make prayers to *Manitou*. The danger is from the dead ones who live. Go away and leave me be."

Nikolas watched the old woman hobble off to pray and turned to Prunie. "What is that old one talking about? You believe in all this stuff?"

"You shouldn't worry about what she saw in the bones. Forget about this, Nikolas. Don't say anything to the others and neither will I." Prunie tried to sound calm. Nikolas hesitated before nodding his agreement.

◀ ▶

When she finished her prayers, a grim-faced Auntie Rose joined the other women. When Sophia asked Rose what was wrong, the older sister said nothing, put down the carving knife and walked away. Auntie Rose kept apart from everyone. She stared into space, silent and alone. Prunie felt uneasy and it showed on her face.

Sophia patted her arm and said, "Don't worry, Prunie. Rose is in one of her moods. She always gets that way whenever she messes with them old bones. She calls it *'seein' visions.'* What she imagines she sees, I ignore. She just wants attention. She'll get over her bad mood and be her regular sassy self in a few hours."

◀ ▶

Nikolas joined the men at their campfire. Uncle Alex discussed the route from the headwaters of Reed Lake to the west bank, then north where moose were to be found.

"I had good luck up at Rabbit Lake 'bout seven, maybe eight seasons ago," Uncle Alex said.

"Then let's head up there," Martin said.

"We'll need canoes," Peter said. "Can't get the big canoe up there."

"We'll borrow from my relatives," Martin said.

"Good," Alex said. "Here's the plan. Martin and Peter will hunt together with me and Freddie as a second team. Nikolas will be the go-between for the two groups."

◀ ▶

That night Prunie walked to the lean-to where Martin rested; puffing on his clay pipe. She crawled into bed.

Martin blew out a puff of smoke, took the pipe from his mouth. "Did you see the look on Auntie Rose's face when she heard we'll go up to Rabbit Lake?" Martin asked.

"I was too busy listening to Uncle's plans to notice," Prunie said. "Auntie Rose has been in a bad mood all day."

Martin gave a big sigh.

"What do you want to tell me?" Prunie asked. "Did Auntie Rose say something to you tonight?"

He phrased his answer carefully. "This is not the first time Rose talked about danger around that lake. When she came here four years ago she told me never to go there if I was alone."

"But you're not going alone," Prunie said. "So what's the problem?"

He rolled on his side and faced his wife. "Auntie Rose said she'd had visions; *warnings*, she called them, about some dead things."

"If she wants to warn you, to protect you, let her do it. Old people, like Auntie Rose, are the only ones who still know how to do such things. If I knew the old protection songs and how to make amulets to protect you, believe me, I'd do it."

"I thought you were a church member."

"I am, but maybe there's something true and powerful in the old ways. I want you back safe and in one piece."

"I'll come back safe. I've not hunted over that way, ever since old Rose spooked me four years ago."

"What did she do?"

"She took me aside and said she wanted to talk. She looked towards Rabbit Lake and started talking to herself as much as to me," Martin explained. "She said the night was full of evil spirits on the other shore; dead things walkin' around and don't I see 'em? I tell her, '*No. I don't see no dead things.*' Then she asks, '*Did you ever hear any whistlin' when you was over there at night?*'

"No." I told her. '*You will some day,*' she said, '*when you hear the whistlin' you'll know. The* wanisid manitous, *evil spirit things is around. Somebody's gonna die.*"

Prunie lay beside her husband. She felt a chill in spite of the warmth of the heavy quilts and blankets. Memories of old legends; stories of the hairy men; the *wendigo;* wild men of the woods, the *ganibod;* the dead people who walk; the under-the-lake-people; the old tales invaded her brain like misty ghosts that wouldn't take clear shape or form. The fear of something ancient, something terrible and deadly, something she knew existed but had never seen nor heard grew within her. She shuddered and Martin, feeling her tremble, asked if she was cold.

"Yes," she said and snuggled against him. She slept fitfully, awakening suddenly in the late night. She was jolted upright in the bed still feeling the tugging, clawed hands of some nightmare creatures, imagined dream horrors.

◄ ►

The camp came alive with morning activity. Supplies were pushed into backpacks. Freddie and Ephraim carried gear to the lakeshore. Prunie and Sophia helped Nettie pour water on the campfires while they waited for Martin, Peter and Nikolas to come up the lake with the canoes borrowed from the villagers. Auntie Rose paced back and forth at the far end of the spit of land and muttered her prayers.

Shouts announced Martin's and the boys' arrival with three smaller canoes. Uncle Alex supervised the placement of packs and people in them. He took his Elder's place in the first canoe before they moved towards the north bank several kilometres away.

◄ ►

Before the second night in the new camp, brush lean-to shelters had been fashioned to face a central fire pit where the women prepared the meals. Smaller "bear-fires" burned in outlying pits.

The third night in camp, a despondent group sat around the fire. Two days without moose sign had passed. Nikolas and his dog brought in rabbits and a goose to provide the camp with fresh meat but the moose remained elusive.

The weather stayed warm. The bushes close to camp were heavy with Manitoba *mashkigimin,* high-bush cranberries; and a few late fruiting *pikwadjish,* wild mushrooms, were found on the forest floor. With a supply of walleyes and pike from the lake, the women prepared daily meals. The hunters grumbled as they ate, and complained every night that the moose must have moved farther northwest from Rabbit Lake.

When Auntie Rose heard this, she developed another bout of sulky silence. The women hoped her moody spell would soon end. Such behaviour disturbed the harmony of the camp.

Each night, campfires provided a sense of safety, holding the thick darkness of the wilderness at bay. For Rose, the shadowy trees concealed *matchi manadad,* very evil things; the dead who live, watching; waiting to steal forward if the fires died.

The nights in this part of Manitoba were cold, silent and, to Rose, threatening. She listened for whispering voices or the whistling calls, but heard nothing. Rose pulled her blanket tighter and recited songs of protection for herself and the group. Her repeated chants lasted until the first grey streaks of false dawn.

◀ ▶

On the fifth morning, a damp haze of fog hung over the forest and camp blurring the outlines of everything it touched. The men sat huddled around the central fire.

Martin spoke to Peter and Uncle Alex. "Ain't no moose for three day's walk. I say we go up past Rabbit Lake. What you think?"

Old Alex rubbed his hands together and held them palms outward to the campfire. "Good idea," he said. "That lake has a big bog at the north end. There's a big sinkhole in the middle of the bog you gotta watch out for, but it's a safe enough place to camp and hunt."

Peter said, "I heard nobody goes up there."

"That sinkhole has a bad name, that's why some hunters don't go there," Uncle Alex said. "It's called the 'death hole.' Been there before. It's a strange place."

Auntie Rose stared at Alex and shook her head vigorously in negation. Martin saw the old uncle telegraph a quick message with his eyes.

Auntie Rose slammed her hand down on the earth and shouted, "No! Never – you can't go there. Something bad will happen!"

Prunie was surprised when her auntie spoke out with such emphatic anger. When Rose disagreed with anything or anyone, she usually turned silent and never shouted.

Alex turned to Rose. "Not the time to speak of visions and deaths." To the other men he said, "It is nothing. Get ready to leave."

Uncle Alex acted as if the harsh exchange had not taken place and said, "We will leave when the sun stands directly over us and camp out by Rabbit Lake."

It was obvious that old Rose did not like this plan at all. She went silent in her sulky manner. This time her silence seemed to convey something more than just disapproval.

Prunie saw a different expression on her auntie's face — a look of fear. It flashed quickly like a burst of flame from bear fat dropped in a campfire. The old woman's expression filled Prunie with a sense of dread.

At noon, the men packed their gear into three small canoes. When the hunters started paddling away, Martin shouted to Rose who stood apart from the others.

"Keep prayin' for us and we're all gonna come back." Martin could not hear the words the old woman whispered to the wind.

◀ ▶

The hunters arrived at Rabbit Lake before nightfall. Peter built a large fire. The bright blaze illuminated the shelters made from tarps and branches. They ate smoked fish and talked.

Nikolas sat close to the fire ring, squatting on his haunches, his arm draped about his dog. He stared north in the direction of the bog. "Uncle Alex, you said people didn't come up here. Is there something you didn't tell us about this place?"

Alex swallowed the bite of smoked pike before he spoke.

"Your Auntie Rose is a superstitious old woman," Alex said. "There was a flat space where the bog is now; a burial site for murdered Cree and Ojibwe people. Generations ago the Dene people from up north fought our people over that flat place — good hunting land. The Dene pretended to leave but came back before dawn and slaughtered all the men in the camp. Old ones say they left the bodies unburied and put a Dene curse on the corpses. The spirits of the dead were unhappy."

"What did our people do?" Martin asked Alex.

"Stories say our people came up here and buried all they could find and built spirit houses over the graves. Maybe it was too late to calm the spirits of those dead men. I don't know. But no one from our tribes ever came back here much after that."

"But that happened years ago," Nikolas said.

"Yes," Alex said. "Right after the bodies were buried, a big fire came through and burned all the trees and brush as well as the grave houses. The rains and heavy snows created high run-off and filled the creeks to overflowing. Creeks changed course and turned the burial ground into a lake for a few years until most of it dried up. Now it's nothing but a bog with that deep sinkhole in the middle."

Uncle Alex knocked tobacco ash from his pipe. "Now it's grown back. Where there's willows and water, you got moose. We'll have good luck tomorrow."

Martin heard gravel crunch and saw Nikolas and his dog leave the fire and walk to the edge of Rabbit Lake. A swift gust of wind grew the fire's embers into flame. In the sudden fire-flare, Martin saw the man and the dog clearly. What Martin saw on Nikolas's face was terror. Nikolas returned and knelt beside his dog and stared into the fire.

"What's the matter?" Martin waited for an answer. None came. "You think maybe bad things live up in that bog?" Nikolas still did not answer. The dog crouched at his side whined and shifted his ears.

Peter put his arm around Nikolas and said, "You're not afraid of an old tale about some things that died there a long time ago, are you?"

Again Nikolas did not answer. He pushed Peter's arm from his shoulder and stood up abruptly. Nikolas stepped out of the ring of firelight; his dog followed at his heels, whimpering. They faced the forest and the bog, watching and listening.

"I need some sleep," Martin yawned. "I'm shootin' moose tomorrow." Martin, Peter and Alex went to the spruce bough shelters.

Freddie stood beside Nikolas. "Don't be payin' any heed to long ago stories. There ain't no such things around today."

"What makes you so sure, Freddie?" Nikolas muttered.

"Because nobody's seen anything for almost a hundred years, that's why I'm sure."

"Maybe they weren't lookin' in the right places, Freddie."

"You're actin' crazy, Nikolas. I'm goin' to bed. Don't let the spooks and *matchi* men get you," Freddie laughed and walked away.

Nikolas stood alone staring into the darkness. The dog growled low in his throat, lifted his ears and pointed his muzzle into the air, sniffing. Nikolas moved back towards the fire. Some innate memory struggled to access ancient warnings. His senses became acute. He heard sounds. They came out of the black night, swirling to his ears on the mists rising from the sinkhole in the bog. The sounds were high-pitched whistles, dropping in tone and fading away to nothingness.

With shaking hands, Nikolas tore open his pouch of sacred tobacco and cedar and offered the contents to the coals. He chanted his prayer so quietly his ears did not hear the words. He prayed, because he now knew the old tales were true. The creatures lived. Dead souls walked the brush forests of Rabbit Lake; the hunting party had invaded their homeland.

◀ ▶

Ephraim tended the fires circling the camp while the women talked story by the big campfire. Rose was over her pouting spells. She told stories of family foibles and escapades which made everyone laugh out loud. The laughter echoed back from the ringing, low hills. The echoes brought a sudden quiet to the gathering of women.

"I think I'd better get to bed before I laugh myself to death," Nettie said.

"Nobody ever dies laughin'," Auntie Rose grumbled. "Death ain't funny at all."

Young Nettie stopped giggling abruptly. "That was a dumb thing to say, Sister Rose." She hurried away.

Prunie put her arm around Rose. "We all say dumb things sometimes."

"You think I'm just a foolish old lady when I tell you what the bones show me. Huh?" Rose sniffed.

"No Auntie. I don't think that."

"You don't believe what I tell you?" Rose followed a spark's skyward flight from the fire with her eyes.

"I didn't say that. It's just that—"

"It's because you're one of these modern Indians hanging around Wekusko or Flin Flon, listening to what white people say. You believe their stories more than our old stories? Our stories kept Ojibwe people protected more than a hundred generations."

"Auntie Rose, it's a different time."

"Don't I know that? Four generations separate you and me."

The young girl touched the weathered hand of her old auntie. "But I do listen, Auntie."

"But do you believe? What I'm gonna tell you now, about things in the bog, you gotta believe. They are real livin' creatures out there that are waitin' to kill someone. I had visions. They are dead things but still alive and eatin' living flesh."

Prunie stiffened at the thought.

She paused and formed her words carefully so as not to anger the old woman. "Auntie, those bog things that could kill our men...What are they?"

"Like a man, but not a man. They are all *nibo*, dead – for long, long time, but still alive somehow. Got hands like ours, but with claws. They are *mask*, ugly *gi-mask*, disfigured."

"Now you're trying to scare me with those old stories about the *wendigo* boogeymen of the woods," Prunie said.

"I'm not tryin' to scare you, child!" Rose pulled away. "I just want you to know there are dead things that walk."

Prunie whispered, "Auntie, don't you think if something like that *did* exist, we would have seen them?"

"They been seen but those who saw them never lived to tell about them. The dead men live in the cursed bog by Rabbit Lake."

"Well, every one of the men has a rifle. If they see any of them up there, they can shoot them and kill them."

"There are some things that can't be killed – by guns, anyway. It'll take more than bullets to kill them bog creatures."

"Why do they live in a bog?"

Rose leaned towards Prunie. "They den in the bogs like beavers and muskrats."

"How could they do that?"

"They go down under the water and dig dens into earth banks at the edge of deep water."

"How do they get out in the winter when the ice freezes thick on the bog?" Prunie asked. "Wouldn't they be trapped with nothing to eat?"

"Them creatures take moose and anything else that wanders into their bog, then stores the meat up for winter. Just like a beaver does with green poplar branches.

"They got holes and tunnels dug up into the woods. They sneak out and roam around whenever they want. Don't make no nevermind if the bog is frozen over or not."

"I see," Prunie said. She smiled at her eighty-eight-year-old auntie and leaned over and kissed her on both cheeks and smoothed the old woman's straggles of coarse white hair back under her floral-printed babushka. "I love you, Auntie Rose."

"I love you too, Prunie. I wish you would send Ephraim to talk the men into comin' away from that bog."

"They'd laugh at us for worrying. The men plan to get winter meat and think that's the place to do it." Prunie stood. "I'm going to get us each a mug of hot coffee. It's getting chilly. Aren't you cold, Auntie?"

The old one shook her head. "I will have a cup anyway."

Rose reached for the spruce root basket of divining bones. She shook the basket vigorously before she dumped the bones on the blanket folded into a square.

"Waugh!" the old woman cried out. "Again it is two who will die!"

◀ ▶

At daybreak, Martin found Nikolas curled up in a ball, next to his dog, his special hat pulled down over his ears, sleeping by the embers of the fire.

When the group woke him, he seemed to be surprised that he was still in the encampment and said, "Waugh! I am still alive!"

The men chuckled. A light dusting of snow in the earliest hours of the morning powdered Nikolas's clothes.

Nikolas shook his head, brushing off the snow with his hands.

"This is good. Snow helps us track moose now," Alex said.

"Today I don't hunt," Nikolas said. "It was foolish of me to fall asleep outside. I couldn't shoot straight today. I'd spoil your hunt. Go without me. Maybe River will help me get some ducks or geese."

"Geese are good eatin', too," Martin offered.

"You get us some geese, Nikolas," Alex said. "We stay with our plan. I go up the east side of the lake with Freddie. Martin and Peter can take the west shore."

Freddie and Alex climbed into their canoe. The pair paddled into fog. Martin and Peter followed in the second canoe. They drew abreast of Uncle Alex's canoe.

"We will return with meat," Peter whispered.

"We'll get two moose apiece," Martin whispered just as Peter had done. Prey could hear a hunter's plans and so they must keep their voices low. The two canoes separated and headed to opposite sides of the lake.

◀ ▶

Nikolas sat by the fire and watched the sun dissipate the fog. The sound of geese honking low overhead brought him to his feet. River jumped up, whining and wagging his tail.

"Stragglers heading to the far end of the lake," he told his Labrador. "They're tired. Let's go get us some geese, River."

The excitement of a hunt pushed the fears of the night from Nikolas's mind. He slid the canoe into the water and River jumped in. He paddled in the direction the geese had flown. Nikolas pushed his leather hat with all its trinkets and totems firmly on his head and bent into his paddling, propelling the canoe forward.

◀ ▶

Peter and Martin paddled the shoreline. No tracks were visible from the shore into the bush. They stopped paddling and let the canoe drift. They searched the willow thickets near a bend. Peter made a sudden hissing sound and pointed to the thick brush near a flat point of beach jutting into the water. The hunter made another sign for "listen" and cupped his hand to his ear. Martin did the same.

Both heard the sound of breaking twigs as something moved quickly away from their canoe. Martin pulled towards the thicket on the shoreline. A louder crashing followed as the something took off running at top speed through the brush.

"Moose," whispered Martin, and beached the prow on the sand. Peter grabbed his rifle and leapt onto the shore. He made signs telling Martin to go upwind and frighten the moose back where he would be waiting. Martin understood and back-paddled. He moved the canoe forward in silence some two hundred metres up the shoreline, jumped from the beached canoe and started inland, making noise to scare the moose back towards Peter.

◀ ▶

Taller hemlocks among the spindly spruce created a thick canopy of interlocking branches. There were no tracks. Peter could hear the snapping of branches and crackling of twigs. He thought more than one animal hurried away. Suddenly the sounds stopped. Peter stopped, dropped to one knee and pointed his rifle in the direction where he had last heard sounds. Peter listened. The sounds he heard were like whispers children make. Over the whisperings came a series of short, low whistles.

◀ ▶

Martin checked the rifle he had slung over his shoulder. He released the safety and began to walk towards his hunting partner. He saw or heard nothing as he sneaked through the thick brush and deadfalls.

◀ ▶

Peter held his rifle at the ready for some time. The animals in front of him had not changed position. He had heard no sounds of movement, just murmurs. The muscles in his left forearm twitched with the strain of holding the heavy weapon. He lowered the rifle to relax his arm.

There was a snap of a twig behind him. Before he could turn something hard and heavy struck the back of his head and he pitched forward, unconscious.

When the hunter came to his senses he was being carried by the grasping hands of many strong creatures that moved at great speed. The creatures held him by the arms and legs and made whispered, lisping sounds and murmurs. As they ran, they called to each other with low whistles.

◀ ▶

Martin heard the sounds of running animals directly ahead. They seemed to be going away from him. He heard murmurs, soft burbling sounds and whistles and could not imagine why, or how, any running moose could make such noises.

◀ ▶

Alex sat on a fallen log and wondered why he had failed to spot any moose.

"The moose is hidin' from me," he told Freddie.

"I'm wonderin' where they went, Uncle Alex."

"Freddie, walk along the shore and see if you can find any tracks. I'll sit here and wait for you."

Minutes passed and Freddie came back. He stood in front of Alex and shrugged his shoulders. "I can't figure it out. I saw moose tracks and they all led up to that bog – the one with the big sinkhole in the middle. Didn't see any moose, though. I did see lots of moose bones and three sets of skulls and antlers all bleached out white."

"Was the tines on the antlers all chewed up by porcupines eatin' on em? Was the bones scattered like bears and wolves had got to them?"

"Nothin' like that. They was all stacked up neat-like. The leg bones in one pile, the skulls in another and the ribs in another pile."

"Why'd anybody stack up moose bones like that?"

"Beats me," Freddie said.

At that moment two shots from a twelve-gauge shotgun rang out.

◀ ▶

Martin stopped in his tracks. The sound of the gunshots echoed. It was Nikolas's shotgun. He pushed his way through the willows towards the gunshots. Martin heard a muffled scream. The tangled branches pulled at his clothing, as if trying to prevent him from reaching Peter.

◀ ▶

Peter could not scream again. One of the creatures pried open his mouth with insistent claws and forced a chunk of lichen-moss into his open mouth. The creatures scurried through the willow and aspen growth towards the bog. Peter's eyes bulged in fear and panic. The choking moss barred the air from his lungs.

Peter heard the whistles grow in volume and the lisping sounds increased to an excited pitch as the creatures dragged Peter into the water. He felt the cold splash against his legs and back as the creatures propelled him feet first into the sinkhole.

The grasping creatures swarmed over his body, forcing him upright in the icy water until only his head remained above surface. Suddenly the whistles reached a crescendo and the things that held him pulled his head under the water. Peter gulped in a last breath of air and choked on the lichen and brackish bog water that rushed in. The grasping claws pulled him down, down…

◀ ▶

Martin pushed on through old deadfalls to the border of Rabbit Lake. He stopped and listened for sounds that might direct him. He heard a sudden series of whistles from the direction of the bog. The whistling rose in volume and then stopped abruptly.

Loons? Could it be loons so late in the season?

He moved down a slope towards the far end of the lake. The water here was dark and looked deep. Martin experienced a brief jolt of unexplainable fear. The water's surface was still and placid. No loons swam there to disturb the black-mirror surface.

◀ ▶

Nikolas heard the gabbling of geese at the far end of Rabbit Lake. He used his canoe paddle to test the depth of the water and found it less than half a metre deep. He pumped the paddle up and down; solid rock was beneath the canoe. He gave his dog a signal to stay.

Nikolas pulled his favourite hat down tight on his head and tied the thongs beneath his chin in a double knot. He did not want to lose the hat when he pushed through brush.

The cackling and the gabbling of the geese lessened. Nikolas crouched low, held aside dangling willow branches and peered through the peephole in the leaves. Nikolas's jaw muscles tightened at what he saw.

A sunken ring of earth, edged with a circle of rock ledges and moss-covered gravel, held a round, dark expanse of water several metres in diameter. A circle of water stared back at him like a giant cycloptic black eye. On the surface, six geese circled in a small bunched flock of frightened birds.

What the hell happened to the rest of the flock? They couldn't have flown away! I would have seen them. He raised his shotgun to fire as he pushed through the willows.

When the remaining birds flapped across the water in rising flight, he fired two shots. Both shots hit the targets and two geese fell into the dark water of the sinkhole.

Nikolas whistled to the waiting dog. River came bounding through the willows and leapt into the water to retrieve the geese. Nikolas watched River swimming at his top speed towards one of the birds.

Now what in the hell happened to the other one? The damned bird is gone. Geese don't sink when you hit them, not right away anyhow. Before Nikolas could concoct an answer, he saw River falter in the middle of the sinkhole. The dog let the bird fall from his mouth and gave a terrified yelp before he was pulled under the surface.

"River!" Nikolas shouted. "River! Hold on boy!"

The man dropped his gun and slid down the mossy incline across the wet gravel and fell into the water. He swam only three strokes towards where the dog had gone down when something clutched at his ankles. The swimming man was held fast in the water. More and more clutching hands tugged at his legs and lower body.

"Oh God!" he cried out just before he was yanked under the black surface.

◀ ▶

When Martin heard yelping and sounds of splashing, he turned to his right towards the sounds. He ran up a slight incline and skidded to a stop. Below him yawned the "death hole." He scanned the area in all directions.

The first thing he saw was Nikolas's hat floating two metres from the pool's edge. Then he saw the dog cowering in a stand of willows. The animal quivered with fright and gave out a keening wail.

Martin hurried around the rim of the sinkhole to the dog.

"Hey there, boy. Where's your boss?"

The dog raised itself on its bleeding forepaws and bared its teeth in a menacing snarl.

"River. What's got into you? What chewed you up like this?"

The Labrador dropped on his belly and did a wiggling crawl backwards through the willows. Martin pushed through the brush and saw the dog, tail between his legs, howling and running as fast as his wounded legs could carry him down the trail to the camp.

He moved back to the sinkhole. Nikolas's hat had floated to the very edge. Martin knelt down to retrieve it. It felt heavy in his hand, as if snagged on something. He set down his rifle and used both hands to pull the leather hat from the water.

The hat gave way suddenly, and Martin fell on his backside onto the slick moss and gravel. Nikolas's severed head, the hat still firmly tied to it, fell into his lap. Martin scrabbled sideways away from the horrible object.

He raised his head and yelled as loud as he could. "Peter! Goddammit, Peter, get over here! Quick!"

Martin moved backwards through the willows just as the dog had done and ran as fast as he could down the same trail.

◀ ▶

Fifteen minutes later, Freddie and Alex knelt looking at moose tracks leading to the edge of the circle of black water.

"Uncle Alex. This is what I wanted to show you."

The old man looked down at the mud. Freddie pointed. Alex saw three sets of tracks; one set made by a big bull.

"That's a big moose. See how deep he sinks into the mud?" Alex said. "That other set of tracks is a cow moose. Her hooves ain't as pointy as the bull's." He moved a few feet to his left. "Look here, Freddie, the cow had a yearling with her, too."

Freddie studied the bull's tracks. His mouth felt dry and he moistened his lips with his tongue. "Somethin' ain't right here. Come and look at this."

Alex looked where Freddie touched the slurred tracks with a willow stick.

"These tracks are real deep and messed up. See how they are bunched up close together with the dew-claws showin' in the prints?"

"I see that." Alex said.

"What does that tell you?"

"It tells me it was a damn big bull moose, and that he was pullin' backwards trying to get away."

"Trying to get away from what?"

"From whatever was tryin' to pull him into the sinkhole."

"Whatever was pulling him in had to be monstrous big," Freddie said.

"Maybe it was several things all pullin' together," Alex replied.

"What?" Freddie scratched his head at the thought.

Alex studied the other tracks. "Something pulled the cow and the yearling calf into the water. Look around, you won't see no tracks comin' out!"

"What do you think happened?"

"I think somethin' got the three moose we been huntin' before we did."

"Whaaat?" Freddie dragged out his question.

"And now I think we best get away from this place fast as we can."

"What about the canoe?"

"Forget about the canoe. What killed them moose will kill us, too. Let's go. Rose knew what she was talkin' about!"

Old Alex started down the trail away from the bog at a wobbly trot.

"What are you talkin' about, Uncle Alex?"

"I'll tell you when we get back to camp. You'd better get a move on if you want to keep livin'."

Martin heard the padding of feet behind him. When he turned, he saw the willows were shaking. He cocked his rifle and held it at waist level, the barrel aimed at the spot where the willows moved.

Alex and Freddie came through the willows and stopped in their tracks when they saw Martin in the trail with his rifle pointed at them.

"Martin! Don't shoot!" Freddie yelled.

Alex saw the fear Martin struggled to hide. "So you know about the bog things?" Uncle Alex said.

"Something killed Nikolas – in the death hole place."

"Let's get as far away from here as we can. Come on. It's a long way to run."

"What about Peter, we can't go off and leave him up there."

"Pretty sure the things got Peter, too."

"Why would you think that? We gotta look for him!" Martin said.

"Old Rose said *two* people would die on this hunt. It's too late to save Peter. He's gone. Them dead, flesh eatin' things – those damned creatures took him or we'd have heard from him by now."

"Martin. Let's go! I wanna get outta here." Freddie ran down the trail.

◀ ▶

Rose sat staring up the trail. Uncle Alex hobbled to his sister. The others rushed to greet the hunters. The group encircled Auntie Rose. The old woman's eyes were open but not seeing.

"Rose," Alex said. There was no response. "Rose?" The old woman's eyes fluttered shut and she began to moan.

Alex shook his sister. "Answer me!"

Sophia explained. "Yesterday, a little time before noon, I heard her scream. Prunie heard it too, and we thought a bear had come into camp."

"About an hour ago, that black dog came runnin' in here. His legs were all chewed up but he wouldn't let anyone get near him," Prunie said.

Ephraim said. "Rose just been sittin' there and mumblin'."

"She began to say words that frightened all of us," Nettie said.

"What in hell did she say?" Alex demanded.

"She called Peter's name. She said *'Matchi wanisid mani-tou* got him' and the words 'they pulled him under. *Madagamiskwa nibi; gi-nibowiiawima manadas matchi ijiwe-bad – wissiniwin, matchi!* The water is moving, he is dead, just a body now; the evil ones are eating!'"

"I thought she'd gone crazy." Sophia swallowed hard and continued. "Next she hollered, 'Nikolas! Look out! Get away from there!'"

"I don't understand what's goin' on," Nettie whimpered.

"I do," Alex said. "What she saw in the bones came true. Peter is dead and Nikolas too. We have to go back to Cranberry and give them the sad news."

Rose exhaled a great breath and shuddered and opened her eyes. "I have seen it all," she said.

"It is finished," the old man said.

"No. It is not finished yet." Rose struggled to her feet. "Are you ready to listen to me now?"

"Say what you want to say, Sister," Sophia said.

"Strike camp and pack up. We must be gone from here before dark comes."

No one doubted the old woman's words. They hiked the trail to Martin's hunting camp, where there was shelter. Uncle Alex and Ephraim coaxed the wounded black dog to follow.

◀ ▶

Alex, Freddie, Sophia and Nettie packed the freight canoe for the return trip to their village. Prunie and Martin insisted Old Rose spend the winter at their cabin and Rose agreed.

Two weeks later, a flotilla of seven canoes from Cranberry Portage made their way to Rabbit Lake. Forty men from Prunie's village carried cans of fuel oil and gasoline two miles inland to the sinkhole.

The men did as Old Rose had instructed them. They spread oil and gasoline on the black surface of the death hole, dropped in a sealed case of dynamite with a timed detonator and hurried down the trail. The resulting explosion was heard miles away. The fire burned for several days, but died out beneath the heavy rains of mid-September.

◀ ▶

When the first heavy frosts crusted the ground, four young men from Flin Flon appeared at Martin's cabin. They told Prunie and Rose they intended to hike to Rabbit Lake and see what remained of the sinkhole.

"There is nothing there. It is finished," Rose said. "You should not go."

The boys were polite to the old woman but paid no attention to her words. They left that afternoon, promising to return the next day. Snow clouds massed in grey billows overhead began to drop light flurries.

Rose made her way to a dark corner of the cabin.

◀ ▶

The boys found the dynamite and fire had obliterated the sinkhole and left metres of burned brush and scorched trees. Farther away from the ruined bog, the taller trees and leafless willows were untouched by the fire. The boys moved into the shelter of the trees and set up a lean-to of canvas and spruce branches before exploring the area.

"Hey, Lucas, look over here. There's a whole bunch of trails and tracks," a slender boy said.

The tracks were barely visible in the quickly melting snow and the slanting late afternoon sun muddled their shape.

"Looks a little like black bear tracks," the slender boy said. "Some prints have claw marks."

"There sure are a lot of them," the boy called Lucas said.

◀ ▶

Four days later, the boys had not returned. At Prunie's urging, Martin and a neighbouring Cree man went to search for them. The first snows of the season had melted and the tracks and trails in the forests surrounding the old bog were no longer visible.

What the men found was the collapsed and destroyed lean-to shelter. The white of the canvass was spattered with rust-red stains.

The boys' backpacks were ripped and scattered about. Two rifles, their stocks broken and the barrels stuffed with chunks of lichen-moss, lay near the campsite.

Martin and his neighbour searched farther into the forest and found four neat piles of human bones. The skulls in one pile, the leg bones in another and the ribs placed in two mounded stacks.

ON THE WINGS OF THIS PRAYER

Richard Van Camp

There are two stories my great grandfather told me. He said a long time ago before *them* – the Shark Throats, he called them, during the time of the warming world – there was a family in the way of the Tar Sands of Alberta. One day as the mother was gathering water, she stepped on teeth in the ice and muskeg. The jaws of an old man, a trapper, had thawed enough to bite her. She ran but she had not escaped. The woman got very sick: buttons of pus boiling through a body rash, the paling, her hands hooking to claws. She asked her husband to bring her glass after glass of water. She was thirsty and panting. He kept bringing her more, yet she never drank. She said something was coming through her. Something starving.

Her voice then turned to a low growl as she began to rock for hours hissing, "Kill me now. Kill me now or I'll kill you all before the sunrise. Do it do it if you love me. Kill me please. Your meat is magnificent and what roars in your veins is calling me. It's calling me to drink you open and warm me so sweetly. Oh let me start with your scars and scabs. Let me. Let me taste you. You'd let me if you love me."

As her husband returned with help, she snapped at the air with her teeth and rasped before striking out wildly at all of them with her nails. After they subdued her, she begged again for all of them to kill her – before the sunrise, she insisted. They tied her fists and feet and ran for more help. When they returned, she was gone. She'd torn her binding and fled, but the strangest thing – the oddest thing – were the glasses of water he'd brought her. They'd all turned to ice. The husband never saw his wife again. They think she was the first and they say she is still here as their queen, that she gives birth to them through her mouth. Hatching them through her over and over. More and more. The Boiled Faces, we call them – *zombies*, our son said – and they remember faces.

The Tar Sands of Alberta had tailing ponds and excavators, and I am sure those teeth belonged to that old trapper who lived out there before them. That old man, no matter how much money the oil companies offered him, would not budge, so they built and dug around him. He quit coming to town. There was a family who went to visit him, to bring him supplies, but he had changed. He had gone to white and had eaten his own lips and fingers. He had stepped in bear traps spiked to the floors on purpose. He could still speak and said the devil was in him now and that they had to cut him up. They had to burn his heart and scatter his ashes after they cut his head off.

They did everything he asked them to, but the land was uncovered and turned for years by excavators, tractors and the curiosity of men. We think those machines must have moved the heavy rocks that covered his limbs. We think his fingers were able to crawl back to the torso and legs and head. We don't think they burned his heart to ashes because they saw him again and he killed many, many people by biting at them. Burning, cutting, stabbing, shooting – all of it was wasted until his family heard of him walking again, so they told the people how to stop him. And that's how we knew. That was how we knew to stop the Boiled Faces with the old ways.

There is a ritual to things now: a lunge shot with the Decapitator through the skull. It's a longer harpoon with a cross-axe on the hilt to ram and split the skull so zombies can't grab you. It detaches so you can begin chopping. Only good one on one. Useless against many. Scramble the brains. This blinds and confuses the body. With a quick twist, the top blade comes off to free the axe. Then you hack the right arm (the reaching one) off before the left (the grabbing one) is to be cut. Then you take the right leg and the left before cutting the heart out. As the heart is burned with a sharpened flare, the Known People turn, look away and chant in Apache, *"Deeyá, deeyá"* for "Leave, leave." We believe that what is left of the soul still rises and the spirit of the person inside will know to look away, as well, so it doesn't need to see what has happened to its body. There is respect and fear in this. Then we bury the limbs far apart and weigh them down with stones. The Known People buried everything and every-one pointing north, even though we've all seen some of them come back marked and scored. (Are they unburying each other or themselves?)

I can still speak Dogrib, me, but Apache is the common tongue for the Known People – or it was before the three of us were banished. For some reason, when the Hair Eaters come, it slows them when you sing or talk to them or chant in the first tongue. It's like they're listening. They weaken when you chant and that's when you take them.

All those old movies were true: body shots are wasted. Even with a shattered spine, they crawl. You'd think by now we'd be used to this, but they've a hot, sweet smell like dead fish that turns your stomach when they near. We then burn their limbs to ashes and scatter them. This is why the air tastes as it does. Their wild, rolling cry is used to paralyze, but it is not as strong as their mother's. I heard it a few times in the sky and felt the strength leave my legs, but our drums drown them out. If you drum you can stop their mewling cry, turn it to ice in their throats. Also, our little group has discovered that The Boiled Faces are terrified of butterflies. They run screaming – as if set to flames – when they see a butterfly and that's why we've camped here. Also, this is why we bottle them. All it takes is one butterfly and when one runs, they all do. It is hilarious. I laugh every time I see this. I wish I could have done the Butterfly Test to the Known People. I bet they would have all run away. I would have laughed so hard I would have thrown myself upon a Decapitator throat-first and not come back.

The zombies took our dogs first, systematically and determinedly. Once the dogs were gone we were blind and deaf to them. I miss the dogs. I can't even think of their names or I will weep. A wise hunter looked where they looked, always, and dogs always know more about storms than humans. And we used the old ways when we took one down with the dogs: we poked their halfway-human-and-mean-as-starving eyes out so they wouldn't see you the next time. We sliced the tips of their ears off and hung them high so they wouldn't hear you the next time, but they do. The new ones can.

I hear of things in the ravaged south (no word from the west), but they, I hope, are rumours: death cults who eat or rape the Shark Throats for power, building sod huts and using their stomach linings for windows. In the east, thousands of people wait with their eyes closed in fields to be taken at once so they can come back to roam together. And they say the new generation of the Boiled Faces can sing themselves back together. Let us pray that this is not true.

Here in the north, the Known People dressed their children in rabbit fur and seal skins. I'm not sure if I agree with the practice of sewing bones under the skin, but I saw that most youths' faces were tattooed in the way of *Kakiniit*, ghost marks in memory of the One Sun. The Known People were greedy to learn our songs for the slowing.

If you are reading this, please know that I tell you these things because I love you and wish for the world a better way. I have sent this back to tell you this, my ancestor: the Tar Sands are ecocide. They will bring Her back. In both stories, it is the Tar Sands to blame. This is how the *Wheetago* will return.

As far as we can tell, the exact pinpoint is around the time when they transport one atom from one part of the world to the other. This has something to do with all of everything during your time. You must stop the Tar Sands. At all costs. If you read this, there is still a spirit with a starving heart there. Waiting to be resurrected.

I've seen them chase down an older couple as they ran in deep, black snow. One Shark Throat – a newer, smaller one, one with a long beak and hooks for thumbs, raced ahead and circled back, floating over the land. He cut his way into their stomachs with his claws. The elders' stomachs opened like mouths and out poured their guts. The larger Hair Eaters began to eat their unravelling intestines as they stumbled away. It was a game to them. The younger one gripped and squeezed their grey, steaming leashes as the half-alive elders tried to scream, but all that came out of their mouths was slop. The younger one began to slowly braid their guts together while pulling them closer, nearer, playing with its food. The others feasted. The younger Hair Eater looked up and saw me and pointed but the others kept gorging. It opened its beak and let out a cry as it started to run towards me. The cry tangled my wings. Their sound: it rings through what is hollow inside you. It finds your marrow and squeezes it to weaken you. And I think once their song touches you, they can hear what you are thinking.

At night, when I sleepwalk, my soul leaves my body and I fly. I could always fly and that was why I had to save Thinksawhile. I spied on the leaders of the Known People. They were boiling and eating old moccasins and mukluks and they were talking of having him fall through the ice and eating him frozen. This explained our last few meals. Oh Creator, the things we've done to survive. That night, we took the boy and his computers and left, travelling downwind, upwind and through the fog. East. Always moving east. Watching the skies for ravens as ravens follow them for what's left.

Four Blankets Woman covered my eyes with ash. "So the new ones can't see you."

"Heh eh," I said. "They are getting smarter, crueller."

She rubbed my back with palms of yarrow. "We need new medicine."

"You know what was beautiful?" I said. "Those elders they tore apart, they never stopped holding hands or trying to…"

"Shhh," she said as she rested on my chest. "I know how to beat them now."

I turned. "How?"

"The new ones have beaks."

"Heh eh."

"And it has a tongue to direct sound?" I nodded.

"I will chant on this to see."

The next morning I woke to find she'd tattooed my eyelids with syllabics. She'd also sliced her left breast open and marked our Decapitators with strange symbols of whips and dots. "For your weapons and wings," she said.

I closed my eyes and looked at the fire to see this magic again. "Are these from heaven?"

"In le," she said, stirring broth. *"Gah.* The Rabbit. There are only two left and they have passed their medicine to me. They told me how to beat them and the Bitch." Thinksawhile looked up from his computer.

"This will cost us one of our lives. We have to choose carefully."

Four Blankets knew the way of the four winds. I had seen her part the clouds. She knew which root and moss to braid to make wick for cooking and heat. Her medicine was rabbit medicine. When she was thirteen, she saved the life of a doe. In turn, she was given *Gah* medicine. Four Blankets Woman had tattooed our tongues, so the Hair Eaters could not hear us speak. Not even in this dream.

She ran soot down her nose. "Whoever we choose will suffer, but it is the only way." The boy was young, weak. I had a blown right knee and couldn't stop talking in my sleep.

"We choose tonight," she said and left to slice her arm to ribbons. This was the cost of a Dream Thrower.

Thinksawhile went back to his computer. "I have an idea," he said. "A way to stop this. A way to undo all that's been done."

I began to braid my hair. "Tell me," I said. And he did.

Before we fled, the sick cooked for us. The sick chanted for us. Scouts left. Our son vanished. Women gave birth to things that were killed immediately (except redheads), and there was a low growl from the cancered earth that trembled us. All Known Elders turned blind. What the last hunter brought was a hand that could be bear with an eye sewn backwards into the palm. Could be human, could be them. Knuckle sockets sucked dry. I touched one and singed my finger. It burns at night when I dream.

Now the air is loaded with ash that coats us and the wings of the butterfly, and my dreams. My dreams.

The Hair Eaters have eaten all the caribou, moose, bear, fox, wolf, bison, buffalo and everything under the earth here. We are too scared to check nets as they feast on our catch underwater and wait for boats. All we have left are creatures of the air: ducks and ptarmigan, geese, swans. We eat roots pretending they are what we used to love.

This message comes from the future. From our Dream Thrower. Remember: there is a hard way and an easy way: stop the Tar Sands and that old man's body from waking up. He – not she – is the beginning of the end. May your children – our ancestors – not know a time of being born hunted as we are all hunted now.

As for us, our season's done, and I miss smiling at my memories. It's getting colder now. Soon the fist of the sun will surrender to frost. We see it on the lower mountains across the way. Soon the butterflies will leave (where do they sleep at night?) and they will find us. They say some humans are farming other humans and making deals with the Hair Eaters. At night, when I lower myself to the cooling earth, as I breathe through my palms to cool my roaring head, my finger burns. I think this is how they are tracking us.

I heard a story once. It warmed even the hearts of the Known People. It was a story outside of Fort Providence. The buffalo ran with two giant horses, two Clydesdales: one white, one brown. When you approached the herd you could clap your hands and the buffalo would look one way, the horses the other. Wolves and the zombies could not come near for trampling and goring. I sometimes think about how the horses and buffalo adopted each other. What was their ritual for each other? I told that story the second night after moving with the Known People, and they marvelled until hunters from that region reported that two giant horse skulls burned among the mountains of bones. They also spoke of lakes now, filled with humans swimming in their own blood. Hundreds of women, men, children, elders, harpooned and buoyed by jerry cans to keep them floating. "It's the adrenaline," a sharpshooter who got away said. "It sweetens our blood. They keep us terrified and once we die, they tear into us. They just keep adding more and more people to these lakes. There were lines of peoples for miles, as far as we could see."

I saw a grey whale once, rolling in shallow water. Hundreds of Hair Eaters poured over the body biting, ripping at the barnacles and sea lice. Others clawed into and reached into the eyes and blowholes. One dove into its mouth. Then others. Then more and more. It thrashed and couldn't get away. The Shark Throats ate their way from the inside until I could see its skeleton. I watched a mile away and heard it scream. Their cries are supposed to be subsonic but I heard it. I still hear it.

I've seen a pack of Hair Eaters down a pack of bison in slush. The lead bull flipped in the air as the opposing Hair Eaters forked to cut him off. As he flipped in the air, two were upon him ripping and tearing at his belly and balls. He was hollowed out completely by the time he landed, still kicking.

We wish you luck. The future is a curse. There are no human trails left. I was born running from them as they are born starving and hunting for us. Now, we carry on in fever. We carry on for you and what you do next.

Four Blankets Woman has thrown two dreams now: one for you and the other to prove it. In your time, Taiwan will shut down their biggest highway for seven suns to allow for the safe passage of one million butterflies. If this is so, you will know this warning to be true.

I pray you remember this when you wake up.

You must remember this.

You must stop the Tar Sands. Do not bring cancer to our Mother. Do not unleash them.

On the wings of this atomized prayer, we reach to you with all we have left.

Now, they have expanded their range to the fullest here and are now crossing the ice of time to reach you – you who live in the time before the sun twins, when fish only had one mouth, when moose knew who they were.

You *can* change the future.

Now wake up.

GROUND ZERO: SAINTE-ANNE-DE-BELLEVUE

Claude Lalumière

From her office window, Agent Parinita Gupta can see both the Jacques Cartier Bridge to the east and the Victoria Bridge to the southwest. Even without her binoculars, it's obvious the situation is chaotic. The pictures and videos from the West Island went viral even before the federal government gave the okay to evacuate the Island of Montreal and blow up all the remaining bridges and tunnels. Every access off the island west of the Decarie Expressway had already been bombed by the military the previous day. There's no way everyone will be able to drive off the island before the deadline. Not a chance in Hell. Even with all the metro, suburban, and Via trains commandeered and diverted to evacuate the maximum amount of people to the east, south, and north, there'll still be hundreds of thousands stuck on the island; evacuation will have to continue by boat and aircraft. Thankfully it's not her job to figure out the logistics of that. Her task is to help implement the directives once the big brains figure it all out. Which is why she was left behind in the Montreal office of CSIS with a skeleton crew of four other agents.

There's a knock at her door. She looks at her watch before peeking at who's there. Less than twenty minutes left before they cut off all road access to and from the island.

"Nita – there's a guy here. A student. Says he has info about the cows." *Cows*, she thinks. Her aunt Padma would be both horrified and smug, railing that it was Kamadhenu the cow goddess wreaking vengeance against the Western world for the industrial farming of cows.

"Gilles – I don't have time to deal with crackpots." She turns back to stare at the bridges, counting down time in her head.

"Yeah, but I checked him out. His dad is CSIS: Dr. Jack Chen. A molecular biologist at HQ in Ottawa. Anti-terrorism forensics."

"Molecular biologist? Fuck. Really?"

Gilles nods.

"Okay. Get him into Room 2 and start recording. Don't question him – wait for me. Stay when I get there, but let me lead. Tell Jocelyne and Stéphane to watch from the other side. Put Derek on lookout, in case the cows come near the building."

"Will do, Nita."

Cows, she thinks again.

◀ ▶

The kid can't be more than in his early twenties. He's tall – over six feet; he doesn't even have a hint of stubble on his baby face; hair so dark it's black, but with a streak of red on the left and a streak of platinum blond on the right. His eyes keep straying to the floor, and he tends to mumble.

Agent Gupta says, "Kid, look at me when I speak to you and when you answer." Then, she repeats: "First – what's your name?"

He focuses straight into her eyes; there's terror written all over his features. He's about to open his mouth, but he pauses at the sound of distant explosions. The bridges.

Nita checks her watch: only five minutes behind schedule. "Kid, we don't have time to waste. Who, what, how, and where. Go."

The kid doesn't have the demeanour of someone who's lying or looking for attention. That makes him earn hers. She gives a subtle nod to Gilles.

The kid collects himself. "My name is Tony. Tony Chen. You know who my father is." He pauses. "Okay. I won't waste time. The cows – it's all my fault. Well, not all of it, but I…I instigated it. But then it got out of control. Completely out of control. I mean, how could I know that there was a secret cult worshipping Hathor and Kamadhenu in the department? Thea never told me."

"Back up, Tony. Explain things. Hathor? Cult? Department? Thea?" But Kamadhenu? Agent Gupta had never heard anyone except Aunt Padma mention the divine mother of all cows. But none of her stories had featured cows like these…

"I'm a second-year Environment student at McGill. Thea was my girlfriend. Well, not really my girlfriend. I'd been trying to get her to—"

"Kid. Tony. Focus. Back to what all this has to do with the cows. Worry about your love life on your own time."

"Okay, okay. So the last time I was home in Ottawa, I snooped around my father's laptop. He thinks it's secure, but I cracked the password and encryptions, no problem."

Tony's self-satisfied grin does not endear him to Parinita.

He continues, "It was mostly boring administrative stuff...until I found a folder called 'China Cattle Projects' – that was gold. But now I wish I hadn't read it."

"What you did with the contents of that folder – that's what caused the...the situation with the cows?"

"Sort of. You see, at the beginning of the school year, the department—"

Nita interrupts him with a gesture. "You mean, Environment at McGill?"

"Yeah, exactly. So, every year, the department organizes this field trip to Sainte-Anne-de-Bellevue, where the university has its agricultural research centre, which includes a dairy farm. That's when I met Thea. She was – I mean, we were appalled at what we found. They give a tour of the dairy farm, like they're proud of how they torture the cows and their calves. All year, we made up plans about what we could do to sabotage the dairy farm and free the cows but never came up with anything practical that was ever really good for the animals. But doing nothing...how was that acceptable? But then, during summer break, I read the files on my dad's computer. And there was our solution. So when I came back we—"

Parinita's phone won't stop buzzing. "Hold that thought, Tony. I'll be right back."

On the phone, it's Burgess from head office. He wants a status report. While he's talking, she looks out the window: the cows have made it downtown. They're eating everything in sight: trees, lampposts, concrete, bricks, windows...everything.

"Agent Gupta...are you listening?"

"Sorry, sir. It's just…the cows are here."

"Inside the office?"

"No, on the street. Downtown."

"Well, they're on schedule."

"They move faster than I thought. Not like cows at all."

Agent Gupta is mesmerized; she'd seen the video – the one that was leaked everywhere, so that the evacuation order would be taken seriously, the one in which the cows tore into armed troops, devouring the soldiers and all their weapons, too – but seeing the cows in the flesh, even from five storeys above ground and a half-dozen blocks away, is…surreal. Too bizarre to accept as true, despite the evidence of her senses. There are holes in their hides, showing bone. How can something that looks so fragile, so barely alive, be so damned impossible to hurt or kill?

The herd laid waste to Sainte-Anne-de-Bellevue yesterday morning – they'd killed the entire population and razed the whole borough: all the buildings, all the vegetation – everything. The army had been sent in, pronto. But no matter what the armed forces threw at the animals – gunfire, artillery, grenades, air strikes – the cows shrugged off, continuing their single-minded destruction of Montreal's West Island.

Derek appears, with a panicked look. He mouths silently, *The cows.*

"Agent Gupta, are you still there?"

The cows are getting too close. "Sir. I'll call you back." She pockets her phone and tells Derek, "Time to move to the secure basement. We'll be safer there. Take the stairs." Derek gathers Stéphane and Jocelyne, while Nita goes into Room 2, to gather Gilles and the kid.

Part of her thinks the kid is a waste of time, but there's something about his manner...he could really know something important. Something that could help her save what's left of Montreal.

At least, Montreal is an island – and the cows have shown no inclination to cross the water. They don't look like they can swim. Then again, they don't look like they can chew through steel and concrete and annihilate a metropolis. Hell, they barely even look alive.

◄ ►

Burgess is furious with Agent Gupta for not following orders, going so far as to threaten she'll face charges of treason. Maybe she's being stupid, but she has to stay and hear the kid's story. Nita hangs up on Burgess a second time, mid-threat. She tells Gilles to take over until further notice. Her last order: she dispatches Derek and Gilles to the airport and Stéphane and Jocelyne to the port, to help coordinate the rest of the remaining air and sea portions of the evacuation.

There's a small kitchen with a fridge attached to the underground CSIS office. Agent Gupta grabs two beers, invites Tony to sit at the table with her, and then says, "Okay. Take a few sips. Then tell me your whole story. But focus. Stick to the cows, and try not to segue every which way before you finish an idea."

Tony nods. They drink in silence for a couple of minutes.

Then Tony asks, "What did you understand from what I've told you already?"

"My best guess is: you and your quasi-girlfriend Thea used top secret CSIS intelligence to unleash a Chinese biological weapon, thinking it would somehow save some cows and further some kind of animal rights agenda. You're lucky I haven't arrested you yet. I don't understand why you brought up the Hindu goddess Kamadhenu or...what was the other name...Haptor?"

"Hathor. The Egyptian cow goddess."

"So your girlfriend is a cross-denominational cow worshipper?" Nita's aunt would love this girl. Maybe she knows these kids. She teaches anthropology at McGill. Or did. The cows have probably eaten the whole campus by now.

"She wasn't my girlfriend. Not really."

"Sorry I brought it up." Nita takes another sip of beer. "Alright. Go on. Explain all this craziness."

"So my minor is chemistry. Plus, I've been around my dad all my life. Chemistry comes easy to me. The Chinese had all kinds of weird, abandoned projects in that folder. One caught my attention, though. When I opened the files on his computer, I got it immediately, what the Chinese had developed."

Nita gestures for him to move on.

"Okay. So this would only work on ruminants, because of their distinctive digestive chemistry. If you added a compound to their feed, it would, in time, toughen their hide so that they'd basically be indestructible; as a side effect, it also made their milk indigestible to humans. It would only take one dose to kick-start the chemical process. Imagine if all the cows could be infected..."

She may think he holds important information, but it's hard for Agent Gupta to sympathize with this young man. The prime minister is right: these environmentalists and animal rights activists are enemies of the state. Terrorists. If she could prove they were responsible for these cows and for the destruction of one of Canada's most beloved cities, the weak-kneed progressive opposition would be neutered in Parliament. CSIS and the RCMP would be empowered to clamp down on these nutjobs once and for all.

Agent Gupta has read about this Chinese project. "You realize that wasn't the goal of the Chinese. They were using cows as test animals. They're trying to make supersoldiers. They don't care about cows. They just want to take over the world." She probably shouldn't be telling him that; none of this information has been released to the public. She appreciates that this government knows how to keep secrets. The Liberals used to blab everything to the public. None of that anymore. Transparency is just another word for weakness. A safe public is an ignorant public. Not that you can tell that to civilians' faces, but it's true nonetheless. But who knows how many secrets this kid has stolen from his careless father?

"I'm not stupid. I guessed that's what the Chinese were up to. But I still thought we could use it to sabotage the meat and dairy industry – without hurting cows or people."

"Okay, okay, Mister Animal Ethics. Back to what actually happened."

"Anyway, the compound was easy to manufacture. All I needed was—"

"The recipe's in our files already. You stole it from us. Skip forward."

Tony resumes his narrative: "So this older Indian lady drove a bunch of us to the farm. We were, like, seven or eight in the back of her van. I didn't know anyone, except Thea. That's when I learned about the cow cult. These people were all part of it. I started to ask questions, but Thea shushed me and said she'd explain later, after. Except there wasn't any *after*. Things went way beyond anything I was expecting as soon as we reached the gates of the farm."

"Enough with the dramatic pauses. What happened?"

"All the others had guns, is what. They shot the two guards. I tried to protest, but then one of the girls trained her gun on me."

"Were they all women?"

"No. But most of them were. I think there were two other guys."

"Go on."

"And then I recognized the old lady. I'm in the science half of the Environment program. But there's a humanities stream, too. We make fun of those students. They're just hippies. Or lazy. Or both. Anyway, this woman taught the Anthropology & Environment class. We all have to take it, even in the sciences, but I still haven't. I had seen her around before, though."

"Wait a minute... When you said *Indian* earlier did you mean First Nations or...?"

"No, I meant *Indian* – like you."

Holy fuck. It could only be her. "Her name?"

"Padma Ven – Ventash, I think?"

"Venktesh. Padma Venktesh."

"Yeah, that's it. You know her?"

It was her. Her aunt. Aunt Padma has unleashed crazy, unkillable demon cows on Montreal. Of course she would. Deranged leftist old bitch. "Yeah, I do. Just go on. I need to hear this. Just skip to the cows. What did the lot of you do to the cows?"

"Once we got to the cows, we fed them the compound. And then this Padma woman ordered the other students to slaughter all the animals quickly, before the formula could take effect. They killed all the cows. They used knives and guns…There was so much blood. Have you ever heard a cow scream? How about dozens of them at the same time? I threw up. It was disgusting. Horrifying."

"Wait a minute. I thought you lot were trying to save the cows. And if you killed them all – what the fuck are they doing eating the whole Island of Montreal?"

"I didn't kill any cows. This crazy woman and her cult did. They tricked me. Anyway, the cows all came back to life."

"So the Chinese formula is really a resurrection formula?"

"No, no…not the compound. Well, I think maybe it played a part. But, really, it was the goddesses who resurrected the cows."

"Goddesses?"

"Yeah. The slaughter of the herd was a ritual. To invoke the two cow goddesses, Hathor of Egypt and Kamadhenu of India. And it worked. The goddesses appeared. They were, like, ugly as all sin and twice as tall as anyone I'd ever seen. And stinky. Even above the stench of the farm and the slaughter, these cow goddesses reeked something fierce. This Padma woman knelt before them and spoke in a language I couldn't understand. In answer, the goddesses walked among the cows. One by one, each cow was kissed simultaneously by the two goddesses – and then came back from the dead. Only, maybe not really alive, either. They still had gaping wounds. And there was blankness to their stare, like the eyes were dead."

"Are you sure about all this, Tony? Were you on any drugs? Tell the truth. I'm not going to bust you for drugs. I'm CSIS. We don't care about that stuff."

"No, ma'am. I was clean sober. Anyway, I was so terrified, even if I'd been on anything, the adrenaline would have scared me into sobriety. There's no doubt about what I saw. I've thought about this. There was no opportunity for anyone to slip me anything either. This is what I saw. This is what happened. But there's more.

"The goddesses said…I'm not sure how I understood them; they seemed to be speaking dozens of languages at the same time. I understood what they said in English, in French, and in Cantonese, but I don't remember hearing any words per se. Anyway, they said the cows needed to feed, that it could not wait. And the cultists, they…Thea, and this teacher, all of them…they gave themselves to the cows."

"Gave themselves? You mean, as…as food?"

"Yes, food. The cows moved like tigers. They were fast, and vicious."

Damn it. Aunt Padma couldn't do the right thing and stick around to take the blame. "How did you escape?"

"By then, no one was holding me. There was nobody left to threaten me. I ran for the van. The teacher had left the keys inside, thank God. And I drove out of there. I was stupid, though. I was right next to a bridge. I should've driven off the island. To Ottawa. But I was freaking out. I drove towards the city instead, to my apartment in Park Ex. I don't even remember the drive itself. When I woke up, I thought I'd dreamed the whole thing. Then on the internet I saw that video of the cows eating those soldiers…"

Agent Gupta sighs. "Kid, this may surprise you, but I believe every crazy word you've just told me. Of course, the fact that there are, defying all logic and sanity, mutant demon zombie cows devouring Montreal kind of helps your credibility."

◀ ▶

Burgess doesn't believe her. "Sir, I know this sounds insane, but everything about this is insane. Say it out loud: *indestructible cows are eating the City of Montreal down to the rubble.* If you patch me through to Dr. Chen, we might have a chance to beat this thing. Or at least tell him it's related to the Chinese supersoldier project. Even if you don't believe me, we have to try something."

"Agent Gupta…"

"Yes, sir."

His sigh is loud in her ear. "I'm sending a helicopter to get you and this young man out of there. We'll discuss this at HQ, not over a wireless connection."

"Yes, sir. Thank you, sir."

"Don't thank me yet. You're still in a lot of trouble."

"Yes, sir."

◀ ▶

The cows haven't gotten to this building yet, but they will soon. Agent Gupta and Tony are standing on the roof, waiting for their ride off the island.

All around them, skyscrapers and hotels are crumbling to the ground, as the cows devour the ground floor of each building. Montreal is unrecognizable. There are none of the city's usual sounds. None of this feels real. Her mind feels sluggish, too, like in a dream. Parinita is fed up with thinking about these cows. She doesn't want any of this to be real. Looking to the east, she stares at Montreal's most iconic building: the Olympic Stadium, an eyesore every Montrealer loathes. *At least we'll finally be rid of it.* She snickers. Tony looks at her quizzically, but she gestures off his unspoken question, suddenly irritated with herself.

Then she hears the unmistakable beat of rotors: their ride is almost here.

Agent Gupta says, "Okay, kid, ready to try to save the world?"

Tony gapes at her with a look of dumb terror.

The floor beneath their feet starts to shake. *Shit.* The cows.

The helicopter is here, but she gestures for it not to land. As it hovers a few feet above the roof, Agent Gupta grabs Tony's arm; they run and climb aboard the vehicle.

The driver flies off even before the pair have strapped themselves in. After Agent Gupta has secured both herself and the kid, she looks back to see the whole block of buildings collapse on itself.

"Kid, I'll make you save the world, whether or not you think you're up to it."

Tony gulps as Agent Gupta holds his stare. She hadn't meant what she told him as encouragement. It was a threat, and she poured every ounce of her anger into every word.

THE FOOD TRUCK OF THE ZOMBIE APOCALYPSE

Beth Wodzinski

I was driving the poutine truck to the Whispering Pines sur-vivor compound when I spotted the hitchhiker.

It's never exactly been safe for an old woman driving alone in the middle of Saskatchewan to stop and pick up hitchhik-ers. But these days? When there's no way to tell if someone's got the Z and their brain just hasn't rotted enough yet to show? Yeah. It's not safe. It's not safe at all.

But come on, he was just a kid, not even old enough to drink, all gangly and stupid-looking like they are at that age. I was still a few hours drive from Whispering Pines; it would take him days to walk there, soft snow up to his ankles and no sign of a sleeping bag. How the hell did he think he was going to survive?

I figured, even if he was infected, well. I may look like your granny, trick elbow and all, but I didn't survive the Z this long without picking up a few tricks.

That sounds brave, and maybe I was even feeling feisty that day. But the *truest* truth was that I'd been missing my husband Carl something fierce. When I saw that helpless kid, all I could think was how bad he needed help – and how much I wished someone had helped Carl when he needed it.

So I slowed, tapped the brake, and came to a halt a dozen feet ahead of him. The road stretched on ahead, covered with pristine snow, unbroken by tracks of either humans or vehicles. Totally silent and perfect and the cold made my elbow ache and I missed Carl.

Oh, God, the hope on this kid's face. He broke into a run, stumbled on a rock or something buried under the snow, and jogged up to the truck waving his arms and yelling.

"Thank you! Thank you! I thought I might be the last person alive!"

I resisted rolling my eyes. But it was hard.

He was an American, I could hear by his voice. Apparently there's a rumour going around that zombies freeze in the winter, so the Americans head up here, thinking they'll be safe. But they don't know a damn thing about surviving outside their comfortable cities. They don't bring enough warm clothes or food and end up freezing to death or starving. Weak and helpless, the lot of them.

Most of them don't even bring guns. I have no idea how they get this far; are American zombies just lazy?

I rolled down the window, and aimed the rifle out it. Now that I was close enough, I saw something that looked suspiciously like blood on his jacket. Maybe this was a bad idea, after all. "Hold it right there."

He froze, and his hopeful puppy-dog face turned wounded. Seriously? His feelings were hurt? He thought I'd just get out of my nice warm armoured truck and give him a big hug?

"I'm clean," he said, raising his hands like we were in some crappy movie. "I swear."

"How'd you get that blood on your jacket?" I asked. I let him leave his hands up. Worst case, it was his own blood that spurted on him when one of the shamblers took a big bite out of him. That would mean it's just a matter of time before the infection wins and he starts shambling hungrily, too. Best case, it was shambler blood that got on him when he killed a bunch of them with an expertly wielded machete or chain saw.

But I didn't see any sign of a machete.

"I'm clean," he said, again, but he didn't answer my question. Oh, hell, kid.

I shot a few feet above his head. He shrieked and jumped away, and flailed his arms up over his head as if that would save him from a bullet.

"How did you get that blood on your jacket?" I asked again, my voice steady.

"Holy crap! Don't shoot! Don't shoot! I'm clean! It's not my blood. I didn't get bit. It's Andrea's, God, it's not mine! It's not mine! Help me, please, don't let me die out here." He was about to start crying.

"Take it off." He hesitated, but I chambered another cartridge, and he hurried to unzip the jacket. He tossed it on the ground beside him, and looked up at me imploringly. "Now the shirt." It was cold and he was shy but I didn't care. I pointed the gun at him until he was stripped all the way down and I could see for myself that he hadn't been bitten. Anywhere.

Finally I was satisfied that every inch of his cold white skin was clean. "Get in."

◀ ▶

I shoved the rifle under my seat; plenty of time to get it out if we ran into some shamblers before we hit Whispering Pines. The truck was safe and warm.

This truck, it was our dream, me and Carl. We'd saved up all our money when we were working, and then when we retired, we bought the truck, equipped it with a deep fryer for the fries, and a big pot for the gravy, and travelled around selling poutine. We had a few good years but now it's just me.

Most people want to hunker down in their compounds where it's safe – relatively safe, that is – but not me. Carl always said I was too damn stubborn for my own good, but I just couldn't see my way clear to hiding out. It felt too much like giving up. So every spring, as soon as the roads were passable, I'd gas up the truck and head out, selling poutine to survivors. Of course, these days I sold more guns and ammo than poutine, but I still kept the fryer oil hot and the gravy bubbling.

It reminds me how things used to be. It reminds me how things might be again some day, if we have the hope and guts enough to make it happen.

"Thank you, thank you," the kid said. "I don't know what I would have done if you hadn't stopped."

"Died, probably," I said, and started up the truck. He'd be safe enough in Whispering Pines for the winter. They'd grumble about taking him in, another mouth to feed, but I was bringing enough food and ammo to buy us both a safe winter. Maybe the kid would even find a way to make himself useful and be able to stay in Whispering Pines come spring. At the very least, he'd probably be handy when it came time to start repopulating the earth. Lucky kid.

"Who was Andrea?"

He swallowed, hard. "My friend," he said, but the way he said it told me she was more than a friend to him. "We came up from Boise together."

He told me his story, one I'd heard a hundred times before. A thousand times. It's the only story anyone has any more: you hear a rumour about some settlement where there might be enough survivors and supplies for you to really be safe, to start thinking about what would happen next. So you start walking. You walk and suffer and starve and freeze and one day you get caught off guard and people die. The lucky ones die fast.

He'd been travelling with five other people, and they'd gotten trapped in a grocery store in Moose Jaw. They'd killed off the shamblers by dumping propane on them and lighting a match, but not before his girl Andrea got bit.

So he'd hugged her and kissed her and locked her in the walk-in freezer. He blushed when he said he kissed her, and I wondered just how enthusiastic that kiss was.

He should have killed her. Freezing zombies doesn't do much, no matter what the Americans believe; it barely even slows them down. It's not like you can just thaw them out later, some magical day when there's a cure. All he did was leave a nasty surprise for whoever opened that freezer next.

"What's your story?" he asked.

But there's only one story. You get caught off guard and people die.

Me and Carl, our version of the story came early, back when we could still pretend everything would be fine, that all the strangeness we'd been hearing about was some American craziness that would never touch us. We had the food truck at a high school hockey game. Carl was crazy about hockey, took the truck to every game he could drive to.

I never quite understood why he wouldn't rather watch the game than be stuck outside selling poutine, but he just said I didn't understand. He loved the whole *world* of hockey, not just the games – and being part of it was magical for him. His old hockey stick from college was hung up in the place of pride, right over the fryer.

It was the third period. Carl left me in charge of the truck. He said he was going to the bathroom, but I knew he was going to watch the game. No problem; he'd come back when the quarter ended and I could handle it until then. Nothing hard about popping fries in hot oil.

The crowd roared. Not an uncommon occurrence at a hockey game, but there was something different about this sound. The sound was more jangly and afraid; there were shrieks.

And there were moans.

I'd never heard anything like it, and I shuddered. Where was Carl? For a moment I wondered if I should lock up the truck and go find him, but some intuition told me to stay where I was.

A guy came stumbling out of the arena, stunned and horrified. "What's going on?" I yelled to him, but he didn't answer. He just ran into the parking lot and disappeared.

Coward.

He was followed by more people, a growing mass of urgent terror-stricken people.

It was an outbreak. A dozen or so infected people converted all at once. Time from initial exposure to full-blown Z can take up to ten days, but there were lots of reports of people converting all at once, even if they'd been infected at different times. It's like a big pep rally. One of the zombies makes it all the way, and then sends out encouraging pheromones or whatever to egg the others on into full conversion.

I saw Carl in the middle of the pack, shoving his way towards me. "Zombies!" he yelled, and then something else. I couldn't hear over the roar of the crowd, but I swear he said to close the truck. He had a cut on his forehead, and blood all over his face. Then undead hands reached for him, and he disappeared into the crowd.

I know he said "Close the truck."

I slammed the service window shut and locked the truck. I turned off the fryer and locked down the gravy vat. I hid, while all around me people shrieked and died and came back to life and turned on each other. The truck rocked as they hurled themselves against it, but it held strong.

The truck was safe.

A lifetime later, silence reigned. The undead had moved on, seeking weaker prey. Slowly, carefully, I unlocked the truck and got out. I looked until dark, but found no trace of Carl among the truly dead.

Sometimes, when I dream about that moment, Carl's already a zombie, and when he pounds his fists against the truck and moans, he's trying to devour me.

In other dreams, all Carl wants is for me to save him.

I did not open the truck.

The truck was safe.

◀ ▶

"So," I said, after I told my story, "are you hungry?" We'd been driving for half an hour, and had settled into a warm companionship. The truck was full of the rich scent of my homemade gravy, and I was ready for dinner. "I'll pull over and get us some poutine."

"What's poutine?"

"French fries, with hot rich gravy, and cheese curds. Good stuff. You'll like it."

He made a face. "Gravy? On fries? Sounds gross."

"No, it's great," I said. He'd locked his girlfriend in a freezer, but thought *poutine* sounded gross?

But wait. He hadn't said *gross*. His voice had slurred a little: *grosh*. No, no. It was impossible. He hadn't been bitten. I'd seen that myself. Then I remembered the kid's little stumble as he ran up to the truck. I should have noticed it.

Then he sneezed. Oh, hell. Everyone knew the signs of Z infection: first the sneezing and a low-grade fever, as if it were just a mild flu. As the disease progresses, you start getting neurological symptoms: slurring speech, difficulty walking. Then your fever spikes and you die. For a moment. Once the first neurological symptoms start, you don't have long.

"Tissues in the glove box," I said, keeping my voice calm. Damn it! I was screwed. Frantically I did the math: how long did I have before the kid fully converted and I had a hungry zombie on my hands? I looked at the kid, and his face was flushed and his eyes bright with fever.

I'd cleverly put the gun under the seat. Because the truck was *safe*.

Damn it.

So much for old age and treachery.

◀ ▶

I slowed the truck and let it cruise to a halt on the side of the road. It's not like we were going to see any other traffic on this road tonight, but old habits die hard.

"Yeah," I said. "Poutine. Let me make you some. You must be starving. I'm kind of hungry, too. And we have a long drive ahead of us." All I could think of was to get some space between us; I was within biting distance of the kid.

All that kissing before he locked his girlfriend in the freezer. The disease is spread through saliva, after all, from bites from the infected. He probably had a cut inside his mouth. It wouldn't take much, just the tiniest break in the skin.

Poor stupid kid. Just trying to get one last kiss before his girlfriend died, and now he's turning into a zombie.

Poor stupid me.

The kid moaned. I was out of time.

I unbuckled my seat belt, said a quick prayer, and stood up. I slid past him into the kitchen. He snarled and grabbed at me, but I wrenched myself away. He was still trapped by his seat belt, and it took him a few seconds to figure it out, press the button, and come lurching after me.

A few seconds was all I needed.

He shambled towards me, reaching out his arms. I'd grabbed Carl's hockey stick from above the fryer, and hit him with it. My trick elbow complained. The kid stepped back a little, then came at me again.

The galley was narrow, with the service window on my left and the fryer and gravy pot on the right. There wasn't much room to manoeuvre, and flight was impossible.

This time I kicked him in the nuts, as hard as I could. I don't think it hurt him; do the dead feel pain? But the force was enough to make him stumble, and he fell against the fryer.

Then I smashed the hockey stick against the back of his head, hard. I forced his face down into the fryer. I keep the oil at 175°C, the perfect temperature for the perfect fries. It's also the perfect temperature to melt the skin off a zombie's head.

The kid – no, the zombie – was stronger than I was, and pushed himself up from the fryer. He moaned and put his hands to his blistering face. His eyes had popped and melted and he couldn't see me.

But he could *smell* me. He took another lurching step towards me.

I grabbed the cleaver I use to chop up bones to make the stock for the gravy. I swung the cleaver with my good arm, and it bit into the kid's neck with a thick and meaty sound.

Everyone thinks it's so damn easy to cut off a zombie's head, but it isn't. It takes strength and persistence and a good sharp blade. The kid was thirty years younger than me and twice as strong – but his eyes and his brain were gone, and I was determined to survive. Finally it was done, and his severed head rolled on the floor, and his body slumped after it.

I stood there in my kitchen, breathing hard, adrenaline coursing through my body. I nudged the body with my foot, but he didn't move. Of course he didn't move.

I stepped over him and went back to the driver's seat, and sat there until my shaking stopped. Then I got out and stripped and looked myself over the best I could. I was pretty sure that little bastard hadn't bitten me, but I wanted to be sure. I'd have someone at Whispering Pines give me another look when I got there.

Then I cleaned out the back of the truck. I used extra bleach and made sure I got every last trace of that kid out of the truck.

When I was certain everything was clean again, I started a fresh vat of oil heating. Fortunately, I'd had the lid on the gravy pot, so I wouldn't be serving up zombie gravy.

I'd chosen safety once before, and Carl had died. Now I knew that even the safety of the truck was an illusion. But I sure as hell wasn't going to let that stop me. Whispering Pines needed poutine and ammo and *hope*; and I would be the one to deliver it to them.

DEAD DRIFT

Chantal Boudreau

Darren sat on his front stoop, sulking and kicking at the dirt. He was freckled-faced and tanned from the summer sun, reddish-blond highlights showing in his brown hair, the result of rarely wearing a hat like he was supposed to. He heaved a heavy sigh and glanced over at his dark-haired friend, Byron, who stood a few feet away, rolling a pebble with his foot. They had had plans for the day, great plans, and now those plans were ruined. What was worse was that the evening's activities, a yard party and clam bake, had had to be postponed as well – and all because of a red tide.

Lower Wedgeport was like many other small fishing villages in Nova Scotia. Unless you had a car and could make your way into the closest town, there wasn't a heck of a lot to do to keep yourself entertained. The village didn't even have a golf course, unlike Pubnico, and the playground down the road from where Darren lived was rotting from weather-wear and had not been all that exciting even when it had been brand new. For fun, you could fish or swim off of the pier, but not during low tide. You could ride your bicycle to the corner store, but Darren didn't have any money and wouldn't get his allowance for three more days and his mother never allowed them to collect on it early. Or you could go digging for clams, but never during a red tide. His father had just informed them that they had announced a red tide on the radio, a proclamation of doom and gloom for Darren and Byron.

With the current tide schedule, fishing and swimming were out of the question and Darren preferred to dig clams anyway. He loved coming home after shovelling through the muck while standing in an ever growing briny puddle, his feet sinking part way into the greyish-brown sludge. He would be plastered from head to toe in the sea-stink riddled ooze, despite wearing his hip-waders. There was nothing like the crusty feeling as it dried onto his skin and hair, crackling in the creases of his joints and flaking off in the spots that brushed together, accompanied by the satisfaction of a pail so full that the topmost clams were prone to sliding off.

Of course, you didn't have a successful day of digging without the yard party that followed. Darren loved the bustle of those parties, Acadian and country music blasting from the radio, beer bottles clanking, people laughing and talking loudly to be heard above the music, and the smell of fresh clams steaming away over the fire pit, just waiting for the opportunity to be dipped in melted butter and slide delightfully down some hungry person's throat. The thought made Darren salivate.

All that had been destroyed by the only thing that could keep them from going on a dig in the middle of summer, during low tide on a sunny day. His disappointment rested as heavily on his heart as his boredom did. His father had pointed out that it wasn't the end of the world; they just had to wait for a better day when the red tide wasn't a health hazard. Then they could dig to their heart's content. It didn't feel that way to Darren. Like most twelve-year-old boys, he lived in the now, and what he wanted to do right now was go digging for clams.

He had tried defying his parents once, and had ventured out with bucket and shovel regardless of the red tide advisory. His mother caught him secretly trying to light a fire in the pit, when she had noticed the clam pot missing and had gone looking for it and Darren. She had sat him down to explain why the red tide made eating clams dangerous.

"Clams are the ocean's water filter. It's how they feed – they draw water in and spurt it out again, keeping anything worth eating for them," she had told him. "If there's anything bad in the water, it sticks with them, and if we eat them, it ends up in us. That's why you can't eat these, Darren. When the red tide hits, it turns them to poison. They may still taste okay, but they could kill you."

"But what's so bad about it. Why would it make us really sick, but not kill the clams?" he had asked.

"I guess they're used to it and they aren't built the same way we are. The poison comes from algae in the water, and they're exposed to a little bit of it all the time. It builds up in their system when there's a lot of it in the water. That's the most I can tell you. I'm not a scientist, but that's what I've read and I know people who have died from eating contaminated clams," she had said.

Darren made a face, remembering her explanation and wishing there was some way around it. He didn't want to die any more than the next person though, so he wouldn't disobey his parents like he had tried to in the past. He'd just have to come up with some other way of entertaining himself and Byron, and forget about the yard party for now.

He got to his feet and shuffled over to Byron, his hands in his pockets.

"Well, there ain't nothing we can do about it. How about you and me go over to the duck pond and see if we can catch a couple of frogs. It's better than sitting around here all day."

Byron shrugged and nodded. Frog hunting had lost its mystique the prior summer, when they had decided it was too babyish an activity for someone their age. Nevertheless, it was a way to pass the time and better than wallowing in ennui. If nothing else, it would take up the few hours they would otherwise have to wait until supper.

"I'll race you there," Darren said, and the two boys ran off towards the pond, laughing and shoving at one another.

◄ ►

It had been two weeks since the end of the red tide advisory, and finally Darren's parents had agreed to reschedule the yard party and clam bake. Darren was so excited his toes were curling in his hip-waders. It didn't matter that he and Byron had been up incredibly late the night before, watching an old zombie movie at Byron's house once everyone else was asleep; tired or not, they were more than willing to dig. Sacrificing sleep had been worth it as well. The zombie movie had been a particularly gory and scary one, a film to which any well-meaning parents would have objected. That was what had made watching it all the more thrilling – knowing that their parents would have considered it taboo.

Darren still had zombies on the brain when they set out with their buckets and shovels for the beach. The flats were dotted with tidal pools and the mud squelched beneath their boots as they searched for the holes in the sand that were the telltale sign of clams hidden below. Darren noted that the tidal pools looked particularly cloudy that day, the silt within greyer than normal, but that wasn't that uncommon a couple days after a storm, and there had been a doozy earlier that week. He also detected a slight oily sheen on their surface. Perhaps a motorboat had overturned or had sunk during the gale-force winds and rough waters, emptying the contents of its gas tank into the ocean. He had seen such things happen before.

"Over here!" Byron yelled, pointing at a patch of mud littered with a multitude of tiny holes. Sometimes the holes led to the tunnelling sea worms that were okay to collect for bait, but were otherwise useless. Finding them, instead of clams, after digging down a certain distance, was always disappointing. Usually, however, an area this big, bearing this many holes, was a good sign it would be clams below and not worms.

Darren and Byron chatted happily together as they dug, their conversation starting with talk about girls, and eventually veering off to a discussion of the movie they had secretly watched the night before. Remembering some of the most violent scenes made Darren's blood run cold, particularly one involving a zombie chewing up one of the lesser characters' face. They laughed when they talked about that moment in the film, but it was more of a posturing thing, trying to prove their bravado, the laughter nervous. The conversation came to an abrupt end as they reached a sizable collection of clams. With a celebratory shout of triumph, the two boys began to load up their buckets, digging off to the sides as they cleared the place where they had started.

It wasn't very long before their buckets were brimming with clams and, lifting their harvest up from the sand, the two boys turned to start towards home. Something, however, caught the corner of Darren's eye, some unexpected movement that seemed out of place. He glanced over at its source, something he had assumed was an oddly shaped chunk of driftwood, draped in drying seaweed and bleached by the sun.

"Did you see that?" Darren asked Byron, pointing towards the whitish-grey clump jutting out from the flats. "I think it moved."

Without bothering to put down their fare, the two boys wandered over to get a better look, thinking that perhaps Darren had spotted some kind of animal hiding among the seaweed, and curious to see exactly what it was. They had seen racoons, skunks and even porcupines lurking along the beach before, as well as a wide variety of birds. It was likely just a seagull or a crow, creatures that commonly scavenged along the shore, but Darren wanted to find out for himself, just in case it was something more interesting.

No animal was visible as they approached, but the closer they got, the less what they were looking at resembled a random piece of driftwood and the more it took on a human form, like an outstretched corpse with tendrils of brownish-grey flesh hanging off of its bleached bones, half-buried in the wet sand. Darren assumed it was the zombie movie from the night before playing tricks on his mind, but that didn't stop his heart from racing.

They didn't get close enough to know for sure. At the point where they were only a few feet away, whatever it was in front of them moved again. Darren was convinced, at that moment, that what he saw was a corpse, denuded of much of its flesh and all of its organs, reaching towards him with a rattling groan. He could make out a worm-eaten face with empty eye sockets and shrivelled chunks of lips, its leathery tongue lolling out of the place where its cheek should have been. Only patches of brittle-looking hair remained attached to the dry off-white skull, barely visible among the seaweed that rested there.

Darren's breath caught in his throat as the bony fingers extended towards him, choking off the scream that wanted out. He didn't wait to gauge Byron's reaction. In a panic, Darren turned and ran.

Byron was actually two steps ahead of him, and the pair galloped away as fast as their legs would carry them, almost tripping several times as the mud clung to their boots, the suction refusing to release them at first. Both boys spilled the topmost clams from their buckets but did not take the time to stop and pick them up, far too frightened to interrupt their flight. In fact, they did not come to a breathless halt until they were practically at Darren's doorstep, gasping for air with limbs trembling.

"What was that?" Byron asked, once he could finally speak again.

"I don't know. I thought it was driftwood until I saw it move, but now I'm not so sure," Darren replied.

Byron's expression shifted from fear to shame. "Maybe that's all it was, just a big ratty piece of driftwood. Do you think we could have been imagining things – because of the movie last night?"

Darren shrugged; he wasn't sure either. He might have been seeing something that wasn't there, his thoughts dwelling on their late night elicit entertainment. "Maybe – I don't know, but if it was just driftwood and seaweed, then why did it move?"

Byron looked thoughtful for a moment, contemplating potential explanations. "Maybe the sand shifted underneath it, or maybe a stiff breeze caught it and made it shake."

Neither boy was willing to go back in order to test this theory. Instead, Darren conceded that Byron must be right.

"If that was a zombie it would have been dead for a while, and we ain't heard anything about nobody going missing around here. You probably guessed it right. We're still spooked from the movie."

Without further mention of the incident, the two boys carried their bounty into the house. The clam bake that night would be extra awesome, with plenty of clams for everyone. They both should be pleased with themselves and thoroughly excited.

So why were the butterflies in Darren's stomach the negative, anxious kind?

◀ ▶

Darren was surprised at the size of the crowd that had shown up for the yard party. Since he and Byron had brought home such a sizable haul, despite the few lost to spillage on the way back, his parents had invited several extra people. The music was already blaring out on the back patio, and the beer bottles were in the process of being pulled out of the cooler and passed around. Darren's father had started the fire in the fire pit and his mother had finished rinsing the clams, tossing any that were broken or appeared to be dead. Most of them seemed shipshape, and she commented that they had so much on hand that they were going to have to steam them in two smaller batches, instead of the usual big one. She said that with a certain amount of pride, mussing Darren's hair before carrying the hefty pot outside.

The boys hung around outside enjoying the hustle and bustle, and snacking on the chips and other party foods that had been laid out on the patio table so that guests would have something to eat while waiting for the main dish to be ready. People seemed jovial, chattering and laughing and relaxing in the patio chairs until the clams were done. Darren had heard that Byron's older brother Trevor had brought his guitar, that he would probably play after they were done eating, and Darren had spotted a couple of giant bags of campfire marshmallows in the kitchen, that they would no doubt get to roast once everyone had eaten their fill of clams.

Before long, Darren's father announced that the clams were almost ready.

"I'll go get the melted butter," Darren's mother said.

"You better hurry. I don't know about anyone else here, but I don't think I'll be able to wait until you get back. I can almost taste those clams already. They're going to be delicious," he told her.

As she passed Byron, the boy reached into the pop cooler, but came up empty handed. He looked thoroughly disappointed.

"No more root beer," he sighed.

"There's more in the fridge," Darren assured him. "Come with me to the kitchen. We'll go get a new batch for the cooler."

The two boys slipped through the patio doors and made a beeline to the fridge. When they arrived, Darren's mother was in the process of giving the big glass bowl of buttery goodness one last stir.

"I'll see you guys out there," she said with a smile, as she lifted the bowl and turned to go. "I bet you anything they started in on those clams without us. Your father was never any good at waiting for anything."

Darren smiled back, but he still had bad butterflies in his stomach. His thoughts kept drifting back to the conversation they had once had about the red tide and the idea that clams were the ocean's filter, ingesting whatever garbage was in the water.

Darren was shocked back into reality by the ice-cold cans of root beer that Byron was foisting into his arms. It had taken longer than expected to get at them, that particular flavour of pop shoved far in the back and therefore difficult to reach. Darren chastised himself for being such a big baby and a scaredy-cat. Zombies weren't real. All smart people knew that. He even promised himself he would go back to the beach tomorrow, when some of his courage had returned, so he could confirm that truth for himself.

Byron was the first through the patio door and into the backyard. Darren paused before stepping out, seeing his father kissing his mother rather vigorously. He rolled his eyes as he placed the cans on the table, waiting for Byron to move out of the way to the cooler. His father was not big on PDAs, which meant he had already had too much beer – how embarrassing. That was when Darren noticed the entire bowl of melted butter had been upended on the patio planking... and nobody seemed to be making a fuss about it.

Puzzled, Darren looked over at his mother, who should have been upset. His father was still kissing her, or so Darren believed at first. Then his father pulled his head back, a few bloodied strands of his mother's face hanging from his clenched teeth. He hadn't been kissing his wife's face, he had been eating it.

The scream that Darren had choked back on the beach now escaped. Flooded with panic, he turned to run back into the house, but Byron's brother, Trevor, was already there, blocking Darren's path. The older boy did not smile or say a word, his eyes as lifeless as Darren's dad's. Instead he lunged for Darren's throat, his teeth bared and a strand of unswallowed but slightly chewed clam dangling from them.

Darren thought it was ironic that all he could see was red, as the tide of zombies swarmed him and joined Trevor in feasting upon his flesh.

HUNGRY GHOSTS

Michael Matheson

Zhou Lei-Fang felt the weight of her long years as an ache in
the marrow of her bones. Kensington Market was noisy
around her with its too-full streets, blaring music, and the
heavy clang and rumble of streetcars rattling along their
tracks; the 505 Dundas eastbound well overdue. Not long
ago she'd have walked the few blocks from Bathurst to
Augusta, but even the short trip from the Toronto Western
Hospital now left her exhausted and crumpled in pain: walking more than a few blocks had become an agony after frac-
turing her hip the year before.

Lei-Fang leaned back against the glass of the TTC shelter and closed her eyes, her breathing ragged, and reflected
on the cold seeping into her flesh. "A fine state for a *wuyi* to
come to," she muttered into the empty enclosure. Queasy
self-loathing sloshed in her guts at her forced reliance on
Western doctors and their endless sea of pills. Six decades
she had ministered to her community, and now after all the
spirits she had sent to their rest, all the ills she had cured, and
all the incantations she had sung, to be slowly falling apart
herself? The heavens had a funny way of showing their gratitude. Her hip throbbed and the arthritis in her hands pre-
vented her from brewing her own remedies, let alone wielding her exorcising spear – not that she'd been called to cast

out a spirit in more than twenty years. Not since Liang Fu's poor, dead, foolish children had gotten their hands on an authentic *jufu* talisman; Lei-Fang still had no idea who had written the inscription for them. Liang Fu's girls had been too young to see the danger in raising a *jiang shi* after watching a copy of *Geung si sin sang*. *Mr. Vampire*, Lei-Fang amended, forcing her thoughts back into English – that was getting harder too; she didn't used to have problems staying in her adopted tongue.

The old *wuyi* sighed and opened her eyes to examine her aching hands. Still long and delicate, they were weathered with age and their joints gnarled. Bao had always loved her hands and she missed the touch of his fingers against hers. Lei-Fang inhaled sharply and wiped her eyes where tears had begun to pool at their edges. She looked west, watching for the streetcar, and caught her reflection in the glass. She frowned, and the elderly woman in the glass frowned back at her.

The 505 clattered along the street, slowing as it bore down on the Bathurst stop. She eased her tired body off the shelter seat with a groan; even broken she stood tall and willowy, her hair bound elegantly back in a bun pinned with a pair of lacquered hair sticks. Lei-Fang reached for her cane as the streetcar came to a rolling stop.

◀ ▶

Lin Quon's control did not falter as he held the delicate brush; his hand moved like a slow river, tracing liquid curves as the chi flowed through his arm, down through his fingers, and into the characters. Stroke by stroke they became words, their black designs forming a neat line down the yellowed paper.

When he was done he closed his eyes, his arm aching from the chi that he had forced through it. He leaned into the plush chair, remembering quiet days like this twenty years ago, here, in his father's study. Remembering the boy he had been, watching his father work with the old characters, straining to force his chi into them. It had been Lin Changgong's pursuit of forbidden knowledge that had driven Quon's mother away from the house on Oxford Street. None of the members of his family spoke her name after she left, only daring to whisper it in quiet rage when Changgong killed himself seven months later.

Quon was still waiting for her to return and explain her decades-long absence, to tell him why she had never come to rescue him from the extended family for whom he was the unworthy son of a failed father, second always to his cousins. He dreamed of her often: dreams where he was a small boy again and she would sweep him up in her arms, hold him close, and never let him go.

He opened his eyes and leaned forward, feeling the ache in his chest that marked the part of him she had taken with her when she went away. In all the time his aunts and uncles had spent raising him, he had thought only of her. And, of course, his father.

It had taken twenty years of failed effort to finally tap the chi necessary to reproduce his father's work – to craft an authentic *jufu*. He held his aching arm in tender fingers as he rose and exhaled slowly. Quon stared down at the talisman on the table. He couldn't bring his mother home with it, but then, the *jufu* wasn't for her.

◀ ▶

Lei-Fang shuffled slowly along Augusta, leaning heavily on her cane as she headed home. She stopped in front of her house, shook her head at her own weakness and breathed deeply, her purse tucked under one arm.

"Wuyi Zhou?" Lei-Fang turned to see Song Xiu standing behind her, Xiu's sleeping daughter, barely six months old, cradled in the young mother's arms. Xiu still carried some of the weight of her pregnancy and Lei-Fang stared at her, trying to picture Xiu without her daughter and could not; in six months the child had become so much a part of her that it seemed as though Xiu had always been a mother. It suited her. "I am sorry to bother you, Wuyi Zhou—"

Lei-Fang waved off the young woman's distress and motioned for Xiu to follow her. "Come inside."

◀ ▶

Lei-Fang settled her weary bones into an inelegant, hard-backed chair, its rigid spine a comfort for her sore back. Like her furniture, the apartment was ascetic; neither she nor Bao had cared for frivolous things. The small shrine to Bao was the only luxury she allowed herself.

The old *wuyi* listened as Xiu rattled around in her kitchen. "You said the cupboard on the right?" Xiu called around a corner.

Lei-Fang smiled. "No, that's the herbal teas. Xiu—"

"Yes?" asked Xiu, peeking around the corner, one arm still holding her sleeping child tightly, a packet of green tea dangling from her other hand as the tiny girl nuzzled in against her shoulder.

"You're going to make the tea while holding your daughter? Ridiculous. You'll burn the child, and I have nothing prepared for that. Give her to me."

Xiu pursed her lips before gently lowering her daughter into Lei-Fang's waiting hands. The baby stirred and cooed in her sleep, but did not wake.

"Go," shooed Lei-Fang. "Brew the tea. She'll be fine."

Lei-Fang held the infant in her arms, watching the unusually quiet child squirm as she slept. Lei-Fang traced the pudgy features of Xiu's child with one long finger, wondering what her own children might have looked like; by the time she and Bao had thought to try, it was too late.

Xiu came in from the kitchen carrying two steaming cups of tea, one in each hand, and Lei-Fang nodded her head at the empty chair across the table. She handed Xiu her daughter once the young woman's arms were empty, and waited while Xiu settled in, hugging her child to her breast and rocking gently back and forth.

"Now," said Lei-Fang as she reached for her tea with both hands, her flesh drinking in the warmth of the cup, "what can I do for you?"

◄ ►

Quon stood in his doorway in the warm evening, brandishing the hundred dollar bill he had promised the two teens, their eyes wide as he held it out for them to take. The elder of the two boys took the proffered money and Quon raised the talisman in his other hand, drawing their attention to it. "*Exactly* as we discussed. Agreed?" The two boys nodded sagely as the younger child took the *jufu* and cradled it in his hands in awe.

Quon waited until the two boys disappeared down Oxford Street before he retrieved his coat from where it hung near the door, and stole into the evening after them.

◀ ▶

"You owe me nothing, Xiu," said Lei-Fang as they walked out into the cool light of the evening.

"Are you sure, Wuyi? It's true that between Xue's being let go and the mat leave things are…tighter…than they were, but we have a little money put aside. And I would not have you think less of me."

"Bao made sure I would be looked after," Lei-Fang tutted as she escorted Xiu and her daughter out.

"But after what you've done for our daughter—"

"You have nothing to worry about, Xiu. She's not possessed. She'll start crying soon enough, you'll see. And then you'll wish it *were* spirit possession," smiled Lei-Fang. "She's healthy, just quiet," Lei-Fang stroked the hair of Xiu's sleeping child. "And unusually well-behaved. Enjoy it while it lasts." Lei-Fang's smile became a grimace as a spasm tightened the muscles of her ribs, and she curled towards the pain.

"Wuyi Zhou?" solicited Xiu, leaning in to steady the old woman.

Lei-Fang shook her head. "It's nothing."

"Are you sure?" asked Xiu, holding Lei-Fang up with one hand while the *wuyi* leaned against her doorway, her cane left inside. "It doesn't seem like nothing."

"It's close enough," Lei-Fang said slowly, trying not to collapse under the weight of her own body. "At my age everything is something. It's knowing which something is worth getting excited about that makes a difference." Lei-Fang breathed her way through the pain, though the tightness in her chest did not fade. "I wouldn't wish this on anyone," she cursed under her breath, and looked pointedly at the young woman whose hand was still on her shoulder. "If at all possible, Xiu, die young enough that your body is still your own."

Xiu stepped back and looked askance at Lei-Fang, instinctively clutching her child tighter to her. "Wuyi?"

"Never mind," Lei-Fang coughed. Some things you couldn't explain. The *wuyi* waved away the young woman's fear. "May you live long enough to appreciate the truth of my words, and not long enough to utter them yourself." The spasm passed and a different kind of tightness settled in. A long shudder passed through her bones and Lei-Fang straightened, her pain forgotten and her spine a steel bar as she listened to something only she could hear. "Do you feel that?" she whispered, turning to the east.

"Feel what?" asked Xiu, following the *wuyi*'s gaze.

"Xiu, does your husband still have his car?"

"Of course. Xue has been making the payments. Barely," Xiu added under her breath, leaning on one hip to better support the weight of the child in her arms.

"Then I will accept your offer of payment, provided you allow me a favour in its stead."

"Of course, Wuyi Zhou. Do you need us to take you somewhere?"

"You and the child can't come for this," Lei-Fang said gently, noting Xiu's relief. The old strength flooded back into her bones, and she flexed her hands, ignoring the arthritic joints.

Xiu nodded, touched the old woman's arm in a silent thank-you, and jogged down the steps before halting and turning back to Lei-Fang. "Where are you going, Wuyi Zhou?"

"We'll know when I get there. Go, child, run along and tell your husband I will need him in a few minutes." Lei-Fang watched Xiu and her daughter disappear down the street, the child half-awake as she curled tiny arms partway around her mother's neck and flattened her face against Xiu's shoulder. Lei-Fang frowned and vanished into the darkness of her house, flicking on a light switch as she passed, the evening settling in quickly now as the sun dipped low in the sky.

In Xiu, Lei-Fang recognized the same concern she had seen in countless mothers who had come to her over the years. Obedient children were always suspect. Lei-Fang never had figured out why. Xiu's daughter wasn't possessed, but someone *had* opened the way. Something was coming; the first steps had been taken and Lei-Fang had felt the cold chill down her spine that spoke of Yin and Yang out of balance: the natural order turned on its head. It had been a long time since she had dealt with a risen spirit. More often it was those who lingered – *po* or *hun* ghosts who for whatever reason, more often than not their murder, couldn't rest – that had to be exorcised. But this… This was as if someone had opened a door into *Diyu*; someone practicing wugu to drag a spirit out of the eighteen Hells and the ten courts of the underworld. Lei-Fang shook her head: it was unwise to take what King Yama had claimed and passed judgement on.

The old *wuyi* – her mind and body clear of pain for the first time in nearly a year, her mind shutting out everything but the task at hand out of long training – looked down into the umbrella stand near her front door. Several umbrellas and her cane poked out of it. And resting in the shallow well, leaning against the wall where it had stood for twenty years, removed only when Lei-Fang had cleaned the wood and oiled the blade, was her spear. Lei-Fang drew it by the haft, feeling the remembered weight, the wood long ago worn smooth from the oils of her hands. Using the spear as a walking stick she went to retrieve her *shenyi* – the formal robe the closest she could come, in Toronto, to wearing the traditional garments of a *wuyi* without drawing unwanted attention.

A horn honked outside, followed shortly after by a knock at her door and the sound of Xue calling "Wuyi Zhou?" through the wood.

"Coming!" called out Lei-Fang, the *wuyi* garbed in her *shenyi* and wielding her exorcising spear. Now all she had to do was figure out how to transport her spear in Xue's car without getting them arrested.

Like two whispering ghosts the boys stole into the shadowed grounds of Mount Pleasant Cemetery. They hoisted the backpack they had brought with them over the high fence, avoiding the open entrances for fear of being seen. The pack landed in the loam with a soft thud and the boys went up and over after it. Joe, the elder of the two, retrieved the bag and pulled their flashlight out, handing it off to his brother, Peter, as they slipped between the graves. They kept the flashlight off, skulking low, bent-kneed, as they made their way to the section of the graveyard their employer had specified. They didn't worry overmuch about the noise their shoes made as they scuttled across the grounds, the cemetery never entirely quiet with the rush of traffic on Yonge, the faraway clatter of subway cars – like the one they had ridden uptown on – heading into and out of Davisville Station on the above-ground tracks, and the lonely calls of night birds echoing from tree to tree.

"So, you think Mom's gonna buy the sleepover story?" asked Peter.

"Yeah, it's good. Bud's covering for us and his parents are out of town, so if Mom calls, she'll have to talk to him."

"Okay," shrugged Peter, trying hard not to shiver in the darkness, despite the warm night. "Hey, Joe," he whispered as they made their way between the graves, his brother glancing back over his shoulder, "do you think that guy's trying to raise a fighter?"

"What, like Lee Pyron?" asked Joe. His brother nodded, and they stopped moving while Joe thought it over, the two of them huddling close together in the deeper shadows of a tall tree, its leaves rustling in a soft wind. "I don't know. I mean, he wasn't wearing robes like one of the *Daoshi*. Still, what else would you want a *jiang shi* for?" He frowned and slipped off, his brother scrambling after him in the late-summer dark.

"Well, if he's not like Jun, do you think he's like Faust the eighth? It must have something to do with the way it worked in *Shaman King*, 'cause what he gave us is all wrong for how the undead worked in *Shikabane Hime*, right?" asked Peter, his nerves wire-taut and his tongue garrulous in the rush of adrenaline and freedom that came with stealing into a grave-yard on a warm summer night, when all the world is still and everything else fades away outside the borders of grass and stone.

"Well, yeah, he gave us a *jufu* to put on the corpse," Joe shrugged, squinting as he tried to read the headstones in the dark. "I can't see a damn thing. Put on the flashlight."

Peter fumbled with the flashlight until the switch caught and the beam played over the grass at their feet. The boys walked in silence, moving a few feet apart as they looked for the grave they needed, Peter swinging the light back and forth like a slow searchlight.

"Where the hell is it?" asked Joe. "Pete, do you see the name? He said there'd be English on the tombstone, too."

"Found it," hissed Peter, his flashlight illuminating a high, narrow tombstone carved from polished stone. Peter thumbed off the flashlight and Joe dug out a pair of collapsible camping shovels from the backpack. The boys assembled them in silence, listening for signs of other nocturnal visitors before they started digging.

◀ ▶

It was dark by the time Quon stood outside the wrought iron fence running parallel to Yonge. Intermittent cars hurtled past, and regular subway cars rattled in the distance behind him. He tapped his fingers on the fence, rubbernecking casually, watching for observers who might notice a grown man fence-hopping into a perfectly accessible graveyard. When the street was relatively clear of pedestrians and there was a lull in the passing traffic he clambered up the fence with a grunt, and half-slid, half-tumbled down the other side.

Quon dusted off his long coat as he rose, striding into the shadows of the concealing trees. He dug his hands deep into the pockets of his overcoat to hide their quivering as he walked between the graves, and forced himself to amble, not wanting to arrive while the boys were still digging. Quon had no taste for the necessarily messy work, only for what followed.

◀ ▶

"Turn in here," said Lei-Fang, pointing left as they drew up between the eastern and western gates of the cemetery, heading north on Mount Pleasant Road, the route bisecting the two halves of the grounds.

Xue angled the car through the stone posts bordering the open gates and slowed the sedan to a crawl. "Where do you want me to wait?" he asked, checking the rearview mirror to make sure no one was coming up behind them. The cemetery appeared utterly deserted in the warm night.

Lei-Fang shook her head. "Don't wait for me. I'll make my own way back."

"Are you sure, Wuyi? Xiu said your hip was still bothering you."

"There's a bus stop not fifty feet from where we're sitting." Lei-Fang turned to glare at Xue, who shrunk back into his seat. "Are you implying that I can't walk fifty feet?"

"I was thinking about all the other walking you'll be doing first," Xue said quietly, avoiding Lei-Fang's gaze.

"Yes, I know," sighed Lei-Fang, "but you can't be here for what's coming. Go home to your wife and child."

"Do you think you'll be here until morning then, if you're planning on taking a bus back?"

"It takes how long it takes," Lei-Fang shrugged as she unbuckled her seat belt, eased herself out of the door and closed it behind her. "The dead are fussy that way," she said through the open passenger side window.

Xue leaned across the car as Lei-Fang went to pull her spear out of the backseat of the sedan. "What should I tell Xiu?"

"Tell her whatever you like," said Lei-Fang, hefting the spear and planting its butt in the ground like a walking stick. "I wouldn't tell her the truth, if it were me," she added, straightening the fall of her *shenyi*, "but that's up to you." Xue frowned at her while Lei-Fang waited for him to leave. "Drive safely," she hinted, tapping one long finger on the haft of her spear.

Xue shook his head as he pulled the wheel hard to the left and did a slow, tight turn. He waved at the *wuyi* as he drove out of the cemetery gates.

Lei-Fang let out the breath she'd been holding, afraid that he would refuse to leave. She couldn't vouch for his safety, and she didn't like the idea of depriving Xiu of a husband and their daughter of her father. The old *wuyi* closed her eyes and reached out for the unnatural flow of chi in the cemetery. It wasn't hard to find: the discordance lit up like a beacon in the midst of so much natural energy. The cemetery was still verdant in the late summer and the imbalance was a rot festering at its heart somewhere to the west. It was still more potential than spirit, but the force at work had called the coming spirit by name, had dragged it up out of *Diyu*. This was no normal *jufu*. Maybe it wasn't meant to be; Lei-Fang wasn't sure.

Knowing just how long the night ahead would be, Lei-Fang shoved aside the pain in her body – let the coming work push it from her mind – and made her way into the depths of the darkened cemetery.

◀ ▶

Joe leaned heavily on the shovel, gulping down lungfuls of air. "Why do they have to bury them so deep?" he huffed up at his brother.

Peter shook his head. "The smell?" They stood atop the excavated wooden coffin, drifts of earth and clumps of grassy loam scattered at their feet. The hole they'd dug was ragged, but wide enough for them to stand beside each other. "So, what, do we just crack it open?"

Joe rubbed his sore back. "I guess. He wasn't real clear on the details of how we *got* to the body."

"All right," Peter shrugged, and jammed his shovel down into the edge of the simple pine box, cracking the wood. "Help me push," he hissed through gritted teeth. Joe tossed his own shovel up over the lip of the hole and helped his younger brother heave on his shovel like a crowbar.

The wood cracked open and fell away with a loud clatter. Both boys went dead still in the wake of the echoing crash, but only the hooting of a lone owl followed the tumult. "Quick, get the *jufu*," said Joe, putting a hand to his face to block the foetid stench of the corpse while Peter crawled out of the hole to go digging in the backpack. The worms had worked their way through the soft pine of the coffin and eaten away at the meat of the body. What was left was a combination of liquefied gristle and dirty bone. Small insects still crawled in and out of the corpse's cavities. "Oh God, that's rank."

"Why does he look like that?" asked Peter, kneeling at the edge of the grave and clutching the *jufu* in both hands.

"Because he's a *real* corpse, not an animated one," spat Joe around the flesh of his hand, fighting back nausea. "Give me the talisman. The sooner we raise him the sooner we can get out of here." Peter leaned in and Joe snatched the paper out of his hands. "I tell you, this better be the best reanimation *ever*."

The bugs skittered away from Joe's hands, disappearing deeper into the dead man as the boy knelt down to drape the *jufu* on the corpse's skull. He positioned it as carefully as he could with one hand, still using the other to cover his nose and mouth, then scrambled out of the grave to be clear of the *jiang shi*'s reach when it rose.

Both boys covered their heads and flattened themselves along the ground. And waited. Several minutes passed while a warm wind blew through the trees, carrying with it the stink of the open grave. When nothing happened, the brothers looked around cautiously and scuttled along the ground to peer over the lip of the pit.

The corpse lay exactly where they had left it, just as dead as it had been before.

"Well, that was a complete waste of time," said Joe, blowing all the air out of his lungs as he stood up and dusted off his pants. Peter rose with him and they moved off to refill their lungs with air that didn't smell of corpse and rot.

"What are we gonna do now?" asked Peter as they gathered up their things. "Should we bury him again?"

"Hell no," spat Joe as he collapsed the shovels. "Let somebody else do it. I'm tired, I'm filthy, and I want to go home and shower. We'll tell Mom we didn't feel like staying over at Bud's the whole night after all. 'Kay?" Peter nodded eagerly as they turned their backs on the dead man to load up the backpack. Neither of them saw the bony hand rise over the lip of the hole, the ruined figure hauling itself out of its own grave one slow foot of earth at a time.

"You wanna put on *Gungrave* when we get back?" Peter asked, his enthusiasm for the undead undaunted by the night's excursion. Behind the two boys the skull of the *jiang shi* rose over the lip of the grave, the *jufu* affixed to the corpse's forehead, the wide talisman trailing down to cover the better part of the dead man's face.

"After digging up a corpse?" Joe spat as the *jiang shi*'s upper half cleared the grave and it buried the claws of one hand in the dirt and heaved its lower half over the rise. "I'm not watching anything with zombies tonight unless there are hot, naked women in it." He paused, then he and Peter looked at each other and said "*Highschool of the Dead*," in unison, grinning in silent agreement as they went back to their packing.

The *jiang shi* rose to its feet, a moaning wind whistling through gaps in its rib cage.

"Hey, do you think we should give that guy his hundred back?"

"What are you, nuts? He totally wasted our time. He's probably laughing his ass off right now."

"Well, I just thought—" Peter stopped short as a rotting, mostly bone hand fell on his shoulder. "What?" he had time to say before the *jiang shi* turned him roughly around and opened its mouth, the gaping hole hidden by the trailing edge of the *jufu*, and inhaled.

◀ ▶

Quon came around a bend in the path, slipping out of the shadow of an enormous tree in time to watch the *jiang shi* toss aside the desiccated husk of Joe. It fell not far from Peter's shrivelled corpse. The dead man straightened and inhaled empty air, then exhaled deeply, clearing its throat before it tried to speak. No sound came out, and the *jiang shi* stared down at its hands, confused.

"Father?" called Quon as loudly as he dared, his eyes wet. He wiped them on the sleeve of his overcoat. He took several steps towards the *jiang shi*, ignoring the dead children on the ground, and the creature stretched out its arms to him.

"Stop! Don't touch him," yelled Lei-Fang, moving around the bole of the tree under which the risen corpse of Lin Changgong stood before his son. Her spear was in both hands, its tip wavering between the two men: the living and the dead.

Quon turned on the *wuyi*. "Who the hell are—"

"There's a reason this magic is forbidden," hissed Lei-Fang. She kept her spear raised as she swept her gaze over the *jiang shi* and the young man. Her shoulders sagged as she took in the two dead boys, barely teenagers. "It's dangerous enough when performed by someone who actually knows the *wugu*," she added, swallowing her anger as she turned back to Quon, "let alone someone who has no idea what they're doing. All that is keeping me from exorcising you to Hell along with *him*," she said, tipping her spear at Changgong, "is that you do not carry the chi of a practitioner. But he cannot remain here; his hunger will only grow. And no matter how deep or how dark you conceal him, Niu Tou and Ma Mian *will* find him and drag him back to *Diyu*."

"*Who?*" asked Quon, unable to parse her words. His hands articulated his confusion, then his anger. "*What are you talking about?*"

"Ox-Head and Horse-Face," said Lei-Fang more patiently than she would have thought possible. "Servants of King Yama who greet the newly dead upon their arrival in *Diyu*, and hunt the souls that escape the underworld; the monsters Yama sent to collect Sun Wukong. You truly think yourself the equal of the Monkey King – the only figure in history ever to defy them? You dragged a spirit out of the eighteen Hells, child. What did you think would happen?"

"No," said Quon, as if by refusing her words he could erase the truth of them. "I brought him back, that's all that matters. I have subverted the laws, as he did before me." Quon pointed behind him, at the *jiang shi* wavering slightly in the wind. "He knows where my mother went when she left us, and he will help me find her. He will help me *bring her back*."

Lei-Fang slumped, glanced at the haggard corpse, and settled her gaze on Quon. "That thing is not your father, child; a *jufu* only restores the body. I don't know how you managed to trap your father's *hun* in his own corpse, but you haven't raised him from the dead. All you've done is pull him out of *Diyu* to bind him to another prison. And if what you say is true, then in life, twenty years ago now, your father condemned two siblings to a fate worse than death. Your father was a monster, child, and you have followed in his footsteps.

But *his* actions killed not only children, but others close to you as well. And if you—" Lei-Fang interrupted herself, pausing to squint at the *jufu* covering the corpse's face. "Why is there a stroke missing in the third character?"

"What?" asked Quon, turning to his father and leaning in to examine the *jufu* while the *jiang shi* stood silent, breathing in and out in imitation of life. "What does that mean?" Quon asked, pivoting back to Lei-Fang.

"It means you don't have control," Lei-Fang whispered as she raised her spear in a defensive position, planted one heel in the loam behind her and squared her shoulders. "Walk *very slowly* towards me," she instructed Quon, not taking her eyes off the *jiang shi* behind him.

"I still don't even know who you *are*—" Quon began, before the corpse of Lin Changgong put a bony hand on Quon's shoulder. "Father?" Quon asked over his shoulder, his voice a breath on the wind, before the *jiang shi* swung him around and inhaled deeply, stifling the scream rising in Quon's throat.

"Oh, *gaisi*," Lei-Fang spat, and lunged forward, ignoring the screaming protest of her hip. She angled her spear over Quon's shoulder as the *jiang shi* threw him aside – the spear tip slashing a tight cut that bisected the *jufu* draped across the *jiang shi*'s face.

Quon hit the ground in a heap as the *jiang shi* stopped moving, the lower half of the *jufu* drifting down to the ground like a fallen leaf. Lei-Fang stood her ground as the *jiang shi*'s corpse bent violently backwards, splaying like a marionette, the ragged, gaping hole where its mouth had once been facing the sky. Lei-Fang braced herself against the piercing, steam-whistle shriek that followed as the trapped *hun* was torn from its own corpse. The empty bones clattered to the ground as the hun of Lin Changgong coalesced before her: an angry, lost spirit, now doomed to wander like a *po* ghost; to drift farther and farther away from his humanity until Niu Tou and Ma Mian could find and claim him.

Lei-Fang looked into Lin Changgong's empty eyes, and thrust her spear into the centre of the *gui hun* floating above her, shouting to frighten him off and speed him on his way.

When the last of Changgong's chi had fled, sent back down to *Diyu*, Lei-Fang hobbled over to Quon, her hip grinding as if newly cracked. She bent down to the young man with a grunt of pain and stared into his mostly glassy eyes, too much of his chi drained by his father for him to linger long in the land of the living.

"I don't want to die," he whispered, his eyes not focusing properly.

"Shh," whispered Lei-Fang, inhaling sharply as she sat on the ground and her hip collided with the earth. She set aside her spear and took him into her arms as she would an infant, and held him there. "What's your name, boy?"

"Quon," he whispered, folding his head against her breast like a small child and hugging himself to her with the failing strength of his limbs.

"Death comes to everyone, Quon."

He glared up at her. "Supposed to make me feel better?" he slurred.

"No."

He looked away from her, and his chest heaved, all the breath going out of his lungs. "You…knew him?" he managed on the exhale.

"I knew *of* him. But I know enough, now, to put together what would be pertinent to you. But ask yourself, Quon: do you want the truth, or do you want comfort?"

"Truth," he said through chattering teeth, his flesh going cold.

Lei-Fang hesitated a moment, then cradled Quon's body to her, and rocked him gently as she spoke. "Twenty years ago a man named Liang Fu, whose name will mean nothing to you, but it's his, and I owe him the respect of using it, came to me. Both his children were dead, their corpses little more than desiccated husks. Like those two," she said, jutting her chin at the two dead boys, though Quon couldn't see the motion. "The police are never keen to investigate things that do not fit into the easy lies the world tells itself. And there were those who said that nothing came of the case because the Liangs were Chinese in a white country. That last part I don't know the truth of. Perhaps. Perhaps not. What mattered was that Liang Fu did not know who to turn to in his grief. Until he was given my name."

"And?" breathed Quon, half-conscious.

Lei-Fang stroked his hair, and swept it away from his face. "I looked into the matter of their death. And I found her – the *jiang shi* who had killed them."

Quon gasped for breath. "My mo—" he began, unable to finish the question.

Lei-Fang nodded, more for herself than Quon. "I exorcised her, but her corpse had been deliberately defaced so that no one could identify her. The police suspected murder, and whoever had given Fu's children the *jufu* had to have known where she was buried. I don't know why he chose to bring her back after what he did to her, but your father is the only man, aside from you, who I have ever known in this country to craft an authentic *jufu*. It's not certain. Very little in life is, but I don't think your mother *abandoned* you, Quon."

Quon said nothing, all the breath in his lungs gone. He clasped the fingers of one hand on her arm.

"Do you hear me, Quon? She didn't leave you," the *wuyi* whispered into his hair, holding his head to her breast.

He drew in a final breath, and exhaled "Don't...leave me," as Lei-Fang held him close.

And when he was dead she held him to her tighter still, and cried over him because his own mother could not.

THE ADVENTURES OF DOREA TRESS

Rhea Rose

I was only a child when Baby bear bit me. That's the part of the story they never tell. He bit me right on the knuckle, tore my delicate flesh clean away as if it were pale tissue, exposing the white pearly bone beneath. That bite hurt like a hundred hellfires, and I bled for days from that wound. Back then I was a star, a golden child on a movie set. I ran from the film shoot into the dark, green woods and got lost.

It took the searchers three days to find me curled up in the roots of a large tree. They had to enlist an old Salish chief to track me. Ricky Joe was an elder, a chief and a shaman, a rare combination, and he'd grown up in this area where the woods and riverbanks were riddled with trails. He'd told the reporters that he could find a yellow-haired fish in a dark, green sea, but he would have to use magic.

And he did.

Legend has it that an ancient Salish family had once lived in these woods, a mother and father, two daughters and a small son. The youngest daughter often misbehaved and played bad tricks on her sister and brother. Over time her

misbehaviour escalated. Her parents tried to punish her mis-
deeds in the hope that she would learn to respect her family.
Instead, she ate her little brother. She tried to eat her sister
but only managed to bite her. She ate her mother and then
began to eat the animals in the woods. Her father took her
sister away and abandoned Little-Daughter to the forest.

I remember the day Ricky Joe found me. His face
appeared from the tangle of sticks and leaves in front of me,
floated in towards me like a large, papery leaf, fallen from a
tree. His teeth were perfect, a mouth full of little white beach
shells, and he smiled down at me and said, "Come out, little yellow hair. These woods aren't friendly. This tree has
been kind, but soon its roots won't let you go." He gave me
his hand, and it was leathery, big and warm. "Take my paw,"
he said, laughing, "and don't bite me." He pulled me gently from the roots. He told me he was over a hundred years
old as he carried me down the trail. He called me Little-
Daughter.

◀ ▶

After awhile I was sent to see Dr. Bruno. My therapist.

Dr. Bruno says that Ricky Joe never really existed, that I'd
made it all up, and that I hadn't run very far that fateful day
before one of the movie people found me and took me to the
hospital. Dr. Bruno says the reason I continue to run the
same trail so many years later is because I was forever-after
traumatized.

Against the advice of my therapist I was going for a little
run in the woods to alleviate my anxiety. Having run this
route often, I knew all the twists and turns on the path, all

the rocks and roots to avoid. I could have run that path through the woods with my eyes closed. The scents on the air, the twilight, the dry sandy earth beneath my feet, and the smell of a long-dead rabbit, rank and bloated, filled my nostrils. I love to run barefoot with my yellow hair streaming behind me.

And come to think of it maybe my eyes *were* closed when I ran into Christopher.

I'm sure Dr. Bruno would nod wisely and agree when I say I fell over this guy and not *for* this guy. I literally ran him down and injured his ankle. When we crashed, we rolled all tangled together down the path.

"I'm so sorry," I apologized over and over. I was on top of him and staring down into his terrified eyes.

"I've been lost for hours out here," he said, clearly shaken.

I tried my cell phone.

"There's no signal up here," I told him. I examined his ankle. I noticed several sharp gashes. They looked like bites. He grabbed my arm for support and pulled himself up to sit.

He whispered. "I don't wish to alarm you," he said, glancing nervously past me and over my shoulder. "These woods are strange. I heard something. I mean – I heard – *some thing.*"

"A bear?" I asked.

He nodded. "Y-y-yes. I mean, I think it was – a bear. I hope it was and not something else. I mean. I think it was. There. Right there in that bush."

I twisted my head awkwardly around, then back the other way. "I don't hear it. Did you smell him? They smell like unwashed laundry, but worse. They just want the berries." I rattled on and on about all the bear facts I knew, until finally, to shut myself up, I picked a nearby huckleberry and ate it.

I picked one for the injured man and offered it to him. He refused. Looking closely at him I saw he was very young, maybe twenty, maybe still a teen. His fair-haired looks gave him a boyish appearance, like my younger brother, if I'd had one.

"Were you bitten by anything?" I asked.

"No. No."

I tried again to see the marks on his leg, but he wouldn't let me look. "What's your name?"

"Christopher." He held out his hand. I shook it, sweaty palm and all.

"My name is—" I hesitated then. In my head I heard Dr. Bruno's voice, *"You are Dorea. Dorea Tress."*

"I'm Dorea."

"You don't seem very sure about that," Christopher said.

"My parents never called me by that name."

"Oh?"

"They called me – Little-Daughter."

He laughed. "Oh, well, nice to meet you, Dorea. Do you come here often – Dorea?"

I nodded. "Yup. This is my running trail."

"A bit secluded isn't it? I mean for a girl, alone in a hundred acres of woods."

"That's the way I like it." I smelled the blood on his leg. I reached for my water bottle. I wanted to wash the wound and get a better look at the injury. I pulled out the rag I carried in my running pouch, squirted the cloth with water and gently began to wipe away the blood. I saw a protrusion pushing his skin out.

"Ooouch!"

"I hate to say it but I think it's broken, Christopher."

◀ ▶

While I waited for Christopher to recover, I told him my story. Christopher rocked his sore leg and listened politely but didn't say much, until I got to the part about these woods. He insisted that these woods weren't magic. I laughed then and told him he was well and truly lost. He got very quiet.

"You need to try standing," I suggested.

"No. It hurts."

"I know but we can't stay here all night. It's getting darker and we have to get inside before nightfall." I looked cautiously over my shoulder. The smell of the blood from his wound was making me nauseous and dizzy. He must have sensed my anxiety because he agreed to try and hop on one leg with me supporting him.

Even with my help he could barely hobble on the crooked, narrow path.

"I don't think I can make it very far."

"No. You can't," I agreed. "There's an old cabin. We can go there for the night."

"Cabin?"

"A small old house."

"I know what a cabin is!" he snapped at me.

"It's abandoned. I used to go there as a child. I stop there sometimes, when I'm out running. It's a pit stop." I laughed. Well, that wasn't entirely true. It was the old cabin built for that movie I was in as a child.

Christopher was a slight young man. I knew I could lift him, carry him, even run with him across my shoulders. I suggested this and he agreed.

I used the fireman's lift to get him into position. I felt strong with him slung across my back and shoulders. A ravenous hunger took hold of me. How long since I had eaten?

"What brought you out to these woods?" I asked.

"Ah, I, ah, lost a pet," he said. He seemed hesitant to talk about his lost pet. "Too bad there's not more of a moon," he said, changing the subject. "It would make finding our way through the woods much easier."

"Don't worry, Christopher, this time I know my way."

◀ ▶

The first thing he noticed when we arrived at the cabin was the three chairs and three beds. I put him down, and he hopped and slid on his one good leg to the kitchen cupboards, opened them and handled the three bowls stacked there. Then he noticed the folder I'd left on the kitchen table. With some effort and squirming on his part, he managed to seat himself at the kitchen table where he picked up the blue file folder. The newspaper and magazine clippings spilled out. He began to read one, then another, quickly skimming through them, looking at the photos.

"These articles about bears, why are they here?" I could taste something in the air then. Slightly sweet like tree syrup and sour too, the kind of musky reek that dampens the air when an animal is frightened. Christopher picked out one article and read it in the small spill of moonlight. "Those articles are mine," I said. Christopher looked at me, a puzzled expression on his face.

"Dr. Bruno says I have to read them until I can accept what has happened."

"These people were all killed by crazed bears, rabid beasts." He read the headlines aloud: "Bear Chews Hot Tubber," "Hiker Eaten," "Children Attacked," "Dogs, Cats, Pets Bitten and Ripped Apart By a 'Crazy' Bear."

Just then something began scratching incessantly at the door. A critter wanted in.

"What's that?" Christopher asked nervously. I went to the door. "No!" Christopher screamed. "Don't open the door!"

But I did open the door.

"What the f—" Christopher climbed up onto the table. The dead rabbit I'd smelled on the trail was at the door. The brown bloated hare burst into the room like a rocket headed for Christopher, straight for his fresh flesh. But I caught the little Thumper before he tore a strip from Christopher. I ripped the rabbit's head from its body. That was the only way to stop it.

"Sorry," I said. I threw the head into the stone fireplace, but not before I checked it for brains; alas, there were none, I'd sucked them out long ago. I lit a wooden match I kept in the drawer. I built a fire using some wood that had already been gathered. Then I took the rabbit carcass and bit into its hide. My teeth and hands ripped skin from muscle and sinew, and I tossed the fur and skin into a corner of the cabin. I threw the bug-ridden carcass into a water-filled cauldron on the wood-burning stove. I stoked the fire. "It's not too bad when it's cooked," I said.

"That rabbit was rotten. Dead and maggoty," Christopher complained.

"I've had worse."

"What? What could be worse?" His eyes looked large and frightened. I saw the moon reflected in his stare.

"Night is upon us – the creatures are coming. They'll be hungry. The rabbit's only the beginning," I said.

I thought I could protect Christopher from every animal monster that came to the cabin. I'd created them. I'd bitten them all. Ricky Joe had known exactly who I was. He'd recognized my work, not as a child actress, but as the spirit that ran through these woods. When time first dawned in this forest, Little-Daughter ran here, misbehaving. As a child I had an insatiable appetite, but these days, Dr. Bruno reminded me, I was all grown up. Still, I wasn't sure if I could save Christopher. "What's – what's happened to you? Are you rabid?" He asked. He threw a magazine article at me. The article Christopher tossed floated towards the roaring fire pit and caught the flames, then became ash. Outside the soft rustle and shuffle of forest creatures beneath the windows grew louder.

Christopher sputtered; his spittle flew across the space between us and landed on my lip. I licked it away. I shouldn't have. That put me over the edge. "They're coming, Chris," I said.

"Christopher!" He insisted that I call him by that great long name.

Christopher crept slowly closer to the fire, perhaps he felt cold, or safer there, or perhaps he sensed the truth about his predicament. His terror was evident in his trembling hands which moved like cautious spiders across the stonework, seeking a crevice to crawl into. He took hold of Baby bear's chair and dragged it over to support his injured leg, but the chair really was too small because the foot and ankle had swollen to an enormous size. The chair broke when he placed his weight on it. It was an old movie chair, designed to break under pressure. Christopher sat hunched over in Papa bear's chair and this made him look small, and fragile, and very, very vulnerable.

He looked at me, his eyes glassy with pain and fear. "I guess rabid is a close description of my behaviour, but you don't die from what I have. You never die, but you don't live happily-ever-after," I tried to explain.

"What then?" he asked meekly.

"It makes me want to bite," I said, gnashing my teeth. I didn't want to gnash my teeth. I didn't want to frighten poor young Christopher. But his spittle on my lips, the smell of his blood, the moon shining through the window, all of these worked against my control, my own personal choice as Dr. Bruno put it. I couldn't help myself, yet the good doctor insisted that I could help myself, and I suppose I *have* helped myself, though not in the manner he'd suggested.

I felt the golden hair on my head, arms and legs bristle. I clenched my teeth and began grinding them; this kind of behaviour was against Dr. Bruno's orders. I tried to talk with my captor. Yet I burned inside, that part of me that would never die wanted out, wanted desperately to take control, and I yearned to taste Christopher's flesh and brains, even though he was a skinny and bony meal. When I noticed how thin he was, I understood why the witch of the woods held Hansel and tried to fatten him up. I wanted to do the same, but then the three bears arrived in the yard, and I forgot my struggle. I became what I was, Little-Daughter.

I heard the bears charging around outside, bumping the walls of the cabin like testy sharks. How on earth could I protect Christopher? He needed more time. The bite I'd given him on the leg was small and for that reason he would take longer to become what he must. I'd promised Dr. Bruno no more eating, and ripping, and swallowing whole, only small bites, and so I had been gentle with Christopher. He seemed like such a gentle young man. These were the small steps I had taken, but good ones, yes, I was doing well, the doctor even said so the last time we spoke. Yet the forest seemed to descend on us, Christopher and me, in this rickety cabin. All the creatures I'd bitten and, hence, the ones they'd bitten, were finding their way through the night to the cabin where they smelled blood and bones and boy.

"Christopher, listen to me."

He didn't look at me, but I continued anyway. "The forest is alive with death. I come out here to run and – well, bite, and gnaw, and chew. I confess. I bit you out there in the woods."

"You bit me?" he asked.

Another crash outside frightened us both, and we leapt atop the table. I stood ready to do battle, while he balanced like a stork. "If any of the critters outside that door get in here you will be eaten. You're pulsing with life. They'll tear you apart and there will be nothing left of you, my woodland friend."

"I'd rather it go that way," he said.

"No! No, you don't know what you're saying. I'm sorry I bit you, but there was nothing left alive in the forest for me to bite. I couldn't stop myself from stalking you. Okay, that's not entirely true. Dr. Bruno says I can stop myself. Yet, con-sistently, my choice has been to *turn* every creature in these woods, and the very worst are the deer. They're horrid. They're savage."

"Whatever," he said. All hope gone from his voice. Then the two zombears crashed through the door. Baby zombear clambered in over the window frame.

◀ ▶

It was over pretty quickly. Papa bear hadn't left any traces of the young man. Christopher would never be back, except as a steaming pile somewhere in the woods. Papa wouldn't even let Baby bear have a bone. Mama bear tried to clean up, but it was too messy; she only made it worse. It wouldn't take much time for everyone to get hungry again in these hundreds of acres of woods...and didn't Christopher say he'd lost his pet? I licked my lips. I'd have to go find it. I was pretty sure I saw a new movie cast and crew out there shooting in the woods, a story about Little Red Riding Hood. Just thinking about her skipping alone along the trail made me drool. She needed a friend.

Once upon a time the three bears lived in Little-Daughter's woods and then worked for the movie industry, that is, until Baby bear bit me. Okay, that's not entirely true. If the three bears hadn't frightened me by waking me from my deep, deep slumber, not with a kiss, but a growl, I probably would not have chomped down on Baby bear first.

THE LAST KATAJJAQ

Carrie-Lea Côté

Wiping the sweat from my brow, I smiled warmly at the woman standing opposite me. Sweat streamed down her face and she was smiling broadly too. The rest of my family and village sat in a circle around us, pounding their boots on the ground in a show of appreciation for the round of *katajjaq* my mother and I had just performed.

Breathless, I smiled wider as my mother clasped my arms and rubbed the tip of her nose to mine. Her eyes were shining with pride.

"You did very well, my little Kanguyak. You kept up so well this time!" She smiled wider and I couldn't help but blush.

It was hard to keep up with the Elders when singing, but with all the practice over the long winter, I was ready to perform for the Spring Ceremony. With a last squeeze on my arm, my mother turned to embrace my father briefly before moving to talk to Qilaq, our Medicine Woman. Our *Angatkut*.

With spring fully here, we had a busy season ahead of us. Mother wanted to make sure that Qilaq's needs were noted, and supplies gathered for her ceremonies and medicines.

I fetched a drink and stood near the tent door, still getting my breath back and enjoying the breeze that came in. Sipping my water from a bone cup, I felt at peace watching the happy milling of people in the multiple-hide tent we set up for larger gatherings.

Distracted as I was, I didn't hear my eldest sister Chulyin come up behind me with my brother Uyarak in tow. I was suddenly shoved gently from behind. Turning quickly, so as not to scuff my new slippers, I saw her laughing face.

"You did good! So good in fact, I think you get to be the big sister now. Enjoy." Grabbing my hand, she put Uyarak's into it, and moved off quickly. I wrinkled my nose at her, and knew for sure that she would be running off to sneak some quiet time with her sweetheart, Nauja. I was also willing to bet that by the end of the spring he would be asking my father for her hand in marriage.

I sighed and looked down at Uyarak. "Did you enjoy the show, little brother?" Sweeping him up into my arms, I carried him over to where some food and drink were set up. It was mostly dried fare, and was small pickings, but it was shared by all. It was also a fitting display, because it served as a reminder of how close we were to our first fishing trip of the year. I always loved the fresh roe from the fish we netted.

"Kanguyak did good! I liked! Uya want to sing too." He clapped his chubby little hands together and squirmed in my grip.

I laughed and put him down beside my youngest brother, Tattilgat. He was fast asleep this late in the evening. To keep Uyarak settled I handed him a strip of dried fish to chew. "You might be able when you're older, Uyarak. But maybe you want to drum, like father?" Uyarak looked in the direction I pointed where our father sat with my uncle, then back to me.

"No. Uya want sing!" He dropped his fish into his lap, took a deep breath and started to make a long series of garbling and grunting sounds. I shrugged and sat down beside him, content to let him fill the little area with his noise, just so long as it didn't wake Tattilgat.

He was more than happy to oblige.

The next morning we were up early to prepare for a day of fishing. I'd like to say we were up before the sun, but it had neared the time of year where the sun never set. The best we got for darkness was around the spring, when the sun swung low and almost disappeared behind the horizon, but not quite. I had crawled from our caribou-hide tent and quickly did up my outer coat, pulling the hood over my head. There was a little bite of cold still left in the spring air.

Mother handed me a piece of sealskin that was thickly lined with fat to chew on, while I helped to stretch out and untangle any knots in the sinew net.

I wasn't yet quite old enough to fish in deeper water with the three-pronged fishing spear, so I got to do the nets with the other children. Tattilgat and Uyarak played loudly in the rocks nearby; I made sure to keep an eye on them. Looking out to the exposed water edge, I saw my uncle showing Chulyin how to hold a spear.

Chewing absently, I hummed while my practiced fingers found tangles and eased them straight. My mind was full of anticipation for the catch we hoped to get today.

I was so absorbed that I almost jumped when one of the other women shouted a warning. I quickly dropped my net and scooped up Tattilgat, looking to where the other women and children were pointing. It wasn't unusual for a starved polar bear to come hunting us this early in the year. I frowned and squinted at the lumbering shape emerging from the tundra, slowly coming towards us. Nets forgotten, a few of the women picked up nearby spears and a few braver children had rocks.

I grabbed hold of Uyarak's hand, and shifted Tattilgat on to my hip. I didn't trust what I saw, and wanted to be able to run if I had to.

The shambling thing looked like a man, standing on two unsteady legs, and its arms stretched out by its sides stiffly. Its clothing was like nothing I had ever seen before. There were parts of it covered with fur and leather, but these were stained and ripped. It looked almost like an animal had been chewing on it for the better part of a season. Also draped here and there was what looked like a shirt, but made with fish scales. Dull grey fish scales with holes in them. The thing took a step, halted, teetered a little, then took another step. Over and over. It moved like nothing natural, and from the fearful talk around me, that sentiment was felt by the others.

What I assumed was hair stuck out in a matted and filth-riddled hood around the head. It looked almost yellow, like a well-tanned hide. Weirder still, the skin was a strange pale greyish-blue colour. Like dirty snow or ice.

As I stood and stared, Uyarak pulled on my hand and made a fearful noise as he backed up. I shook my head and looked down at him; his little cheeks were streaked with tears.

I looked back at the thing coming nearer to us. Its mouth opened and closed. Opened and closed like a landed fish. Its teeth clicking together sharply in the cold air each time its mouth closed.

And then it moaned.

A horrible, loud and guttural sound. The hairs on the back of my neck stood straight up and I shivered.

"An Evil Spirit! Grab the children and get away from here!" One of the women in the group broke the trance we were in, retreating as she shouted.

The cry was taken up by the others around me, and wasting no time, I followed Uyarak's insistent pull away from the shambling thing.

One of the men ran from the edge of the water towards the creature, his spear held high and with intent. His steps faltered over the uneven and rocky ground, but his strike was true. He yelled as he drove his spear straight and deep into the chest of the creature, tearing flesh and cracking bones with a horrible wet noise. We could hear the wet "'thunk" from where we stood; his face was a grimace as he drove it deeper still. And suddenly Qilaq screamed.

"Umiak! NO! It is a *tuurngait*! It will not die by a spear! Run! Run now! Umiak!"

Umiak turned and looked towards us, as if deciding. He took his eyes off the creature too long, and it lurched towards him, grabbing him with hands whose fingers were nothing but sharp bone ends.

We watched in frozen horror as the *tuurngait*'s mouth snapped as quickly as a bear's, latching onto Umiak's neck and tearing a great hunk of flesh away. The blood spurted strongly, pouring down the side of his neck in great gouts timed with his heartbeat.

Umiak screamed and screamed and screamed.

I quickly turned Uyarak's face into my thigh and covered Tattilgat's ears.

The screaming increased as the *tuurngait* pulled Umiak tighter to its body. We could hear his bones breaking as it did, and then it took another large chunk from his body with another ripping bite. This time from his shoulder.

Umiak flailed and knocked its feet out from under it, bringing them both to the rocky ground beneath.

The hunters of the village stood ringed around the unarmed women and children, bone weapons ready, but really, everyone just stared in horror. No one sure how to even approach the writhing tangle that was the creature and Umiak.

Qilaq kept screaming for us to stay back. It was hard to hear her over Umiak.

He kept screaming and screaming, shriller and shriller each time the *tuurngait's* head pulled back violently with another piece of his flesh in its jaws. His body jerked as he fought with all he had against the creature that was slowly and methodically eating him alive. As Umiak groped along the ground, his hand closed upon a rock. He brought that up in a hard swing, smashing it right into the temple of the blood-stained, yellow-haired creature. Caving its temple in. It bellowed loudly and flopped onto Umiak, twitching once, and then was still.

Umiak's thrashing stilled a heartbeat later, and his eyes stared into the sky, past pain now as his blood continued to sink into the cold rocky ground.

I sobbed and held my brothers tighter. I heard Umiak's mate scream, and was sure she would have run to him, but for Qilaq's warning, and the hands of her family holding her back.

She sobbed and cried his name over and over, and before long the rest of the village had taken up her note of grief.

Our voices rose into the air to grieve the man who had slain the evil spirit.

We milled about as a group around the fire in the Gathering Tent.

It was quieter, and so very, very different from the gathering just the night before.

Once Qilaq had deemed it safe for us to approach Umiak and the demon, Umiak's family had cleaned, dressed and wrapped his body for burial.

It lay covered with stones on a sledge far outside the village. His family would drag it out to the tundra to bury under a cairn in the morning when the sky was brighter.

The *tuurngait* had been festooned with amulets of Qilaq's making.

Amulets to appease it.

Amulets begging it to not continue its wrath among our people.

And other amulets whose sole purpose was to beg the forgiveness of the Spirits that had sent the *tuurngait* in their anger.

Once Qilaq had decided there were enough, it was weighted with rocks, wrapped in a hide, and pushed over the edge of a fishing boat to sink down into the icy depths of the ocean.

Now the Elders argued what steps to take next.

I had long ago given up on listening to the yelling of the village. So far removed from the normal, quiet and lengthy debates I was used to, this one raged and would not be reasoned with.

I sat as far from the tent door as I could, my knees were drawn up and I rocked myself back and forth, wishing comfort, but unable to find it. My brothers were both cuddled in the embrace of my parents, and even Chulyin found comfort in Nauja's arms. I was left on my own at the moment, and couldn't remember feeling so alone in my life.

The yelling had ceased to be original a while ago, and now the same things were yelled back and forth.

"We should leave immediately! We obviously have done something to anger the Spirits, and shouldn't stay here!"

"We should stay and find out why the Spirits are so angry, and fix what has been done!"

"Find out what happened!"

"Leave!"

"Stay!"

"NO!"

"YES!"

It went on and on and yet never came closer to the end. Things were so unruly that even people who traditionally had very little say in the decision-making process were yelling.

The quietest of the Elders was Qilaq. She sat there, smoking her pipe and looking at each member of the village evenly. Quietly.

I used to feel warmth in me when she singled me out for her attentions, but tonight, it made me shiver that every so often her gaze lingered on me, and then started to roam again.

I bit my lip and tried to make myself smaller as I wedged my body closer in between two of my cousins who continued to yell at the top of their lungs.

It was madness in the tent, and several of the younger children had started to cry at this point.

Finally, Qilaq stood up and cleared her throat. I watched in amazement as she was ignored and had to raise her hands above her head and call for attention before she was noticed.

Such disrespect wasn't even shown by children.

"This is solving nothing, and is making everything else worse. Your voices have all been heard. Loudly. Repeatedly. And now I will ask that everyone except the Elders who help me in my Walking to leave. Take your children home and hang your worries outside your tents. I will talk with the Spirits tonight, and tomorrow we will discuss what I have learned."

It was a relief to my ears that the yelling had stopped, and a relief to my heart that Qilaq would talk with the Spirits. The faith we had in our *Angatkut* was absolute, and with a few parting grumbles, the people of our village slowly left the tent, family by family.

I couldn't scurry after my mother and father fast enough.

The next morning started slowly. So few of us found sleep easily that night, except for my brothers. I was sure it was the same in other tents and families too. Mother and Father whispered most of the night, and I could hear Chulyin tossing in her furs. Sleep didn't come to me easily, either. I kept worrying about what would happen to our village and our people if we had to leave our summer camp. Having enough time to store up food was a major concern in our short season.

My mother came over to me and gave me a quick embrace before handing me a small strip of dried whale. I took it and looked up to her for an inkling of support. But she was too withdrawn into her own thoughts to notice me. Mechanically, I started to chew on the dried meat.

Umiak's father had gone to check on the body, ensuring that no animals had disturbed it while we slept.

Of his mate, there was no sign that morning.

I assumed she was still in her family tent.

We didn't mill around long before Qilaq came out of the Gathering Tent. She was heavily assisted by Buniq, the woman who would take her place when she went to join the Spirits.

Qilaq looked tired. Exhausted even. Her skin had a grey pallor to it, and her eyes seemed to have shrunk back into her head, leaving the skin to hang in deep bags beneath them.

I shifted my feet and wished I could have held on to my mother's hand, but she was holding Tattilgat. I looked briefly to the rest of my family, and again, Father was holding on to Uyarak, and Chulyin was with Nauja.

I sniffled a little and hugged myself, continuing to chew the whale meat.

Qilaq coughed, still supported by Buniq, and everyone quieted immediately, intent on what she had learned as she Walked among the Spirits while we slept.

"My children…What I learned, what I heard, while Walking last night. We cannot stay here—" A sudden murmuring rose from the crowd, and Buniq raised her hand for silence in Qilaq's stead. She frowned her disapproval at the interruption. "As I was saying. We cannot stay here. There is no anger in our Spirits, and that was no *tuurngait*. The Spirits tell me that the thing who took our Umiak away from us is a creature that has no Name to the Other World, and cannot be stopped without heavy consequences. And there will be more of them." As she paused to gather her words and a breath, an uneasy mumble started up among the families. They were scared.

"We must leave this place and go farther north along the coast. We will meet up with Brother Tribes, and pass the warning on to them. If they take heed, it will be up to them, but our immediate concern will be getting food for the winter. I have learned that these creatures slow in the cold. That they will stop during the winter months, but beyond that I cannot See any more." Qilaq sighed heavily and looked to each of us, her eyes bright with unshed tears.

Holding her closely, Buniq looked at the older woman, then to the gathering.

"We will leave today as soon as the proper words are said over Umiak's Journey to *Anguta*."

As if that were the dismissal we were waiting for, the group slowly started to dissolve. Each family heading back to their tents to repack what had just been set up mere weeks before. Father exchanged a long look with Mother, before heading to the tent with her.

I pocketed the rest of my whale meat and slowly started to follow. I would be expected to carry part of the camp.

It was then we heard the scream.

Umiak's father came tearing into the camp, his hand clamped around a heavily bleeding wound on his arm.

"My son is taken! Taken by the *tuurngait* that killed him!"

His brother grabbed him on his shoulders and shook him gently. "The creature is no *tuurngait*, Akiak. Qilaq says this. Surely you mean a bear has gotten Umiak's body?"

Akiak shook his brother off violently and pulled his jacket sleeve up, exposing the bleeding, half-circle-shaped wound where a piece was missing from his arm. "It is a *tuurngait* I tell you! It has possessed my son! Listen to me! Umiak walks!" He turned and gestured frantically back the way he had come. "I went to the sledge, and his body was missing! I feared it was a bear and looked for scat or a sign of my son, but it was my son who found me! He walks and he has attacked me! Just as the yellow-haired creature did!"

I could actually FEEL the fear rising in the crowd. Nothing that Qilaq or Buniq yelled helped to stop the panic now. There was a mad rush to get our tents packed and to get on our way.

The need to leave this place behind had grown exponentially.

Among the panic and disorder, no one save those closest to Qilaq, and myself, took notice when she collapsed. With a cry, I rushed to where she lay on the ground. I feared that the elder woman had suffered an illness of some sort. The kind of illness that attacks the heart of the elderly in times of high stress.

It was with a pang of joy I saw her chest rise and fall gently.

Amidst the raised noise of our camp packing up, and the fear we had lost our *Angatkut* before we were ready to say goodbye, no one heard the quiet shuffle and hesitant scuff of slippered feet.

No one heard the gurgling, wet, meaty sound that leaves a mouth with no throat.

But everyone heard the scream from Umiak's mate, Mauja.

Her shriek cut through the chilled spring air like the wind itself. Turning, we looked to see that she had fallen to her knees in the stones, surely cutting herself in the process. Tears streamed down her cheeks while one hand covered her open mouth, and the other pointed a shaky finger towards a shambling figure entering the ring of tents.

Step. Pause. Teeter. Step.

Step. Pause. Teeter. Step.

Mauja's face was contorted as she started to wail again, collapsing so her face lay buried in the rocks as she sobbed.

Umiak stood there, still dressed in his burial finery, his hair still mostly tucked into an elaborate braid. He was scuffed all over from when he clawed out from under the rocks that had protected him. And the wounds that the yellow-haired creature had given him stood out like dark pits in the paleness that was his dead flesh. No longer bleeding a true red blood, but oozing something unnatural.

There was a mad scramble as people tried to get away from the creature that Umiak had become.

All but Mauja, who still knelt in the rocks and the mud, crying for her mate.

The creature that was Umiak took notice of the keening woman, its face contorting into a frown, and slowly, with less hesitant steps, made its way towards her.

I stood frozen in horror as no one moved to help.

As no one called out to her to run.

I yelled for Mauja to run, to stand and get away. But she either didn't hear, or ignored me, as she continued to kneel and rock back and forth, her face covered by her hands.

And I swallowed a sudden surge of bile as I watched that shuffling figure approach Mauja, its arms outstretched.

Kneeling on the ground in front of her, it covered her rocking body with its own. The wounds along its neck, shoulder and arms dripped and ran with orange and yellow ooze. The fluid seeped down and along her neck, into her hair and down her back, sliding to coat the suede that protected her arms.

I could hear the muffled, high-pitched shriek from Mauja increasing in volume, covered as she was by the creature. It responded by grabbing her tighter, uttering a low, gurgling moan, and spewing more fluid along her back from the crater in its throat.

I couldn't take it any longer, just standing there watching. No one was moving to help her; they were all running around panicked, or standing and watching.

I couldn't let her be eaten and die like her mate had.

Grabbing a large rock, I ran towards the creature with a scream, hoping to drive it off. But I was prepared to destroy it with a blow to the temple, like Umiak had done to the yellow-haired creature.

The creature looked up, its milky, clouded eyes somehow focusing on me. It lumbered upright and I heard Mauja scream Umiak's name again. Rock raised, I jumped towards the creature, aiming high to its head.

I never saw the backhanded blow it dealt me.

I felt the fisted hand of the creature slam into my cheek, shattering the bone. The sickening crack echoed inside my head and the pain flared brightly. I felt the pop of my eye rupturing, the fluid gushing from the socket and the pain blinding me in an instant. I bit my tongue from the force of the blow, my teeth cracking like hazelnuts and the taste of my own blood filling my mouth. My head whipped around sharply, and instantly after the crack of my cheek breaking, I heard more snapping noises within my body. My head spun to the side at an impossible angle.

I never felt the ground as it rushed up to meet me.

It felt like no time had passed, but at the same time the world had ended.

I heard crying, could hear my mother calling my name over and over. I could feel wetness on my face. But it was probably from my eye, or the blood that poured from the open wound on my head. I was lying propped up on my mother's lap. I opened my eye to look up at her, and she cried all the more to see me awake.

Straining my eye in its socket, I tried to see what had become of Mauja.

Of the thing that was Umiak.

Had I saved her?

Akiak was kneeling on the ground, his son cradled in his arms. Umiak's form was still, and the body full of spears. Mauja lay beside him, and her mother stood above her still form, tearing her hair and crying. Mauja's blank, open eyes stared at me from a head turned the wrong way on her neck, and she drew no more breath.

I looked back up to my mother, my eye filling with tears. I tried to lift my hand to her cheek to offer comfort. It was then I realized that I couldn't move my hand.

Couldn't feel her hugging me tightly.

Couldn't feel the cold rocky ground beneath my body.

Couldn't feel my heart beat in my chest.

And I couldn't breathe.

My mouth opened and closed as I desperately tried to fill my lungs with air. I could hear the air moving in my body. But my heart no longer beat, and the blood no longer moved through my system.

My mother wailed harder and pulled me tighter to her, pressing my face to her neck as she rocked me back and forth, her sobs shaking my body. Over her shoulder I could see my father holding on to my brothers.

My vision was greying at the edges and I could hear the gasping noises I was making growing louder. My face hurt so much. I wished it would stop.

Opening my mouth again, my mother's ear was so close, surely she would hear.

"...I...I was...so...p-proud...I...got to sing...the *katajjaq...*"

MOTHER DOWN THE WELL

Ursula Pflug

I wanted more than anything to keep a stone tablet, but they always slipped out of my grasp back into the water. I felt there must be some rule I was missing. They were covered with inscriptions of course; that was the whole point of tablets. Without inscriptions they'd just have been meaningless slabs of stone. Once they'd slid back into the pond I couldn't remember the inscriptions anyway, so it was just the same as if they'd been blank, as if I hadn't read them, hadn't held so much wonder in my hands. Finally, one day a tablet stayed in my hands without being pulled back into the water, as if there was a giant down there tugging with all her might. Needless to say I felt stoked, pretty much like Moses, in fact. I wasn't expecting proclamations that I could share with multitudes though, or even just my village, but hoping for something more personal. A fortune cookie, a horoscope. Some light thing to cheer and sustain me when all else had failed.

I had trouble making out the engraved words, what with all the slime and chipping, so I left the tablet by the pond and went up to the house to get the wheelbarrow. My friend Blue was sitting on my back steps; he asked me what was up.

"I have a tablet," I said. "It's heavy so I'm going to get it into the wheelbarrow and bring it up to the well and scour it so I can read what it says."

Blue smiled. "I don't believe in that whole stone tablets business," he said, "but even if I did, aren't you supposed to get them up on mountaintops and not out of the lake?"

"Pond," I said. "Siena got hers out of the water too. She found it upriver. Maybe some places it's mountains but here it's water."

When he was around, Blue stopped by fairly regularly to see if I needed his muscles for anything. He is a big strong man with long blond hair and dark roots.

"Me either, really, but they're just so tantalizing. Siena got one that said…"

Blue smiled, as though now that I'd cloaked it as a bit of neighbourly competitiveness, my craziness made all kinds of newfound sense. "What did Siena's tablet say?" he asked.

"It said her third child would be a great leader of his people. Siena is confused because she couldn't have any more after her second daughter; all the doctors said so."

"She could always adapt a third one," Blue said, "in hopes of fulfilling the prophecy."

"You mean adopt," I said.

"I try very hard to mean what I say," Blue said, "and say what I mean."

He followed me back to the pond where my tablet lay in the grass. A long crack running through its middle, right where the words were.

"Tricky," he said.

"No doubt."

We headed back to the barnyard to get the wheelbarrow. It was between the well and the house, and I avoided the well like I always do, giving a little shudder.

"Why do you always avoid the well," Blue asked, "giving a little shudder?"

"My mother fell in before I was born."

"Really, Clarissa? You never told me you had a mother. I didn't want to pry so I didn't ask, but I always assumed you'd grown up without one."

I looked at Blue. He is a friend I can stand. Most people really just want to take advantage of your kind heart, should you be lucky enough to be in possession of one. They want to complain and borrow things and not return them and call that poor assemblage friendship, when really what you've been praying for is the friend who can help you map it all out, say the insightful thing, help you disentangle the sheets of fabric softener from the wash as it were. Help get your mom out of the well she fell in before you were born.

"I have spent my whole life coming up with ways to try and fish her out," I said.

"I take it none worked," Blue said.

"So it would seem."

"Getting mothers out of wells is something I have a little experience with, actually," he said.

"Really?" I asked, casually as I could so as not to give away the as-yet-unfounded hope I felt.

Talking about such things, we took the wheelbarrow down to the pond. Blue and I tried to lift the tablet in but it was too heavy, even with him on one end. That made me wonder whether the giantess who lived at the bottom of the pond hadn't pushed a little to help me get my tablet out onto the grass. The grass was wet, the tablet was wet; it was late October and the sky was overcast. I'd worn thick socks and rubber boots so my feet were okay but I needed an extra sweater under my sweater. I wanted to get this thing done so I could get back inside and have homemade squash soup and tea, perennial favourites for dinner.

"We'll lay the wheelbarrow on its side," I said, "then we'll tug the tablet into it; then you'll right the wheelbarrow with me holding the tablet to prevent it from slipping out again."

Blue rolled his eyes as if I might find this much exertion and coordination a stretch, but he didn't offer an alternate plan so we went ahead with mine, which turned out to be successful. We took turns pushing; Blue's turns were longer than mine. It was hard going through the long wet grass; there hasn't been much of a path down to the pond since I sold the last of the cows.

By the time we got to the barnyard we were so exhausted we dumped the tablet out of the wheelbarrow instead of gently laying it on its side, and even more gently sliding the tablet out onto the gritty dirt. Because of our carelessness it split in half right along the big diagonal crack, making an inordinately loud cracking sound as it did so, almost like thunder.

I thought I might cry, it was all so pitiful: the old well, the split tablet, the dirty barnyard. I'd tried planting flowers but even tansy and comfrey hadn't taken.

To cheer me up Blue said, "I told you I don't believe in tablets. I also don't believe in divine messages being accompanied by cracks of thunder."

"I'll just run up to the house and get a brush and some scouring powder," I said.

"Scouring powder?" Blue asked.

"You don't believe in scouring powder?" I asked.

"Just the syntax is unfamiliar. I call it Comet Cleanser or Old Dutch."

I came back from the house clutching a wire brush and a bottle brush and a brush for floors. The truth is I hate brushes now, the way the bristles are all shoddy and made of plastic.

"I'd go gentle with the wire one," Blue said. "That tablet is made of limestone and flakes easily. I wouldn't want to brush away what's left of the words."

"No ma'am," I said. I say this all the time, to anyone and everyone, including small girls and grandfathers. It is true I particularly like saying it to big strong young men like Blue, because that makes it funnier.

I cleaned out the carved words on my stone tablet as gently as I could with the sharp corner of a scraper and the wire brush. The well itself is open and level with the ground; no wonder, I sometimes think, that my mother fell in. There used to be a wall around it, a fieldstone-and-muck deal made a hundred years ago. Its crumbling accelerated at some point and I worried all the crumbles would make the water gritty, so I took it down. More truthfully, I called Blue and he came over and helped.

We teamed up to push the two halves of the tablet back together.

"Did you hear a clicking sound when they snicked together?" I asked.

"Clicking and snicking sounds we believe in," he said.

"The crack didn't disappear, though. The halves didn't melt back together."

"Accompanied by a hissing sealing sound," Blue said.

"And maybe some smoke," I laughed.

"I can make it out okay now but I think you should be the one to read it aloud," Blue said.

"Raise Your Mother," I said, after first reading it inside my head a couple of times to make sure I'd gotten it right.

"Well, that's kind of anticlimactic, isn't it?" he asked.

"Come in for soup and tea?" I shrugged.

"I would, Clarissa, but I've got a dinner date," Blue said.

After he had gone I stayed a moment alone by the well and thought about my mother. Trying to get her out of the well was a project that made me feel stupid so much more than it ever made me feel smart. I'd turn over stones and ask them what I should do and they'd answer me with a stony silence. I'd make tea and forget to drink it. I'd walk until my legs ached. I spent as much time as I could outside, communing with nature, with tree spirits; seeing myself or the fate of the world in the flight of a bird or the curve of the current around a submerged rock.

I'd wear necklaces that had once belonged to my mother or her mother or my beloved aunt, sometimes all three at once, thinking it would help. I'd stay up late worrying about my brother Dave, alone across the continent. After Father died I was alone too, but I stayed on at the family farm in eastern Ontario, so it was as if everyone was still there even when they weren't, Grandma and Grandpa and Father. And of course Mother was still alive, just living down the well.

I've only ever heard her voice the once, although Dave, who was there, has never been a hundred per cent sure it was even hers.

◀ ▶

After I retrieved the stone tablet, a doe came out of the woods every sunset for a fortnight to raid the gardens along the river, eating our lettuces. She was so pretty that we mainly forgave her foraging and just gathered on our verandahs to watch. My friend Siena kept her garden right up near the house, and after a couple of days the doe overcame her shyness and investigated Siena's kale. We stood together drinking tea and Siena pointed, showing me how the deer's left ear was split. We discussed whether this was the result of a wound or whether she'd been born that way. Siena also told me she had named the deer Georgia O'Keeffe. She seemed relieved when I didn't laugh at this affectation and was even familiar with the famous artist's work. I suggested that Georgia – the deer not the artist – was skilled like me and my mother at bridging dimensions, and that if I could only teach her to speak English we could have the nicest conversation about our metaphysical work.

"Or you could learn to talk deer," Siena nodded agreeably. "And how do you know Georgia-the-artist didn't know how to bridge dimensions? Many artists and writers do, you know."

"Of course. And equally many, or almost equally many, don't know that's what they're actually doing when they create. I just can't ask her, because she's dead, and wherever she is now is a place I don't know how to get to and ask things."

"How do you know your mother could, then?"

"For starters, she had another name for it. She called it exploring portals. It's why my grandparents bought the place next door. My mother said there was a particularly powerful portal in the well."

"Well, that explains a lot," Siena said.

"Agreed," I said.

"If it's true. Maybe she's been dead all this time and you're just telling yourself otherwise."

I laughed at Siena's joke and said goodbye so I could go home and plant. I expanded the gardens so much I didn't know what to do with all the food I grew. It was an earwiggy summer because of the damp but the insects left my crops alone. This seemed a boon from nature I had to repay and so I hugged trees on a daily basis, whispered to them to tell Ms. O'Keeffe to stop raiding our gardens. I can speak tree but not deer, but you gotta figure a tree and a deer could likely converse.

Lovely as Georgia was, I was worried come November deer season someone upriver would kill her in revenge for eating all their succulent young beans, which would make her flesh so very tasty and tender. Maybe the trees told her this advice of mine for she did eat all my beet tops, but my beet tops only, and I was able to push the dark red globes back into the ground where they simply grew new leaves, palest green streaked with crimson. She also ate my beet tops in a pattern, leaving interesting designs in my rows. At first I thought my eyes were fooling me but after the third time I realized she was mimicking her famous namesake, leaving art behind everywhere she went.

It was because of this succession of events that I felt closer than ever before to raising my mother. It wasn't just retrieving a stone tablet and reading its self-evident yet powerful message, or my special relationship with Georgia O'Keeffe that gave me hope, but the fact that sometimes now when I called down the well my mother answered back, a cool burbling cry that let me know she was submerged but employing some method she knew for breathing underwater.

My aunt's and grandmother's necklaces were beautiful, green jade and red carnelian respectively, but my mother's was the nicest, opulently beaded from coral and amber and finely wrought silver filigree. I knew that once she emerged from the well I would have to give it back. I didn't mind because I was looking forward to the conversations we would have.

"Have you ever noticed how people may be called Blue or Red, but rarely Green or Purple and certainly never Orange?" I imagined asking her. "Why is that?"

"What did you think the tablets were for?" I imagined her asking back, while putting on the necklace I'd been so careful not to lose.

The only time she ever spoke aloud was twenty years ago. She said, "Magic is a skill that can take generations to learn, and many incarnations."

Dave and I had turned thirty and thirty-one that year. We stared at the speaker we had set up beside the well, astonished, waiting for more. Then Dave proposed that maybe someone had hacked the transmitter and interposed a recording of a woman's voice uttering these cryptic words, just to embitter us. After all, we didn't know what her voice actually sounded like, did we? I felt more likely that it indeed was our mother, and that she was trying to explain how she had abandoned us in favour of the study of magic, so compelling a task she couldn't give it up, not even for us.

Dave nodded when I told him my opinion, but still he was gone west before Easter and only returned three Christmases out of ten. He's invited me to Vancouver Island but I've always used the excuse that it's too hard to find someone reliable to look after the livestock. Of course the last cow has been sold for some years now, so I wonder what is still holding me back?

I think maybe my mother didn't throw herself in the well; I think maybe she jumped. Everyone knows there is an inter-dimensional portal down there. Before he died, my grandfather even told me it was a selling point. Perennial gardens, good barn, older farmhouse with new 200-amp service; steel roof; wood/oil furnace; portal.

"What's this?" my mother apparently asked. She was just a young unmarried lady back then.

"I don't know," the real estate rep said. "It must be a typo. I've never heard of a portal before. I'll go home and check the master listing."

"I know what a portal is," my eighteen-year-old mother allegedly said. "Magic, of course, is not at heart either wand waving or spell weaving or the gathering by moonlight of certain types of nuts, berries and owl innards but a form of thought," she apparently continued. "The other things in the aforementioned or any other list are just supports, but without mastering the type of thinking that is called magical, all your crystals and ceremonies may be worse than useless."

My grandmother fished a pen out of her purse and wrote it down right away. This speech was the first, and almost the last clue that there was anything different about my mother. Whether Grandma got my mother's words right or not we have no way of knowing, because our grandfather didn't also copy down this strange proclamation. And my mother certainly didn't write down her channeled wisdom. Maybe if she had, she'd have had the strength of will to stay out of wells. She might've written books and inspirational tracts she could've sold and bought me and Dave new school clothes come September, instead of the church sale and Value Village rags Pa was able to provide.

And so they bought the place. Sometimes people assume we've been living here for generations, beneficiaries of a land grant. It is true that during the Irish Famine the local government gave away lots of hundred-acre tracts of swamp and brush and bush to starving farmers from Ireland. That was what the Williams Treaty was all about, swindling the local Mississauga out of what they had left, so it could be given away for free to white folk. Blue and his cousins still complain about it and why wouldn't they?

Mainly, the only people who think we're a land grant family are newcomers, for the old timers around here still know exactly who is who and some of them are old enough to find it a point of scorn that my best friend is indigenous. I figure that along with a lot of other things that is their problem more than it is mine.

My mother jumped down the well the day after her wedding to a local settler boy. Everyone thought her young husband must just have been awful until a beautiful baby girl floated to the surface nine months later. That would've been me. Dave followed a year later, although how Pa impregnated Ma once she was living down the well I was too shy to ever ask.

Pa did a fine job raising us. I think he missed my mother a lot and wished he had been able to provide whatever it was she got suckling at the portal down the well, but of course he could not. Special as he may have been, he couldn't provide her with whatever other dimensional flavour it was she loved best, for it simply doesn't exist here on Earth, not now and probably never. Ma never did tell me what it was either.

◀ ▶

This year's harvest was a bumper crop in everything the earwigs didn't eat, although I've had better-tasting tomatoes; they prefer things on the dry side. Siena and I bottled for weeks. Come November, Blue went hunting; he said it was how he gardened. Successful on the second day, he brought me half a deer for my freezer once they'd done cutting and wrapping it at the organic abattoir. I thanked him and he asked whether he could tan the hide in my barnyard. He lives in a little apartment in town, so there is nowhere to tan a hide unless he does it in the parking lot of his building, which wouldn't work for a number of reasons.

I said okay. Once he was done with the hide he nailed it up in my barn and said I was welcome to it. This seemed puzzling to me but I figured he had his own reasons for doing things, as well as his own ways. When I went and checked I saw the hide had a telltale slit in its ear. This made me sad. Would I be able to eat this beautiful wild creature we had fed all summer? Had Georgia been easy to kill because she was half tame from snacking on our carrots while we stood by and watched? Had my whispered warnings to the trees gone unheard after all? I didn't know whether to tell Blue the story or not. I didn't want to make him feel bad, for the food and the skin were beautiful gifts and he would not have shot her had he known she was our pet. As to the mother-raising operation, he suggested we try sinking rare earth magnets into the well.

◀ ▶

We worked most of the morning and half the afternoon with a complicated assemblage of pulleys and ropes, magnets, delicious snacks, and photographs of my brother and me when we were babies. The snacks were for us, not for my mother. Like a baby in amniotic fluid, we figured she had been nourished by the earth herself while she was sunk. When we finally got her up we stood discussing how to get her back to the farmhouse. It was because she was too heavy to carry. Blue is a really big and really strong man but he couldn't lift her, not even a few inches off the ground. We finally got her into the wheelbarrow, but it took the two of us. I am as shrimpy as they come but was still able to help with the leverage. It all seemed like a rerun of our tablets adventure except so much more important. Would she split in half if I dumped her accidentally? And what would her insides look like if that happened?

We trundled her up to the house. Blue kept saying he'd never seen anything like it, and he'd gotten a few women up out of wells.

"Anything like what?" I asked.

"The amount of water," he said. "The wheelbarrow keeps filling. We've had to empty it four times between the well and the house."

"True. It's as much water each time as a king-size duvet you've just removed from a machine where the spinner doesn't work," I said.

"It's got to be magic on that count," Blue pointed out.

"How so?" I asked.

"More water than the body of one small woman can contain," he said.

"It must be some portal down there."

"That's what they've always said," he agreed.

Artificial respiration. They used to teach it to all the children at swimming class. Maybe it was so that should their mothers throw themselves down wells, the children could perform this trick once they were fished out. And once they were able to breathe by themselves again, their mothers' eyes would open. That was my hope anyway.

We got her up onto the table in the farmhouse, an old varnished job, slightly better than the one you use for slaughtering chickens on. Then I pinched her nose shut tight and pushed air into her lungs, over and over and over. You are supposed to give up after three minutes, or is it twenty? When do you make that decision, and how? Blue said I should just keep going, since magic was involved. I said I didn't believe in magic.

"Portals then," he said. "Call it portals."

Those I believe in.

I kept going, breathing into her mouth, and then the moment came when her chest started to rise and fall, rise and fall.

Rise and fall, rise and fall.

"Well, that'll be that then," Blue said, making for the door.

"Stay for soup and tea?"

"Dinner date, Clarissa."

I meant to thank him profusely but he was already gone.

I sat and looked at my mother whom I had never seen before, even though she had carried me for nine months and given birth to me from inside the bottom of a well. It was the original water birth.

Her eyes were open and she was breathing. I put pillows under her but left her on the table as she was still too heavy to move. The pillows soaked through immediately. She was dribbling big puddles all the time as if she were an unending source of water.

"For the last fifty years I have been sure my life would have been different if I had only had a normal mother like other folks, and not a drowned one," I told her. "Waterlogged, silent, unmoving. Your hands waving feebly, not that Dave and I could even see them except when we attached water-proof video cameras to poles and stuck them down the well."

I think that is what sent my little brother to Vic in the end. He couldn't stand Christmas after first our grandparents and then Pa died. Just me and Dave left, sending cameras and mics down the well, hoping Ma would wave and offer Christmas wishes.

"Why are people never called Orange?" I asked, after try-ing to help her sit up for the fourth time.

"Give me back my necklace," she gurgled.

I went and got it from the bathroom and clasped it around her neck, gently as I could. She didn't thank me. She fingered the necklace as if she knew each bead from memory but didn't look down at it. She didn't speak again either. Mainly she dripped and dribbled.

After a couple of days I got tired of all the mopping. I put her back in the wheelbarrow and took her to the barn. She had drained so much water I could push her on my own now. Even in the barn she was still spitting water. Finally I hung her up, thinking it might help. Thin rivulets streamed out of her fingers and her feet. I began to realize she had probably been drowned all this time, after all. While our resuscitative methods seemed to have worked, her breathing and even her speech probably weren't breathing and speech per se, so much as some kind of enteric nervous system response.

◀   ▶

Blue has been scarce. Maybe getting mothers out of wells is more exhausting than he makes it look. No one calls anymore except the telemarketers. I keep making lists and forgetting them. I make tea and forget to drink it. I stay up late worrying about my brother. I wear my grandmother's and my aunt's necklaces, but I don't think they're helping.

When I go down to check on Ma she blinks at me, or maybe I just think she does. She fingers her own necklace almost constantly, wearing away the filigree. Georgia O'Keeffe's skin is nailed to the wall beside her. I think one day I will use it to make a coat for my mother. She would like a deerskin coat I think, after having spent decades down a well. The damp must have seeped into her bones something fierce.

RAT PATROL

Kevin Cockle

"Well, that oughta do it," Arthur Low said, arching his stiff back after placing the last of the warfarin-laced rolled-oat squares in Travis McGuinn's massive bale stacks. Could have used barium carbonate or zinc phosphide out here, but Travis had grandchildren and warfarin would be safer if there were any mishaps. The bait squares were also obviously marked – little pieces of brightly coloured confetti woven into the oats. Most kids knew that meant rat poison, kept their hands to themselves.

"Yep," said Travis, squinting up at the bright blue sky, measuring the chance of precipitation through force of habit. "Well, thought I'd better have you check. Could'a sworn I saw a rat among the bales, day before last."

Probably a hedgehog, thought Arthur. *Or a ground squirrel.* "Did the right thing," Low said as he removed his ball cap, revealing an almost entirely bald head – a thin grey line held its ground from ear to ear at the back. False sightings were common, but keeping Alberta rat-free was no joke and even though Arthur Low was the pest control officer in these parts, it was up to everyone to be vigilant. Arthur didn't mind the false alarms. He'd have to check these farms and ranches any-way – every building, every structure at least once a year – but coming out when people called made things more social.

"Looks like a sprinkle on the way, prob'ly around 5:00 or 6:00 or so. Good to…" Travis prattled on as Arthur nodded, shifting his gaze and attention back to the truck. Jake Saunders was toeing dirt, looking restless. Low felt the twinge of a smile on his lips, fought it down. Kid was itching for mischief right about now – have to give him something to do.

"…you know?" Travis said, waiting for a response. Arthur double-clutched, opened his mouth to say something, when Jake hollered from the truck, "Hey, Arthur – phone's ringing."

"Excuse me, Trav," Arthur said, big hand reassuring on the smaller man's arm: saved by the bell. Low ate up the distance with bow-legged strides, getting to the cab and taking the big hand-held unit from the boy.

"Ya-lo – this is Arthur." John Lockey's brassy voice scraped loud over the cell – even Jake could hear it. "Calm down, son," Arthur said, dropping his voice to instill some order. He listened as Lockey screeched, Jake staring up with an interested frown. Arthur's face had gone rigid, blue eyes steeling up as he nodded, taking in the info.

"Sit tight, Johnny, okay?" Arthur said when the voice finally stopped squawking. "I'm over at McGuinn's right now, but I'm on my way. You get Agnes and Jean back in the house and tell 'em to stay there. And you stand up to Jean if you have to, John, you hear me? You tell her to stay clear of Hank until I get there. You understand me?" There was throttled agreement – as though the prospect of standing up to Jean Dolan was only slightly less daunting than facing down the minions of Hell.

Arthur switched the phone off and made eye contact with Jake long enough for the kid to say, "What?"

Arthur didn't know what to say right off the bat. He went with, "Get in the truck," and promptly followed his own advice.

They pulled out of McGuinn's with a tornado trail of dust beneath the Ford's back wheels, Arthur driving fast, the wind rushing in through Jake's open window.

Jake Saunders. Arthur Low was sixty years old, had never had kids, his first and only wife having died in the attempt some forty years ago. Never remarried, and as the years went by he'd forgotten about wanting certain things – got so he didn't need them. He was friendly enough, not what you'd call cold, but he kept his distance from folks, until eventually things just got smooth and even and easy. What people knew of him, they tended to like, and Arthur stopped them right there. So when Todd Evers had asked him to take Jake on for the summer, Arthur had said the only thing that made sense: "No bloody way!"

"Come on, Artie." Todd had grown up not so far away in Brooks, knew Low through family connections. Evers had fought his way up Tory ranks to Minister of Agriculture under the McCullough administration, and the old "Mr. Low" of Todd's youth had been replaced by "Artie" in lockstep with the rise. Arthur didn't much care for politicians, but as he was the "rat patrol" for the southeastern edge of the province, he dealt with the Department of Agriculture on a regular basis. Evers wasn't bad, as the breed went.

"What do I know about kids?" Arthur shook his head.

"What does anyone know about kids? Look, my sister Tracey's got her hands full. Husband bolted, she's got two younger daughters to look after and this kid Jake's on the verge, you know? Caught him with a little weed – nothing

serious, but she doesn't know where he got it, who he's hanging with. This kid needs some old-time upbringing, Art.
You're the steadiest hand I know, and I'll bet you could use
the help over the summer. Think of him as unpaid labour."

"I pretty much got that covered."

"That's funny – you're a funny cowboy – I like that.
Seriously."

"But…where will he stay? What will he do?"

"Mattress on a floor, Art – the harder the better. Put him
in a tent out back the cabin. Make him mow lawns and carry
heavy shit, you know? He's thirteen. He needs to get his act
together or he'll get to a place where I can't step in anymore,
you know?"

On and on like that. Todd Evers hadn't gotten to where
he was by being unpersuasive, and Arthur knew eventually
he'd be taking on an apprentice, but before he gave in he
fixed Todd with a meaningful stare and asked him point-
blank: "What if I have to take care of badness while he's
around?"

Evers had smiled indulgently, like young men new to
power always seemed to do. Like they knew all the answers.
"Oh. Yeah, that. When was the last time you had to deal with
any of that?"

"Maybe five, six years ago," Arthur admitted. "But that's
only counting when It takes shape so you can handle It. You
can't tell me It hasn't been active for the last little while. You
can't tell me everything that's happened the last few years –
that's all just been back luck."

"Yeah, well. From what I understand, the peak threat
from the region came back in the thirties – It doesn't have the
juice to seriously hurt people anymore. Look, if it so happens

the kid sees something scary, maybe that's not so bad. Maybe if a kid got a sense that there's something bad at the end of the road for kids who make lousy decisions – maybe that's not such a bad thing. But you and I both know the worst he'll see is some traps and a whole lot of hard labour."

"That ain't the worst," Arthur had said, having seen "the worst" firsthand. "Not by a long shot."

Jake busted up the reverie with one of his sudden questions, forcing Arthur to refocus on the present. "Why you got so many hats?" the kid blurted. Johnny Cash rumbled on the radio, barely audible over the wind.

"What?" Arthur said.

"You got about fifty ball caps hanging on the wall at the cabin. But you always wear this same old beat-up 'Toro' cap. What's with all the hats?"

Arthur shrugged. "People give me hats – I collect 'em."

"You collect hats," Jake grinned, shaking his head. Arthur grinned too. Couldn't help himself. Kid brought it out of him.

It hadn't been as bad, as awkward, as Arthur had thought. Jake wasn't some juvenile delinquent – he was shy, reserved, but he wasn't hard-bitten or looking for trouble. He was lazy by nature, and drifted where the wind tended to blow, but he wasn't like those kids Arthur saw on the news, shooting up stores and rampaging through schools. Jake was the kind of kid who took his cues from the strongest person in his immediate vicinity, for good or ill. And when Arthur had been the only person around, and Jake had learned how the townsfolk, farmers and ranchers all respected "the rat-patrol man," Jake had responded in kind. Kid hadn't enjoyed the 5:00 a.m. starts, hardy Scottish porridge breakfasts and manual labour at first, but he'd come around. Got so he'd dry dishes without being asked, while Arthur washed. Seemed to enjoy watching CFL games – Arthur in his big old E-Z chair, Jake sitting cross-legged on the floor. By and by, Arthur had to admit, taking care of the kid wasn't a chore. He hadn't realized how empty his little cabin had become, until he'd let someone else in.

The Ford surged off gravel onto blacktop, roaring along down Highway 41 as Arthur coaxed the engine to sixty (he still reckoned in miles per hour). He'd been putting off buying a new truck for a couple of years, wanting to squeeze every last drop of utility out of the existing one, but now he could have used some brand-new horsepower. Out of the corner of his right eye, Arthur spotted an abandoned farmhouse leaning atop a low hill, grey and seemingly fragile, yet refusing to go down. Countryside was full of such stubborn relics. Reminded him of the people. Reminded him of Hank and Jeannie Dolan.

Hank Dolan. Arthur shook his head. Stress of the mad cow scare, the ongoing crush of financial problems, and a sudden stroke had used Hank up in a series of unrelenting hammer blows. It had been sickening to watch – Hank making desperate moves, working harder, worrying more – and every decision just turning on him and biting him back like fangs in the face. Death had come as a release after all those trials – for Hank, and for Jean – but of course, even then, there had been mistakes to be made.

Jean Dolan was as shrewd a business person as you could find – had no qualms about making pragmatic decisions. Some of the local ladies even accused her of being *too* pragmatic – like she enjoyed the feel of making tough decisions, and having everyone know she was making them. After the funeral, she'd wasted no time restructuring – got the books prettied up for final liquidation, started divestiture with single-minded focus. She was getting out, and neither her love of the land, nor her memories of the previous life would stop her from making the best damn deals she could. But what Arthur still couldn't figure was why she insisted on handling the funeral the way she had. She'd been ruthless, even merciless with every other consideration since, but when it had come to Hank's remains, Jeannie'd been downright sentimental.

They'd buried Henry Dolan whole, in the little cemetery that bordered on Smith's and Crowley's – the one that held bodies stretching back to the flu epidemics of 1918. Some of *those* bodies hadn't stayed put either, had to be handled by the men who would eventually be legitimized and funded by the province as "rat patrols." Arthur had warned her against it, but in the end Jeannie Dolan did what Jeannie Dolan wanted. Truth is, the harder Arthur had pressed, the more resolved Jean had been to go ahead. Couldn't really blame her, but Arthur had had a bad feeling about the whole thing – the queasy inevitability of it, like getting Hank into that particular ground might have been the point all along.

Jake fiddled with the radio, searching for and finally picking up a weak signal out of Lethbridge: the monotone thumping of some rap artist. Arthur winced. Jake started nodding his head in time with the so-called music, riding his arm out the window like an airplane wing in the wind.

"You know the Empire State Building in New York? The top of it?" Jake said, nimble mind taking off on its own tangent. Arthur and Jake had logged a ton of miles in the old Ford over the summer and Jake's abrupt musings had helped to make that time fly.

"Yeah?" Arthur said, perplexed, but knowing that resolution was right around the corner.

"It's supposed to be a docking port for airships. Is that wild or what? In the thirties, they figured Zeppelins would cross the Atlantic and anchor-up on the Empire State Building. Guess they tried it once and it didn't work. But still. That's cool."

Arthur chuckled – the kid's curiosity was mind-boggling. Some of that had gotten him into trouble, but overall it was an endearing quality. Arthur wondered how many kids knew that about the Empire State Building. He wondered how many kids thought about airships at all, these days.

Suddenly the feeling hit Arthur like a sandbag in the stomach: how fond he'd grown of the kid in a few short weeks. It had been nothing but early mornings, chores, long drives, routine border checks, trap laying and investigations, but the gaps had been filled in by Jake's inquisitiveness, good-natured grumbling and quirky sense of humour. It had been a unique summer for Arthur Low, the most memorable, maybe the best of his life since Emily had passed. He wouldn't ask, wouldn't even bring it up, but if Todd Evers suggested that Jake should spend next summer helping out on patrol, that would be just fine with Arthur.

There was, however, the little matter of Hank Dolan come back to life that needed to be tended to first.

Jake wouldn't necessarily be in danger over at Dolan's – most of the time, people rarely got more than badly spooked by these events. Evers had been right about that – badness was reduced to mean little tricks and illusions these days, but this thing with Hank – it was positively muscular, bringing him all the way back like that. Arthur hated having to expose Jake like this, but there wasn't time to take the kid home first, and besides – when it came right down to it – Arthur wanted him where he could see him. "Jacob," Arthur said, reaching to turn off the radio.

"Yeah?"

"When we get to Jeannie Dolan's, you stay right with me until I figure out what's what, all right?"

"Sure, yeah."

"Yeah. Don't go wandering off."

"They got rats? Real rats? Finally!"

"Yeah," Arthur said, face grim. "Maybe they do."

◀ ▶

"Up at Crowley's they had that dog, went wild and killed a couple hogs, then went after Jimmy Crowley, remember?" John Lockey said, trying to recall other instances of badness in his lifetime. Agnes Dolan, Jean's older sister, sat in the rocking chair, gently squeaking back and forth. Jean sat with one broad hip on the porch rail, rifle across her lap, occasionally turning and looking over her shoulder past the circular barn.

"And when I was little, supposedly this drilling crew went missing, just left all their stuff out in the open," Johnny continued. "Nobody found anything except the rig and the sheds and tools and stuff."

Jean nodded. "Yep, that's true. The dog wasn't nothing though – just rabies. Nobody got hurt."

"You remember Grandma telling us those stories about the flu?" Agnes piped up, eyes wide, looking frail and small in her pink summer dress. With her white hair tugged back into a disapproving bun, she was just about as opposite in build and appearance to her sister as a woman could be. "Whole towns got killed off around here and then just disappeared. There's towns around here that ain't even on maps anymore – just old houses and broken-down fences. Died faster than the census takers could keep track."

"The flu's the flu – nothing supernatural about that," Jean said, brushing a fly away from her ear. "True enough about the ghost towns though."

"And you don't want to be going to those towns either," Agnes said, warming to her recollections. "Maybe they got cleaned out and maybe they didn't. That was before the rat men you know." She took a sip of Coke, then kept on babbling. "I 'member Grandma telling me, 'It's just bad land, Agnes' – that's what she used to say. Just something about this place don't like people living here. Saves Itself up till times get bad, then comes on strong, gets people when they're at their most vulnerable." That got a look from Jean, because it sounded right. Times had sure as hell been bad lately. On top of that, she'd been missing Hank, what with making plans to go and leave all the memories behind. She'd been missing him, and now…here he was.

"*Jesus!*" John shoved himself up off the wall and pointed – Jean stood and turned. Coming around the western curve of the round barn, trailing his hand along the wooden wall of it, Hank Dolan wandered, like he'd never seen the place before. Jean swallowed, clutched the gun up tight. Agnes caught her breath, stopped rocking, and gripped her woven God's eye the harder.

Hank looked around, shuffled to the old water pump, ran his hand across it. Occasionally as he turned, his eyes shone silver, and his face bore no expression. He scuffed at dirt, rubbed his hands on the sides of his jeans. No plan, no hurry. He seemed lost, aimless, random.

But eventually, he saw them on the porch.

"Get inside," Jean said, bringing the gun barrel up. She was a big woman, Jeannie Dolan was, shoulders and forearms like a man. When she barred your way, you paid attention.

"But Arthur said…" John began.

"You take my sister inside, you hear?"

"But Arthur said you should go inside too – I told you that – we all should."

Hank began walking towards the porch, eyes shining. Eyes staring. Fixated now, no longer random.

Jean moved to the steps and primed her weapon. She felt her own eyes get moist at the sight of the only man she had ever loved, spat out from this spoiled ground and returned to her like some massive, cosmic taunt. She cursed herself for not having listened to Arthur Low on this. "Henry John Dolan!" Jean shouted. "Don't come any closer. I'll put you down, Hank, you know I will."

Hank stopped. Nodded. He raised his right hand in an old familiar gesture, the one that said, "All right, Jean, you win," and turned away. Now he was interested in the barn again. Started heading over towards it.

Jean felt her throat tighten, forced herself to swallow down those tears. *Hurry Arthur*, she thought. *For God's sake, hurry.*

◀ ▶

The Ford cut off asphalt and tore onto loose gravel again, churning up a comet's tail of dust as Arthur took the back road to Dolan's. Coming in from the north, they could look across the grazing field with its clumps of foxtail and crocus, see the distinctive round bow of the grey-green barn, and as they progressed, they could see the main house in back. The Dolan place was old, but elegant, with white clapboard siding and a pointed turret on the western side. They drove right through the open gate, geared down as they passed round the back of the house, then took a curling route into the courtyard out front. No dogs to greet them, Arthur noticed. Nobody around anywhere. Arthur took a good look at all his compass points before he cut the engine.

Arthur and Jake got out of the cab, went round the back of the truck. Jake wasn't bowlegged, but he walked as though he were – he'd picked up a lot of Arthur's mannerisms over the last few weeks. In the back of the truck there were lockboxes nailed into the bed – long and white – holding the poisons, traps and tools of the rat patrol trade. Jake was nonchalant as he assumed he'd seen the contents before, but when Arthur hauled out a sawed-off, large-bore shotgun, Jake whistled and said, "Holy shit!"

"Watch your language," Arthur mumbled by rote. He reached for another object from the same box: a foot-long knife in a leather scabbard. Arthur pulled the thick blade out to check the edge, and the fierce steel gleamed in the sunlight.

"What are those markings?" Jake asked, taking in the bone pommel and queer designs on the sheath.

"Zulu words, I'm told." Arthur was low key, didn't want to get into it. The knife had been handed down from previous rat patrol men, originally brought to the country by an RCMP officer who had served in the Boer War and spent some time exploring Africa afterward. Something about the weapon solved certain problems peculiar to Southern Alberta – Arthur had no idea why. But if Hank Dolan really were up and around, Arthur would likely need the knife more than he would the shotgun.

They headed towards the house.

Steps creaked underfoot as they made the porch, tired old nails groaning under the weight. A half-empty plastic bottle of Coke stood beside the rocking chair. Arthur progressed to the door, knocked on it.

The curtain at the window to the right of the door moved, then the door opened: Jeannie stood armed and ready, eyes red, but stern.

"Arthur," she said, tone warning him not to say he told her so.

"Where is he?" Arthur asked.

"He's in the barn. Went in about fifteen minutes ago, hasn't come out."

"Who you got with you?"

"Just Agnes and Johnny. I called and cancelled the other fella I had coming in today."

"All right. You remember Jacob?"

"Surely. Afternoon, Jake."

"Mrs. Dolan."

"Take him inside, will you?"

Jake perked up, sensing an adult conspiracy to cheat him out of a rat sighting. "Hey man, I'm your backup!"

"Hey 'man' – you're staying inside. Have a cookie. I'll be right back."

Jean opened the screen door wide for Jake, exchanged a hard look with Arthur. Arthur set off towards the barn without a backward glance.

The doors were open. Arthur approached cautiously, but his boots announced his presence by crunching gravel – whatever was in there would know he was coming. He came in off the left flank, shotgun forward, then stepped past the threshold.

It was gloomy, but not dark – open loft doors illuminated golden motes of hay and dust suspended in midair. Great spools of wire lay off to the left, alongside old hand-tools, branding irons, gas cans, couple old kerosene lamps, wooden planks. The animal pens had been dismantled to make room for storage, but the steel stanchion posts were still there. Centre of the barn was taken up by the silo, but Arthur knew the tack room lay on the far side. He could smell hay from the loft, and cattle musk still prevailed despite the absence, forever, of the animals.

Just to the right of the silo stood the Dolan's green and yellow '49 Farmall Cub – still the finest vintage tractor this side of Empress. And on the runner of that classic machine sat Hank Dolan, hands on his thighs, head inclined as he stared at the ground between his legs. Made sense he'd wind up at the Cub. Even pragmatic old Jean hadn't been able to bring herself to sell it, Hank had loved it so.

"Hank?" Arthur said.

"Come on in," Hank said, voice thick with phlegm, but clearly recognizable as the man who had once been Jean

Dolan's husband. He was young again, brought back at his best.

Arthur stalked cautiously into the relative cool of the barn. He could hear Hank's breathing, the rattle of it, thick and croupy in his chest.

"How you doing, Hank?" Arthur asked, close enough to blow the man's head clean off his shoulders, if it came to it.

"I'm all right. I'm handling it." Hank looked up, and his eyes, nose, and mouth shone with a silver light, as though his head were a jack-o'-lantern, lit with a harsh magnesium bulb inside. "This is why they pay you the big bucks, eh, Art?"

Arthur smiled. "Guess so."

"You ever wonder about it? How the government knows about this land, always has known? Weird ain't it? Why wouldn't they just warn people outright? Make it official."

"Easier to just have a rat patrol, Hank. Have us look after things. Just easier, that's all." Arthur thought of Todd Evers. Current generation of politicians weren't even sure there was a problem – were starting to doubt there ever had been.

"Yeah. 'Spose so." Hank rubbed his jeans, a nervous gesture without any anxiety attached to it. More a memory of a mannerism – doing the things that Hank Dolan would have done. Arthur repressed a shudder. "You gonna shoot me, Arthur?" Hank added, "That how it's done?"

"Depends. You gonna hurt anybody?"

"Maybe, yeah. I feel it, you know? Deep down, this feeling. Like I want to hurt Jeannie. Burn the house down. Head on over to Crowley's and do some things there too. It's ugly, but I'm still controlling it."

For now, Arthur thought. "You still angry?" Arthur said, referring to the mad cow disaster that had ultimately killed

Hank Dolan in the first place: the desperation and the macro-economic lunacy of it all.

"I guess so. There's that rage, yeah. But that's not why It chose me."

"No?"

"Nah, it ain't interested in me. It's using me 'cause I'm weak. Knows I wanted to see Jean again before she left for good – used that on me to get me here. But mostly It wants Jeannie. You know that's really what It always wants: the strong. Don't come any stronger than Jeannie. It'll cut me loose on her if It has to, but It's hoping to break her instead."

"Break her?"

"Sure – get to her. Can't be easy on her, seeing me again. That's what this land does – disheartens folks, discourages 'em. Gets 'em to quit. That's what it's really all about. Take on the strong and beat them down. I still can't figure why."

"Well, not much to figure," Arthur reasoned. "Something doesn't want us here. Never has."

"Yeah." Hank straightened, looked around. "It's so strange, seeing things from this side. Everything's all bright, washed out, until you get to a building or a piece of machinery or something. Then it's kind of shaded, like black-and-white TV. I think I can see why It hates us, just can't put it into words."

"Hank," Arthur paused, not knowing how to put it, not knowing how much longer to wait. "When you want to go, you just tell me, all right?"

Hank nodded, face stiff, but conveying the essence of sadness in eyeless sockets, glowing mouth. "I appreciate that, Arthur. I'm glad you're here."

"No problem."

"Arthur? You know you're one of the strong too, right?"

"What?"

Hank turned to stare at Arthur, looked as though he might be struggling with the words. "You're one of the ones It really wants. You and Jeannie."

"What are you talking about?"

"Something's different about you now, I can see that, and It can see it too. You're open, Arthur, just a bit. It's sniffing around you these days, sniffing at something It ain't smelled on you before."

"What's that?"

"Weakness. You got a weakness, buddy. I think it's that kid."

Arthur shifted his weight. He didn't like Hank talking about Jake. Jake wasn't part of this discussion.

"That don't make any sense, Hank."

"Sure it does. That's how It operates. Looks for something It can use on you, then gets after you with it. Like me and Jeannie. Only you haven't had anything It could use. Till now."

"Nothing's getting after me, and nothing's getting after Jake. I can guarantee you that."

"Let me do you a favour, Arthur. Let me show you something."

"What?"

"Let me show you something. I'll show you something before I go. I think you have to look me in the eyes to see it."

"Hank..." Arthur raised the shotgun on instinct.

"You look and I'll show you something. I think it's important, Arthur. If you can't see your own weakness, maybe you can see it through me."

Arthur looked. For three steady heartbeats, all he saw was starlight pulsing out from a dead man's head, but on the fourth beat...

The barn door tilted open just a bit further – rusty hinges singing out a tortured tune – revealing a figure so brightly backlit that Arthur couldn't make it out. Then, as the figure stepped forward, it was clearly recognizable as Jake. It was Jake with his face and his yellow tee shirt covered, just drenched in blood. Only when the kid started to smile, and raised his right fist in a gesture of awful triumph, could Arthur understand. "Couldn't have done it without you…" a voice gurgled in Arthur's head. The sound was throaty and ragged – lungs bogged down in mucus and blood.

Arthur staggered back a few feet, mind reeling from the vision: *That wasn't real! It hadn't happened.*

It hadn't happened…

But it could.

"Hank…" Arthur said, warning at the edge of his voice. He hadn't seen Hank stand up from the runner, hadn't seen him take that prowling step forward.

"You better get to it," Hank said. "Don't think I can hold on much longer."

◀ ▶

The Ford's engine idled, shaking the truck as Arthur gazed across the road at the silhouette of that old abandoned farmhouse on the low hill. Sun was setting, casting thrilling shadows around the house, spilling in golden between the cracks. House had no business standing upright after all this time, all that weather. The wood had been burned grey by seventy-odd years of prairie sun, withered by seventy-odd years of prairie winter.

Arthur had dispelled Hank with the Zulu knife, and Dolan had gone easy, painlessly – not wanting to fight it. Then Arthur had spread symbolic bait-squares around the barn, blessing – at least that was the term he used – the squares with the knife and memorized ritual. The words and gestures meant nothing to him – he assumed both were African, but he really had no clue. Whatever the origin, the practice would make the Dolan farm safe for a while.

He'd had a long heart-to-heart with Jean, about a lot of things. Put her mind to rest about Hank, but also, squared things about Jake. Jean had agreed Jake could stay the night while Arthur gathered up the boy's things. In the morning, John Lockey would drive Jake back to Edmonton, back to his mother, and away from this particularly nasty stretch of land along the southeastern border of Alberta. Arthur hadn't even said goodbye, hoping the sting of it would keep the kid away for good and all. The look of Jake's face, his mouth glistening black with blood, was never far from Arthur's mind, and every time he caught a glimpse of that vision, his skin writhed enough to make him twitch.

But Jeannie'd rattled him just before he left. "What if," she said, after they'd gone through it all, "what if It *wants* you to send the boy away? What if you're stronger having him here? You can't trust a vision that came from…you know. *That.* Could be just a trick, like It does. A trick to manipulate you into giving up something that could make you even tougher than you already are. Having a kid around's like a second chance for you, Arthur. Maybe It doesn't want to see you happy – you ever thought about that?"

Arthur hadn't known what to say. The implication was that maybe all along, decisions he had made about his life and his situation had somehow been…guided, nudged along without him knowing, but in the end, he couldn't get his mind around it. It was too subtle, too cute, and he didn't have a chess-player's mentality. He was stone steady, that's what he was, that's what he brought to the dance. He knew the land around here measured Its victories in inches, got to people one sadness, one doubt at a time, and It had the patience to wear a man down like rain on rock, but Arthur wouldn't play those games. *I'm still here*, Arthur thought. *Jake or no Jake, you still got me to deal with.*

Couldn't take his eyes off that old house though, and truth was, he had no idea why he'd stopped. Seen the damn thing a thousand times, and countless others like it. Arthur Low was no poet – his mother quoting Blake was about as close to the stuff as he'd ever gotten – but looking at the wooden ruin with the sun going down behind it, he had what he assumed must be a purely poetic impulse…

I'm just like that house, Arthur thought.

So picturesque.

So empty.

He shook his head, felt himself blushing, wondering where the hell he'd gotten a fool notion like that. Arthur pulled his arm in, kicked the Ford into drive. He accelerated off the shoulder, headed down Highway 41 like a man with duties, responsibilities, and purpose. Behind him, something that did know a little poetry, something that was subtle, and ancient, and didn't mind playing games at all, laughed a vicious laugh in the warm prairie wind.

THE DEAD OF WINTER

Brian Dolton

1: DENNIS BARR

Yuri's late.

We don't hold much with schedules up here – running bush planes ain't like running a railroad – but there's one simple rule: If the sun goes down, and you ain't back at base, you're late. So there we all are, Jeff and Eddie and Lana and me, bundled up in the cold of a Yukon twilight, waiting on Yuri. Ain't all the way dark yet – there's a long two hours 'tween the sun going down and true night coming on – but we're an hour into that and the wind is bitter and the first stars are coming out and it ain't no lie to say I'm a worried man. Because the frozen North can kill you.

Jeff looks worried, too, but then he always looks worried. And Jeff, well, it's that old Curtiss Robin he cares about, not Yuri. Lana's just the opposite. She hates them planes, but she sure loves her husband. Must do, to have come with him all the way from Russia. Her real name's Ilyana or some such but we all call her Lana, which is a big joke because she sure don't look nothing like Lana Turner. She has black hair and she's thin like a rake – sure ain't no sweater girl! Don't get me wrong, she's still a looker. But she's only got eyes for Yuri.

Don't rightly know if Eddie looks worried or not. He's so bundled up I can't see his face. He's a good mechanic but he sure don't care for the Yukon winter. Reckon he'll be off out and find himself another job soon as he can, back down Vancouver way. I hear it don't freeze proper down there. Crazy, if you ask me. How do you know it's winter if it don't freeze hard, eh?

And me? Sure, like I say, I'm worried. Yuri's as good a pilot as I ever met, but if the north wants you dead, then you're dead, and that's all there is to it.

Then Eddie jumps like he's been bit.

"You hear that?" he says. Well, truth is, I don't hear too good, but all of us is straining to see if we can hear anything over the thin hiss of ice in the blow. And it's there. It ain't right; sounds like it's struggling, cutting in and out, but could just be the way the wind works, bringing us snatches of it here and there, and throwing 'em away the rest of the time. But it's there. Yuri's comin' home.

Lana's got her hands together like she's praying. Jeff's got his hands on his hips. Looks to me like he can't wait to chew Yuri out for worrying us all like that. Some men I know, they'd do that to hide the fact that deep down they care, and they're damn relieved. But I've known Jeff for thirty years and I'll tell you this: that ain't the kind of man he is. He just don't like nobody.

The plane's sliding in with the wind across it. Shouldn't handle like that, which means either something's wrong with the plane or with the pilot. I know where my money is. Yuri, I tell you, he could fly a decent plane through a blizzard and land it anywhere you told him. But a plane that's messed up? Ain't a pilot in the world can make a broken plane fly good.

Nothing we can do but watch. The left ski hits and bounces, then the right, which doesn't kick up much snow. It's broken off halfway back by the looks of it. Then the left ski's down again and the snow's flying up like it always does, so for a moment we can't see nothing. Then the motor cuts out and the plane might as well be a stone, just skidding along the ice. Not that it matters much; it's down, and it sure don't look like it's gonna be taking off again anytime soon. Jeff starts running towards it, which is damn stupid for two reasons. First, there ain't much snow on top of the ice, so he'll likely go end over end; and second, the plane's gonna slide right on past us before it runs out of momentum.

That's how I'm the first one to the plane, not Jeff. And soon as I get close to it, I know there's been a problem. Plane looks like it's been chewed up and spit out. One of the wing struts is hanging by a thread, the whole right-hand side is scraped raw like something's clawed all the way down it, and the door on that side is missing. How Yuri ain't frozen to death I got no idea. But he's there in the cockpit. I wait beside the plane while the others come up, and while Yuri gets himself out of the seat. He don't look much better than the plane; his thick jacket is torn, he's missing one glove, and there's blood frozen in his beard.

"Visky" is the first word out of his mouth. Now I know what folks say about Russkies and booze, what with their vodka, but Yuri ain't much for drinking. If the first thing he needs is hard liquor, something bad happened.

"What the hell you done to my plane, you Rooshan bastard?" Yep, that's Jeff. All heart. Yuri's clambering down onto the ice and, hell, if his right ear ain't hanging off the side of his head. Looks like it'll fall off if you give it a sharp tug.

"What happened? You all right, fella?" I ask him.

"Visky!" he growls, emphatically, and he fixes Jeff with a glare that don't look like he's inviting no argument. Yuri ain't a big guy, not like those cartoon Russkies built like bears. He ain't much taller than Eddie – hell, even Lana tops him by an inch or so – but I seen him fight and I'll tell you this: I'd take him on my side against pretty much any man in the territory. So Jeff just steps aside, but he ain't paying too much heed to Yuri. He's looking at the plane and I can see him tallying up what it's gonna cost to get it back up in the air – money and time both.

Asshole.

So Lana's jabbering on at Yuri in Russian, and Eddie's almost hopping up and down alongside him wanting to know what the hell happened. I figure I'll catch up to them by the time they've found the whisky and Yuri's knocked back a shot or two, so I stay back with Jeff.

"Must have flown it through the treetops," Jeff says. "Jesus. Every last cent this is gonna cost comes outta his pay."

I shake my head.

"Reckon there's more to it than that. Yuri ain't no tree-clip-per."

"It's dark," Jeff says. "Could have come in too low."

"How 'bout we let Yuri tell us what happened? Come on, Jeff. Ain't like we're going to work on this till morning."

He still has his hands on his hips.

"Coming out of his pay, I swear it," he says. I'd kinda like to deck him but he's the boss so it'd be a bad move. So I just clap him on the shoulder and turn to head on back towards the office. Jeff stays out there. The hell with him. Plane can be fixed; Eddie and me, we could put the damn thing back together if you chopped it up with an axe. Pilots, not planes, are what really counts up here.

By the time I get inside the office, Yuri's sitting there practically on top of the stove, tin mug in his hands. Lana's fussing over his ear, still jabbering on in Russian. Yuri's hands are shaking – the one with the glove on as well as the one without, so I figure it ain't just the blood getting back into them.

He's a scared man.

"Look like you seen a ghost," I say, trying to sound like I'm joking, "but ain't no ghost beat up that plane. What happened out there, Yuri?"

"You von't believe it," he mumbles.

"I've heard some tall tales in my time," I say. "When I was a kid, old Bill Lemmon told me about a winter that got so cold even the flames on the fire froze solid, and he snapped them off one by one. Your story better than that?"

Yuri takes a swig of whisky. As he's swallowing it down, the door opens and Jeff barges in.

"You want to tell me what the hell this is?" he asks, tossing something at Yuri. Yuri jumps like a whipped dog. The thing lands right by the stove and we all stare at it.

Darned if it ain't a severed human hand.

Eddie swears, and Lana mutters something in Russian, and me, it feels like my eyes are going to bug out of my head. Yuri looks at the hand like it's going to jump up and throttle him, then he shuffles slowly towards it and kicks it across the room, into the farthest corner.

"Where in God's name did that come from?" Eddie asks.

"The plane," Jeff says, his voice clipped, taut. "Clinging to the left-hand strut. Had to pry it off with a knife; frozen hard. Yuri, you better have a damn good explanation for this."

"You von't believe it," he says again.

"Just tell us, you sumbitch," Jeff says. Now like I say, he ain't much for being pleasant to folks, but I can tell that frozen hand's got him shaken, too. It don't make no sense.

"Whose hand is it, Yuri?" I ask, gentle, kinda like I'm talking to a kid.

He takes another gulp of whisky.

"Kathy Devlin," he says.

"You chopped off Kathy Devlin's hand?" Jeff asks. I feel like slapping him. "Fella, you're plumb loco. When Malcolm finds out…"

"Malcolm's dead," Yuri interrupts.

"Dead? What, you chop him up too, you Rooshan bastard? I oughta—"

I interrupt him

"Jeff, will you just shut your trap and let Yuri tell us the damn story?"

Jeff glares at me. There's silence for a minute.

"It better be a good one," he says in the end, looking at Yuri.

"Nothing good about it," Yuri says, and takes another drink.

And the whisky gets passed around. I figure we're going to need it.

2: YURI LERMONTOV

Devlin's Hole is my second stop of the day. Isn't even noon when I come in from the east. Figure something is wrong straightaway. In winter, two things can kill you; too much fire, or not enough. Devlin's had both problems. I am coming upwind and I see no smoke, so I do not land first pass. Their place is back off the lake, about quarter of a mile. So I fly low over it and what I see...is not good. Their cabin is in rocky hollow, cliffs on either side. Why it's called Devlin's Hole, I'm guessing. Is sheltered from wind on two sides. All trees in hollow cleared but plenty just above. No shortage of wood for winter fire. Is big stack of chopped wood up under outcrop just behind cabin. More wood than cabin has left. Burned to the ground. Very bad. Only charred timbers showing. Cannot tell from air how long ago it happened – could be day, could be week – so I swing plane round to come in and make landing. Get as far up to end of lake as I can. And get him turned round, ready to make it out quick if need to.

Hard work, getting through snow to cabin. Is bitter cold. Breath freeze in scarf. Have to pull scarf down to call out. Careful not to take big deep breath. Lungs would freeze.

I call out. No answer. Only own voice, echoing back off rocks. I call again, and again. Nothing.

Is bad, I am thinking. Careless with fire somehow, cabin started burning. Accident. Cannot have accident in winter up here. Winter always trying to kill you. Never give it chance.

Burned timbers are cold. No heat left. Does not mean much. Blow out fire, ashes are cold in an hour, less.

But then I see something. There is arm, sticking out from under timbers. I know is dead, of course, but I try to lift up timber, see if I can uncover body.

No body. Very odd. Just arm. Looks like has been hacked off, just below shoulder. With axe.

No rest of body I can find.

Have bad feeling now. Fire? Fire can be accident. Chopping off arm with axe? Not accident. I pick up arm. Frozen solid. Shirt sleeve, jacket sleeve, torn up some, lots of dry blood. No glove. Fingers curved like claws. Nails torn. More blood. Almost as if Malcolm was dragging himself away from fire. But cannot be, if arm only. Unless maybe someone moved Malcolm's body.

I stand there in ruined cabin. Snow drifts on wind. Only sound is my breath. I call out again. Nothing. Silence.

I look for tracks in snow. Has not snowed for almost a week. But snow is soft and wind blows this way and that. Not easy to find tracks, but tracks are there. I follow.

Tracks head to woods. I stand on edge of trees. Wind makes them sway, all together. Like forest is alive. Like living creature.

No. Stupid idea. I follow trail into wood.

I do not have to go far. It is dark under trees but not too dark. Before long I see someone. Body, resting against base of big tree. Axe in right hand. Big axe. Kind of axe could chop off man's arm.

I call out but no answer. Slowly I move forward. No sign of movement. I am careful. Winter can make people crazy. Maybe Kathy crazy enough to kill Malcolm. Crazy enough to burn cabin, though? Have to be special kind of crazy to do that in winter.

Body is Kathy Devlin. Blood on her face, chin, like maybe someone hit her in mouth. Eyes are blue and cold as sky. I say little prayer.

Makes no sense. What happened here? Where is rest of Malcolm? I think maybe they fight, she kill him, then run into wood. But what made them do this?

I see something lying next to her in snow. Pencil. Ha! If she has pencil, maybe somewhere she has paper. Maybe written something. But wind...cold wind could have blown papers anywhere. Snow could have covered them. Is pointless to look...

But then I see breast pocket of jacket. Folded paper sticking out.

I take out, very careful, and read.

3: KATHY DEVLIN

I'm going to die out here. It's a week until the plane is due. I hope someone will find me and read this.

I pray God that He will take me after what I did. I pray He takes Malcolm, too.

I didn't want to kill him. But at the end, he just wasn't himself. He wasn't – I don't know. It's like he wasn't even human.

I think it started with the wolf. Malcolm came back with a bad bite on his hand. He'd bandaged it up but I took a look and redressed it. He said there'd been a wolf in one of the traps. It was still barely alive when he found it, and it had gnawed most of the way through its leg. He shot it, of course, right through the head. But he said it was the strangest thing; when he got to the body, the wolf bit him. It must have been some reflex, or maybe somehow his shot hadn't quite killed it. He said it still seemed to be squirming even after he'd cut its throat for good measure. Even after he'd skinned it, it was still moving some. That's what he said. It sounded like crazy talk but he swore it was true.

The bite seemed to bother him over the next few days. I changed the dressings and it seemed to be healing up right but he said it felt like the teeth were still there in the wound. Which they weren't, of course, it was good and clean. But he said it was like he could still feel the bite, all the time. And he seemed to get hungry real quick. I started making more food, giving him bigger helpings, but it didn't help. Always hungry, he said. But aside from that, and the bite, he was still Malcolm. At least for a while.

I don't have much paper. What to tell. Today, maybe two weeks after the bite, he really went crazy. He woke up in the night almost howling with hunger. I went to try and see what I could find to cook up on the stove. I had my back to him when suddenly he grabbed me and – I swear this is true – he bit me. Bit me! Hard, on the arm, like he wanted to tear off a chunk of my flesh. I yelled at him to ask what he was doing and he didn't answer. Just kind of growled, like he wasn't a man anymore, like he was an animal. I backed away from him. He kept coming at me. His jaws were snapping. Biting. I was scared as all get out. He wouldn't say anything, I couldn't reach him. His eyes were just fixed.

Really, he was looking at me like...like I was just food. Just meat.

I didn't know what to do. The axe was by the door. I picked it up, I think just to warn him. You know, by holding it, show him he couldn't attack me like that. I mean, dear God, he's my husband. I didn't want to hurt him. I hoped maybe he'd calm down.

But he didn't. He kept coming at me. I just backed away at first, even swinging the axe a couple times just to keep him away from me. But he wouldn't stop. He wouldn't stop. I was circling round the cabin backwards and he was just growling and snapping his teeth and he wouldn't stop.

I tried to hit him with the back of the axe first. You know, use it more like a hammer. I thought if I could knock him out maybe I could tie him up until he came to his senses. And if he didn't, well, maybe I could keep him tied up until the plane came and they could take him to a doctor and find out what was wrong with him. But when I hit him, and I hit him pretty hard, it didn't do a thing. Drew blood, sure, but he just kept on staring and snapping his teeth and coming after me.

So I switched the axe round and hefted it up.

And, dear God, I hit him with it.

I got him in the shoulder. Not too hard because, you know, he's my husband and I didn't want to hurt him more than I had to. I didn't want to have him bleeding to death or anything. But he didn't even seem to *notice*. He grabbed at the axe as I pulled it back out. He was bleeding, bleeding hard, but he didn't scream with pain and he should have.

And he just kept snapping his teeth all the time.

I think I went a bit crazy then, myself. I started hitting him again, trying to knock him down, trying to stop him. I say trying but I don't really know. I wasn't thinking it through. I was just so scared.

I don't even know exactly what happened. I don't know if it was him or me who knocked open the stove. I don't quite know how, but suddenly his pants were on fire. I don't think he realized it. He was still chasing me round and I was still hitting him with the axe and he didn't seem to notice that I'd all but chopped off his arm and that he was on fire.

He blundered around and then he wasn't the only thing on fire. The cabin was burning and I knew I had to get out but he was between me and the door.

Oh, God, I am so sorry. Please forgive me.

I swung the axe with all my strength and I hit him in the neck. His head didn't quite come off but I broke his neck and his head tilted over like it wasn't properly fixed on and, oh God, oh God, *he was still biting and growling at me!* I mean there was no way he could do that. I remember just screaming and I was crying and I dropped the axe to tell him I was so sorry for, you know, for killing him, even though I hadn't.

He hit me in the face, then. Hard. I think he broke my nose. I fell down and he was on top of me, biting with his head all twisted off to the side. I managed to squirm out from under him and I grabbed the axe again and before he could get up I hit him again.

I cut off his arm. It fell to the ground and he looked at the stump of the arm like, I don't know, more like he was just curious about it. And his arm was there on the ground and I swear to holy God *it was still moving.* Dragging itself towards me.

I hit him once more in the neck. His head came off and rolled away. His body stumbled, dropped to its knees, but it was still moving too. That's when I knew he was dead and a demon or something had got into him. I just started praying and praying, saying everything I could remember from the Bible. And the cabin was really burning now. And there was his body on its knees, flailing around, and his head off to one side still biting, biting, biting, and his arm crawling towards me.

I guess…I guess I hoped that if I couldn't kill it with the axe, maybe fire would do it. So I ran out of the cabin and I ran to the woodpile and I swear to God it was the only thing I could think to do. I just took an armload of wood and I threw it into the cabin to burn that damned thing that had taken my husband from me. And I just threw it on in, more and more of it, until the cabin was just a roaring furnace and I couldn't get close enough to do any more.

I just picked up the axe and waited.

Nothing came out. I waited some more and then I turned and walked away. I was crying for my poor husband and I was crying for me because without the cabin I figure I'm probably going to die out here. And I hurt where he bit me – like I can still feel his teeth – and where he broke my nose and I hurt down inside worst of all because maybe God won't believe me and maybe I really did kill my husband and Lord knows that's a sin, Lord knows that's a sin, but I swear all this is true and it's real, even though it sounds crazy.

So I sat down in the woods and figured I'd best make my peace with God and write down what happened and I swear every word of this is true as God is my witness no matter how crazy it sounds.

It's strange. I should be freezing but I don't really feel cold. I don't feel cold at all.

I'm just so very very hungry.

4: YURI LERMONTOV

Is crazy story. Maybe Kathy went crazy. Would not be first woman to kill husband with axe. Maybe did not mean to burn cabin down. Maybe hoped someone would find her before cold killed her. Maybe thought story would help when police came asking questions.

Maybe.

Kathy's body frozen hard. But she is not big woman. I can get her across shoulders, bring her back to plane. Have done this too many times before. Winter. It kills, I bring them back for proper burial. Is right thing to do.

Is already late. I put Kathy in passenger seat. Legs stick up off floor so I have to tilt her forward. Much pushing and shoving. But in she goes and I strap her in place. I know, sound stupid. Is habit, I think. Then I go round to pilot side. Shout once more. Not sure why. No answer. Just wind. Just cold.

I climb into plane and start up engine. Cough, splutter, the usual. Then turns, and we start along lake. Trail spray of snow and then up in the air. Hands are frozen, but engine makes much heat. Soon, warm enough to take off hat, scarf.

I look to my right. Frozen Kathy sitting there. Beginning maybe to melt a little. Drip of water from tip of chin. Pink water, because of blood on face.

I stop looking at her. Check ground, check compass, check instruments. All good. Heading home.

Noise beside me. Like little gurgle in throat. I look at Kathy again. Almost jump out of seat; she is looking back at me. Eyes still frozen, but head turned. After moment, I laugh. Heat from engine is thawing her out some. Neck must have been at odd angle, has thawed, head has turned. Nothing to worry about.

Then she makes noise again. Opens mouth. Tries to bite me.

I am shouting. Do not remember words. Bad swears, I think. I push myself away from her. She cannot reach me. Body strapped in place. But I hear teeth snapping, like angry dog.

In shock, have forgotten where I am.

Have let go of controls. Not good. Is windy. Plane slips sideways and starts to drop. I grab stick. Have to fly plane. Pull back, bring back up level. Crash would likely kill me. If not, cold would finish job double quick.

Kathy moving in seat next to me. Growling, like some kind of animal. I hit her in face. I do not care if she is woman. She is dead and tries to bite me. Anyone do that, I hit them in face.

She bites. I am wearing thick glove. Is good; if not, maybe she bite off finger. She bite very hard. I yell and pull hand free, out of glove. She shakes glove in mouth, like cat shaking mouse.

She still have axe in right hand.

I reach out, grab it, try to pull it from her. Maybe first I am just afraid she might hit me with it. But then I think of Malcolm and severed arm and think maybe axe can chop her up like she did him.

I hear teeth, snapping, right next my ear. I don't want being bit. But I need axe. So I hit her with elbow, try to get time to grab axe from her. She move slow. Mostly still frozen, I think. Just barely starting thaw. I pull axe and hear her arm crack, like snapping frozen branch. She still hold on, though.

I hit her again in face. Is not nice to hit woman. But she is not woman. She is like some kind of monster. Like vampire or demon or some creature, I don't know. So I hit and hit and hit and then I grab axe again and this time it comes free and I have axe.

Is good to have axe. But plane is not flying itself. I have to grab stick, work rudder, everything. I am doing this and I feel pain in right ear. I yell and turn and she has got left hand holding my ear. Fingers are like pliers. Ice-cold pliers. She is trying to pull me close so she can bite me, I think; her mouth is going all the time, teeth snapping like she is hungry, hungry, hungry. I pull away. Feels like I leave some of my ear behind.

I want to push her out of plane. But body is strapped in.

Heh. I have axe.

I swing best I can. Cockpit small, not easy. Do not want break instruments. Only want to break strap. Well, maybe strap, maybe Kathy too. No. Is not Kathy, like Malcolm was not Malcolm.

But if I break strap, maybe she can reach to bite me. I do not want to be bitten. Maybe if bitten I will become like Malcolm, like her. I do not want this.

So first thing, I must get door open on her side. So I can push her out of plane. Is not easy. She is still most frozen, stiff, but left arm is clawing at me, trying to get hold. I use handle of axe, push it across her, try to open door. Does not open at first. I say little prayer and maybe God is listening because of how close I am and I push and door opens. Plane lurch, tilt to that side. Is exactly what I want.

I pull axe back, switch it round, and swing hard at strap. It break. I tilt plane even more. She try to hold on.

I push her out of plane.

I am very happy for moment. Then over sound of engine, over sound of wind, I hear click-click-click.

Teeth, snapping, open and closed, open and closed.

She is holding on to wing strut. One hand. Good grip, just like grip she had on axe.

I swear some more. Prayer, swear. Shrug. It is how it is.

She is still clinging to strut. Plane is tilting, swinging. I am half in wrong side of plane. Losing control. In danger of falling out.

I swing axe one more time. I hit hard.

Something breaks. Kathy falls. Plane still swinging. Wind strong. Hand, face, frozen. I think for moment I fall out after her. But then get good grip with left hand. Brace right leg. Pull. Push.

Back in plane. Trees very close. Haul on stick. Plane crashes through tops of trees. Branches break, maybe bits of plane break. Haul on stick some more. Nose lifts. Plane climbs.

I circle twice, big wide circles as I climb and try to get bearings.

Then fly home.

5: DENNIS BARR

Yuri looks at the mug on the desk. Eddie reaches for the whisky, but Yuri shakes his head.

"That's one hell of a story, Yuri," Jeff says. "Now, you want to tell us what *really* happened?"

Yuri stands up. His fists are bunched, he's angry and I can't say I blame him. Sure, it's a crazy story, but he ain't crazy. Just pissed as all get out.

And that's when Eddie suddenly lets out a yell and points at Jeff. And Yuri's eyes bulge and Lana swears in Russian and

I look over; at first I don't see nothin' but then Jeff leaps to his feet and he brushes at his arm and something drops to the floor.

We all stare at it. It's moving like some big, slow spider, but it ain't no spider.

It's Kathy Devlin's hand. The fingers are reaching and curling, dragging it across the floor.

For a moment we all stare. Then Yuri stomps on it, just like you'd squash a bug. His big boot comes down on it once, twice, more. I hear what might be bones cracking. But it keeps on moving. Be pitiful if it were some critter, dragging itself along with a broken back. But it sure as hell ain't getting any pity from me.

"Open the stove!" Yuri says, and I realize then what he's thinking. I'm looking round to find something I can scoop the damned hand up with, 'cause there is no way on God's earth I'm touching that thing. Moment later, I got my mug and Yuri's, and together I reach down and scoop up the hand with 'em, my arms stretched way out in front of me to keep that thing as far away as I possibly can. Lana's got the front of the stove open and I just toss the lot in, mugs and hand and all. Yuri kicks the stove shut and we all just glare at it. I can see it, in my head; the fingers twitching as the flesh starts to crisp up, starts to burn away. See it trying to claw its way out of the fire. But there's no chance. That stove is hot as Hell, which I figure is kind of appropriate, because there sure ain't nothing godly about any of this.

Hell, if I don't kind of imagine it screaming.

We're silent, all of us. Even Jeff ain't got nothing to say at first. It's Eddie who speaks.

"Well, that's it. I quit. I'm getting out of this place."

Like I said, I figured he was planning on quitting. Didn't reckon on anything like this being the final straw, though.

"We should all leave," Lana says.

"Quitters," Jeff grunts. His face is white, but he's trying to tough it out. "That hand ain't gonna hurt anyone now."

"No," Lana says. "But that hand was frozen hard. And when it got warm enough, it came back to life."

"Too warm now to do a damn thing," Jeff says. He laughs. It ain't much of a laugh.

"*Da.* But thaw comes in what, two months, maybe three? And somewhere out there is rest of Kathy Devlin. Hungry Kathy Devlin."

And I realize what she's saying.

The frozen North can kill you, sure. We all know that. We fight our way through winter and when spring comes we breathe a big, long sigh of relief.

But what if you're in even more danger when the thaw comes?

ESCAPE

Tessa J. Brown

There's something about the stench of rotting flesh. You can get used to almost anything else. I had a friend whose cat pissed on everything – every single day, that cat would piss on a chair, or up against a wall, or hell, just in the middle of the goddamn floor. The stench was incredible. If you went to visit him, you could smell it in the hallway when you got off the elevator. Going into his apartment you would hold your breath, gag, try to breathe through your mouth, anything to avoid smelling the air. But he never smelled a damn thing. He was completely oblivious, and if anybody ever said anything, he'd look at them like they were nuts.

The fact is that if, for whatever reason, you had to spend a couple of hours there, you'd start to forget about it too. Your nose would just gradually adjust, as if the air had always smelled of cat piss.

But flesh, human flesh rotting is something entirely different. It permeates everything, just like the cat piss, but it never goes away. You smell it all the time. It fills your mouth – you can feel it on the back of your tongue when you breathe, taste it, practically see it in the air. It's everywhere. Before there were so many of them it worked almost like a warning. You could smell them coming before you could see them, before you could even hear them moan. But as their numbers grew, the smell grew too. Now it's everywhere, even if you're alone. There isn't one of them for miles, so far as I can tell, and I can still smell it. It's like the world is rotting with them.

Jim succumbed to the infection last week. I never even noticed they got him – almost didn't realize he was infected until it was too late. Still don't understand why the bastard didn't tell me: none of us wanted to end up like that. I ended it when the fever took him over. Dumped the body off the roof. So that's the last of us. I'm the last of us.

I've started talking to the monkeys. Nice thing about being trapped in the biodome – even if I'm the last human alive, at least I'm not the only animal in here. If the things were any bigger they'd probably be dangerous, but as it is they mostly stay out of my way, clambering around high above me, chattering furiously. I guess they'll die when the generator goes, when the reality of a Canadian winter finally sets in. Poor little buggers. I feel like I should find some way to save them, or at least to put them out of their misery. I guess we're all as fucked as each other.

Some of the animals are saveable – I could break the skylights in most of the other habitats, at least let the birds escape. Can't really see any way to help the land animals, though, and the sea creatures are super fucked. The predators will finish off their food supply and then they'll gradually starve to death.

I wonder if that'll happen to the things outside. Somehow I can't imagine them starving to death. But what are they going to do when there are no more humans? Maybe they'll die, really die, as soon as the last of us does. Or maybe they'll just wander the earth, mindless, purpose-

less and hungry until they finally rot away. With enough supplies, in the right place, we might even outlast them. But I'm
not in the right place, and I sure as hell don't have enough
supplies. I can't even catch the fish in the ocean habitat – as
a matter of fact, I'm kind of scared of them. The fruit in the
tropical enclosure will only last so long, and we exhausted
the crappy sandwich supply from the café a week ago. The
plan wasn't long-term survival. The plan was to come to the
biodome, hang out for a couple of days in a comfortable and
attractive environment, and then get picked up by rescue
helicopters by noon on the third day. But the rescue helicopters seem to have missed the memo, and the radio's picking
up nothing but emergency signals and static – I'm on my
own here.

I've been sleeping in the security office since Jim died: I
was in there last night, fast asleep – or as fast asleep as I ever
get these days – when the motion sensors went off. It's lucky
the generator's still up; it's the only warning system I've got. I
switched on the security monitors as I loaded my handgun.
Only three shots left. Not like I was going to find more ammo
anytime soon.

The enclosures were dark, simulating night in the animals' natural habitats. I squinted, peering intently at each
screen, and checked that the security office's door was
locked. There was movement in the tropical habitat. Shit. I
hoped there was only one of them.

I grabbed a flashlight from the equipment cupboard – no
sense leaving it until morning. Might as well deal with it
while I knew exactly where the thing was. I turned the lock
with exaggerated care and waved the flashlight's beam in a
wide arc across the foyer. Empty as I'd left it. I edged along,

pressing my back to the wall as I went, holding the gun and the large, heavy flashlight out in front of me. At least if I ran out of bullets I could use it as a weapon. I just wished I were a better shot.

A dark, slippery trail wound its way into the tropical habitat – it was barefoot, but only one of the feet left proper, human-looking prints: beside it there was just an extended drag mark, shining a dark brownish-red in my flashlight's glow. One of the thing's legs must have been dragging behind it. The smell intensified as I stepped towards the curtain between me and the door to the jungle. I tasted bile at the back of my throat – couldn't complain, though. It sure as hell tasted better than that smell. I thought of the old-fashioned plague masks, long-beaked and featureless, full of flowers and herbs to cover the scent of death and disease, and I wished that I had one. What do they say about wishes and horses? I swallowed hard and stepped through the curtain, pushing open the door, listening intently for the telltale moan. That's the only advantage with these things: they never come at you silently.

I heard a moan off to my left and turned, shining the light along the walkway. Damn it – where the hell was this thing? I held the gun out in front of me, aiming along the flashlight's beam. I could hear the moaning, closer now, and I shivered as every hair on my body stood at attention. Where the fuck was it? Another moan, to my left again – but there wasn't anything to my left. It had to be off the walkway. I heaved a sigh of relief. Holy crap. The damn thing had fallen straight into the crocodile enclosure.

I held my flashlight close to my face, staring down its beam until I saw a croc's eyes glowing red, half-concealed in the water – it held the creature clamped tightly between its jaws. As I watched, the croc leapt upwards, muscles rippling as it tossed its head back, prey still firmly in its grasp, ripping off bite-sized chunks of the thing's rotting flesh. Its strength was incredible. Its sense of smell must have been non-existent.

The light attracted the once-human thing's attention – it looked up at me and reached out, its hands opening and shutting uselessly. There was nothing left behind those eyes. The croc lashed upwards again and the thing's head snapped back, bones shattering as it was flung upwards again. Below its waist, its legs were a mangled ruin. The croc dropped it into the shallow water and dug its teeth into the creature's torso, writhing furiously, whipping its head from side to side to pull out the thing's innards.

I gagged, spitting bile over the railing. The creature reached down, pushing at the croc's head uselessly, mouth opening and shutting as its intestines were pulled out; a long, tangled rope, pale and malodorous. Jesus. Poor fucker. I couldn't even tell if it had been a man or a woman. *Who were you?* I thought as I stared into its uncomprehending eyes. I remembered the last meal I had shared with Jim – we'd been trying to remember all the best lines from *Ghostbusters*, laughing and arguing over what they would have done in this situation. I raised my gun, aiming carefully at the thing's head. I squeezed the trigger slowly, exhaling, but the croc reared up suddenly, ripping another chunk out of its stomach, and the bullet slammed uselessly into the earth. High above me, the monkeys screamed and chattered as the sound of the shot echoed through their woods. Birds screeched in surprise, taking to the air.

"Fuck," I muttered. As if I could afford to waste ammo like this. Still, I took aim again. I counted slowly in my head as I stared down into the thing's ruined face. One. Two. Three. I fired. Its head snapped back as the bullet shattered its skull seconds before the croc tossed it into the air again.

I stood for a moment, listening to the offended cries of the animals, the splashing of the water as the croc enjoyed its meal. A bead of sweat rolled down my neck. Then, watching the shadows around me carefully for movement, I walked back to the security office and locked the door behind me. I flicked the monitors on again, staring at each in turn, over and over again, until the hum of electricity lulled me into a fitful sleep.

When I woke up, the monitors showed the bright, warm light of early fall spilling into the foyer. I picked up my gun and took the heavy flashlight for backup as I patrolled the dome, checking each door and window. How the hell had that thing gotten in here? Glass crunched under my feet as I rounded a corner. Shit. One of the massive windows stood before me, utterly shattered – how could I not have heard it? How the hell was I supposed to fix it? How the hell was I supposed to fix any of this? My shoulders slumped – I was suddenly filled with a strange sense of relief. There really was nothing I could do now. No haven to wait in, no rescue forthcoming. They would get in.

I've been sitting here for a couple of hours. One of the tamarins came down pretty close, and I've been having a chat with him. Cute little guy. I wish I could do more for him. I climbed around in each of the habitats, smashing windows, opening up vents. Nearly broke my neck – cut my hand pretty badly, too. Most of the birds have flown out already.

The monkeys are good climbers – I'll bet they could get out, too, but I don't know where they would go. Hell, maybe they'll head south. I'd say they've got about a month before the first frost. How fast do monkeys move, anyway? I don't know. It's just nice to think they might get out of this alive.

My stomach is aching a bit – it's been a while since I ate this much, even if I did share half with the animals. I ate all of the fruit I'd collected over the past couple of days. No more supplies now: no going back. The light through the smashed window is incredibly bright, lancing down through the thick canopy above me. The air is still warm and wet, but for once I don't think I can smell them. Everything is fresh and green and alive. I can still hear the birds calling to each other, squawking and flapping high above. It's a little weird to see them all mixed together like this – huge blue macaws and pink ibises, little grey and black catbirds and bright bluebirds from the Laurentians, black guillemots and king eiders from the arctic habitat, all flying around at once. Makes me laugh. It's such a beautiful day that I could almost believe the past few weeks have been nothing but a dream. But I guess I'm in luck: I've got one bullet left.

HALF GHOST

Linda DeMeulemeester

They call me *s'igee sha'awu'*, because I am the child of a spirit — a half ghost. When my father arrived from the spirit world, our summer village gathered on the beach. My people watched the waves lap the supernatural vessel and tug it to our jagged shore. Dead, leafless trees planted on the deck held billowing shreds of clouds that drifted between his ghostly world and ours.

The skin of the dead men on that ship had faded until it was almost as white as those clouds. The spirit men could not speak our language but we understood that they found our world displeasing. I am told they crawled off their ship on hands and knees and remained animate for only a few short days. Perhaps they arrived only so my people could wrap them and leave them in the living trees thinking it would please the spirits of the old ones on the coast.

I like to think my father lingered because of my mother.

As the crow chief's daughter, Guna' was chosen and then offered as a wife to a dead man. Lying with a spirit has its price. My father soon refused to draw breath and returned to his ghost world, but he longed for her, I think. Impatient, he claimed her again and she left her own body behind. Her journey, I am told, was wracked in agony and fever as Guna' kept one foot in our world long enough to birth me.

I am already half a ghost, one that is neither fully alive nor fully dead. It makes sense that they send me on the traverse to be the wife of the man who had two wives die in winter – each claimed by the hungry demon, the *widjigo*. It makes sense but I fear it.

"Each man must have a wife to traverse the traps – to mend the fur skins as they wear thin, to render the bear fat and scrape the caribou's gut," my clan auntie explains to me. "But once the *widjigo* has claimed a family, the demon will return if winter lingers too long."

"So why send me?" My voice sounds bitter, but truly it is cracked with terror.

"Sha'awu, what do you have to fear?" my clan mother scolds. "You will have an advantage over others if the *widjigo* creeps into your camp. You are already half-dead."

And then what, I think. Clan auntie spits out the bitter aftertaste of the tanning juices from chewing my moccasin lining until it is soft and smooth. I like to think this shows affection. I say no more, but inside me I don't feel as if I half-belong in the spirit world. My skin *is* pale like the dead – but I bleed red blood. I know this. Clan auntie's spit turns into brown frost as soon as it hits the ground. The temperature plunges already – a harbinger of a cruel winter as the ice shield stretches its arms in early greeting. I shiver and not from the cold.

The village prepares to move inland for winter and travel from camp to camp – a harsh choice but the Northerners will soon travel south for winter's harshest months, and if we stay there will be war. All families pack up – they will cling to the tree line chasing the caribou, but my future husband and I will be forced closer to their territory as we tend the

traplines and avoid the Northerners. It is the most perilous
route.

My mother's mother, Nokomis, has bidden me to come
visit her at her lodge the night before I leave. Only Nokomis
rests as my people work. She has chosen to stay behind this
year. She does not fear the Northerners; she says she will join
my mother in the ghost world before they arrive. If only I had
her courage. On my way to her lodge, the new moccasins
crunch through dry powdered snow even though the long
nights have not yet fallen. Again a shiver of trepidation travels
down my spine. When I arrive, my Nokomis has a deerskin
bundle prepared.

I try and show gratitude but my hands are heavy as I fum-
ble with the gifts inside – ivory awls carved from walrus tusk
filed sharp to pierce the toughest hide. Seal gut stretched thin
and sleek to mend and darn, and a precious necklace of purple and white shells – a treasure of my mother's. My eyes
water.

Nokomis flashes a toothless grin, pleased by how I love her
gifts. Then as the smile disappears in a fold of wrinkles, she
goes to the corner of her house and lifts up birch boughs and
pulls up an object wrapped in beaver fur. I see a flash of silver.
She moves towards me, gingerly carrying the object as if it
might burn her.

"This is from your father." She places the object in my
hand. "I have kept it away from the rest of the villagers because
I fear the menace of its otherworldliness. But I dreamed of a
use for it – a desperate use."

I unwrap the object and pull out a knife – but what a
strange knife – with a blade so thin and cruel. I touch it and
pull my finger away as blood beads on my fingertip – red blood.

"A spirit knife," I gasp.

Nokomis nods,."To fight the *widjigo*. Keep it on you always, Sha'awu, day or night – for what the others don't tell you – what I suspect – is that the *widjigo* can appear in many forms – both strange…and familiar…"

Her words freeze my heart, and I tuck the forbidden blade in the folds of my underclothes. There is no village feast for my wedding or farewells as I pack my belongings on my new husband's toboggan. The snow has already begun to fall – it is the persistent flakes of many blizzards to come.

Dzagwa'a is handsome, except for the scar on his face, a red bite mark. Still, he has fine features and the bitter winds that carve sharp lines into our faces have only chiseled deeply around his eyes. But those eyes... Staring indirectly at my husband's face, I fully realize I am joined to a haunted man. I suppose he sees me, a half ghost, as a fitting wife, though he says little – simply gives orders in a way that sounds similar to the snapping of our dogs; to bundle our trap snares more safely at the front of the toboggan, and tuck the moose skins more firmly in the corners before I lace them with thick moose gut. Then we are off.

Our marriage falls into the divided tasks of man and wife – the tasks of survival. He carves a shelter for us from the ice – I seal any tear of our clothes with gut. I cook what we have brought and what we find but there is precious little of that. At night we fight the gnawing hunger by drawing what warmth we can from each other. But Dzagwa'a is a silent man given to murmuring feverishly in his sleep. He cries out, and I tell him I am nearby. I cannot tell if he is pleased with me, or if I am pleased with him. I like to think it is because we must only focus on surviving.

Twenty days out our first dog dies. We find it frozen and half-eaten in the cold morning light. At night the black skies dance with the cold blue flames of the Great Fire People, surely a bad omen. I glance once more at my haunted man – his eyes are fading and becoming soulless.

The twenty-first day out and the scraps of the dog carcass have already gone – fed to the other dogs to keep them moving, and fed to us in a weak broth. Then the second dog dies – again, some beast has crept into our camp and devoured most of it. The terrified whimpers of the other dogs are pitiful.

Twenty-five days out and two more dogs die. The traplines have been mostly barren, and I know in my freezing heart I am joined to a bad luck man, and even when his arms entwine me each night they no longer offer warmth. He grows colder by the waning moon.

Each night the Fire People's flames mock us – "See, up here in the sky we are warm and down there your world turns to ice." Our bellies are empty when we limp into an abandoned winter house with only two dogs left – the house where his last wife was taken by the *widjigo*. I shudder as the birch bark creaks and groans in the punishing wind. Daylight has abandoned us for good now, and we unpack our belongings in the twilight and the howling.

When our last dogs are attacked and devoured, I scrape the remaining flesh off their bones and make the broth stretch for days. Then we are faced with two choices. One is to wait in the house until we die or until the *widjigo* comes hunting for us, or two, we walk near a camp of the Northerners which is by a river, and drill through the ice.

If we are undetected, we can hope for fish, but if we're caught we can pray for a quicker death. My husband chooses the latter, and I must follow him. The bitter nights are hard on him – even the scar on his face has grown angry and red. I like to think he is waging battle against the dark spirit that rides him for both our sakes, even if the bad luck man is married to a half ghost.

We pick a frozen day so cold that when we spit, it freezes before it hits the ground. It is not good to travel on such a day. The trick is to walk fast, but the ice covers bog and this can be treacherous – to watch the shadows below the ice is wearing and we go too slowly as we hunger. My heart sinks when we pass the stone cairn – the Northerners' warning not to trespass. Soon we spy moving black dots of the others ahead in the gloom, and almost too late we are forced to retreat, but not until we stumble on a trapline and take the rabbit.

Our house awaits – a dark shadow of impending death in the pure white snow. How can the *widjigo* not be drawn here? We have stolen food from the traplines of the Northerners – they will search for us soon. I can only wish they find us before the *widjigo*. But we eat our stolen meat and we sleep and we wait. No dogs are left outside to die.

A blizzard rages. The snow we have packed around our house and the furs we huddle inside each night can no longer keep us warm. For the first time in our marriage we have time to sit and speak with each other, but only the occasional hollow whisper escapes our lips. What is there to speak of, except the unspeakable? Perhaps death will find us first – will my father and mother await me? This is what I hope.

A ragged groan whispers to me as the birch bark of our house shifts and buckles under heavy snow. I awaken from a troubled sleep as the hunger gnaws my belly. It is so cold. I shift to lie on my back and as I begin to drift, a weight presses down upon my chest and hips. I fear to open my eyes. I fear to breathe, thinking the hungry demon has stolen upon me. But I drink in the smell of sweat and skin and musk – the familiar scents of Dzagwa'a.

I open my eyes in relief – only to stare into an emaciated face where my husband's gums have pulled away from his teeth and the skin shrivels from his eyes — the eyes of madness. The scar on his face has opened, and the flesh surrounding it has turned grey.

It is then I inhale another scent – the stench of death.

In a lingering and languid grasp, his lover's touch, his hands caress — but I do not trust those eyes. I'm wildly thinking there are worse things than a clean death. I remember Nokomis's words: *Widjigo can appear to be both strange and familiar,* and with dread as thick as the frost that covers our land, I know my husband has been possessed.

His hands draw up towards my face, his mouth opens as if his jaw has become unhinged and the smell of sweet rot makes me gag. I suddenly realize if his teeth sink into my flesh, even if he rips away my throat, my death will not be clean, so I reach for the leather belt between my shift and my furs.

I draw out the spirit blade. I have intent only to force him back. Nevertheless, I am weak and my hand slashes wildly. The blade buries deep – I like to think my father's hand guided it, but I am not sure this is so. The blood that seeps from my husband's throat drives a hunger lust in me.

I can no longer be certain who the *widjigo* has possessed. How can I fight the dark spirit swelling inside my own head, taking over my lungs, my heart, and my gut? Once more, I slash with the silver knife, the tool from the spirit world.

There is a bite mark on my arm, and I stab at it. The clean agony clears my head and drives the *widjigo* out. I drag my husband's body from the house and leave it out back where the snow will shroud him.

Admittedly, I lick the blood that has showered my skin. I like to think this is my husband's gift.

The blizzard rages for two more days and as soon as it lifts the Northerners come hunting for who had poached their traps. They discover me alone in the winter house, and I am willing to leave this world. But they back away.

They call out in their terrified voices, and when there is a scream outside the house, I know they've discovered my husband, his flesh stripped away.

◄ ►

The ice on the river groans and trembles and cracks, but I see no point in returning to my summer village. Soon bog berries will cover the tundra. And the Northerners leave fish and seal and a fine delicacy of whale blubber inside the rock cairn – so I may reach it and scavengers cannot. They leave me this offering so I will not go hunt.

I am no half ghost anymore.

AUTHOR BIOGRAPHIES

Chantal Boudreau is an accountant/author/illustrator who lives in Nova Scotia, Canada. She is a Horror Writers Association member, she writes and illustrates predominantly horror, dark fantasy and fantasy and has had several of her stories published in a variety of horror anthologies, in online journals and magazines and as stand-alone digital shorts. *Fervor*, her debut novel, a dystopian science fantasy tale, was released by May December Publications, followed by its sequels, *Elevation* and *Transcendence*. *Magic University*, the first in her fantasy series, *Masters & Renegades*, was followed by the sequel *Casualties of War*. She has also published a YA tribal dark fantasy trilogy, *The Snowy Barrens Trilogy*. Read more about her at www.chantellyb.wordpress.com

Tessa J. Brown is a writer and performer based in, and inspired by, the City of Montreal.

Richard Van Camp is a proud member of the Dogrib (Tlicho) Nation from Fort Smith, Northwest Territories. He has published a novel, *The Lesser Blessed*, which is now a feature film with First Generation Films; his collections of short fiction include *Angel Wing Splash Pattern, The Moon of Letting Go and Other Stories,* and *Godless but Loyal to Heaven*. He is the author of the three baby books *Welcome Song for Baby: A Lullaby for Newborns, Nighty Night: A Bedtime Song for Babies* and *Little You,* and he has two comic books out with the Healthy Aboriginal Network: *Kiss Me Deadly* and *Path of the Warrior*. You can visit Richard on Facebook, Twitter or at www.richardvancamp.com

Jacques L. Condor (Maka Tai Meh, his given First Nations tribal name) is a French-Canadian, Native American of the Abenaki-Mesquaki tribes. He has lived in major cities, small towns and bush villages in Alaska and the Pacific Northwest for fifty-plus years. In the 1980's and 90's he taught at schools, colleges, museums, and on reserves, about the culture, history and arts of his tribes; he held this position for twenty years in the Federal Government's Indian Education Programs. Now 85, Condor writes short stories and novellas based on the legends and tales of both Natives and the "old-time" sourdoughs and pioneers he had collected over the decades. He has published five books on Alaska. Recently, his work appeared in five anthologies: *Icefloes*, *Northwest Passages, A Cascadian Odyssey, Queer Dimensions*, and *Queer Gothic Tales*.

Kevin Cockle is an Alberta-based horror and dark-fantasy author, who draws nightmarish inspiration from the seemingly mundane realms of politics, economics, and science. A regular contributor to On Spec Magazine, Kevin's work has appeared in numerous anthologies, including the Tesseracts series; the Chilling Tales series; Evolve, and more. In 2012, Kevin optioned a screenplay based on his story "Spawning Ground" for a movie now in pre-production.

Carrie-Lea Côté from Calgary has stories in *Fifty Shades of Decay*, and *Fur Planets* "Roar Volume 5." When not writing she spends her time sculpting, reading and wishing cheetahs were native to the plains of Alberta. Her Twitter is @cattpaws and her Goodreads account is Carrie-Lea Cote.

Linda DeMeulemeester grew up listening to stories of the burial trees her grandfather had seen in British Columbia's north during his visits to Haida Gwaii. The fog shrouded rainforest later served as inspiration for her award winning and bestselling spooky children's series, *Grim Hill*, which has been translated into French, Spanish and Korean. Linda's speculative short fiction has been published in zines and magazines *ChiZine, Twilight Tales, Neo-opsis, Storyteller,* and in anthologies *Under the Needle's Eye, Escape Clause* and *Wyrd Wravings*. When she writes grown-up tales, they're still spooky but are less inclined to have a happy ending...

Brian Dolton is an Englishman, now transplanted to a small town in New Mexico. He's travelled to more than thirty countries, and has ridden a camel in the Sahara, played volleyball on a sandbar in the middle of the Pacific, and stayed in a Buddhist monastery on a sacred mountain in Japan. When he's not being distracted by work, travel, or cats, he writes.

Gemma Files is a former film critic and teacher turned award-winning horror author, who is best known for her *Hexslinger* series (*A Book of Tongues, A Rope of Thorns* and *A Tree of Bones*). She has also published two collections of short work – *Kissing Carrion*, which takes its title from the story of the same name reprinted here, and *The Worm in Every Heart* – and two chapbooks of poetry. Recent work can be found in *Beneath Ceaseless Skies, The Three-Lobed Burning Eye, Clockwork Phoenix 4* and *The Grimscribe's Puppets*, a tribute to the work of Thomas Ligotti. She was born in England and raised in Toronto, where she lives with her family, and is hard at work on her fourth novel.

Ada Hoffmann finds writing much more satisfying than actually talking to people. Her work has appeared in *Strange Horizons, AE,* and *Imaginarium 2012: The Best Canadian Speculative Writing.* She also blogs about autism in SF at http://ada-hoffmann.livejournal.com/

Tyler Keevil was born in Edmonton and grew up in Vancouver, Canada. His speculative fiction has appeared in a wide range of magazines and anthologies, including *Black Static, Interzone, Leading Edge, Neo-Opsis,* and *On Spec.* In 2010 Parthian Books released his debut novel, *Fireball,* which was longlisted for Wales Book of the Year, shortlisted for the Guardian Not the Booker prize, and received the Media Wales People's Prize 2011. His next novel, *The Drive,* was published this summer. He currently lives in Mid Wales with his wife and son.

Claude Lalumière is the author of two books: the collection *Objects of Worship* and the mosaic novella *The Door to Lost Pages.* He has edited or co-edited twelve anthologies, including three being released in 2013: *Masked Mosaic: Canadian Super Stories* (co-edited with Camille Alexa), *Bibliotheca Fantastica* (co-edited with Don Pizarro), and *Super Stories of Heroes & Villains.* With Rupert Bottenberg, Claude is the co-creator of the multimedia cryptomythology project Lost Myths. www.lostmyths.net and www.lostmyths.net/claude

Michael Matheson is a Toronto writer, editor, and book reviewer. An editorial assistant with *ChiZine Publications,* and a submissions editor with *Apex Magazine,* his reviews have appeared in *Chiaroscuro Magazine, Innsmouth Free*

Press, and the *Globe and Mail*. More of his fiction can be found in, among other places, the anthologies *Chilling Tales 2*, *Future Lovecraft*, *Mark of the Beast*, and *One Buck Horror Vol. 6*.

Jamie Mason is a Canadian sci-fi/fantasy writer whose short stories have appeared in *On Spec, Abyss & Apex* and the *Canadian Science Fiction Review*. His novel *ECHO* was published in June 2011 by Drollerie Press. He lives on Vancouver Island. Learn more at www.jamiescribbles.com

Ursula Pflug is author of the novel *Green Music* and the story collection *After the Fires*. Her new collection, *Harvesting the Moon*, is forthcoming in 2013. A new novel, *The Alphabet Stones*, is also due in 2013. Pflug is editing *They Have To Take You In*, a forthcoming Hidden Brook Press anthology fundraiser for The Dana Fund. Currently, she edits flash fiction for *The Link*, co-organizes the Cat Sass Reading Series and teaches at Loyalist College.

Rhea Rose lives in Port Coquitlam, BC, and is originally from Etobicoke, Ontario. Her short stories and poetry have appeared in anthologies in both Canada and the United States. Her writing has been nominated for both the Rhysling Award for poetry and the Canadian Aurora award. Her most recent work has appeared in *Masked Mosaic: Canadian Super Stories* and *Tesseracts 17*.

Simon Strantzas is the author of the critically acclaimed short story collections *Beneath the Surface, Cold to the Touch*, and *Nightingale Songs*, as well as the editor of *Shadows Edge*.

His writing has appeared in *The Mammoth Book of Best New Horror*, and *The Year's Best Dark Fantasy & Horror*, and has been nominated for the British Fantasy Award. He lives in Toronto, Canada, with his wife and an unyielding hunger for the flesh of the living. For more information, please visit www.strantzas.com.

E. Catherine Tobler lives and writes in Colorado. Her fiction has appeared in *Clarkesworld*, *Realms of Fantasy*, and *LCRW* among others. She is a Sturgeon Award finalist, and the senior editor at *Shimmer Magazine*.

Beth Wodzinski, publisher of *Shimmer Magazine*, really loves poutine, dinosaurs, cephalopods, and choose your own adventure stories. If you choose to follow her on twitter, she's @bethwodzinski. If you prefer to read her blog, it's at www.bethwodzinski.com

Melissa Yuan-Innes is an emergency doctor, but she's never sewed up a zombie – yet. She writes strange and funny stories, most of which can be tracked down through www.melissayuaninnes.net.

"Escape" by Tessa J. Brown was originally published in *Re-Vamp*, 2011.

"Rat Patrol" by Kevin Cockle was originally published in *On Spec*, 2005.

"Kissing Carrion" by Gemma Files was originally published in *Kissing Carrion*, 2003.

"On the Wings of This Prayer" by Richard Van Camp was originally published in *Godless but Loyal to Heaven*, 2012.

"Waiting for Jenny Rex" by Melissa Yuan-Ines was originally published in *Full Unit Hookup*, 2003.

All other stories are original to this anthology.

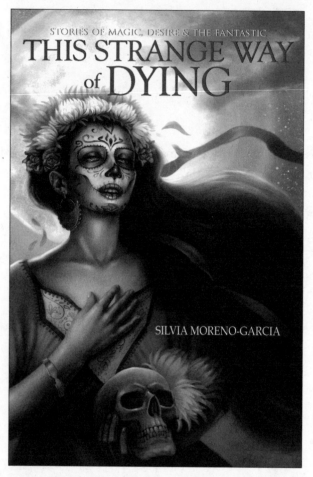

Exile's $15,000 Carter V. Cooper Short Fiction Competition

FOR CANADIAN WRITERS ONLY

$10,000 for the Best Story by an Emerging Writer
$5,000 for the Best Story by a Writer at Any Career Point

The 12 short listed are published in the annual *CVC Short Fiction Anthology* series as well as *ELQ/Exile: The Literary Quarterly*

Exile's $2,500 Gwendolyn MacEwen Poetry Competition

FOR CANADIAN WRITERS ONLY

$2,000 for the Best Suite of Poetry
$500 for the Best Poem

Winners are published in *ELQ/Exile: The Literary Quarterly*

These annual competitions open in October and January
details at: www.TheExileWriters.com